FIRST DATE

A new arrival. White—as a *ghost!* That man needs more sun or something. He's wiping his hands on his pants. Nice suit, though, wrinkled as it is. His shoes need a shine, and his face definitely needs a shave. Decent eyes—

That are looking at me.

Squinting.

Look at all those crow's feet. He's about, what, forty?

I look away from him and focus on the condensation streaming down my water glass. He wasn't looking at me, I mean, he *couldn't* be looking at me . . .

I look back.

It's him. It's Joe. It has to be. He, um, he even looks like a Joe, whatever that—

His lips are moving, forming my name.

Where's my voice? Gone. I can only nod and stare at the water making puddles in a circle around my glass.

Dearest Lord Jesus, what have I gotten myself into?

Books by J. J. Murray

RENEE AND JAY

SOMETHING REAL

ORIGINAL LOVE

I'M YOUR GIRL

CAN'T GET ENOUGH OF YOUR LOVE

TOO MUCH OF A GOOD THING

THE REAL THING

SHE'S THE ONE

I'LL BE YOUR EVERYTHING

Published by Kensington Publishing Corporation

too much of
a good thing

J.J. Murray

KENSINGTON PUBLISHING CORP.
http://www.kensingtonbooks.com

KENSINGTON BOOKS are published by

Kensington Publishing Corp.
119 West 40th Street
New York, NY 10018

All Kensington Titles, Imprints, and Distributed Lines are
available at special quantity discounts for bulk purchases for
sales promotions, premiums, fund-raising, and educational
or institutional use.

Special book excerpts or customized printings can also be
created to fit specific needs. For details, write or phone the
office of the Kensington special sales manager: Kensington
Publishing Corp., 119 West 40th Street, New York, NY 10018,
attn: Special Sales Department, Phone: 1-800-221-2647.

Kensington and the K logo Reg. U.S. Pat. & TM Off.

ISBN-13: 978-0-7582-6876-1
ISBN-10: 0-7582-6876-9

First trade paperback printing: February 2009
First mass market printing: February 2012

10 9 8 7 6 5 4 3 2 1

Printed in the United States of America

1

Joe Murphy

Aimless, Breathless, and Clueless:
Widowed Father of Three Needs Prayer!

I hope you can help me. My wife (38) passed in August (breast cancer), leaving me with two boys (13 and 16) and a girl (17). As the sole breadwinner, I was rarely home before six, and my wife did everything else. Sad to say, but I appreciate her more now than when she was alive.

Our house is a wreck, and the kids hate each other and me. While my church has been wonderful in helping us, the closest family I have to help us out are in Canada. I'm not sleeping, not eating, and not recovering.

Will you pray for us?

Joe

2

Shawna Mitchell

I help folks as much as I can by replying to their posts at LivingWithDeath.com, a site for the grieving, but there are so many needy people at that site. I had my own grief to deal with, my own husband, Rodney, dying eight years ago from colon cancer when he was only forty. But as soon as I started posting my own coping techniques, all learned on the job as the widowed mother of two girls and a boy, I started to heal.

"Give and it will be given to you," the Bible tells us, and it's true. The more help I give, the more healing I receive.

I check out the newest posts every morning while the kids get ready for school, and Joe's post stops me today. "Father of Three"—a single parent of three like me, and their ages are close to my kids' ages—girls eight and seventeen, boy fifteen. Joe says he is not necessarily in need of "help"—he's in need of "prayer." That really touches me. Ninety percent of the posts at LivingWithDeath.com are "Help me *now!*" letters. I'm sure Joe wants and needs help,

or why would he have asked someone to share and bear his
burdens? But simply asking for prayer—I can do that for him.

"Father, help Joe, and help his family," I pray.

He mentions that his wife (who was the same age as
me) "passed," not died, so maybe he's from the South. I
haven't heard that phrase anywhere but the South. Joe took
his wife for granted, just as I took Rodney for granted. You
never truly know what you have until it's gone. Our church,
Pilgrim Baptist, has helped us, too. The folks at Pilgrim
have been a weekly source of strength, giving my children
extralong hugs and holy handshakes as if they've adopted
my kids. Family who could help Joe is far away. Rodney's
mama lived in Texas before she passed, and most of the
Mitchell clan lives in or around Atlanta, while my kids and
I live in Roanoke, Virginia. We are not a hop, skip, or jump
away from any "free" help either. Joe's house is a "wreck,"
and his kids hate him. Our apartment isn't a wreck, and
after eight years, my kids don't hate me as much anymore.

I know exactly how Joe is feeling. My older two, Crystal
and Junior, hated me, each other, their new baby sister, Toni,
our apartment, their teachers, God, the food they ate, their
clothes, their shoes, the dusty old TV that sometimes worked,
life itself—anything, in fact, that they *could* hate. My youngest? Toni never knew her daddy at all, just all that tension
and me, and though she's capable of monumental temper
tantrums, she has been such a mostly *quiet* blessing so far in
comparison to her brother and sister.

And so has Priscilla62, a faceless saint of a person who
posted "Embracing the End" at LivingWithDeath.com several years ago. Her poem is so amazing that I printed it out
and have it taped inside the front cover of my well-thumbed
copy of *Streams in the Desert,* that timeless book of daily
devotions. I read Priscilla62's poem before I even brush my
teeth every single morning, and her words comfort me in
ways I cannot fully explain.

"Embracing the End"

The end of something is often uncomfortable.

The end of
a paddle,
a needle,
a tank of gas,
a cliff,
a rope,
a marriage,
a life.

What's so hard is the sense of imminent pain—
the sense of falling with no net.
We try to avoid the end,
deny the end,
delay the end;
even run from the end,
because we know that
embracing the end
will be like hugging a cactus—
causing unbelievable pain and many scars.
Embracing the end is also hard
because we can't even imagine
a new beginning.
The present, no matter how painful and horrible,
feels familiar and even "safe."
In fact, the better the present and recent past have been,
the more inconceivable something "different" seems.

So we wander in a "no-man's land,"
like a jackrabbit zigzagging across a desert—
not just unable to embrace the end,
but also unable to embrace the beginning of something else.

On *top* of that, we feel guilty
for our cowardice,
for our indecision,
for our fears,
for our tears,
for still wanting a miracle.

We are hard on ourselves,
condemning of ourselves without good reason.

Just look at Jesus—

From the beginning of His life,
He KNEW what His end would be.
He knew
the pain,
the torture,
the ridicule,
the loneliness,
the abandonment,
and the death
He would face.

He also KNEW the amazing beginning
His death would purchase—
forgiveness for the whole world
and the beginning of
a new relationship with God Himself.

He knew all this
Before He entered Gethsemane.
He prayed all alone for hours.
Oh, at first His friends were there,
but even they abandoned His pain for their sleep.

Jesus threw Himself on the ground;
His face in the dirt.
He groaned,

He grieved,
He agonized.
His sweat was like
great drops of blood.

And He prayed
that He would not have to face
the end.

He begged and pleaded
not once,
but three times—
"Father, remove this from Me!"

He embraced the end
With the words:
"Not my will, but Yours be done."

He rose to face His end
and OUR new beginning.

Embracing the end
requires the death of life's dreams
AND the hope that new ones are possible—
The knowledge that we are not falling
without a net,
that underneath are
the Everlasting Arms,
a glimpse that the God of the past
is the God of the future;
is the God of NOW.

Given that four-letter word "TIME,"
God can take the most horrible end
and create a new beginning—
full of good
full of purpose
full of God's glory.

My life since Rodney's death hasn't exactly been full of God's glory, but moving into Terrace Apartments, aka "The Castle," at the intersection of Wasena Avenue and Maiden Lane seven years ago saved us and made our lives, well, glorious.

It still doesn't make sense. How can you remove your family from a nice two-story house with everyone—including the baby—having his or her own room? How can you uproot your family from a nice flat yard containing a million flowers you planted yourself to a white brick apartment complex that looks more like a government-built White Castle than a home? What was I thinking?

Well, I was thinking that you take them to a new place to leave the ghost of their daddy behind, since he died in our bed with all of us around him. You take them to a new place to save yourself money you don't have for mortgage, insurance, and property tax payments if you want to keep alive your husband's dream of sending all three of your kids to college. You take them to a new place to be somewhat closer to your first real job as an assistant manager at a McDonald's. You take them to a new place to escape the old memories . . . Even if it is to a 225-unit monstrosity built in 1950 on nine acres overlooking the muddy Roanoke River.

Colon cancer. End stage before Rodney, me, or anyone else, for that matter, knew what hit him. We had spent ten adventurous years together, mainly at Camp Lejeune, North Carolina, where Rodney moved up in rank from corporal in Desert Storm to a master gunnery sergeant thinking seriously about becoming an officer and being a career marine. "But," he had said, "my kids won't know me," so he became a full-time marine recruiter here in Roanoke instead. He was only three years from his "twenty," just a thousand days from retiring with full pay and benefits. Despite all his duties, he somehow found time to coach Little League, Pee Wee football, and an AAU basketball team. Strong. Virile. A heart as big as his chest. Yet cancer laid him low because they didn't catch it in time. Of course, Rodney was the kind of man who only went to the doctor if he was on his last legs—meaning never. I should have made him go before he hit forty. I should have driven him myself. Instead I watched him vanish before my eyes, watched him disappear little by little over three months, his big, strong arms reduced to sticks—

"Ma-uh-*ma!* Crystal's using *my* brush again!" Toni screams.

The child can scream, and our neighbors on all sides in all directions—including upstairs and downstairs—know it. I'm always afraid they'll dial 9-1-1 on me because of those screams.

"Crystal!" I *yell.* I don't scream. I *yell.* "Use your own brush! Toni, stop all that noise! You're scaring the neighbors. Junior, have you put on deodorant?"

"Yes," Junior says, coming to me from the kitchen.

"We have to be out the door in ten minutes, y'all!"

"Haraka, haraka, haina baraka," Junior says in his deepening, mannish-boy voice.

He's learning Swahili from some of the African kids here and, by extension, so am I. "I know, I know. 'Hurry, hurry has no blessing,' right?"

He nods. He's becoming something miraculous, this child, something bigger and wiser than me and Rodney combined, and he's not nearly as hateful as he used to be.

"We need to get up earlier," I say.

He nods, and then he returns to the kitchen.

Who am I kidding? I've been saying "We need to get up earlier" for eight years.

Now, where was I? Oh, yeah. Terrace Apartments, our home.

Everybody lives in Terrace Apartments, and I mean, everybody: black, white, Muslim, Christian, and Jew, old, young, plump, thin, foreign, and domestic. The Castle contains Vietnamese boat people who escaped the Communists almost thirty years ago, Bosnians who fled war and ethnic cleansing, Cubans floating away from Castro, Liberians es-

caping civil war, and, most recently, Somali Bantu, a perse-
cuted minority fleeing civil war, famine, random killings,
and virtual slavery in East Africa. They have all come to The
Castle as refugees, and I guess I'm a refugee from grief, but
my grief doesn't even compare to theirs. I lost a husband.
Many here are the last remaining members of their *entire*
families. Some have lost everyone and everything dear to
them, while I still have all my children.

Physically anyway. As for their minds and spirits, I'm not
so sure.

The Castle is the United Nations in Roanoke, Virginia, of
all places. People from Sierra Leone, Albania, Afghanistan,
the Sudan, Haiti, and Iraq also live here. Why Roanoke? We
have a low cost of living, cheap housing, decent schools, a
low crime rate, and, despite the South's close-minded image,
Roanokers are generally accepting people.

When Rodney and I moved to Roanoke, we found an average city. Nothing too good and nothing too bad ever seems
to happen in Roanoke. Decent. This is a decent place full of
decent, hardworking folks who value education, old people,
the flag, this country, and the president—as long as he (or
she) is a Democrat. Roanoke has made many national Top
Ten lists, but we're never at the top. We're middling. That's
it. Roanoke is a middling town in the middle of the mountains where folks are middle-of-the-road and generally have
average middles.

But after Rodney died, the four of us looked so strange to
the people already living at The Castle when we first moved
in. We had no colorful clothes, no accents other than this
Southern twang I've infected my children with, no terrible
tales of refugee camps or boat rides on menacing seas or
walks through African deserts. Yet, these people have wel-
comed us, have embraced us, and have ultimately saved us.

There are so many stories walking around here. Carlos
Caballero spent twenty years in Cuban prisons being tor-

tured, and now his daughter, Soima, recites the Spanish version of "The Pledge of Allegiance" nearly every morning at Patrick Henry High School, where Crystal and Junior go to school. Rema Mdame, a Somali Bantu and a devout Christian friend, spent *ten* years in a refugee camp. She arrived at The Castle with three children and one on the way just a few months ago, and now she shops at Mick or Mack over in Grandin Village like a seasoned pro after cleaning rooms at Brandon Oaks Retirement Community. And Amina, the pretty little girl teaching Swahili to Junior—and that better be *all* that child teaches my boy now that he's a man-child with peach fuzz on his chin—Amina would rather walk to school barefoot carrying her books on her head than ride the bus carrying a backpack. I know Junior's smitten with her. I catch him trying to balance his books on his round head, and his new school shoes still look new even after a month of school. This is good because those shoes have to last him at least until Christmas.

The Castle has definitely been an education for me and my kids, and one day I will cancel my cable because of it. I can spend hours at the windows watching the Third World walk by, wearing colorful scarves and head coverings and handmade dresses. I can hear Spanish, and Bosnian, and Creole, and Arabic, and Pashto mixing with bold attempts at English. I can feel and see the village taking care of its own people. My kids get as much of an education after school here as they do in school. The Castle is a place where difference is normal, where skin color, fabric, hair, and even noses defy convention. There's so much texture here, so much . . . life. *Atangaye na jua hujuwa*—"A person who wanders around by day a lot, learns a lot." I have learned so much in my wanderings around here.

And it's nice to live around other people who don't have much. I know that sounds strange, but daily it makes a difference for me. No one in The Castle is in competition to get the "next best thing" to show off. My busted, dented, dusty, and paid-off Nissan Sentra looks right at home next to ancient Buicks, Chevrolets, and Fords parked around The Castle. We're not poor—we just don't have much money. Rema once told me, "Lacking money is not necessarily the same as being poor," and I know she's right.

Whenever the ice-cream truck comes around, I no longer feel the need to give my children money, ever since the day I saw Rema calming her four children with one phrase as the ice-cream truck rolled away. My kids hear "No," but they have to keep negotiating. Rema's kids had just walked away smiling while mine stewed long into the night because they didn't get any overpriced ice cream. I just had to find out what she told her kids.

" 'Ah,' " Rema said. " 'I tell them I live as I can afford, not as you wish.' "

Trust me—if you say that line five times a day to each child, your kids will stop pestering you for *anything*.

I wouldn't live anywhere else but The Castle now.

A *long* time ago after watching *The Color Purple,* I got it into my head to become a missionary to Africa. Now, I guess I'm kind of a missionary here among these people. Or maybe, and I'm believing this more and more, these people named Isha and Nuri and Hijiro and Yussuf and Sabtow are missionaries to *us*. Rema says, " 'God is our neighbor when our brother is absent,' " and I truly believe God is *in* our neighbors.

What time is it? Geez, we're running late, but I can't leave Joe hanging. "Okay, Mr. Man-in-a-similar-predicament."

I start to type:

Joe:

I'll pray for you

"Msema pweke hakosi," Junior says from the front door. "Huh?" I ask. That's a new one. "What does it mean?"

"It means, 'One who talks to himself or herself cannot be wrong.'" He smiles. "You were talking to yourself again, Mama."

"I was?"

"You're praying for someone named Joe, right?"

I was talking to myself, all right. Hmm. "Let me finish, okay? And help your sister with her backpack."

I finish typing:

Joe:

I'll pray for you. Have you tried having a family meeting to get everything out into the open? It hurts, but it can start you and your family on the way to healing. Let me know how it goes.

Shawna

"Mama, you at it again?" Crystal asks from the hallway, Toni trailing behind.

I hit the SEND button. "At what again?"

"Trying to save the world one e-mail at a time," Crystal says.

I stand in an attempt to dress Crystal down with my eyes, but I can't since she's *almost* wearing her clothes again. Deep V top showing more cleavage than I have (Rodney's people are big-breasted) and a whole lot of flat stomach and pierced belly button (I wish I could show off that much!), tight black jeans, and no panty line. She has to be wearing a thong again.

"Girl, you cannot go to school looking like that. They'll send you home." Again. I'm praying for a cold spell so she'll have to cover up all that skin, but Roanoke doesn't start to really cool off until mid-October.

"They won't send me home for this." She poses.

Junior shakes his head. *"Kizuri chajiuza kibaya chajitem-beza."*

"Mama, he's doing it again!" Crystal whines. "Why can't you just speak English for a change? You ain't African."

"Tell her what it means, Junior," I say, hoping it's something deep.

"It means 'A good thing sells itself,' " he says, " 'while a bad thing advertises itself.' "

So true. Miss Thing is advertising Miss Bad Thing today. If I weren't her mama, I'd say, "What's that child selling?"

Junior smiles at Crystal. "You are a flag blowing in the wind, my sister."

"I ain't advertising nothing," Crystal says, teeth clenched, a finger in Junior's face.

"Speak English," Junior says, and he opens the door, Toni zipping around them out to the sidewalk, Junior drifting through the door.

"I *am* speaking English, African Boy," Crystal says, practically stepping on the backs of his feet. "You're only learning that stuff cuz you want to get with Amina . . ."

After I get a sweatshirt that Crystal will wear all day *or else* to cover up all that skin, I lock up, chuckling to myself. I used to hate any kind of arguing in my house, and Rodney did, too. We argued softly, reasonably, without raising our voices. But now, I don't mind the yelling so much, mainly because of something Rema told me. She said something so beautiful in Swahili to me one day when I had to go outside to separate Crystal's flailing (and sharp) fingernails from Junior's face.

"What does it mean?" I had asked.

In her lilting voice, Rema said, " 'Hot water not burn down house.' "

Hot water does not burn down a house.

In other words, fussing doesn't destroy a family.

At the rate we're fussing, though, we're bound to be the strongest family that ever lived.

I can live with that.

3

Joe

Wow.

Sixty people answered my post, but not many said they would pray for us. Some give advice: "Get a nanny . . . " "Hire a housekeeper . . . " "Move to a new house . . . " "Move back home to your family in Canada . . . " "Go to church more often . . . " "Read this book I wrote . . . " "Call this toll-free hotline." One even suggested I cart all three of them off to military school.

Though that particular idea is tempting, I cannot live alone in this house in Wasena. This was Cheryl's dream house, all eighteen hundred square feet of it. She refinished the hardwood floors, she updated the kitchen, she nagged me to build the fence, the deck, and the playhouse, and . . . Okay, she didn't nag me. She would just drop hints for days and weeks, and, like water dropping on a stone, eventually she'd get through to me.

God, I miss her.

I look back at all the advice. One person asks where Cheryl's family is and why don't they help. Cheryl was from Oregon, a navy brat, the youngest of five, and her folks passed within a year of each other about six years ago. We had already lost touch with her brothers and sisters completely before Cheryl died. As for my family, my brother is a missionary in Irian Jaya, but he and my parents e-mail me often enough.

I just feel so alone in all this.

I'm not quite alone. Arnie Roberts, a retired army chaplain and member at Shenandoah Baptist where we've attended since Rose was born, stepped in and helped me with the funeral. Arnie is all short hair, spit, and polish, the fittest seventy-year-old I've ever known. He's been a mighty prayer warrior and friend, calling regularly to catch up and sitting with us during the morning service. My kids call him Uncle Arnie, and that suits him fine. I'm not sure if he adopted us or we adopted him, but he is one powerful church brother to have, sharpening me and my walk with the Lord as "iron sharpeneth iron" (Proverbs 27:17).

I just wish Arnie weren't so pushy about me finding another wife. "Get yourself another Proverbs 31 woman," he tells me. Cheryl fit some of the qualities of the woman described in that famous passage, a passage usually read on Mother's Day, but, honestly, I don't think there are that many women *who have ever lived* who match the Proverbs 31 woman, who is worth "far above rubies." This particular woman has to be able to sew, shop, cook, clean, take care of her family, work eighteen-hour days, do charitable work, and somehow find time to work in the garden. "She will do him good," the Bible says. "Strength and honor are her clothing." If I ever found a woman like that . . .

I think I did once. Cheryl was her name.

I browsed a few websites claiming they could find me my soul mate ("She's out there waiting for YOU!!!") in sixty days or less ("Guaranteed, or your money back!!!") and read post after post titled "LOOKING/PRAYING FOR A PROVERBS 31 WOMAN." At first, I was surprised that so many women responded to these posts, but when I read what these women had to say, I wasn't surprised at all. "That woman doesn't exist, you foolish men" is how most of the nicer ones began. "She's just an example of the woman God wants us to be . . ." "She is the model, and the rest of us *real* women are the clay . . ." "Why waste your entire life looking for this woman when the woman of your dreams might be sitting in front of you at church?"

"I'm on the lookout, Joe," Arnie says, "always on the lookout."

I'm not sure I should be taking advice from Arnie, a life-long bachelor, at all, but it's nice to know someone is on the lookout for me.

Arnie and all these folks who sent me e-mails mean well, and I'm sure every bit of their advice is rooted in reality, but only Shawna has given me something concrete, something constructive I can do right now.

I go to the foot of the stairs. "Family meeting in the kitchen in five minutes!"

I expect to hear a door or two opening, the familiar "What'd you say?" echoing throughout the house. But I hear nothing, not a single squeaking bed, shuffling chair, or footstep.

I climb halfway up. "Family meeting! In the kitchen! Now!"

"Now" arrives ten minutes later, Joey showing up first. "I was just finishing my homework," he says.

Joey is a good kid, hardworking and smart, a better athlete and student than I ever was, excelling in soccer, basketball, baseball, math, and science. I'm hoping he'll rub off on his little brother, Jimmy, who has turned into a little hellion since Cheryl died. Jimmy thinks nothing of slamming doors, "borrowing" Joey's stuff, or harassing Joey while he tries to do his homework. Joey has asked for a lock on his bedroom door, but I don't want that.

I pray it never comes to that.

"You had homework on a Friday night?" I ask.

"Just some reading."

He is Cheryl's son, all right. While Rose, Jimmy, and I would vegetate in front of the TV most nights, Joey and Cheryl would be off by themselves in another room putting together a puzzle, playing Scrabble, or reading quietly. Though he looks more like me than Jimmy does, I don't really know Joey all that well, and that scares me. I don't know my own child. I don't know what's going through his head, I don't know why he's suddenly shy, and I don't know why he stays inside all the time. He and Jimmy used to tear all over the neighborhood on their bikes or go down to Wasena Park and ride skateboards and play basketball.

Rose arrives next, looking like death. No father should ever feel this way about his firstborn, but I can't help it. She has become what she calls a Victorian Goth. "And not just because Queen Victoria smoked marijuana to help her cramps," she tells me after church last week. Rose has suddenly decided to like corsets, long black gowns, and red ballet slippers. She makes me buy Cheer Dark to keep all her dark clothes nice and Gothic. Her room is a shrine to death with Edgar Allan Poe's head filling most of one poster on her door. The rest of her room is dedicated to *The Rocky Horror Picture Show,* huge bloody red lips everywhere. Joey tells me the Goth look "went out years ago, Dad." I'm hoping it's just a case of old-fashioned, teenaged rebellion. Just a month ago, she was wearing Levi's, Nike, and Gap, and had a poster of the U.S. women's soccer team on the wall. She used to wear makeup, but now she wears no makeup at all, saying she prefers to look *un*natural.

"What's this all about?" Rose demands.

"We need to have a family meeting," I say.

"To discuss what?"

"This family?" I smile.

Rose slumps into a chair, her gown rustling around her. "Is this going to take long?"

"It might," I say.

"Whoopee," she says.

Jimmy finally trips down the stairs. "What are you all doing?"

It must be a commercial break. Jimmy didn't hear me yelling up the stairs at all.

"Family meeting, doofus," Rose says.

"A what?" Jimmy asks.

"Family meeting," Joey says softly.

Jimmy takes a seat, what used to be Cheryl's, at the other end of the table. "And no one invited me?"

Jimmy is the he-man in the family, preferring to use his fists and mouth more than his mind. He has always been a little ornery, but since Cheryl left us, he's been trouble with a capital *T*. He has been suspended from the bus for extorting "seat rent" from other kids, sent to the office twice for bullying, and is in danger already of repeating the seventh grade—and it's only mid-September.

"Okay, I've called this meeting so we can air out whatever has been bothering you since . . ." I sigh. "Since Mom died."

I brace for an onslaught of grief, despair, angst, and anguish.

Nothing happens. The mantel clock over the fireplace in the other room ticks on.

"I can go first," I say.

Louder silence.

"Okay, um, I have to admit that I am the least prepared single parent who has ever lived."

I expect a reaction, especially from Rose, but still no one speaks. Should I press on? I wanted *them* to talk, not me. This meeting isn't for me—it's for them—yet here I am doing all the talking.

I shrug. "I am not a good cook. You all know that."

Fast food is my forte, and I've even gotten it alphabetized. Most Mondays I stop at the Crossroads Mall McDonald's on the way home from work, double cheeseburgers and fries from the dollar menu for everyone. On Tuesdays, I hit

Western Sizzlin when I'm running late for the Tuesday Special: chopped steak, baked potato or fries, green beans, and roll. Wednesdays is for Wendy's chili and taco salads. Thursdays we eat the family pack from Taco Bell. Friday we splurge and go to Five Guys Burgers and Fries over in Salem for the best burgers and fries on the planet. Saturdays we sometimes go to Sonic, and Sundays we eat Szechuan if Arnie isn't treating us to Golden Corral or K&W Cafeteria after church. When I'm not rushed or late or too bushed to cook, I mainly do Hamburger Helper with a side vegetable, garlic bread or rolls, and applesauce.

If I include the $42 a week I pay for their school breakfasts and lunches, I spend roughly $170 a week on food, which isn't that bad. At least I don't think it's that bad. Cheryl did all the shopping for us before, so I don't know. I know it's not as healthy as it could be, that they should be consistently getting more fruits and vegetables, but . . .

"Any comments on my, um, cooking?"

The mantel clock ticks on.

"Okay, uh . . . I'm also not very good at doing the dishes." This is why we use Styrofoam plates, and plastic spoons, forks, and cups. I'm sure we have our own section at the landfill by now. "And you know I'm terrible at cleaning up."

A few blinks, but otherwise . . . I need to take the battery out of that clock!

"And, Rose, you know I do not shop well. What were you telling me the other day in the mall? That I wouldn't know a good price if it bit me? Well, I . . ."

Rose yawns.

Oh, this is going *so* well.

"But most of all, I'm sad. I'm sad because I haven't seen any of you smile or heard any of you laugh since . . ." My voice catches. "Since the funeral."

"You haven't either," Rose says.

One of them spoke! But I can *still* hear that clock!

"You're right, Rose. I haven't had much to smile about lately." I look at Jimmy first.

"What?" Jimmy asks.

"Son, I liked school when I was there a million years ago, but I do not particularly like going there as an adult."

"So don't come," Jimmy says with a scowl. "They can just put me in detention."

"I don't want you to be in detention, Jimmy."

He smiles. "Neither do I, but . . ." He shrugs.

The school has urged me to consider what they call "drug intervention" to control what they think is a "clear-cut case of ADHD," but I don't believe it. Jimmy is just expressing his sorrow through rage. I wanted him to play football in August, but we missed signing up because of . . . because of Cheryl's passing.

I turn to Rose. "And didn't you used to do homework?"

"Yeah," she says. "So?"

Rose's answer for everything these days.

"Look, I want to smile and laugh again. Don't you? Don't you want to smile and laugh and get goofy again like we used to?"

"I miss her," Joey says, softly, as if saying it only to himself.

I look at Jimmy and Rose, but their faces betray nothing, not a single drop of emotion. "What do you miss about her most, Joey?"

Joey looks at the table. "The way she helped me with my homework. She would help me, but she wouldn't give me the answer. She would . . . coax me, you know?"

Rose exhales sharply. "All you ever think about is school! You are *such* a geek."

Joey doesn't respond, retreating into that silent world of his.

"He's not a geek, Rose," I say, flexing fatherly muscles I'm still developing, "and I don't want you referring to your brother that way."

"Whatever," Rose says, using her second-most favorite word.

"Jimmy, what do you miss most about Mommy?" I ask.

Jimmy shrugs, his eyes drifting to the ceiling. "I dunno."

"You have to miss something," I say.

He shrugs again. "I dunno."

He has to miss *something!* "Well, think about it, and I'll ask you again in a few minutes."

"Like I said," Jimmy says, "I don't know, all right? Gosh."

"Gosh" translates to "leave me alone." I turn to Rose. "What do you miss most?"

She shakes her head slightly. "I miss the fact that with Mom we *didn't* have to have stupid family meetings."

I nod. "You're right. We didn't have to meet like this to talk. We just . . . talked."

And here I have to call a family meeting to talk to my own kids when I could be talking to them all the time. I am such a fool. I come home with the food, dump it on the kitchen table, yell "Dinner!" up the stairs, and then they come, grab their share, and disappear into their rooms. We haven't been communicating. We rush around all morning to get ready for school and work, barking at each other. They go off to their buses, they come home at different times, I'm usually late, and they live in their rooms.

"From now on, then," I decide, "we'll eat dinner together every night like we used to."

"You're not going to cook, are you?" Rose asks.

I wince. "I probably shouldn't. You could, couldn't you?"

Rose shakes her head. "Mom never taught me, remember?"

"Well," I say, "you watched her, didn't you?"

"Yeah, but watching isn't learning," she says.

Maybe I'll hire a cook. No. I can't afford that. "Well, at least we can sit down and eat whatever I bring home or attempt to cook."

More silence. I'll take that as agreement and move on.

I sit back. "I know this is a silly way to communicate, but I had to do something. And this sure beats the screaming and yelling and fussing and cussing"—I stare Jimmy down—"that I hear just about every day in this house."

No reactions.

How do I get them all on the same page? How can I get them to live in the house that their mother decorated, kept, and filled with love?

I have to be around more often. It's as simple as that.

"I'm taking tomorrow off," I say.

Three sets of eyebrows twitch. For my job at Progressive Insurance I usually work on Saturday mornings because so many accidents happen on Friday nights, but tomorrow I'm staying home.

"And," I add, "we're going to do some spring cleaning."

"But it isn't spring," Jimmy says.

"You know what I mean. We're going to clean this house top to bottom, every nook and cranny—"

"What's a cranny?" Jimmy interrupts.

"Everywhere," I say. "I want this house to shine again. I want this house to look as if your mother still lives here, okay?"

Joey nods. Rose rolls her eyes. Jimmy slumps lower in his chair. At least they're finally reacting.

"We'll be up at the crack of dawn," I say, "so get to bed early, okay?"

More nothing.

"Okay, um, meeting adjourned."

Then something miraculous happens. They *don't* tear up the stairs. They leave quietly without a single "stupid-this" or "dork-that" or a "Leave me alone!" or a "Cut it out, puke breath!"

Silence.

I'm onto something.

I think.

And I have to get online to thank Shawna.

4

Shawna

After a long day managing a McDonald's, a trip to Kroger with Toni, and a quick meal of fried pork chops, Jiffy cornbread, and green beans, I sit in front of the computer while Toni watches the Cartoon Network, Crystal "advertises" outside, and Junior goes for a walk with Amina to Wasena Park.

Joe's reply brings a smile to my lips:

> Shawna:
>
> It worked! So far, anyway. Thank you. We are cleaning the house from top to bottom tomorrow as a family. Any foreseeable problems?
>
> Joe

We cleaned house after Rodney died, too, and I fully intended to stay in that house until I realized that my McDonald's pay was not enough to keep paying on that house and keep up the kids' college funds. Everything was tripping along fine

that day until we started running into Rodney—his clothes
in the laundry room, his size 14 shoes under the bed, his pictures in photo albums, his coats in the closet, all his many
uniforms. We ended up bawling together on the bed where
we last saw him alive, half the house still a mess.

Joe needs to know all this, too.

Joe:

This may be hard to do, but save your bedroom for
last. And unless you want to blow through five boxes
of tissues, avoid photo albums.

Shawna

"What show is that?" I ask Toni.
No response.
"Toni, what are you watching?"
"I dunno, Mommy," she replies with attitude, lying face-
down on the couch, her eyes glued to three creepy-looking
white boys with pasty skin.
"Well, what's it about?"
"Three silly boys," she sighs.
"What are their names?"
"Eddie."
"All three of them are named Eddie?"
She nods.
Only in America.
I'm about to do some surfing, when a message from Joe
appears in my mailbox:

Shawna:

Luckily, Cheryl's room is the cleanest in the house,
and since she took most of the pictures, I think we're
okay with the photo albums since she won't be in
many of them. What, if anything, should I do with her

clothes? Rose has become a Goth and wouldn't wear any of Cheryl's old clothes.

Joe

Hmm. "Rose may surprise you, Joe," I whisper.
"Who are you talking to, Mommy?" Toni asks.
She doesn't hear me address her directly, but she can hear me whisper to myself. "Just talking to myself, honey."
I type:

Joe:

Give Rose first dibs on the clothes anyway. She's still her mama's daughter down deep, right? Otherwise, Goodwill, Salvation Army, your church, even some schools could use them.

Shawna

And then . . . I wait. This doesn't normally happen to me. Most folks say a quick thank you, and then I never hear from them again. Yet here's this man somewhere in the world having a conversation with me.
When his next message appears in my mailbox, I check it quickly:

Shawna:

Will do. Have I thanked you yet? I probably haven't. Sorry. THANK YOU for your prayers and advice. Is there anything I can do for you? I've been praying a LOT these days, and I know I can add you to my list.

Joe

Whoo. A man I don't know wants to pray for me, to put me in God's thoughts. And in a way, he'll be keeping me in his own thoughts, too. How much of my life do I tell? I try to keep my personal life personal. I mean, I'm hoping that God has another man out there for me, but I can't be revealing my heart to strangers online. Even local men don't want to hear that I have three kids. This man, though . . . something about his focus on God, his kindness, his obvious ability to communicate with my soul . . .

And to think he's waiting at his keyboard for *my* reply!

Joe:

I am a widow with three children: Crystal (18), Toni (8), and Junior (15). I have been hanging on for eight years. I can always use a little prayer. Thank YOU.

Shawna

My fingertips are sweating. Why? What is happening to me? It's only a random man. He just needs my help, and I'm doing my best to—

"Whatcha doin'?" Toni asks, suddenly appearing next to me.

"Um, just checking my mail."

"From who?"

I look into her baby browns, her eyelashes so long, so thick, so Rodney. "A person who needs my help."

"Oh. What's his name?"

And so perceptive! "How do you know it's a man?"

She points at the screen. "Joe is a boy's name."

Little by little, my youngest child's ability to read is eroding my privacy. "Yes, I'm helping a man named Joe, and he has three kids just like us."

"Yeah?"

"Yeah."

"What are their names?" she asks.

Hmm. I only know Rose. "Well, the girl's name is Rose, and—"

Another message from Joe appears. I click on it and read:

Shawna:

Does it get any easier?

Toni frowns. "Does *what* get any easier?"

"Oh, life, living," I tell her.

"Oh," she says. "Well, does it?"

"Yes, honey," I say. At least I hope so, Lord Jesus, I hope so. "Is your homework done?"

"It's Friday, Mama," Toni says with a long, slow blink.

It is. Where'd Thursday go? Weeks end without my knowledge or permission sometimes.

I have to stop working six days a week. Except for Sunday, every day seems like a Monday. McDonald's has been wonderful about my crazy schedule, though at first they weren't. But once they realized that this mother-of-three runs one of the tightest, most efficient (and therefore more profitable) ships in Ronald McDonald's golden-arched navy, they let me schedule myself. And the hours are almost perfect. I work 8:30 to 3:30 Monday through Saturday, about a forty-two-hour week. I see my kids onto their buses in the morning and get home in time to collect Toni from hers. Crystal and Junior are so-called "latchkey kids," but the village takes care of them. Other managers call me in to work every now and then to solve a crisis, and when one or more of my kids is sick, I just plain don't work until they're well.

As a mother is supposed to do.

"Mama?"

She has caught me daydreaming again. "Yes, Toni?"

"Didn't you hear me?"

Were her lips moving while my mind was traveling? I'll

bet they were. Toni is chatty. "I, um, I didn't understand your question, honey."

"It wasn't a question, Mommy. Look." She points at the screen. "It's Joe."

"Oh."

One click later, and I'm smiling:

Shawna:

Sorry about that. I hit the wrong button before I was done with my message. What I meant to say:

Does raising children on your own get any easier? I feel like I'm treading water surrounded by two sharks and a dolphin. Rose has the sharpest teeth, Jimmy has the most teeth, and Joey is, well, a dolphin. I can't figure him out yet. He's lurking or something, I don't know. He's so much like his mother—quiet, intuitive, reserved, intelligent. I guess it's his silence that scares me so much. It's almost scary that he's half-mine. Sorry to ramble. I used to be so organized.

Joe

"So did I, Joe," I whisper.

"Huh?"

"Just talking to myself again," I say, hitting the REPLY button.

"You're writing to him *again?*"

Why not? It's Friday night, and I'm talking to a single man. "Joe and I are having a conversation."

"So why don't you just call him on the phone?"

Toni is perceptive and logical, though I wish she didn't have such a bossy tone. Where'd she learn that tone? Oh, yeah. Her older sister. "I don't have his phone number, honey." Though it would be easier to chat with Joe, we'd lose the anonymous intimacy of the Internet. We'd also lose the ability to delete something before we actually "say" it. Phone conversations are permanent. E-mail correspondence is, um, take-back-able.

"Why don't you ask him for his phone number?" Toni asks.

"Well, honey, I can't—"

"Ask *who* for *his* phone number?"

Crystal's home? I didn't even hear her come in.

She looks over my shoulder at the screen. "Who's Joe?"

For eight years, Crystal has been the child with flames in her eyes, the protector of all that was Rodney. In her own heartbreaking way, she has kept me loving her daddy for eight long years, stopping most of my thoughts of finding someone else dead in their tracks with those flaming eyes of hers. Four years ago, I almost dated a slightly younger man, Clifford Smalls, the piano player at Pilgrim Baptist, our church. He had some nice hands and a quiet way about him, but he was always trying to separate me from my kids, almost ignoring the fact that I had three of them hanging on me. On the one and only date I was to have with Clifford, I took the kids with us to the movie. "Couldn't you get a babysitter?" he had asked. Crystal had overheard and set him straight: "I ain't no baby, and if you want to be with my mama, we are part of the deal." Clifford didn't bother me again. He still plays piano at Pilgrim, and I still watch his hands, those soft, strong—

"Who is Joe?" Crystal asks again, this time louder and with more venom.

"Joe is a man Mommy is trying to help," Toni says. "He has three kids just like us, and their names are Rose, Joey, and Jimmy."

Toni is perceptive, logical, a quick reader, and helpful—though this is not really the time for Toni to help her mama, not with Crystal's eyes on fire.

"How long has *Joe* been goin' on, Mama?" Crystal asks.

"Two days," I say. I stare at the blinking cursor to avoid Crystal's fiery eyes. And now I have completely forgotten what was in Joe's e-mail. "And if you'll both excuse me, I'd like to write him back."

"Where's he from?" Crystal asks, not moving.

I blink. Here come twenty (or more) questions. "I don't know. We've just, um, we've just met."

"Uh-huh." Crystal leans on my chair.

"Really. I don't know anything about him other than what your sister told you."

She drops her face in front of mine, holding me with a withering stare, a stare she learned from me. "So you're on-line with a stranger?"

Here we go with *my* "The Internet Is a Dangerous Place" sermon in reverse. She thinks she has me, but she doesn't. "His name is Joe. He's not a stranger."

"So he *says*." Crystal stares harder. "That might not be his real name."

She is so good at echoing me. "I believe him."

"He could be a sexual predator, Mama," Crystal says.

Shoot. She has that speech of mine memorized. But after eight years of hunching on Rodney's pillow, a sexual predator doesn't sound very bad to me right now.

"What's a sexual predder, Mommy?" Toni asks.

"I'll tell you later." I look up at Crystal's smoldering brown eyes. "Look, I'm helping Joe through his grief just as I've done for hundreds of people, Crystal. That's all."

Her eyes relax a little. "So he's nobody special, huh?"

He could be, but I can't answer her question at all. If I say, "No," I'd be lying. I have something in common with a man who is out there on the Internet waiting for my reply. And if I say, "Yes" or "I hope so," I'll have to endure twenty more questions and solar flares coming from Crystal's eyes. In times like these, a sermon usually does the trick.

"This man needs my help, Crystal, and I'm so grateful that God, in His infinite wisdom, has blessed me with the gift of—"

Crystal leaves. All I have to do is mention God, and she's

out of my face. She hasn't gone completely heathen—yet, and I pray to God that *never* happens—but when we go to church, Crystal is not really there. She has practically renounced God for stealing her daddy away, keeping her eyes open during prayers at dinner (I've peeked), keeping her beautiful voice silent during hymns, and definitely keeping her mind closed during the sermon.

But Toni is still there, singing and clapping and praising the Lord. And, unfortunately, Toni is still *here* beside me while I'm trying to "talk" to a man.

I stare at her. "You need me for something?"

She shakes her head. "No."

"Are you through watching TV?"

She nods, runs to the TV, turns it off, and returns to me. "Can I watch?"

I blink. "You want to watch?"

She nods.

She wants to be nosy. I am so entertaining. At least she won't be watching three silly white boys named Eddie. "Well, come on." I set her on my lap.

I click back, reread Joe's letter, then begin:

Dear Joe:

It won't get any easier unless

"Unless what?" Toni asks.

"Toni, please. I'll read it to you when I'm done."

"I can read, Mama."

Dear Joe:

It won't get any easier unless you reorganize and get your priorities in order. Devise a set daily schedule that includes family time, like an outing, a game, a TV show you all enjoy, a video you all pick out. If necessary, put up a daily schedule of chores

Which reminds me . . . "Is your brother still at the park?"

"No. He's in his room."

My children are becoming increasingly sneaky. "When did he come back?"

"A couple minutes ago."

"Well, what's he doing?"

"I dunno. His door's closed."

"Well, run tell him to dry the dishes and take out the trash."

Instead of moving from my lap, Toni yells, "Junior! Take out the—"

"Hush!" I say with a squeeze of her leg. "I said to run *tell* him, not yell *at* him."

"Oh."

She drops off my lap and runs to Junior's door, bellowing at the top of her lungs again. Time to type fast.

If necessary, put up a daily schedule of chores that rotates with each child.

Toni's back. I need a bigger apartment so she'll have a longer run. "Junior says he'll do it when he finishes his chapter." She climbs onto my lap. "What are you saying now?"

I sigh. "Grown-up stuff."

I watch her lips move as she reads. Oh, well.

As to the "sharks" in your house, I hear you. I have a piranha, a guppy, and a dolphin of my own.

"We don't have fish, Mama," Toni says.

"I'm talking about you all."

"Oh." She frowns. "Am I a guppy or a dolphin?"

"You're definitely the guppy, little and cute and easy to take care of." For the most part. She has her piranha moments, though.

"Oh. Right." She rolls her eyes. "What's a pur-ran-ha?"

"A vicious fish."

Her eyes widen. "Crystal."

"That's right." I keep typing:

But as to the "half-mine" part, Joe, they're ALL yours
now, 100%. That's the part that still scares me. We are
completely responsible for the lives of three children.
And don't ever be sorry to ramble. There is much
sense in what you say.

I sigh. That last sentence was something Rodney used to
say to our kids and to me when we *weren't* making any
sense. It would always make Crystal giggle, and I think she
purposely said goofy things so that he would say, "There is
much sense in what you say." I don't even know if Crystal
has the ability to giggle anymore.

Let me know how tomorrow goes.

I smile. I've just asked him to write back without asking
him to write back. And now all I need is a Bible verse to help
him through. Which one? There are so many highlighted in
my Bible. I could hit him with Ecclesiastes 3:1: "To every
thing there is a season, and a time to every purpose under the
heaven." Hmm. Kind of dry, that verse. Not enough life. The
Psalms are more uplifting.

Let me know how tomorrow goes.

Shawna

"But thou, O LORD, art a shield for me; my glory, and
the lifter up of mine head." (Psalm 3:3)

I hit the SEND button.

"Why did you put that Bible verse in there, Mommy?" Toni asks.

"To lift up his spirits." I squeeze her shoulder. "It's getting late, Little Miss Guppy."

She groans.

"And you need a bath."

"Aw, Mama!" she whines.

Yeah. Aw, Mama.

That phrase is music to my ears.

While I'm making my child take a bath to remove some of her guppy funk, I know there are probably other single-parent women my age out on the town. For whatever reason, I have never been that way. I hang with my kids. I'm so old-fashioned. I just can't see myself dropping off my kids with a friend or getting a babysitter so I can go to happy hour. My happy *hours* are with my kids. My coworkers tell me that I need to go out more. Why? I have responsibilities—three, to be exact. "You need to find you a new man," they say. Why? I haven't finished with the gifts Rodney left me to enjoy.

Speaking of my surprise gift—Toni—I had better make sure she washes behind her ears.

It should be the highlight of my evening.

5

Joe

Shawna:

Cleanup was interesting. I had intended to throw out a lot of stuff, but the kids wouldn't let me, claiming Cheryl's items one by one. Rose now has most of her mom's clothes, Joey has all of Cheryl's books (they're stacked all over his room), and Jimmy has the photo albums.

And I was the only one crying. Why is that?

When I put up the chores schedule, before I could even explain it, Rose and Jimmy jumped me. Joey was willing, but those two . . . I took the list down. I need a firmer hand or something, don't I?

Anyway, we made it through another day together, and I guess that's really all that matters.

Thank you for your prayers.

Joe

"The Lord is good, a strong hold in the day of trouble; and he knoweth them that trust in him" (Nahum 1:7)

6

Shawna

Nahum? Is this man Jewish? I have to look that one up in the Old Testament. It doesn't necessarily mean he's Jewish. Maybe he just knows his Bible. I like that.

Dear Joe:

Your children WERE crying—on the inside. Perhaps if they see you letting it out, they'll do the same. There's no telling with kids. I expected Crystal to cry the most, but she cried the least. Junior cried himself to sleep, and Toni (who was a newborn) just cried and cried because she could.

Sorry to break it to you, but you do need a firmer hand now that Cheryl is gone. Sometimes I wish I had three hands, one for each child.

Rodney was the gentle "enforcer," the "good cop" to my "bad cop." I have had to learn not to be as firm as I once was. Joe obviously is a teddy bear with his kids.

Yes, it will feel strange to be the rule-maker and rules-enforcer, but you have to do it. Try putting up that chores list again, and just leave it there. Your kids may surprise you.

Now what? All I'm doing is answering his letters. I'm not really talking to him. I want to ask more about Cheryl for some reason. It's not as if I'm checking out, well, my competition. It's just . . . curiosity. That's it. I'm just curious. No harm in being curious.

Tell me about Cheryl.

Shawna

And now I need another verse. Flipping through the Psalms, I find the perfect verse.

"He shall call upon me, and I will answer him: I will be with him in trouble, I will deliver him." (Psalm 91:15)

Hmm. Maybe that verse is too forward. I mean, Joe *has* called upon me, and I have answered him. I am with him in his trouble, but am I delivering him? Only God can do that.
I delete the verse and find another:

"Lead me to the rock that is higher than I." (Psalm 61:2)

Better. Joe needs to *be* a rock now. I hit SEND.

7

Joe

Dear Shawna:

Putting up the chores list worked! Not at first. Only Joey did his, but eventually they pitched in. Thank you. I guess subtle works when in your face fails.

You want to know about Cheryl. Cheryl was amazing, happy, content, unafraid, resourceful. I miss her.

Which reminds me: How much should I be spending on food? Is $170 a week too much for four people? It's not breaking me (yet), but I have a feeling I'm spending too much.

Joe

PS: I like your verses. They have lifted my spirits. This verse always lifts me up: "They that wait upon the Lord shall renew their strength." (Isaiah 40:31)

I hit SEND and wait, my fingers itching to reply to her reply. I'm finally talking to a person who knows and completely understands what I'm going through, unlike Arnie, and I'm finding it hard to concentrate in my daily life. I compose long letters to Shawna while I'm driving from one dented fender to another, listing all my various shortcomings as a father and single parent, but when I sit in front of the computer, I forget everything I want to tell her.

The little bell in the computer dings. She wrote back already? That means she's sitting out there waiting for me? No, she's not just waiting to write back to me. She just happens to be online, that's all. Or maybe . . . Nah. I'm the only person who would sit and wait for an e-mail to arrive. That's how exciting my life has been recently.

Dear Joe:

You are spending WAY too much on groceries. You should be able to get by on $90 a week (or less). Do you ever use coupons? Do your kids put items into your cart without your knowledge?

I hesitate to tell Shawna about all our fast food meals. And as for coupons, Cheryl did that for us. I will have to start clipping now—and buying groceries instead of hitting the drive-thru.

Are you making a list? You have to, and STICK to the list. Otherwise, you'll buy much more than you could possibly eat. And don't go to the store hungry. You buy much more food when you're hungry.

Shawna

No Bible verse today. I hope everything is all right. I reread her e-mail. She sounds stressed, even a little angry.

Maybe I'm dumping too much on her. I'll just write less often. That's probably it. I'm asking too many questions. I'm also making myself sound helpless when, with God's gracious help, I'm not.

I shut off the computer.

8

Shawna

Joe hasn't written in a while. Maybe that means he's doing okay, and for that I'm happy. But I miss "talking" to him. Was there anything in my last e-mail that turned him off? Was I too pushy? I *was* ordering him around a bit. I shouldn't have been so direct.

Weeks pass, and each day I check my e-mail—in the morning, when Toni is doing her homework after school, after dinner, and just before I go to bed. No word from Joe. And for some strange reason, I find myself thinking and praying about this man at the oddest times. I'm trying to survive a lunch rush shorthanded with a cashier who can't hit the right button to save her life, and suddenly I think of Joe and his food bills. I'm taking a deposit to the bank, and I think about, well, Joe and his food bills. That was a lot of money to spend on groceries. Are they big people or what? I mean, maybe they're big-boned, but come on! My kids would outgrow the apartment if I spent that much each week.

I just can't get that man out of my mind.

I almost write him several times before he writes me, you know, just to see how he's holding up, and I even write an extremely long-winded letter about Rodney that I delete before sending.

"Wait," I say aloud, "on the Lord."

That verse is becoming a mantra to me. It's a good verse, don't get me wrong, but when the Lord has you waiting for eight years, it starts to get old. "I'm not Job, Lord," I whisper nightly. "I'm just plain old Shawna."

Then, out of the blue, Joe writes to me again:

Shawna:

Sorry I haven't written. But once again, I need your help. If I'm getting too needy, please let me know. I don't want to burden you with our problems.

Halloween is coming up, and though we don't really "celebrate" it, Cheryl made a big deal out of making hundreds of cookies, bagging them, the works. The neighborhood kids are expecting her cookies. What do I do?

Also, parent-teacher conferences are coming up, and these will be the first I ever go to. What should I expect? I know Jimmy's and Rose's grades have fallen, so I'm bracing for the worst.

Again, sorry I haven't written. I hope you and your family are safe and healthy.

Joe

Without hesitating, I reply:

Dear Joe:

I'm glad you wrote to me. I've been thinking a lot about you.

Whoa. That is *way* too forward, even for me. I delete the last sentence and type:

I've been praying a lot for you and your family.

Yes, that's safer. I have been praying, but my prayers are becoming less prayerful.

Cheryl's baking sounds like a tradition, and traditions are hard to break. Why not have the kids help you bake those cookies? And save some for me!

Hmm. If the kids make those cookies . . . "Then the neighborhood kids might stop coming around," I whisper. I don't know if I'd eat anyone's home-baked cookies at Halloween.

And as for PT conferences, relax. I have a cousin who teaches, and she tells me that she's just as nervous as the parents are. Focus on helping your kids, and things should go smoothly.

I can't end this letter here. Once again, all I've done is given him advice. I know it's what he wants, but it may not be what he *really* needs.

Joe, I feel that I have to warn you about the upcoming holidays. There are quite a few traditions wrapped up in Thanksgiving and Christmas, and now those traditions will change. Rodney used to play Santa with the kids, letting them sit on his lap, asking them what they wanted. He'd have them write it all down or draw it for him, and then they'd put it in his briefcase.

It was such a simple tradition, but the kids couldn't have Christmas without it. That first Christmas without him—I wish I could forget it. I tried to play Santa, but they wouldn't

even come near me. I tried to get them to write it all down,
but they wouldn't. Then I went out and overspent on toys I
thought they wanted. I didn't realize that all they really
wanted was their daddy. Time to level with Joe:

I tried to play Santa, but I'm not Rodney. I'm too
skinny.

I can't believe I typed that! I mean, it's true, but what if
Joe likes his women with a little meat on their bones? Cheryl
baked lots of cookies, and whenever I bake, I sample. Should
I leave it in the e-mail? I want him to get to know me . . .
don't I?
I decide to leave it.

Your first Christmas is going to be hard, no matter
how hard you try to make it go smoothly and peace-
fully. They get better. You'll just have to start a few
new traditions to replace Cheryl's.

And Joe, please keep writing to me. I don't think
you're needy. I think you're

Where am I going with this? Lord, why are my fingers
more romantic than my mind? Joe could be in North Dakota
or Maine or someplace cold where I do not want to go.
    *I know I'm lonely, Lord, but please help me keep my head
about all this. Amen.*
I delete the entire last paragraph and write:

Joe, you can write to me anytime. Everyone is needy
at some point. I only hope I can help you.

Shawna

And now I need a verse that says what I'm feeling better
than I can. I have to let Joe know I'm here for him, no matter

what. I flip through the book of John, dancing my fingers through all the verses I've highlighted. Ah. This is the one:

"Him that cometh to me I will in no wise cast out."
(John 6:37)

I hit SEND.
And then I pray.

9

Joe

Shawna. She is the answer to my prayers. Through her beautifully written, heartfelt words, she has gotten me and my family through the hardest six weeks of the year.

Maybe the *second* hardest six weeks of my life.

Christmas was *so* hard. I got them to make lists, and I broke the bank getting them everything they asked for. But there was no joy. They kept looking for Cheryl, expecting her to come out of the kitchen to say, "Breakfast is served! Wash up!" They missed her opening the lingerie and saying, "Ooh, la *la!*" And I'm sure they all wanted to hear her sing along with the carols blasting from the little radio in the kitchen as she prepared the Christmas meal.

I've only wept, really wept, a few times in my life. This was one of them. I just couldn't stop crying.

And yet, Shawna has seen me through. There's not much I can count on now, but I can always count on her. My prayers for her go something like this: "Lord God, thank You for Shawna. Bless her and her family. Keep her safe . . . And keep her writing to me."

I've become so selfish about her, hogging the downstairs

computer. The kids must think I'm doing something for work because they don't pry. I wonder what they'd think if they knew I was outsourcing our family problems to a perfect stranger who has been perfect in all the advice she's given to me.

But Shawna isn't that much of a stranger anymore. We're sharing our lives together, even the daily nothingness that makes up most of life. We talk about trips to the dentist, getting and paying for braces, the weather, car troubles, the price of gas, how to clean an oven without gassing up the house, even what direction toilet paper should go on the dispenser. It's all so . . . homey.

But I thank God daily for this "conversation" we're having. I don't want it to end. We sit, maybe thousands of miles apart, and "talk" to each other over hot chocolate or sweet tea or coffee. We've become . . . friends.

But just when we get into a rhythm, when the kids are starting to show signs of life and laughter, Rose gets into some serious trouble at school.

Serious, as in "Daddy, they may expel me" trouble. Serious, as in "Daddy, I may be arrested" trouble. Serious, as in "Daddy, I'm wearing handcuffs."

I feel the weight of the entire world on my shoulders as I enter the main office at Patrick Henry and see my daughter in handcuffs. "I'm Joe Murphy," I say, not looking at Rose.

A secretary whisks me into a conference room, and several folks introduce themselves, as if I really care who they are. My daughter is still sitting outside the room in handcuffs for the entire world to see.

"Would it be possible for Rose to come in?" I ask, still standing.

"We'd like to talk to you first, if you don't mind," a woman says.

She looks as if she's in charge. Is she the new principal? Mrs. . . . Thompson, I think. Yeah.

"Well, I mind." I start to sweat. "I mind that my daughter is sitting out there in handcuffs. I mind that she's not in here while we talk about her. And I really mind that she's wearing handcuffs at all. What could she possibly have done to warrant those?"

Then they take turns telling me, their words a series of verbal punches. "She cursed out a large group of black students, calling them, um, calling them 'niggers' . . ." "After we brought her back to my office, she assaulted two deans and a security guard . . ." "One of the deans had to go to his doctor for treatment."

It isn't possible! Not Rose! She wouldn't hurt a fly! "My . . . daughter. She did all that?" In one day?

A series of nods.

I take my seat. "Um, what started it all?" I ask.

"We're not sure," Mrs. Thompson says.

I'm sweating again. "Well, have you asked her or anyone else?"

"We tried to find out what caused her outburst, but she has been difficult," another woman says. "We've been waiting for your arrival."

"What do you mean, 'difficult'?" I ask.

"She's been, um, singing the national anthem and calling us Nazis."

My hair feels as if it's graying and thinning at the same time. Where did my little girl go? "Now, by 'assault,' what exactly do you mean?"

And again, they give me a tag-team answer: "She kicked one of the deans in the shin . . ." "She punched the security officer in the chest . . ." "She kneed the other dean in the groin . . ." "Oh, and her language was positively horrific."

I look at the floor and blow out a stale breath.

"Is she on any kind of medication, Mr. Murphy?"

I look up. "No." Lord, where is the defense for any of

Rose's actions? "No. She's not . . . taking anything." I look at my hands. "I can't believe this happened. It's not like her at all."

"She has, um, changed a great deal, Mr. Murphy, since last year," yet another woman says.

I look at this woman. "You're . . . her counselor, right?"

She nods. "I'm Mrs. Grady."

"Yes, Mrs. Grady, Rose has changed quite a bit since her mother died. But she's never been in any trouble like this."

"I have read through her file, Mr. Murphy, and you're right," Mrs. Thompson says. "She was a model student last year and made the A–B honor roll. Is she getting any kind of counseling?"

"No." Which is my fault. She obviously needs it. I had thought that just being with the rest of us would be enough therapy and that time itself would heal the rest of her wounds.

"Well, Mr. Murphy, because of the nature of these assaults, Rose will have to go before the DRC in ten days," Mrs. Thompson says.

I wait for her to explain what "DRC" means. She doesn't. "And what's the DRC?"

"The Discipline Review Committee," she says, as if those are the only words that can be abbreviated that way.

"And what does it do?" I ask.

She blinks at me. "They will *review* your daughter's actions and determine what *discipline* to give her."

Oh. Good name for a committee. "And who's on the committee?"

She sighs. I must be exasperating her. "We are."

I look at the others around the table, and they are looking more and more uncomfortable. "So why will you wait ten days to discipline Rose when you could make that decision today?" I ask. "You're all here, aren't you?"

That's when the paper shuffling begins. "We, um, we want to review your daughter's transcripts and permanent file and talk to her teachers," she says. "That takes time."

"So . . . Rose won't be attending classes until the DRC makes its determination ten days from now," I say. "Is that right?"

"Right."

"But," I say, "didn't you just read through her file, Mrs. Thompson?"

She hesitates. "We, uh, we have procedures that we must follow in cases like this."

I lean back. "So these kinds of cases, as you call them, happen all the time?"

Silence. Hmm. Maybe they do. They must have good damage control here.

"As a condition of her return to school in ten days to meet with the DRC," Mrs. Thompson says, plowing on, "we strongly suggest that she begin counseling sessions." She nods at Mrs. Grady, who gives me several flyers. "And if the committee allows her to return to PH, she must agree to multi-cultural sensitivity sessions for the rest of the semester. They will meet twice a week during her lunch hour. In addition—"

"Could Rose come in now?" I interrupt. "She needs to hear all this."

They let Rose come in, her handcuffs gone, and she sits next to me, her eyes on her hands.

"Rose, we were just telling your father what happened," Mrs. Thompson says.

I shake my head. "You've told me what Rose did, but you really haven't told me all that happened." I turn to Rose. "Rose, honey, what happened? What made you . . . snap like that?"

10

Shawna

Crystal comes in hot and bothered from school today, which is nothing new. What is new is that she's *sweaty,* hot, and bothered.

"Where have you been?"

"Basketball practice."

"What?"

She slumps down on the couch. "I'm playing basketball. We had open gym. I told Junior to tell you."

Crystal is playing basketball? This is amazing. And Junior didn't tell me? That's even more amazing. I didn't even know Crystal had any talent in *any* sport. And where is Junior?

"So, during your senior year you just decide to play basketball."

"Yeah, and I'll need some new shoes."

I feel a ka-CHING coming on. I prepare to say, "I live as I can afford, not as you wish."

"Coach is getting us a nice discount on the shoes. They're so cool."

Okay, a small *ka-ching.* "How much?"

"She said we'll only have to pay thirty."

I think we can handle that. "But don't you have to have a physical first?"

"I got a free one."

I stare at her. "Without my consent?"

She winces. "I, um, put your name on it."

"You forged my signature?"

"Yeah. Sorry. I didn't think you'd let me play because of my grades."

"And I wouldn't have!" This irks me to no end. "I thought you were through forging my signature." She once signed all her interim reports before I could see them. Junior had given me his, I had asked for hers . . . Long story short, she got busted. "You really shouldn't be doing anything but studying."

"Yes, ma'am."

I squint. Hmm. She must want to play basketball really badly. She's being polite. I like a polite Crystal. "Well, did you pass your physical?"

"Yes."

"Good." I sigh. "For forging my signature, no TV or phone for a week."

"Oh, Mama, it was only—"

"And dishes for *two* weeks for not thinking you did anything wrong."

She sighs. "Yes, ma'am. But can I play?"

I hold up the "Mama finger," shaking it back and forth. "You can play, but only if you keep *all* your grades C or higher."

"Deal," she says.

I blink. That was too easy. I should have said "B or higher." Shoot.

But why is she still sitting there? Crystal usually arrives in a whirlwind, says her piece, and disappears. Something's up, I can just feel it.

"Mama, something happened at school today."

I knew it. "What happened?" I ask, making it sound like, "What did *you* do?"

"*I* didn't get in trouble."

Thank You, Jesus.

"Mama, this white girl just . . . went off. I've never seen anything like it. She just . . . blew up."

My eyes pop.

"I mean she just lost it entirely, calling my friends 'a bunch of niggers.' "

My muscles tense. "She didn't."

"She did."

Of all the ridiculous . . . When is that word going to die? I grope for words and can't find them, my anger rising. Why would any child take her life into her own hands like that? And why is this racism still out there? We're in the twenty-first century now. "She just . . . walked up to your friends and started calling them . . ."

"Yeah."

"Why on earth would she do such a thing?"

"I dunno. She was one of those Goth chicks I've been telling you about, Mama. She's a freak. She wears corsets and fishnet stockings." She shudders. "Freaky. Then later, I heard she punched out two deans and a security guard. They arrested her. I'll bet they expel her." Crystal stands. "Just another day at PH, Mama. What's for dinner?"

That girl could have been seriously hurt for what she said. I'm surprised Crystal's friends didn't dispense some justice with their fists. What is this world coming to? I don't want to dwell on this, but it's hard not to. When are we going to be past all this, Lord Jesus? All this name-calling and racist nonsense.

To calm down, I go to the computer to tell Joe about Crystal playing basketball, but there's already an e-mail from Joe in there, simply titled: "I NEED HELP."

Shawna:

I am at a complete loss. Rose was arrested today and charged with assault.

This is creepy. I am not calming down.

I told you how she dresses, but what I didn't tell you was how the other kids tease her. A group of kids called her a dyke, and she said some awful, racial things to them. When some deans tried to calm her down, she lost her mind. She may be charged with assault, and she could be expelled. As it is, she's been suspended for ten days.

I don't know what to do or say, Shawna. Please help me.

Joe

I minimize the screen and knock on the door to the bathroom, where Crystal has just finished taking a shower. "Crystal?"

"I'll be out in a minute."

"Oh, that's okay. Take your time. Um, what was that girl's name?"

"Which girl?"

"The one who went off today."

"Rose, I think."

Rose. What . . . ? It couldn't be . . .

"She rides my bus. Or at least she *used* to ride my bus." She opens the door, towels on her head and body. "I seriously doubt she's crazy enough to ride our bus after today."

Oh, dear Jesus, Jesus, Jesus.

"You okay, Mama?"

"Yeah. I'm fine."

I go back to the computer and sit in front of the screen for the longest time doing nothing. This *can't* be a coincidence. What are the chances?

Joe lives in this neighborhood?

The girl who went crazy today is *his* daughter? The girl who uses the N-word and beats up on authority figures is his oldest?

And that means . . . Joe is white.

Joe is white.

Well, the Internet is an anonymous place where race usually doesn't make a difference, but does it matter now?

White or not and whether it matters to me or not, Joe is going through hell right now. I open up his e-mail and write a reply:

Dear Joe:

Nothing like what you described has ever happened to me, so I doubt I can be much help. Know that you and Rose are in my thoughts.

Hear her out. Talk to her. Be there for her. Get away from the house for a while if you can. I'll be praying.

Shawna

I send it to Joe.

And instead of being overly angry at Rose for what she said to Crystal's friends, I pray for her. *Lord, You said to bless those that curse you, and even though she didn't curse me or my family directly, she cursed my race. You know how that hurts me, Lord, and I hope You can help that hurt go away. I'm praying that You bless Rose tonight. And help Joe. Amen.*

And then, I cry for the two of them, wondering if I should try to meet him. I want to, but if Rose behaves this way, maybe Joe . . .

Lord Jesus, just . . . help.

11

Joe

Rose still isn't talking to me, even after three days' suspension. "I'm here for you, Rose," I said that first night. "I'm here for you. Tell me how I can help you."

She just hasn't come to me yet, and it breaks my heart.

It also breaks my heart that I don't know how to discipline her. Cheryl and I never had to discipline her much at all. We might have sent her to bed early or cut back on her phone time, but we had no contingencies for this kind of . . . aberrant behavior.

While the school has graciously decided to drop the assault charges if Rose attends the sensitivity sessions, all this will go on her permanent record and may limit her college choices. I'm angry with her, but I can't help but be angry at those kids as well. Only Rose has to attend sensitivity training for using the N-word, but none of the kids who called her a dyke will have to go since Rose wouldn't tell anyone their names, and the administration didn't seem too keen on finding out who those kids were.

For her punishment, I've cut off all screens—TV and computer—and her phone privileges, and I've forbidden her to leave the house during her suspension unless I'm with her. She can only read or do the makeup work Joey brings home for her. I just don't know if she feels even an iota of remorse for what's she's done.

On Saturday, I take Shawna's advice again and we all get out of the house. We browse Books-A-Million and get mocha somethings that taste great but hurt my wallet. We pick up a few things at K-Mart including a few old videos on sale that we can watch later. One of them just happens to be *Metropolis,* a movie I heard Rose talking about one day with Joey. Maybe she'll open up while we watch, since it's a silent film.

Since the boys are always hungry, and since they don't want to go clear across town to Sonic, we stop at the Cross-roads McDonald's, the boys crowding me at the counter.

"I want a number one large," Jimmy says.

I turn to Joey. "The same," Joey says.

"Rose?"

She doesn't look up. "I'm not hungry."

"How about some fries at least?" I ask.

"Whatever," she says, and she drifts to the nearest booth.

I smile at the cashier. "I'll have another number one, I guess."

The cashier presses a few buttons. "Super-sized?"

"Sure." Rose can have my fries. "Um, and a strawberry shake."

"Can I have a shake?" Jimmy asks.

"It's for Rose," I say.

"Oh," Jimmy says.

"She needs it," Joey adds.

I smile at my son in spite of this cloud hanging over us. Some of Joey's friends have been treating him differently since Rose's outburst. He's had some tough bus rides this week. "Um, y'all go get your drinks. I'll bring it when it's ready." I hand them their cups, and they go to the fountain.

"You have your hands full," the cashier says.

What she doesn't know.

"Giving your wife the day off, huh?"

I sigh. "Something like that."

After we eat, we try to decide what to do next. I don't want to go back to the house just yet. I don't want Rose to close her bedroom door for another evening. Jimmy wants to go to the skate park at Wasena and since neither Joey nor Rose complains, we go to Wasena Park.

While Jimmy skates and Joey wanders down by the river, Rose wanders into a stand of trees beside a picnic shelter where, of all things, a trio of medieval knights practices their swordsmanship. Are they even allowed to wield swords like that? Is this legal? Rose, however, seems interested, and she even looks the part in her gown.

"Are you going to be okay here?" I ask her.

"Yeah."

"I'll, um, I'll be . . ." And I walk away toward the swings before I can finish because I don't know where I'm supposed to be at a time like this. I want to go back to when I was pushing my kids on these very swings, Cheryl right beside me, watching them rise higher and higher into the air, listening to their laughter, their cries of "Higher, Daddy, higher!" I wish I could go back to when Rose was a little girl in pigtails, her ribbons like angels' wings—

"Hey, mister, can you push me?"

A little black girl sitting on the first swing motions to me.

"*Can* you push me?" she asks again.

"Uh, sure." I look around for the girl's mother and only see a black boy nearby sitting on a bench with another black girl wearing a wildly colored dress, her head covered by a scarf.

"Thanks," the little girl says.

Then I push her, lost in her giggles and sighs. *This is how I want it to be, Lord. Something as simple as swings, Lord. That's all I'm asking. Something pure and—*

"I'll do it."

I turn and see the black boy standing beside me.

"That's my sister."

"Oh, uh, sure thing. She, um, she asked me . . ."

The boy steps between the swing and me, whispering something to the girl. I back away feeling totally useless and helpless, one child mourning in the trees, another child mourning down by the river, the last child mourning by hurting himself on a skateboard. I'm standing in the middle of a park, feeling further from my kids than at any time in my life.

And the tears come.

Lord, I'm waiting on You, but I'm not sure how much longer I can wait.

I see Rose talking to one of the swordsmen. At least she's talking to someone. I see Joey skipping stones across the river. His mother taught him how to do that. I cross the field to check on Jimmy and see him talking to a group of kids. They seem to be comparing bruises.

They're all right. They're coping. They won't miss me if I walk up the hill to our house . . . where I pour out a little of my heart to Shawna:

Shawna:

I did what you suggested. I got out of the house today. We went shopping and ate out at McDonald's. The cashier said that I had my hands full, and I certainly do. She also asked if I was giving my wife the day off, and I got depressed. Then at the park, my family scattered. I was pushing this little girl on the swings just as I pushed all my kids before, but even that was taken away from me. I'm on my last legs, Shawna. My heart is broken.

Pray especially hard for us today.

Joe

12

Shawna

As I read Joe's latest e-mail, my heart breaks a little, too. He tries so hard, and what does he get? Just when he's making progress, it all falls apart. *Lord, why is life so unfair sometimes?* I don't even know how to begin to mend this man's heart.

The door slams open, Toni rushing in and giving me a hug. "Hi, Mama."

Hugs can mend hearts. I'm feeling better already. "What have you been doing?"

"Swinging."

"Yeah? All by yourself?" This child is notorious for "picking up" men to push her on the swings in the hopes that I'll meet her future daddy this way. I can't count how many times I've had to get up off that bench down at Wasena to "meet" these guys, some of them nice, some of them right creepy.

"A nice man pushed me for a while until Junior came over."

Joe? No, it couldn't be, could it? *Lord, what are You up to here?* "He did?"

"Yeah. Junior never pushes me. He's always talking to Amina."

I look into her eyes. "What did the nice man look like?"

She shrugs. "Like a nice man. He was kinda tall, too. And he didn't have a wedding ring on."

I smile. I only *once* said for her to look for men without wedding rings, and now she makes sure *every* time. "Why did you ask this particular man to push you?"

"He looked kinda sad, Mama."

I hug her. "I'm sure you made his day."

"I would have, but Junior came over and scared him away."

"He what?"

"I'm thirsty. Can I have some juice?"

"Sure. Uh, wash your hands first."

My hands are tingling. Has my Joe just pushed Toni on a swing? Are Joe's kids just down the hill at the park? Has my son just "met" Joe? *Oh, Lord, all this timing of Yours is driving me crazy! First Rose and now this? What, heavenly Father, are You up to?*

I know that God places the answers right in front of us all the time, only we don't always see them. And in this case, God seems to be working on getting us together. I think.

I hope.

And what have I been doing? I've been stalling. I've been holding out. I haven't let Joe know how I feel.

What am I waiting for? A sign? The Lord is practically planting signs in plain view for me, tripping me with these signs. I should have splinters by now, and my shins should be bruised.

But I have to be sure.

Joe:

This may seem strange, but bear with me. Could you describe your hometown and your house to me?

Shawna

Short and sweet.

Just like me.

What's Junior always saying? *"Lipitalo, hupishwa."* "Things don't just happen by accident."

They happen by design.

13

Joe

This is a strange request, but I have nothing better to do.

Shawna:

I live in Roanoke, Virginia, in a little section called Wasena, just up the hill from Wasena Park and the Roanoke River. As for the house, it's a house with a front porch, back deck, playhouse for the kids, brown brick with yellow siding.

I know you have a reason for asking, but I'm curious to know why.

By the way, where do you live?

Joe

14

Shawna

*N*ow what?

My "man-in-a-similar-predicament" lives right down the street! I've probably seen him in the park. Two of my children have met him, and my oldest daughter thinks his daughter is a freak.

I need to get out of the house. "Toni?"

"Yes?"

"We're going for a walk."

"Why?" she whines.

I pull on a jacket. "Because it's a nice day."

And I want to see Joe's house.

It doesn't take long to see it. I find it just a few blocks away. Wide front porch, deck in back, playhouse, a PROGRESSIVE INSURANCE Jeep Cherokee parked on the street and a green van parked in the driveway. It's a nice house with brown brick and yellow siding, a house I pass whenever I go to the Kroger at Towers Mall. I squint up at the mailbox next to the front door on the porch. "Murphy." Joe Murphy.

"Why are we stopping, Mama?"

"No reason, honey. Let's get back."

"But we just started our walk."

I am confusing this child to death. "It's getting chilly, and I need to start dinner."

"You're crazy, Mama."

When we get back to The Castle, I see Rema and her kids outside. "Toni, why don't you go play with them while I talk to Rema?"

"Mama," Toni whine-whispers, "I don't understand what they're saying most of the time."

"Try listening with your heart, then," I tell her.

"But they, um, smell." She wrinkles up her nose for good measure.

"They what?"

"They smell funny, Mama."

I wrinkle up my nose and sniff her hair. "So do you, now go on."

"I don't—" she starts to say, but I add a pair of fierce eyes to my wrinkled nose. She rolls her eyes and sighs, and off she goes, dragging her feet. That child is eight going on seventeen sometimes.

Rema, in her traditional multicolored dress, sits under a tree, her feet bare, though it has to be in the low forties. I sit next to her, watching Toni playing with Rema's kids.

"Rema, I need some advice."

She smiles. "What kind of advice?"

I pick up and drop a clod of dirt. "Um, well, it's pretty complicated."

"Heart advice, then," she says.

"Yes."

She nods. "You look like a decision is fighting your mind."

She's the most perceptive woman I know. "You're right. I have quite a few battles going on up here." I tap my forehead.

She points at my heart. "And there, too, hmm?"

I nod.

"Your heart desires a man?"

Why are my hands sweaty? Oh, yeah. She put "heart," "desires," and "man" in the same sentence. "Yes."

"Ah. What the heart desires is medicine to it. This man must be the person to heal you."

Joe is my healer? Maybe he is. "But I'm not sure of him. There's so much I don't know about him, and what I don't know could hurt me, you know?"

She laughs. "You are far too picky."

"I am not."

She laughs again. "You are the pickiest woman I know. Everyone here knows it. To be so long without a man when you can have any man."

"Oh, I don't know about that." *Any* man? Is she kidding?

"You are young," Rema says. "And beautiful." She smiles. "And picky."

I sigh. "It's true. I'm just . . ." I sigh again. "I didn't think I was ready."

She leans closely to me. "Ready? For love? Love is always ready. Love is like honey. Once you dip your hand in honey, you do not dip it only once. You dip and dip and dip . . ." She smiles. "You can never get enough of a taste so sweet."

It's so true! I need a new honey! I need me a new sweetie! "What should I do?"

She shrugs. "It is said that love lasts if you eat grapes. Go eat grapes."

She can't be serious. "That's it? Just eat grapes."

She shakes her head at me. "You must be *with* the man at the time."

"But I'm not with him!"

"Not yet." She nods. "You are deep in love with him, yes?"

Say what? "Oh, I don't think I'm *deep* in love with him. I'm in some pretty intense *like* maybe, but love? No, I don't think so."

She folds her arms in front of her. "Then why do you ask heart advice from me?"

Do I . . . *love* Joe . . . like that? "I don't know, Rema, I mean—"

"Go," she interrupts. "Go to him. I will watch your child."

"I just can't . . . go to him," I say, mimicking her accent.

She blinks. "Go. Now."

I stand. "Just, um . . ."

"Go."

"Um, Toni," I call out, "you be good, now."

"I will," Toni says.

"Eat grapes," Rema says.

Grapes. It can't be that simple. I rush inside, glad to be completely alone for once in what seems like years, and type:

Joe:

I, too, live in Roanoke. I want to meet you. Can you meet me at El Toreo on Peters Creek on Monday at around one?

Shawna

And by meeting on Monday, I'll have time to get some grapes after church tomorrow. Are they even in season? What kind? Green or red? Seedless?

I'll just have to get a variety, and if the kids wonder why, I'll just eat more grapes.

15

Joe

She's *here?*
She's here.

Out of all the folks who e-mailed me, I latched on to her, and . . . she's *here?*

She's here.

God, I just prayed to You an hour ago, and You've answered me already? Why pay attention to me with all that's going on in the world? I don't deserve . . .

No. Sorry. You wouldn't give this to me unless I needed it. It's not a matter of deserving. You see my need, and You supply it.

Thank you.

Shawna:

I would love to meet you. See you at one.

Joe

16

Shawna

I have to be crazy to meet a man that I "met" online—especially for lunch at El Toreo, considering I'm dressed in my McDonald's uniform and know that whatever I eat here will wake me up at 3 AM with: "You have five seconds to get to the bathroom."

I am *so* nervous!

I haven't been across a table from a man since . . .

And I can't stop eating these tortilla chips and salsa, which is heavy on the cilantro, and I can't stop checking the door whenever anyone male comes inside.

And there are no grapes on the menu, except for grape soda. I wonder if grape soda counts . . .

I'm early. I had to come early, I guess, so I will be properly crazy by the time Joe gets here. It feels so weird to sit in a Mexican restaurant on my lunch break waiting for a man, who just happens to be after my heart.

Joe. I think his name and feel wonderful. Joe is a searcher like me. We both want reasons for why things happen, for why people we love die from cancer. His wife had breast cancer at such a young age! I'm thirty-eight now, and I check my breasts so much for anything suspicious they're practically afraid of my fingers, hiding all up in my bra.

Where *is* he? He could already be here watching me make a pig of myself with these tortilla chips. But *he* doesn't know who *I* am . . . does he?

Why did I choose El Toreo? Maybe he'll think I'm Hispanic. No, he wouldn't think that, as black as I am. And Mexican food is almost as all-American as Mickey D's is now. Even McDonald's has breakfast burritos, for goodness' sake—

Is that him?

No.

A carryout order. Too old for me, anyway. Rodney was older than me by almost ten years, but this guy—looking at me with my mouth full of tortilla chips—

I need more water.

More soda.

More something.

I wish I had some grapes.

17

Joe

If I drum on this steering wheel any more I'll have bruised fingertips.

Why'd I drive Cheryl's mommy van to meet Shawna? What a dump! The kids never clean up after themselves.

Check that.

I need to have the kids clean up after themselves.

I should have parked farther away, like at that car wash over there. The van could sure use a wash. There's enough tree sap on this van to . . . to do what? I'm not thinking clearly.

"Get out of the van, Joe," I whisper.

"But what if she doesn't like me?" I whisper back.

More drumming.

"She'll like you. She already likes you."

All those e-mails. All those times my fingertips dripped sweat on the keys—like they're doing now on the steering wheel.

I'm already late. I was *never* late before. I was *always* on time. Cheryl and I had a child every two years like clockwork, their birthdays spaced throughout the year so we wouldn't go broke throwing them swim parties and Chuck E. Cheese parties and Thunder Valley parties and laser tag parties—

We haven't had a party since . . . Cheryl. Whose birthday is next? Lord, I can't remember. Is it Jimmy's?

How did Cheryl do it? Every morning I heard, "Brush your teeth, wash your face, lotion your body, and wear clean underwear." They always wore ironed clothing and ate a wholesome breakfast, had a bag lunch, took secure book bags filled with the right books to school, and Cheryl never missed a signature on a note from school. If Rose, Joey, and Jimmy have taken their vitamins and have fresh breath when they leave for school, it's a good day for me.

Shawna will be mad that I'm late. What excuse can I use? Lunch-hour traffic? It's never that bad in Roanoke. The weather? No rain, just a crisp, cold, clear February sky that might turn into a little snow shower later.

"Get out of the van."

Here we go.

I wish I had a towel for my hands.

18

Shawna

Joe isn't showing. Or he *did* show and I scared him away because I smell like French fries. Online he hasn't seemed like a "looks-matter" kind of man, but how can you really tell?

"Are you ready to order?"

Young Hispanic males keep sneaking up on me, asking the same question. They've been so patient, even giving me another basket of chips and more salsa. "I guess I'll have a beef burrito to go."

"Okay."

What will *that* look like? Walking into McDonald's where I am the Queen Bee carrying a burrito from El Toreo? I can always sneak in the back or leave it in the car to eat on my break. But it will get cold if I leave it there. If hot burritos tear up my intestines, what will a cold burrito do? Oh, I know I can warm it up, but I can't—

A new arrival. White—as a *ghost!* That man needs more sun or something. He's wiping his hands on his pants. Nice suit, though, wrinkled as it is. His shoes need a shine, and his face definitely needs a shave. Decent eyes—

That are looking at me.

Squinting.

Look at all those crow's-feet. He's about, what, forty?

I look away from him and focus on the condensation streaming down my water glass. He wasn't looking at me, I mean, he *couldn't* be looking at *me* . . .

I look back.

It's him. It's Joe. It has to be. He, um, he even looks like a Joe, whatever that—

His lips are moving, forming my name.

Where's my voice? Gone. I can only nod and stare at the water making puddles in a circle around my glass.

Dearest Lord Jesus, what have I gotten myself into?

19

Joe

Shawna is black.
And beautiful.

But let's get back to the black part. She didn't sound
"black" online. Oh, what's *that* supposed to mean? We all
sound . . . monoracial or something like that when we're online. That's one of the glories of the Internet. No one has a
race or ethnicity. There are no walls, just two or more minds
connecting in cyberspace.

And she looks familiar. McDonald's at Crossroads. My
God, she's been taking my orders for years. I wonder if she
remembers me.

Geez, will I *ever* get to her table?

Eyes. She has a pair of dark eyes. I'll bet that when she
smiles, those dark eyes—

Ow.

I have bumped into her table, and she has had to grab for
her glass before it topples over.

"Joe?" she asks. A soft voice. A kind voice. A voice . . .
that's trying not to laugh at me, I'm sure. She's probably
thinking I'm blind or have poor depth perception.

"Yeah. Um, Shawna. Sorry I'm late." I look behind me for no reason, no reason at all, at the tile floor, for no reason at all. *There's nothing there, Joe! If you've seen one floor . . .* "Um, traffic was bad from—"

No. Look at her! She's been your lifeline these past six months.

I turn to those dark eyes. "Shawna, I've been sitting in the parking lot afraid to come in." Honesty is always the best policy. "So, I'll understand if you—"

"Why don't you sit down, Joe?"

"Sit?"

She smiles. Yeah, I knew her eyes would light up like that. "Yes, sit down, Joe, before you fall down."

"Right." I sit, immediately grabbing for a tortilla chip. "Have you been waiting long?" What a *stupid* question! Of course she's been waiting long, and *I'm* the reason!

"Not too long." She sips her water. "Joe, why didn't you tell me you were white?"

The tortilla chip slips out of my grasp, spinning on the table. "It, um, I guess it never came up in all our conversations. I mean, you didn't tell me you were . . . um . . ."

"Black?"

Beautiful. So direct. So . . . conversational, so to-the-point like all our online conversations have been. "Yeah."

"We talked about so many things." She shakes her head. "Does it matter to you?"

"No." And it doesn't. She saved me from the abyss.

"Really?"

"No. Does it matter to you?"

She takes a deep breath, and I hold mine.

20

Shawna

No, of *course* it doesn't matter to me. This man has a beautiful mind and the purest of hearts.

But as for my kids?

It might matter to my kids. And his kids. And his family and my family, even though they live far away. And my co-workers. And his coworkers. And the people in this town . . .

"No, uh, Joe. In fact, it's an unexpected blessing. And anyway, we're, um, we're too far along in our, um, friendship, to let that stand in our way." Am I pushing it? He seems unaffected, but I've never really been able to tell with white men. His face hasn't moved. "I mean, it's been, what, five or six months?"

"Yeah. And this is kind of our first date, right?"

I want to touch his hand, to feel the man who has nearly felt up my entire soul with a bunch of letters on a computer screen. "Joe, we've been, um, dating nearly every day for close to six months, right?"

"You're right. Has it been six months?"

I nod.

Oh, no! Here comes my burrito. "I, um, I already ordered." And that is a *huge* burrito! I can't eat all that! Not after all these tortilla chips! And why does it have to be wrapped up in foil and stuck in a paper bag? Oh, yeah. I ordered it to go. "Joe, do you, um, do you like beef burritos?"

"Sure."

Finally, he smiles. Good. My feet can stop running laps under this table.

I turn to the waiter. "Two forks, please."

Then . . . we eat a beef burrito resting on aluminum foil on a table at El Toreo.

It is so . . . normal.

Even a little romantic.

I like this.

I'm even letting him have more than half of the burrito.

21

Joe

"So, how's Rose doing?" she asks.

"Better. Church yesterday seemed to help." I can't take my eyes off . . . my hands. Why is it so hard to look at her face? And if my hands are so chapped and dry, why are they still sweating?

"Church always helps. Makes the rest of the week bearable sometimes."

I glance up to smile at her to find that she's looking at her hands, too. I wonder if hers are sweating as well. It's funny, but after all we've been through, we're just two shy middle-aged parents who don't know what to say or do.

We *must* be made for each other.

"I've been meaning to ask you how you figured out I was here in Roanoke."

She looks up. "Well, we have met before at McDonald's. Big Mac, large fries, Coke, right?" She looks back at her hands. "You've been coming in for lunch for years."

"And you remember my face?"

She looks at my face, and my face gets hot. She has dark brown laser beams for eyes. "I remember the regulars."

"But . . . there has to be more to it. When did you know that I, um, was the Joe who had been writing to you?" That made *no* sense.

"I don't know where to begin, but . . ." She sighs. "You've already met my youngest daughter."

"I have?"

"Yeah. You pushed her in a swing on Saturday."

The little girl . . . "That was Toni?"

"Yeah. That's a little game she plays to find herself a daddy." She quickly looks away. "And my son came over . . ."

"To protect her. I understand." So he wasn't angry with me. He was just being a good brother.

"And my daughter knows your daughter from what happened at PH."

Oh, no! "Was she one of the ones who Rose—"

She shakes her head. "No. The ones she, um, spoke to were friends of hers, though."

So it has even affected Crystal. "Wait. That means Joey, Junior, Rose, and Crystal ride the same bus."

She nods.

"So, they might all know each other already."

She sits back, her eyes drifting up to mine. "Yeah, I guess. But riding the bus and really knowing who you're riding with isn't necessarily the same thing."

True. "Okay, our kids have a passing knowledge of each other. That's something."

She nods.

Now what? I hear more silence, and instead of the ticking of a clock, I hear Mexican music. "Shawna, I want to take you out to eat, to a movie, to a show, something, but . . ."

"But what?" She smiles, and my heart hurts.

"But I'm not sure how we can get away from our kids to do that."

"Crystal or Junior will mind Toni."

"And I guess Rose can mind the boys." I try to laugh but

end up coughing. "But trying to explain to them where I was going, um, might get ugly."

Her eyes drop.

"Oh," I say, "I didn't mean . . . I just want this to work, you know?"

Her eyes rise. "Me, too."

"Okay, then . . . I haven't been on a date in . . ." How long has it been? "In a long time."

"Same here."

At least we're in this predicament together. "The last date I went on I think Cheryl and I went out for ice cream." I smile. "Back when Baskin-Robbins only had a dozen flavors. How about you?"

She counts on her fingers. "*Whew*. Close to twenty years? The older Bush was president."

I feel a *lot* better now. "Where do people—couples . . ." That sounds so strange. "Where do couples go out around here? Cheryl and I only went on family dates." My fingers start drumming on the table again. "How about some ice cream?"

"And a walk in the park?"

A walk! Why didn't I think of that? "Sure."

"Tonight?"

More Mexican music with lots of guitar, the tempo fast and frenetic, as if it's background music to this scene. "Sure." I swallow. "Tonight, uh, after dinner, say . . . seven thirty?" We ought to be through with dinner by—

"Seven thirty would be fine."

Wow. She's really eager. My hands are practically dripping.

"I'll just, um . . . walk down to your house, okay?" she asks.

This is really about to happen. "Sure."

She squeezes my hand, and I squeeze back. Nice eyes. Very nice eyes.

22

Shawna

I can't believe I've just forced this man into a date in only a few hours and we're holding greasy hands across a table in public and—

What am I thinking? *Am* I thinking? I can't believe I just said I'd walk down to *his* place. He should pick me up, right?

"I *could* pick you up," he offers.

Cute. He's . . . cute. "Yeah. Maybe you better." I give him directions, which is pretty silly, considering he only has to cruise up the street a few blocks. I look at our hands. Such contrasts, such—

He pulls his hands away. "I, uh, I should go."

I check my watch. I'm late! "Me, too."

We stand together and step out from the table. He leans in—oh, my beating heart—and gives me the most delicious hug right there in El Toreo.

"See you soon," he says.

Soon.

Too soon?

I have to get back to work, rush home and throw a meal together, make myself prettier, and . . . and . . .

I got a hug today . . . a hug from a man. Oh, getting hugs from my children is heavenly, don't get me wrong, but a hug from a man . . .

A man-hug.

My body feels ten years younger already.

Unlike the movies where the clock never seems to move, the rest of my shift flies by, and instead of whipping up a meal, I bring home Quarter Pounder meals for everyone, something I do maybe once or twice a year.

And that's when my children get suspicious.

"Why aren't you cooking tonight, Mama?" Crystal asks.

I ignore her and concentrate on the fries. These aren't that crispy. They should have changed the oil in the fry vats—

"Something wrong, Mama?" Junior asks.

"No," I say, picking up and barely nibbling at a fry.

They keep looking at each other, and other than Toni smacking her lips over her fries, the kitchen is silent.

"So why . . ." Crystal says.

I have no idea what I'm about to say. "I was tired, okay? I didn't feel like cooking."

Silence. They don't believe me.

Here we go . . . "Okay, okay. I *was* tired, and I didn't want to rush because . . ." *Help me here, Lord Jesus.* "Because I am going out for ice cream with a friend later this evening."

"A friend?" Crystal says. "Rema?"

Who *is* about the only true friend I have other than a few wonderful Christian women at church, but Rema and I rarely even get to go clothes shopping or holiday shopping together because of our work schedules. "His name is Joe."

Toni stops smacking her lips. "Joe? The man on the computer?"

I look at Crystal. "Yes." I flash my don't-you-say-a-word eyes.

Crystal pushes away from the table, shaking her head,

folding her arms in front of her. My don't-you-say-a-word eyes must still be working.

"Joe will be picking me up at seven thirty," I say to Crystal the Angry, "and I'll need you to babysit Toni."

"I'm not a baby," Toni says.

"I know you aren't, honey, but you're too young to be here by—"

"And what if I had plans?" Crystal interrupts. My don't-you-say-a-word eyes only work for so long, I guess.

"On a Monday night?" I ask. "On a school night? You know the rules."

"I can't believe this," Crystal says, and she leaves the table.

At least she didn't throw her half-eaten Quarter Pounder at me.

I look at Junior. "We'll be out about an hour or so. I think."

"Cool," Junior says. "Take your time. We'll be all right."

Toni leaves her chair, gives me a hug, and then returns to her fries. I'd ask her what the hug was for, but I already know.

She thinks she's getting herself a daddy.

And . . . maybe . . . who knows—other than God, of course—what might happen.

23

Joe

"I'm taking a friend out for ice cream tonight," I state as nonchalantly as I can while my fingers ooze pints of sweat under the dinner table. "I shouldn't be out long."

"A friend? Who?" Jimmy asks.

"A woman named Shawna," I say. "I have been writing to her for about six months online, and it turns out she lives right here in Roanoke. Just up the street, as a matter of fact. I want to take her out to thank her for helping me, you know?"

The mantel clock ticks on.

"I'll be taking her to Katie's and then we'll probably walk around a bit," I say, "but I'm sure I'll be back by eight thirty at the latest."

More silence.

That wasn't so bad. I must have the least suspicious kids on the planet.

24

Shawna

WhatdoIwearwhatdoIwearwhatdoIwear . . .
For goodness' sake, Shawna, it's only ice cream and a walk in the park. Jeans, Nikes, a sweatshirt, and a coat. Okay, it's weird to get ice cream in February and go walking in a park with snow in the forecast, but it's a beginning. I don't have to put on airs to get some fresh air.

WhatdoIdowithmyhairwithmyhairwithmyplainol'dull-and—

A hat.

It's February, we'll be eating ice cream, it's cold, it may snow, my hair needs a wash.

I put on a plain black knit hat and pose in front of the mirror over my dresser. Very chic. Very . . .

Plain. Oh, God, I am so plain. I have a decent smile, a medium nose, ordinary eyes, scary eyebrows, a body that doesn't look as if it's been pregnant three times—

It's only ice cream. Just a cone with one scoop . . . or should I get it in a cup? Do I want him to see me licking on an ice-cream cone? It could be kind of seductive—

Sorry, Lord. I'll put it in a cup, okay?

"Mama, he's here!" Toni yells from outside my door.

I look at my watch. He's early. Ten minutes early.

I grab my coat and open the door to see Toni jumping up and down in front of me.

"He's the man who pushed me on the swing!" she shouts.

I look past Toni to Junior, who only smiles and points to the door.

"I'll, uh, I'll get it," I say, moving toward the door. I wish I had heard him knock. He must have knocked softly. Yeah, Joe's been knocking softly on my heart for so long, and it's about time I opened the door.

I put my hand on the knob and look back to see if Crystal is around. Nope. Hmm. Not a good sign, but at least there won't be any drama. I open the door.

"Hi," Joe says.

"Hi," I say. "Want to come in for a minute? I'm almost ready."

"Sure."

He steps inside, nodding at Junior and Toni.

"Hi, Joe," Toni says. "Remember me?"

He nods. "Sure. At the park on the swings."

"I'll, uh, I'll . . ." I return to my room, throw a brush through my hair until it almost looks fuller, and toss the hat on the floor. My ears will just have to be cold. I return to the front door. "Ready." I turn to Junior. "I'll be back in a few—"

"Just go, Mama," Junior says.

"Oh, okay," I say.

Joe steps aside, I walk out the door, Junior closing the door behind us.

"Well," I say, and it's the only thing I can think to say.

"Yeah," he says.

We are just a couple of kids!

He holds out his hand, and I take it, and hand in hand we walk to a green minivan. He opens my door, I get in, he gets in, he backs out . . .

I exhale.

Have I been holding my breath the entire time? I feel light-headed.

"You look nice," he says.

"Thank you," I say.

"Any, um, difficulties?" he asks.

"Just Crystal," I say. "Any difficulties on your end?"

He shakes his head. "No."

"Really?" I ask.

"Really. None visible, anyway. I'm sure Rose will say something eventually."

I nod. "Um, Joe, you do know it's February, right?"

"Yes."

"And we're about to get ice cream and go walking out-side."

He doesn't speak right away. "Oh. Would you rather do something else?"

The answers I could give him . . . *Lord, it's been eight years, right?* "I'm just saying that we're crazy for doing this."

He smiles. "Yep."

I watch the scenery, such as it is, roll by and giggle inside my head. I like Joe. I mean, I actually *like* him. We're not ex-actly soul mate material, but . . . he has a sense of humor, he's polite, and he's willing to take risks.

We walk hand in hand again into Katie's, a well-lit, clean ice-cream parlor that also sells plush toys, Beanie Babies, and party supplies. As I had expected, we're the only two crazy customers out on a chilly February night. We each get one scoop in a cup of Moose Tracks, vanilla ice cream loaded with caramel candies, and then we walk around Tow-ers Mall looking into store windows.

This is *so* romantic!

25

Joe

I wish this were more romantic.

I also wish we had gotten cones so we could still hold hands.

That might make this a little more romantic.

When we finish our ice cream outside Kroger, I reach for Shawna's hand. "Let's find a park."

"I have a better idea," she says, and she pulls me inside Kroger.

Kroger? A date at a grocery store?

I hesitate and tug a little.

"Come on, Joe. It will be fun."

I let her pull me to the fresh produce section where she studies and touches and lifts and weighs grapes, of all things.

"You like grapes?" I ask. Another stupid question.

"Don't you?" she asks.

"Sure."

But when she ends up buying nearly eight *pounds* of grapes, I start to wonder. Does she make her own wine? Are her kids grape addicts or something?

I offer to pay for the grapes, but Shawna shakes her head. "We're going Dutch, Joe. This is on me." And once she pays for the grapes, she hands me nearly half of them. "Eat up," she says.

Grapes? On top of ice cream?

She takes a grape from one of her bunches and pushes it into my mouth. Sweet. Delicious. I get a vision of Shawna feeding me grapes while I recline . . .

Whoa.

This is romantic.

"How is it?" she asks.

"Sweet," I say. I take a grape from my bag and put it on her lips. She doesn't bite into it right away, slowly, painfully using her tongue to take that grape into her mouth.

This . . . this is passionate.

"It *is* sweet," she says.

"How, uh, how hungry are you?" I ask, and as soon as I ask, I know I turn beet red.

"I'll eat whatever food you feed me, Joe," she says.

My heart is thudding. "Um, let's get back to the van where it's warmer."

The van warms up long before the heater finally kicks in because we feed each other grapes. One at a time. Slowly. Passionately.

"I am fit to burst," she says after we've gone through at least two bunches. She holds up one last grape. "This is your last grape tonight, Joe." Then she puts it between her lips . . .

I remove my seat belt so I don't have to strain as much and look into her soft brown eyes. I tilt my head slightly and get close enough for my lips to touch the grape—

And she sucks the grape and my lips right next to her lips for the briefest of moments.

"Hey," I say, pulling back. "That was my grape."

"You want another chance?" she asks.

I check the clock on the radio. Nine fifteen? We've been

out for almost two hours? I watch her eyes travel to her watch.

"I want another chance," I say, "when we have more time."

She smiles. "Yeah?"

"Yeah. And we'll need more than eight pounds."

She fans the air in front of her face with her hand. "Why, Mr. Murphy, you're so fresh."

Fresh. That's what all this is. Fresh and new and alive and—

She holds up another grape. "Just one more?"

"Shawna," I say, "then we'll be here all night."

She nods and places the grape on my lips. "We better go."

I hold the grape between my lips so she can "kiss" a grape away from me, but she turns away and puts on her seat belt.

I pull the grape into my mouth.

Not nearly as sweet.

26

Shawna

Well, I almost got kissed anyway.

I need to slow down. *We* need to slow down. It's obvious that we more than like each other, and it's also obvious that Joe's holding back a little. I understand. Here I am, another woman in what has to be his wife's van, trying to entice him to a kiss using grapes.

At least I know what Rema meant, and we *will* be eating more grapes.

One at a time.

We get to The Castle about nine thirty, and Joe walks me to the door. "I had a really—"

But then his hands are holding my face, his nose touching mine, and I can't finish my sentence. "I had a really . . . too," he says.

Here it comes. A kiss eight years in the making. A seedless grapeless kiss.

But instead of a kiss, he slides his hands down my face to my neck, to my shoulders, down my arms, to my waist . . .

Another hug, this one longer, deeper. I kiss his neck without thinking, and he kisses me on the cheek. "Don't eat all the grapes," he whispers.

"I won't," I whisper back. "Do you want my phone number, Mr. Murphy?"

"Sure."

I whisper it to him once, and he whispers it back. I get goose bumps. Whispering sure is a memorable thing to do.

He steps back, I turn and unlock the door, he steps farther back, I step inside.

End of date.

Whew!

I feel twenty years younger.

I have just been on a date with a man, my breath has to smell like grapes, and I got a kiss on the cheek. And now I'm going to get online with him.

I feel so *close* to him right now!

Or should I call him? He shouldn't be too hard to find in the phone book. But what if one of his kids answers? I'll just act like a bad driver (which I'm not) who has had an accident. I find a listing for "Murphy, C and J." Joe hasn't gotten around to removing the *C.* Hmm. That's pretty telling right there. Maybe I shouldn't—

I dial the number . . .

And it's busy. Maybe a *real* bad driver is calling him. Either that or Rose or one of his sons is on the phone. Hmm. I'll just have to write him, then.

Dear Joe:

I had so much fun tonight. It was good to get out of the apartment and get some calories and fresh air. And grapes.

Oh, this letter is about as intimate as filing my nails. I need to start over.

Dear Joe:

You have a nice booty.

Oh, I can't tell him *that!* Man, I am so hyper right now,
and I only had one scoop of ice cream. I delete the booty
line.

Dear Joe:

I wish we had more time together tonight. I wish you
were with me right now.

I do. I should have a man to snuggle up with after a date. I
should have a man to massage my feet after a hard day. I
should have a man rubbing my back, my neck, my lower
back—
I look at the screen. I guess this will have to do for now,
but I'm not satisfied with this alone. I need to touch him. I
need him to touch me. I mean, this e-mailing is keeping in
touch, but it's not the kind of touching I want to do. And I
want more than a peck on the cheek.

If your work schedule allows it, please visit me at
McDonald's this week. I'll be working 8:30-3:30 Monday through Saturday.

Am I begging here? Do I sound too desperate? I *am* desperate! But wait—I don't even know if he feels the same
way as I do yet. I have to know that he's as desperate for me
as I am for him. He *did* kiss me on the lips. Sort of. After I
tricked him. And I told him to write me, and he will. I'll just
have to wait for his e-mail. Yeah. I'll just have to wait on the
Lord a little longer.

27

Joe

I told her I'd write her, but I can't put into words how I feel.
I write a series of really bad beginnings:

My dearest Shawna:

How I enjoyed this evening with you so close to
me . . .

Dearest Shawna:

I wish you were with me right now so I wouldn't have
to write another boring e-mail . . .

Shawna, my dear:

I'm not sure what I'm feeling right now, and I'm
finding it hard to put into words all that I'm feeling for
you . . .

But what if, after seeing me "in action," she doesn't feel
the same way I feel?
It's so hard to figure out tone and attitude from an e-mail,

though from what I've written, I know that I'm gushing too much. Was I this way with Cheryl? Am I a gusher? I don't come from gushing people, so what's happening to me? I eat a few grapes, and I start to gush. I blame the grapes.

I *have* to hear her voice. That's the only way I'll be able to tell if we're . . . If we're what? An item? That's so old-fashioned. A couple? Significant others? Main squeezes?

I delete the latest gushing e-mail and write:

Dear Shawna,

I miss you already. As soon as Joey gets off the phone, I will call you. How late will you stay up?

Joe

The first part is kind of gushy, but the second part shows I'm kind of pushy. I want her to know that I'm a man of action, despite my seeming inability to kiss a woman on the lips when she obviously wanted me to.

On the *cheek?* What was I thinking?

This e-mail isn't very romantic at all. Should I change the ending to "your friend, Joe"?

Just send the darn thing, stupid.

28

Shawna

I'm saved! He misses me! Yes!

Dear Joe:

I'll stay up as long as it takes.

Shawna

For thirty minutes . . . then forty . . . fifty—c'mon, Joey, give us a break here, huh?—I wait, pacing my feet in front of me, the phone in my hand. The kids are all asleep, I should be asleep, the world outside is asleep as flurries drift down . . . and now my hand is asleep from holding on to this phone for so long.

The phone rings, and I catch it on the first half ring, taking a deep breath, lowering my voice, and saying, "Hello?"

"Hi," he says.

"Hi."

I hear him exhale. It's like we've been running some endurance race and we've finally made it to the finish line.

"I had the worst time writing you, Shawna," he says.

"Me, too, I mean, I had the worst time writing to you, too."

"When can I see you again?"

Music to my ears! "Is tomorrow too soon?" I have no time to be subtle now.

"Where?"

"Come to McDonald's."

He laughs. "I plan to. Daily. Hourly. I might spend my whole day there. There are lots of fender-benders in the Crossroads parking lot."

More music. "I usually take a break around one thirty. Do you, um, do you like coffee?"

"Yes," he whispers, "the darker the better."

Oh . . . my. "Um, I, uh . . . Well." I'm warming up. Are the kitchen windows fogging? *Whoo.* "Um, do you like apple pies?"

"Sure."

"Good. Okay. It's a date." A daily date for hot, dark coffee and some steaming apple pie.

"Shawna, can I be honest with you?"

Strange question, but . . . "Haven't you always been honest with me?"

"Yes, but this is different."

"I'm all ears." And dancing feet!

"Whenever everything is falling apart here, I think about you and pray for you, and it makes me feel better."

Oh, the man can pluck my soul.

"I know it doesn't make sense, but I've been praying that you would keep writing to me, praying that you wouldn't forget about me, afraid I was trying too hard, writing too much, asking too many questions. I was hoping that I wasn't becoming a burden to you."

He's practically strumming my soul now. "You've never been a burden to me, Joe. You have gotten me through so many hard days, you just don't know."

"I have?"

"Yes." And nights, too, but I don't want to tell him that yet.

"Shawna, I'm beginning to believe that all this is a part of God's plan for me, for us. Do you . . . feel that way, too?"

I giggle. It's not the most appropriate time to do so, but I actually giggle. And then I can't stop giggling. I'm laughing in my kitchen with tears in my eyes because I'm so happy.

"Are you all right?"

"Of course I am, Joe. I haven't been this happy in a long time, and true happiness comes from God, so . . . yes. This feels right. It feels . . . heavenly. It's like a heavenly conspiracy or something."

"We're being manipulated," he says.

"By forces beyond our control," I add.

"Right."

I wipe my eyes. "Then you know we have to involve our kids."

"I know, I know." He sighs. "But I can't think of a way to break it to them gently. My kids think we're just friends. Can you think of a way to let them know we're, um, more than friends?"

I sigh. "No. I can't. They're going to be hurt, maybe even shocked."

"Yeah."

"But Toni and Junior don't mind."

"Toni is so cute."

I smile. "Thank you. I hope she stays that way. Crystal is going to be the toughest sell. She's been my chaperone for so long. What about your kids?"

Joe sighs. "Joey might be okay with it, and probably Jimmy. But Rose . . . There's no telling how Rose will react."

I shouldn't have to do all this thinking at . . . one in the morning?

"Do you think we're rushing?" he asks.

"Joe, I don't think we're moving fast enough."

He doesn't respond.

"Joe?"

"I'm just . . . Aren't I supposed to be in mourning? This time last year I was carrying my wife to the bathroom, and now . . ."

He's having doubts. That's why I only got a peck on the cheek. I know I would have had my doubts this soon after Rodney's death. I can't blame him. "It has happened kind of fast—for you, I mean. For me, it can't happen fast enough."

"Shawna, I think—and hope—that I've found someone to love, and I hope that someone is you."

Oh, that wonderful L-word!

"I just wish . . . I wish there was more time in between, you know? More time for some wounds to heal. But that isn't fair to you."

"I can wait." I smile. "I *will* wait. I mean, I have waited, right? Just . . ."

"Just what?"

"Just don't keep me waiting too long, okay?" I have to be realistic about this.

I'm a couple years shy of forty, and for whatever reason, that seems to be the cut-off line for romance in this country and this city. Thirty-nine-year-olds can get some action, but "forty" is another "F-word" to the men around here.

"I don't want to wait."

Whoo. He sounds so sure. Maybe I can coax him a little. "Joe, you have made me feel so special, so needed, so alive. As long as you stop by for coffee and an apple pie every day until you're sure, I can wait." Though I really don't want to. I am a heart deep in love.

My God. I love him.

I love him.

"I love you, Joe."

"I love you, too, Shawna."

Unlike the movies where music swells and the sun suddenly comes up or sets into a brilliant display of God's handiwork, nothing happens. Nothing.

Nothing visible anyway.

Inside, though. Yeah. There are some fireworks going off and marching bands playing and waterfalls of happiness crashing on all sorts of rocks.

Hollywood will never be able to film all *that*.

29

Joe

For the next several weeks, I drink coffee and eat apple pies with Shawna. Her crew has already figured "us" out, and Shawna tells me they're happy for us.

"Mainly because I'm being less of a taskmaster with them," she says. "It's hard to be mean when you're so happy. Besides, I'm the only Bible many of them will ever read, so I'm a much better witness when I'm happy."

The only Bible many of them will ever read. What an awesome statement.

Shawna and I talk about anything and everything, but mostly we discuss our kids. It's all been so strange and wonderful. When Cheryl was alive, I used to talk mostly about my house, what Cheryl had me building, my job, where I planned to travel on vacation. Now here I am talking about the three people who have become my life.

Shawna is an incredible listener. It is so nice to talk to an adult. I don't have to explain myself nearly as much, don't have to fuss at all, and definitely don't have to raise my voice. We're two still, small voices talking to each other in a booth at McDonald's. Sure, it's not what most people would say is romantic, but it's romantic enough for me.

"What's it like being an insurance adjuster?" she asks today, the first time she has ever asked me about my job.

"It's okay. Most folks are glad to see me because I cut them checks on the spot. I meet people by accident, you know."

She laughs softly. "Things just don't happen by accident, Joe. Look at us."

I take another sip, another bite of pie, and collect my thoughts. Unlike when I'm talking to my kids, I can actually take a few moments to think when I'm around Shawna. As rushed as all this has been, we take our time when we talk. There's no hurry at all.

"Joe?"

Okay, sometimes there's some hurry. "Sorry. I was lost in some thoughts."

"Any good ones?"

I smile. "They were all about you, so they were all good."

"You're trying to get another free apple pie today, aren't you?"

"Maybe. Or . . ."

"Or what?"

"Maybe I'll get another hug today."

She widens her eyes. "Slow down, now. You don't want us moving too fast, now."

We have *yet* to kiss. Crazy. We love each other, we've hugged, and we haven't kissed. "You know I want to do so much more."

She licks her lower lip, softening her eyes. "You want to make my day, huh?"

"Yes."

"And my nights, too?"

Whew. She's good at this game. I am such a novice. "Yes. You know I do."

"Just checking." She looks away, a smile creasing her pretty face.

"Why do you do that?"

She looks back. "Do what?"

30

Shawna

I have been flirting my booty off with this man. I haven't flirted like this *ever,* and it seems to be working.

I cannot let this man's heart rest for a single moment.

I want him to leave here each day wishing he could drive me home, take me into my room, and . . . *Sorry, Lord. You know what I mean.* I have to keep him wanting me twenty-four hours a day.

"I mean, we're sitting here talking, right?"

"Right," I whisper. It is a soft, sultry whisper, one I've almost perfected.

"And you're looking at me the entire time licking your lips while I'm trying not to slurp my coffee or make a pig of myself with these pies, and as soon as I get going, you stop me with a smile or a look or that whisper of yours and I can't think."

My plan is working. "Yeah?"

"Shawna, I can't get two sentences together in my head when I'm around you that don't involve . . ." His face reddens.

"That don't involve what?"

He shakes his head. "There you go again."

"What?"

"You're flirting with me again."

I bat my eyes at him. "You've noticed."

"I can't help but notice. From the second I walk in here until I leave, it's like you're trying to seduce me."

"I am?" *Lord, You know that's what I'm doing, and I know it's very un-Christian of me, but* someone *has to do it.* "Does it bother you?"

"Yes."

My eyes pop.

"I mean, no, it doesn't bother me as in making me angry or anything like that. It just . . . keeps me up at night, you know?"

Finally. I'm affecting him in the bedroom. Good for me. *Sorry, Lord. It's just nice to know that I still got it. I am almost forty, You know.*

"Shawna, what I'm trying to say, and I'm saying it very badly, is that you don't have to seduce me. Aside from my kids, I can think of no one else all day and all night. I can't sleep, I don't eat, I get lost on my way to customers—and I've lived in this town much of my life."

"You get lost?"

"Yeah. I'll be driving and listening to the radio and suddenly I'll look around and say, 'Where am I?'"

"You do?" My routine should be copied into a how-to book on seduction.

"Shawna, you have me, okay? I'm yours."

"All mine?"

"All yours. Are you, uh, are you . . ."

"Finish your sentence, Joe." I'm trying to get him to talk sexy to me, something he most likely never did with Cheryl. I have to be able to talk about making love with the man I'm with, and not just the "Want some? Sure." type of talking. We have to be able to communicate sexually, and if I can't get him to talk here at a McDonald's about it, well . . .

"Do you think of me that way?"

"What way?" Say it, Joe. Spit it out!

"Do you make love to me in your head as much as I make love to you in mine?"

I nod. *Sorry, Lord.* "Are you, I mean, are we up in there doing it right now?"

He looks up. Maybe he's apologizing to God for what he's about to say, too.

"Shawna, you keep me awake *all* night."

Okay, now I'm getting hot and bothered in a good way. I need to cool us off. "All night, huh? Well, what are we going to do about that?"

He sets his jaw and purses his lips. I've learned this is a sign that he is about to announce a decision. "We need to figure out a way for our kids to have 'us' in their lives."

I smile inside. Time for a test. "Joe, I'm sorry to tell you this, but until you prove to me that we are an 'us,' I don't know if I can help you."

His face drains of the little color he has. "You don't know . . . But what about—"

"Joe, you have to prove it to me."

"Prove it? How am I going to prove it?"

I lick my lower lip. His mouth always opens slightly when I do that.

"Right here? Right now?" he asks.

I nod.

He leans closer. "How?"

"Well, you could kiss me on the lips. That will give me a little proof. As you know, I haven't been kissed on the lips for a long time, Joe, and I'm wondering how much you really, really want me."

He slides into my side of the booth, takes my face into his hands, and kisses me.

Tasty. Like apple pies and coffee. I'll bet his kisses will taste even better with some grapes.

"Thank you, Joe."

"I want to do much more, Shawna."

"Yeah? What kind of things do you want to do?"

"Intimate things."

He's still so shy! "How intimate?"

"The kind of intimate things you do late at night when all the kids are asleep, with candles lit and soft music playing and we've turned the air conditioner off and it's hot and steamy and sweaty and we can't get enough of each other—"

I kiss him to stop him from starting a fire right here in this booth. He's *not* so shy after all! "That sounds . . . good, Joe." I can't go back to work now and yell at a bunch of teenagers! I need to sleep all this off or take a long, cold shower or something. "So, we need to win over our kids." I pull out a pen and write: "Family Outings" on it. "Let's make a list of family outings where we can bump into each other often." *Sorry, Lord.* I slide a few inches away from Joe. "Let's make a long list."

He nods.

"Um, okay. Let's see . . . Crystal has a game at PH this Friday. Why don't you bring your family to that?"

"Sure. But Rose is still on punishment."

As she should be. "So just you and the boys can go."

"But going to a girls' basketball game? That might be a hard sell."

"There's a JV boy's game followed by the girl's game followed by the boy's varsity game. That's at least four hours of basketball, most of it male."

"Right. I didn't mean . . ."

I stop him with my eyes.

"Sure. That would be great."

I write it down. "Her season is almost over, though. What else could we do?"

31

Joe

"I have some ideas, but they're all going to sound lame."
And my heart is finally slowing down. Where did all
that . . . lust come from? Maybe Shawna brings it out of me.
No. It's all me, Lord. You're right.

"Where have you taken your kids before?"

This is going to be the lame part. "Moto-Cross and Monster Trucks at the Salem Civic Center."

"Oh."

"Loud, muddy, destructive. Jimmy had a ball."

She writes it down.

"And, uh, hockey games."

Shawna blinks.

"Rose actually likes to go."

"Yeah?"

"The players are cute."

Shawna writes it down.

"Let's see, there's always Putt-Putt when the weather
warms up."

She drops the pen. "Joe, don't take this the wrong way,

but . . . Monster Trucks, hockey, and golf are not part of my kids' culture."

"I know. Unfortunately, I've made them part of ours. Sorry."

She picks up the pen. "Okay, what else?"

"What about Festival in the Park?"

"Isn't that in May?"

Three months from now. "I think so."

She writes it down. "Well, I guess all this is something to work towards."

"Um, after that is the Salem Fair."

She doesn't write it down. "We can't afford that."

"Neither can we, but we go with the Val-Pak coupons. Even then, we spend . . . a hundred bucks or so. And I hate every minute of it. So crowded, rude people, a fight last year . . . No, don't write it down."

She writes it down anyway. "Toni and Jimmy will have fun. Maybe we'll only take those two and leave before it gets dark."

"Sure."

She smiles. "There's always church . . ."

My turn to blink.

"We worship the same God, Joe. Just in different ways."

I hadn't thought of this at all! "The kids have attended Shenandoah Baptist their entire lives."

She frowns. "Yeah. Church might be a problem. My kids like Pilgrim Baptist. Is there an interracial church in Roanoke?"

"I don't know."

"I never thought I'd have to leave Pilgrim to get a man. Hmm. Are you thinking what I'm thinking?"

"This is hard." And it is.

"That's what I'm thinking, too. And where will we live?"

A huge "huh" escapes my lips before I can stop it.

"We are talking about a serious commitment, aren't we, Joe?"

"Yes, but . . ."

"Look, Joe. We're two grown folks, right?"

"Right."

"And we're too old, or at least I'm too old, to beat around the bush. If you're feeling for me what I'm feeling for you, we are going to get together and get married . . . aren't we?"

"Yes, Shawna. That's what I want."

"It's what I want, too. And when we . . . blend our families, we will have to make a whole lot of changes that our kids just won't like much. They may even hate us for it. Are you ready for that?"

32

Shawna

Lord, it's sounding as if I'm trying to talk myself out of everything, but I'm not. I just want Joe to know what I think might happen.

"They've already been through so much," he says.

"And so have we, Joe. *So have we.* Don't *we* deserve some happiness?"

He nods. "I am happy, Shawna, happier than I ever thought I'd be after all that's happened. And you're the reason."

I touch his hand. "Thank you. You're sweet. But look, we've been straight with each other, right?"

"Right."

"So why are we beating around the bush so much with our kids? I love you, you love me, and two people who love each other should be together no matter what."

He doesn't agree right away, and that scares me. "We're not even beating anywhere near the bush, Shawna, and I think I know why."

"Tell me."

"It's because we love our kids, too."

He's right. We don't want them to have any pain that can be avoided. I have spent the last eight years protecting them from pain, and here I am preparing some pain for them. "I know, Joe. I understand."

"But . . ."

I look up.

"But if we do this right, and we do it with love, and we pray about it a lot, I know it can work out," he says.

"We're going to have to pray without ceasing, Joe."

"I know."

I look at the list. "And this list . . ."

"I know. It's a crummy list."

I drop the pen. "We're just going to tell them. Tonight."

"Yes." He sighs. "Any ideas on how to tell them?"

"I haven't the slightest idea." I smile. "Out loud?"

33

Joe

"Family meeting!"

They troop down the stairs quickly this time. They're starting to respond to me more and more because of my firmer hand.

Either that or there's nothing on TV.

"What's this one about, Dad?" Jimmy asks.

"I'll tell you as soon as you're all seated."

They sit, looking up at me. I think I liked them better when they were looking everywhere *but* me. My legs start to quiver, so I sit.

"You okay, Dad?" Joey asks.

"Yes. Thanks for asking." This is so hard! Where to begin? I almost want to ask them to bow their heads and pray with me. *I know You are here, Lord. Help me.*

"Well?" Rose asks.

"Okay, this is important, and I want you all to listen with your heart as well as your ears. Just . . . really listen." I take one of the deepest breaths of my life. "You know the woman I went out with the other night? She's more than a friend."

No reaction. The mantel clock ticks on.

I sigh. "I've been kind of dating her for a little while now, and—"

"When?" Rose asks with acid in her voice.

Jesus, now would be a good time for You to come back. "Well, we haven't exactly been dating. I had been talking to her online for a while—"

"Online?" Rose asks.

"Yes, but that was before we realized we were both from Roanoke. We've had a lunch date, an ice-cream date, we've been talking on the phone for a while now, and I see her at her work—"

"What's her name, Dad?" Joey asks.

I look at Joey, who I hope will not grimace, frown, or wince. "Shawna. Shawna Mitchell. Junior Mitchell's mother."

Joey . . . smiles. *Thank you, son.*

And Rose isn't reacting at all. Maybe she's okay with Shawna being black. She didn't say much the other night. "And—"

"How old is she?" Jimmy asks.

"What does her age have to do with anything?" I ask him.

"I dunno," Jimmy says. "Just wondering."

"Sorry, Jimmy, I . . . I think she's in her late thirties, and—"

"You think?" Rose says. "You don't know?"

"It's not polite to ask a woman's age, Rose," I say.

No reaction.

"Well," I continue, "as you may know, she has three kids. Let's see, Crystal is eighteen, and—"

"Three kids?" Rose asks.

Rose is getting on my nerves. "Yes. Junior is sixteen, and Toni is eight."

"Junior and Crystal ride our bus," Joey says.

And then, Rose's face changes. Oh, Lord, her *face!* I have never seen that face! I will have nightmares about that face!

"Them? " Rose asks, her voice shaking. She stands. "You have *got* to be kidding!"

"I wouldn't kid about something this important, Rose."

Her mouth opens and shuts several times before she asks, "How important?"

I take a deep breath. "Shawna and I are talking about getting married."

Rose closes her eyes. "You're . . . you're out of your mind."

She turns, runs to the stairs, and stomps up before I can speak. Her door slams. The mantel clock ticks. Has my heart stopped? *Oh, Lord, please help her understand.*

I look at my sons. "So, um, what do you two think? Are you okay with it?"

Joey nods. Jimmy doesn't move.

"What do you think, Jimmy?"

Jimmy's eyes seem so far away.

"Uh, well," I say, "we have a whole lot to work out before then, so—"

Jimmy bolts from the table, taking the stairs two at a time.

"Jimmy, come back!" I yell, but another slamming door silences the house. I look at Joey. "Thanks for not leaving."

"You're welcome."

"I knew they'd have trouble, but . . ."

"I think it's cool, Dad."

Oh, here come the tears. "It is cool. It's so cool it's positively cold."

Joey laughs.

"I'm going to need your help, Joey. We need to help them understand. When we get married, and we *will* get married, we'll all be living in the same house together."

"Where?"

Excellent question. "I don't know where for sure. Probably here, with some modifications. But we haven't thought that far ahead yet. If we had enough money—and we don't— we'd need . . . seven bedrooms and at least, what, four bathrooms? I don't even know where to look for a house like that."

"Junior and I can share a room."

"True, but . . ." I look upstairs. "Can you see Crystal and Rose in the same room?"

"Dad," Joey says, "I can't even see Crystal and Rose in the same house."

Neither can I.

34

Shawna

I take a little quiet time in my room reading Psalm 23. *Lord, be my shepherd tonight, and comfort me with that rod and staff of Yours.*

I'm going to need it.

And keep that rod and staff handy, Lord. If Crystal gets out of line, You have my permission to jerk her back into the fold.

I approach them after dinner while the three of them are doing their homework at the kitchen table. Crystal's recent presence here at the table surprises me, but I have that basketball coach to thank. That coach is a godsend, checking her grades often, keeping her out of practice if she falls behind in class. I look at Junior, who is blossoming into a man, and at Toni, who is so full of life.

Lord, please keep them this way after I tell them . . .

"Mama, are you all right?" Junior asks.

"Yes." I sit at the head of the table.

After hearing several of my sighs, they look up at me.

"I have something to tell you," I say, "so y'all can take a break for a few minutes."

Pen, pencil, and crayon drop instantaneously. They obviously needed a break.

"You know I don't like to beat around the bush, so I'll tell it to you straight." Inhale. Stop your feet from running. Set your jaw like Joe does. Open your mouth . . . Exhale. Get scared. Ask your youngest child to sit on your lap for comfort. "Come here, Toni."

She comes to me, sitting on my lap.

Try again. Don't look at Crystal. Look only at Toni. "Joe and I intend to get married."

"Good," Junior says immediately. "Good."

Oh, that boy makes me want to cry!

Crystal still hasn't breathed, but Toni lights up. "Really?"

"Really," I tell her. "I know this won't be easy—"

"You can say *that* again!" Crystal shouts.

Put your eyes back in your head. Wait for the ringing in your ears to stop. Check your youngest child. Toni is squinting. Look sideways at your oldest, fire-breathing daughter. Hug your youngest child, using your youngest child as a shield.

"You're hooking up with . . ." Crystal picks up her pen again. She has a weapon. Watch the weapon. "He's white, Mama."

Slow down your racing heart. Give up trying to slow down your racing heart. Your heart is just going to race. "Yes."

"This is a joke, right?" Crystal asks.

Don't look at her, don't look . . . Okay, look. Crystal is staring hard at me, probing my face. "No joke."

"But he's . . . and his daughter . . ."

Pray that the pen point is dull.

"Have you *lost* your *mind,* Mama?"

Laugh, but not too hard. Smile. Don't scare your youngest child. "A little. Love can make you crazy, I guess."

Crystal stands. "Crazy ain't the word, Mama. Dumb is the word. Stupid is the word. Messed-up is the word."

"That's a hyphenated word," Junior says.

"Shut up, Junior." Crystal starts to gather her books and notebooks.

"Sit down, Crystal. I'm not through talking."

"Well, I'm through listening," she says, waving the pen in my face.

"I said, *sit . . . down*."

Crystal comes back but won't sit, standing behind her chair and fuming. At least she came back.

"I have spent the last eight years just being your mama, and, don't get me wrong, I have treasured each and every moment. I never thought I'd meet a man who could even *compete* with your daddy, but I have."

"Who is white," Crystal hisses, "and who has a freak for a daughter."

"Nyana-so ninyu do doun, keh do za-nyohndeke," Junior says.

We both look at him for the translation.

" 'Smoke does not affect honeybees alone,' " he says. " 'Honey-gatherers are also affected.' "

Crystal's shoulders droop. "What's *that* supposed to mean?"

"I don't know exactly, but Amina says that when people are gossiping, kind of like what goes around, comes around."

"Are you calling me a freak, Junior?"

I think he is doing *exactly* that, but I am staying completely out of this one.

"No, but you don't know anything about Rose," Junior says. "And the little that you do know is not enough to call her a freak."

Thank you, Junior.

"And," I add, feeling more confident, thanks to my man-child, "whether you like it or not, Crystal, she will be living in the same house as you."

Crystal is absolutely speechless. I have completely shut her up. This in itself is a miracle.

"Now, I don't know where we're all going to live, and it might be a little cramped at the beginning, but . . . y'all are about to get two more brothers and a sister, and I am *going* to get a husband."

Crystal looks at the ceiling. "And you don't care how it will affect us?"

"Oh, I care."

"Right," she says sarcastically.

"I do. And I almost cared too much what y'all might think and almost talked myself out of being with this man. But then it hit me, and don't you say a thing about this, Crystal. *God* brought this man into my life, and if God brings a man into your life, you don't . . . say . . . no."

Crystal throws her head back and sighs. "But, Mama, you met him online!"

"God's in the Internet, too." He has to be. He prepared Joe for me there.

"I can't believe you're doing this to me, Mama!" She starts for her room again. "I can't believe any of this."

"You think I'm doing this to *you?* This isn't about you, Crystal. God has provided another good man for me, and if you try, you'll see that he *is* a good man. I care what you all think and feel, I do. But I've been lonely, and I hope you never know what it's like to be wanting someone to hold, night after night after night." Here come the tears.

"Don't cry, Mama," Toni says.

I can't help it. "Crystal, he makes me happy. All I want you to do is to give it a chance, just . . . give Joe and his family a chance."

Crystal punches a wall. "So when's the wedding?"

"We haven't gotten that far yet, but . . . soon."

"Before or after I graduate?"

I don't like the way she's talking or what she's talking about. "Weddings take time to plan. Maybe by the end of the summer or early next fall."

"Uh-huh." She rubs her knuckles. "Well, the second I graduate I'm moving out, Mama, and you *won't* have to give me a wedding invitation."

Then she storms off, leaving me with a hurricane of emotions inside because . . .

Because I may have just lost my daughter.

Junior stands and hugs my shoulders. "I'm happy for you, Mama."

"Me, too," Toni says, and she kisses my cheek.

"Thank you both."

"Chanda chema hurikwa pete," Junior says. " 'A handsome finger gets the ring.' "

I look at my ring finger, ashy and callused from dishwashing, cooking, living thirty-eight years . . . "It's not that handsome."

"Handsome enough," Junior says.

"I don't think he's marrying me for my hands." I lower my voice, because I'm sure Crystal is still listening. "We have to work on Crystal. I know this is going to be hard, but be supernice to her, okay? She'll probably still move out."

"She's stubborn," Junior says.

"Yes," Toni says.

They've noticed. "But I want her last days with us to be happy so she'll come back."

"How is she going to move out?" Junior asks. "She's never had a job."

"When a Mitchell sets her mind to it," I say, "a Mitchell can do just about anything. And maybe when she's gone, she'll miss us enough to come back."

"You are so wise, Mama," Junior says.

"I am?"

"Mtoto akililia wembe mpe. 'When a child cries for a razor, give it to her.' "

"Say what?"

"It's Amina's way of saying to learn by experience."

"Oh." I squeeze his forearm. "You really like Amina, don't you?"

"Yes."

"I saw them kissing, Mama," Toni adds.

I giggle. "I got my first kiss today, as a matter of fact." I look at Junior. "I'm sure you two are way ahead of me, but be careful, okay? I'm glad God brought her to you, Junior, but don't have God bringing me a grandchild just yet, okay?"

"We won't until we are married, Mama."

I blink. "You're *that* serious about her?" At sixteen?

"Yes."

He's so sure. "So you know how I feel about Joe. And if you have any reservations about him, any at all, you'll let me know, won't you?"

Junior shrugs. "But your mind is set, right?"

"It is."

He smiles. "So any reservations I have won't change anything, right?"

"Right."

There is much sense in what my son says.

35

Joe

I'm standing in the upstairs hallway in front of two closed doors. Should I go in to see Jimmy, or should I see Rose first? Jimmy might listen to reason more . . . maybe.

I knock. "May I come in?"

After twenty seconds, I open the door and see a surprisingly neat room for a change, only a sock or two lying around. Jimmy lies on his bed with his face to the window.

I shut the door behind me. "I thought we could talk."

"About what?"

"My announcement."

Jimmy shrugs.

"I didn't expect you to understand everything."

He turns his head. "I don't understand anything about it." And he's crying? My rock of a he-man has been crying? How often can my heart break before being damaged beyond repair?

I sit on the end of his bed. "Maybe I can help you, Jimmy. What don't you understand?"

"Mom just died, right?"

I sigh. "That was over six months ago, Jimmy."

"So? Aren't you supposed to wait or something?"

"I've been wrestling with that very question, too, Jimmy. I've tried to wait, but . . . I want to be with Shawna."

"Well, it isn't fair."

"What's not fair?"

"It isn't fair to Mom."

That hurts, but it makes sense. I don't disagree.

"And it isn't fair to me." Huge tears drop from his eyes, every drop shaking my heart to pieces. "I miss Mom. Don't you miss Mom?"

Here come my tears again. Will my eyes ever be empty? "I think about your mom every day and every night, Jimmy. Yes, I miss her."

"So why? Why do you want to be with Shawna and her kids instead of us?"

Jimmy's logic sometimes escapes me, but this time, I think I understand. He's afraid of being replaced. I wipe my face with his bedspread. "Jimmy, I will be with you every day like always. That's not going to change."

"Right."

"It won't. I promise. You'll always be my son, and I'll always be with you."

He sits up. "Well, I'm not sharing my room with anyone."

"I hope you won't have to, son."

"Like we have enough money to live in a house big enough for all of us."

"We'll figure something out, and if we have to add on to a house—even this house—I know I can count on you to help me."

His eyes brighten. "Help you do what?"

"Well, you helped with the deck and the playhouse, remember?" He'd only cut and nailed a few boards, but he was so proud of himself. " 'Look what I helped make, Mommy,' " he'd told Cheryl.

"But what about till then?"

Jimmy is so immediate, so *now* about things. "Well, hmm," I say. "What do you think?"

"Huh?"

"What do you think we should do? How would you solve the problem?"

He slides back to sit more upright against his headboard. "Well . . . we could get some bunk beds. We could probably put two in here."

Great idea. "For the men." And I'm looking at a boy who is fast becoming one.

"Yeah."

"Should we put the beds in your room or Joey's room?"

"This room's bigger."

So true. We even measured it one day. "What about the ladies?"

"I guess . . . the other two, what are their names again?"

"Toni and Crystal."

He nods. "They could take Joey's room."

And this child is having trouble in school? He's a genius!

"Rose can keep her room," he says.

I don't want to hit him with "What if Crystal wants a room of her own?" Jimmy is just working out in space what he can't quite grasp with his mind yet, but if that helps him figure it out, I'm glad.

"We may have to add another bathroom," I say. "I've never done one of those."

"Where would we put it?"

Good question. "In the basement, I guess. Maybe a standup shower, sink, and toilet for the men only. I'm sure the ladies will appreciate that. I'm sure it can be done." Though a shower would probably be enough. "We'd probably have to take a jackhammer to the floor down there."

"Yeah." His eyes are suddenly dry. Whatever this child lacks in book sense, he makes up in common sense. "It'll be kind of nice not to be the youngest anymore."

Ah, the dreaded little brother–brat status will vanish. I'm fully familiar with that.

"Is, um, Shawna a good cook?"

"The best." I'm assuming here, but her kids look healthy enough. "She's a manager at McDonald's."

"Yeah?"

Is that a glimmer of a smile? It is.

"Can we get free food?" he asks.

"I don't know," I say with a laugh. "I'm sure we'll get a discount."

"Cool."

Thank you, Jesus . . . for McDonald's. I never thought I would ever pray that. "Well . . ."

"Are you going to talk to Rose now?"

"I'm going to try."

"Good luck."

"Thanks."

I'm going to need luck and prayer and guidance and courage and strength and . . .

36

Shawna

I don't want a fight tonight, but hot water never burned down a house, so here goes.

Crystal is in her room on the phone, to LaTonya, no doubt. I knock once and open the door. "Let me know when you're done. I want to talk to you."

Crystal looks away, a scowl on her lips. "LaTonya, I'll call you back." She turns off the phone and drops it onto the bed. "What's to talk about?"

I sit on the edge of her bed. "How you're feeling."

"You really want to know?"

"Yes."

"I feel worse than I've ever felt in my entire life, Mama."

I smile. "Say what you mean, child. Don't beat around the bush."

She turns away. "That's how I feel."

I look at her daddy's picture on her nightstand. Sorry, Rodney, but you're the reason. This child is still in love with you. "How so?"

"Huh?"

"You say you feel worse than you've ever felt before. I want to know how so."

She sighs. "Could you find a man more *unlike* daddy than Joe-Bob?"

"His name is Joe." But what's his middle name? What if it *is* Robert? "And he's not that different from your daddy."

"Are you blind, Mama?" She whips out her fingers, counting on wicked-looking fingernails. "He's white, he's short, he's not in *any* kind of shape, he dresses terribly, he has *no* kind of rhythm—"

"How do you know all that?"

"He's white, isn't he?"

"So he's white," I say. "And as for his appearance"— which I kind of like a lot—"so what? And he's not that short."

"He's shorter than me."

I ignore her. "While I like what I see, that's not why I want to be with him. He has touched my soul, and whenever I think about him, I feel good inside. And for whatever reason, he doesn't seem to mind my appearance. I mean, I'm black, I'm short, I'm not in *any* kind of shape, and I dress terribly, too."

No response at all, her face a mask. That *hurts!* She could have at least disagreed a little.

"So, what's *really* your problem with all of this?" I ask.

"I told you."

I have to make her say it. "I don't think you have. Spit it out."

She crunches up her lips and starts chewing on her tongue, something I wish she would do more often to keep from speaking. "He's not Daddy."

Time for some hard truths. "You're right. He isn't your daddy, and he will never be your daddy. In fact, I doubt he will even attempt to be your daddy. Joe isn't crazy."

She almost smiles.

"He'd have to be right out of his mind to try to be your

daddy, Crystal. You are a one-daddy girl, and if Joe ever even says something that sounds daddylike to you, I'm going to cut him off with an 'uh-huh, Joe-Bob, don't go there.'"

She almost giggles.

"He knows you're a grown woman now and you don't need a stepfather to give you any advice or, God forbid, tell *you* what to do. I'm the only one who can do that, at least until you graduate. After that?" I shrug. "You're on your own."

She almost gasps.

This reverse psychology stuff is fun!

"What?"

"You said you wanted to leave us after you graduate. I won't stand in your way. It's what you want to do, right?"

"Yeah."

She sounds so unsure! I'm getting to her.

"So go on and do it. No sense staying with us if you're not one hundred percent sure about us."

"You mean . . . you'd *let* me move out?"

Well, maybe reverse psychology isn't so fun after all. "I'll even help you pack and move into your new place. I had always hoped I would be moving you to some college or university away from here, but . . . there will be time for that. You *will* be taking classes this fall at Virginia Western, though. Your daddy started your college fund the day he knew I was carrying you inside me, so that is *not* negotiable. A year or two at Western, and then . . ."

She's squinting. She's waiting for the "catch," only there isn't going to be one.

"You're kidding about all this, right?"

"No."

"You'd let me go like that?"

Lord Jesus, I know I am going to have to let her go one day, but does it have to be today?

"Crystal, I will never let you go. You're in my heart forever. You're with me when I wake up, and you're with me when I go to sleep wherever I am and wherever you are. And if you feel moving out is the best thing for you to do, then . . . I'm okay with it." Did I just say all that to my firstborn child? What kind of mother am I? "So, um, what are your plans?"

"Plans?"

She hasn't thought about *any* of this at all! I still have the upper hand. "Well, if you move out, you'll need a job first." *Please, Lord, let reality set in to her rash words and make her doubt those plans.*

"So I'll get a job."

My turn to play twenty questions. "Doing what?"

"I don't know, uh . . . I'll get a job at the mall."

I nod. "Smart move. You don't want to work fast food. The grease messes up your hair something terrible, and I ought to know. Any particular store?"

"Well, maybe Footaction or Foot Locker."

"*Whew.* That's good."

"Why?"

"So we can get discounts on shoes, girl. Y'all go through them so fast. Toni will grow three sizes at least this year. Um, isn't there a Lady Foot Locker?"

"Why would I want to work there?"

"I'm sure men come in there to buy shoes for their ladies."

"Right, Mama."

I shrug. "It was just an idea." I pace a little. "What about"—what stores are in the mall, a place I avoid until Christmas?—"Victoria's Secret?"

Crystal blinks.

"What? I'm going to be needing some ling-er-ee, right?"

"Gross!"

"I have to look sexy for my man, right?"

"Mama, I don't *even* want to hear about that."

"What about ... ." What's that creepy store she went into looking for "body apparel," also known as nose rings, tongue studs, and other pain-inducing jewelry? "Hot something."

She sighs. "It's called Hot Topic, and they only have white people working in there."

"So you'll be the first black woman working there. You go in there every time we go to the mall. Didn't you get your latest belly button ring from there?" The things a modern mother has to say to her daughter.

"Yeah. So?"

I take her hands.

"What?"

Time to smooth out a few things, or at least try to. "Do you remember how you reacted when Daddy died?"

Her face clouds over. She remembers. "What does this have to do with Hot Topic?"

Everything. "Just bear with me. Do you remember?"

She sighs. "I remember."

I wish I could erase those memories. "Do you remember how much you changed in a very short period of time from a straight-A student in the PLATO program to a not-so-straight-A student in regular classes?"

She drops my hands. "I told you I remembered."

"But that wasn't all, was it? You used to play sports year round, do a little cheerleading. You remember that, girl?"

"I told you I did."

I had better not push her too far. "Well, Rose is going through similar changes."

"But what does—"

"Let me finish. Please?"

"Whatever."

That word should be removed from the English language. I push on. "Joe tells me that Rose used to be a whole lot different than she is now. Normal looking, he tells me. Jeans and sweatshirts and Nikes and hair bows. The typical white girl."

"I can't believe that, Mama. She's so out there. That doesn't happen to someone overnight."

Hold that thought. "I know, it's hard for me to believe, too. She played on the freshman soccer team, got top grades—all that. But when her mama died, she . . . changed. Think about it: what if I had dropped dead right before *your* junior year?"

"Don't say that."

"I'm not planning on dying until you're old and gray and we can compare wrinkles. I'm just saying . . . What if you lost me? How would you have changed?"

"I wouldn't have gone Goth!"

I laugh. "Lord, I hope not. Black people wearing more black?"

She smiles. "There are a few black Goth kids at PH."

I move closer to her. "What I'm trying to say is that *something* would have changed in your life. Something major. The way Rose dresses, the way Rose acts, the things she shouldn't have said to your friends—this is the way she's trying to cope with losing her mama. I agree with you that it's freaky, but that doesn't make Rose a freak. She is still a scared little girl under all that . . . cloth. She misses her mama as much as you miss your daddy. I'm not sure, but I'll bet Rose is as much against her daddy being with me as you are."

That thought makes me shudder inside. Two strong-willed teenaged girls can be a potent combination against anything. Wasn't Joan of Arc a teenager? I mean, I want these two to tolerate each other, not put their heads together to gang up on me.

"What I'm trying to say is that you two have a lot more in common than not."

"Mama, she'll never be my friend, not after what she said to my friends."

"She lost it for a few minutes on one day of a long school

year. I lose it a lot more often than that, don't I? Are you going to judge her for a few minutes?"

Crystal is silent. She knows better.

"Well, I hope you don't. Your daddy and I raised you better than that."

"So what does all this have to do with me getting a job at . . . Hot Topic?" Her voice trails away. "Because Rose shops there."

"I'll bet she has a discount card and everything."

"But how is having a job there . . . ? Mama, I think you've lost it again."

"Look, you are pierced, are you not?"

"Yeah. So?"

I should never have pierced her ears. She didn't cry or even wince. "And I know you are tattooed."

She looks away.

"And you've been tattooed long before you turned eighteen. I don't know where you went to get that barbwire tattoo around your ankle or that rose on your back, but . . ."

Crystal looks exasperated. Good.

"You think I wouldn't find out? I still come in and check on you every night, girl. It's an old habit I may find hard to break when you move out. You have never made it through the night without kicking the covers off. The rose I like. Stylish. Kinda fly."

She rolls her eyes.

"But the barbwire?"

"It's a snake, Mama." She rolls up the leg of her sweats. "See. There's the head, and that's the tail."

"Oh." I think I liked it better when it was barbwire. "I guess what I'm hoping is that Rose will see you differently if you work at that store or even if you just apply to work there."

"They won't hire me."

I shake my head. "Stranger things have already happened, Crystal. And even if you work at, say, JCPenney . . ."

"Ew."

"Where *I* like to shop. Even if you worked somewhere else, at least you'll have that store in common to shop at."

She leans back into her pillow. "You really want this to work out, don't you?"

"Yeah. I do. And if having you move out is part of the solution, so be it. I *don't* want you to leave, Crystal, don't get me wrong. I may help you move out, but I will be crying the entire time and probably weeping for days afterwards. I love this man, and his kids are part of the package."

"Some package."

"It's a tall order, huh?"

"Yes." She sighs. "Dag, Mama, you're asking a lot."

"I wouldn't ask if I didn't think you could handle it. You've kept me sane, and happy, and needed, Crystal. Help me help a *man* keep me sane, and happy, and needed."

She sighs again. "I . . . I don't know. My friends . . . I mean, if *I* can't understand how you can do this, they won't . . ." She sighs yet again. Isn't there enough oxygen in this room? "I mean, how is all this going to look? Can you honestly say you'll be proud to hold his hand at Pilgrim?"

"Yes."

"Daddy still has friends there, too."

I shrug. "And your point is?"

"Just that . . . I would be embarrassed, Mama." She looks away. "I already am. This will get out. It's too juicy not to. They're going to say, 'There goes the girl whose mama likes cream in her coffee' or 'There goes the girl whose mama is a sellout.'"

Whoa. Would they really say that?

"And I don't have all that many friends." She looks down at her hands. "I may lose a few of them."

This is where I'm supposed to say, "Well, then they really weren't your friends if that happens." This is where I'm supposed to say, "It's none of their business anyway." This is where I'm supposed to say something that will make all this better.

And I can't think of *anything* to say.

"Just wanted you to know how all this will affect me, and Junior and Toni to some extent, too." She finally looks at me. "And as for college, Mama, even at Virginia Western . . ." She shakes her head. "I don't want to go. At all."

I blink. "Say what? Your daddy—"

"Keep Daddy out of this, Mama," Crystal says with a snarl. "We wouldn't be in this mess if you had been thinking about Daddy." She snaps up her phone and punches in a number. "Now, do you mind? I have to finish talking to LaTonya."

Which is as good as saying, "You are dismissed." I let her have her victory, silently backing out and leaving her room. We'll just have to agree to disagree. I'll just leave her be. She just needs time, that's all. She'll see.

But she did hit the nail on the head. We wouldn't be in this mess if I had been thinking about her daddy.

And that depresses me *so* much.

37

Joe

One down, one . . . *really* down. *Lord, help me know what to say to Rose and when to say it.*

I knock on Edgar Allen Poe's face. "Rose, may I come in?"

I hear a commotion inside. What is she doing? I crack open the door and see Rose packing clothes into an old duffel bag, one we used to use for camping trips. She's leaving? *Now* what do I say?

I start to close the door, then think better of it, for whose escape I'm not sure. "I take it that you're leaving."

"Uh-huh."

"May I ask where you're going?"

"Kim's."

Kim. Another Goth girl. Great. "Is it okay with Kim's mother?"

"Uh-huh."

I drift toward her desk, noticing a series of dark, foreboding sketches of . . . I have no idea what these creatures are, but they're definitely not angels. Fuzzy demons? "Are you going to ask me for my permission?"

She finally turns and looks at me. "Did you ask me for my permission? No."

I walked right into that one. "I didn't know I needed your permission to be happy, Rose."

"Well, you did." She tries to zip up the duffel bag, but it catches on several pieces of black clothing.

"I'll do it," I say, pressing her clothes inside and zipping it shut. Now why did I do *that?* "I can carry it downstairs for you." And why did I *say* that? I shouldn't be helping her leave, should I? "Is, um, is Kim picking you up?"

"I was planning to walk."

I lift the duffel bag. "This duffel weighs a ton, Rose. I'll drop you off." And why did I say *that?* I am practically rushing her out of the house! Why am I doing all this? *Lord, is this what I'm supposed to be saying and doing?*

"You'll . . . drop me off?"

"Sure." I hoist up the duffel bag, bearing most of its weight with my back. "Ready?"

She hesitates. "Um, yeah."

She seems unsure of herself. "Do you have your toothbrush?"

"Oh. Um, I haven't gotten it from the bathroom yet."

Anger certainly makes us unorganized. "I'll take this down while you make sure you have everything you need."

As I trudge down the stairs I feel two sets of eyes—the boys, standing in their doorways looking out at me. Quite a show this is becoming. I wonder how it ends. *I'm leaving this in Your hands, Father.*

Rose comes down with a full dress bag and her book bag *twenty* minutes later. "Ready."

She's stubborn, yet she took twenty more minutes to pack. What does this mean? "Um, what's Kim's number, you know, in case of emergency?"

"I'll uh . . ." She leaves the hallway and goes to the kitchen. "I'm writing it on the message board," she calls out.

"Okay." I am surprised how calm I am. I should be begging her not to go, and yet here I am about to take her away from here.

She returns to me. "Well, I guess we should go."

I look up the stairs to where Joey and Jimmy now sit like miniature gargoyles perched on the top of some cathedral. "Don't you want to say good-bye to your brothers?"

Rose only glances at them. "Bye, Jimmy. Bye, Joey."

"Where are you going, Rose?" Jimmy asks.

"To Kim's," Rose says.

"Why?" Jimmy asks.

"Why?" Rose shakes her head furiously. "Jimmy, you were at our family meeting. You heard what he's planning to do."

"But *I'm* not going anywhere," Jimmy says.

"Because you have nowhere to *go,* doofus." She looks at Joey. "Joey, you can't pretend you like this idea."

"I don't have to pretend," Joey says. "It's what Dad wants. That's enough for me."

Lord, thank You for faithful sons . . . and a daughter who is still faithful to her mother. I feel guilty about not being as faithful to Cheryl as Rose is, but don't I have to move on?

Rose makes two tight fists. "Hell-*o!* He's marrying a *black* woman!"

"She's a woman who happens to be black," Joey says, sounding much more calm than I'm feeling.

And why can't I speak? *Lord, why are You holding my tongue?*

"And he was writing her online for months before he even knew that, Rose," Joey adds. "He fell in love with *her,* not her color."

I stare at him. How did he know?

"Junior told me, Dad," Joey says.

Rose turns on me. "For *months,* huh? Mom was barely in the ground, huh? Oh, how you must have *loved* her!"

Oh, too soon . . . too soon! That's what this is all about. I should have waited longer! "I still love your mother, and I always will." *Thanks for letting go of my tongue, God.*

"You expect me to believe that?"

"Yes," I say.

"Well, I don't believe you."

How can I help her to believe me? "Rose, you still love her, and Jimmy still loves her, and Joey still loves her. I would never doubt your love for her. Never. Mom may be gone, but our love for her isn't gone. Love is eternal."

Rose doesn't say anything. The angels must be holding *her* tongue now.

"I will not leave this house because it's her house. When Shawna and I get married, we will live in this house." Why am I making this decision right now? It feels right, but . . . "Crystal and Toni can have Joey's room, the boys will make a bunkhouse out of Jimmy's room, and you'll still have your room." And suddenly I'm being decisive. It feels good.

"Oh, Dad, like I care about any of that."

I know she cares. Her room is her sanctuary, her inner sanctum. "Then tell me what you do care about."

"Mom!"

"She's gone, Rose," I say. "We have to go on living."

"Am I the only one in this house who still cares about Mom? Huh?"

Jimmy jumps up. "No!"

I turn and see my youngest, his face contorted beyond belief. Rose even sucks in her breath.

"I miss her cookies," Jimmy says. "I miss eating her cookies when I came home from school. I miss when she used to play catch with me in the backyard. I miss walking down to the park with her to shoot some baskets, and we'd play horse and she'd let me win. I miss . . . *everything* about her. And I don't want you to leave, too." He begins to sob.

Rose looks at me and back at Jimmy. "I'm just going to Kim's for a few days, Jimmy."

"And that's what Mom told me before she died," Jimmy says, tears dripping from his eyes. "Just a few days, Jimmy, it'll seem like a few days." He wipes his nose on his shirt. "Mom's not coming back, Rose, and if you go, I won't get to hear her voice anymore. You have Mom's voice."

I feel this fire in my chest, and though I want to comfort him, hold him, thank him for finally saying all the things that are in his head, I can't move. All the horrible things Rose says to him and all the names she calls him have been okay all this time because in Jimmy's mind, his mom is still talking to him. He has just been trying to get a rise out of his sister to hear his mother's voice.

Ticking mantel clock, a sobbing boy, and a heavy bag. *Help us, Father.*

"I'm not going away forever, Jimmy," Rose says. "I'm just going to stay at Kim's for a little while, that's all. Like a sleepover."

Jimmy looks up. "Just . . . don't stay away too long." He goes back to his room and gently closes his door.

I nod to Joey, he nods, and he goes into Jimmy's room. We must have first-son ESP or something.

I lift the bag. "Kim lives over on . . . Sherwood?"

"No," Rose says, most of the passion gone from her voice. "Avon."

"That's close enough to walk to PH, isn't it?"

"Yeah."

"Okay. Um, do you have lunch money?"

Her shoulders sag. I think she's finally realizing how hard it is to leave your house, even with her father helping her. There are so many little things—and little brothers—to think about.

I take a ten from my wallet. "Will this be enough to get

you through the week? I've got more up on my dresser, I think."

She takes the money. "This will be enough."

"Even for breakfast each day?"

Another sigh. "Well, um, not really."

"I'll get you some more."

I walk up the stairs to my bedroom, check the dresser, and only find a crumpled five and some change. I look into Cheryl's eyes staring at me from our wedding picture. "No, honey, I don't know what I'm doing," I whisper. "I wish you were here."

I return to Rose and smooth out the five before handing it to her. "All right, then," I say. I get my coat and Rose's fur monstrosity, handing it to her while I slip into my coat. I open the door and start to drag the duffel bag over the threshold.

"Wait."

Music to my ears. "Did you forget something?" Like the fact that your family loves you, that I love you, and that your little brother can't have you taking his mother's voice away from him?

"Um, I just remembered that Kim has a big test to study for, and I'd only get in her way. Maybe tomorrow night."

Or maybe never, I want to add, but I don't. "Yeah." I drag the bag back in, shutting the door. "Should we leave this down here?" Mainly so I don't get a hernia tonight banging it back up the stairs.

"Uh, no, there are some things in there I may need for to-morrow."

I will carry this load of bricks slowly, then. "I'll, uh, I'll just carry it back up, then."

"Yeah."

She leaves me for the kitchen, and I hear a few drawers opening. Lord, I have missed those sounds. They remind me of Cheryl so much. Jimmy's door opens with a little whine, two boys asking me questions with their eyes. I give them a thumbs-up. They close the door. I hoist the bag to the bottom step, and for some reason, it seems lighter.

"Dad?" Rose calls out. "Do we have any vanilla extract?"

Oh . . . I'm crying again, this time over some vanilla extract. "Um, if it's anywhere, it's in the pantry on the . . . second shelf from the top."

"Found it!"

Looks like we're going to have some cookies.

Thank You, Lord, for little boys and their love of cookies.

38

Shawna

I am dying to know how it's going or how it went over at Joe's house.

And it's driving Junior crazy. And I hope it's driving Miss Have-To-Talk-To-LaTonya crazy, too.

We've been watching Tyler Perry's *Madea's Class Reunion* again at an ear-splitting volume, and even though I've seen it at least fifteen times, howling and giggling and carrying on, I can't keep still on the couch. Whenever they break into Gospel songs, I hum along and sway.

"Call him, Mama," Junior says. "Please."

I sit up like a proper lady should. "Joe will call me when he is good and ready. Besides, I am an old-fashioned girl. I do not call men on the phone. They call me. As it should be." I smile. "I must school you on how to date a lady, Junior. A boy should *always* call the girl."

"Then I'll call him for you." He hits PAUSE, goes to the kitchen, and returns with the phone. "What's his number?"

"Like I said—"

"You're driving me crazy, Mama. I like this video, but it's hard to enjoy it when your mama can't keep her feet still."

I have been doing a couch dance. "I'm feeling the Spirit, boy."

He sits. "Mama, it's like you're having a track meet in here." He thrusts the phone to me. "Call him."

I take the phone. "Oh, all right. If you *really* want me to call him." I call the number.

"Hello?"

"Hi, Joe. Can you hold one second?" I cover the mouthpiece and look at Junior. "Do you mind? We'd like some privacy."

He rolls his eyes. "Can't you go into your own room or something?"

"Toni's sleeping."

"But I want to finish watching the video."

"You've seen it a dozen times, Junior."

He doesn't move.

"Oh, all right." I stand and try to mimic Crystal's exaggerated movements, which is hard to do since she's so much taller than I am. "Dag, I'll just go into the kitchen, then. Gosh, Junior. You think you own this place or something."

Junior smiles. "That was the worst impersonation of Crystal I have ever seen or heard."

"I think I was pretty accurate," I say. I pose in front of Crystal's door. "Take that, Miss Drama Queen."

Crystal's door opens. "Mama," she says, "I am *not* a drama queen."

I stand as straight as I can and roll my neck, waving my free hand in the air. "Like, I'm so totally beautiful that I can say whatever I want in this house."

She shuts her door. Fine. I return to the couch.

Junior points at the phone. "You're keeping Joe waiting, Mama."

"Like, okay," I say, and I strut into the kitchen, hearing a tiny little giggle behind me. I uncover the mouthpiece as I go to the sink. "Sorry about that, Joe. Crystal and I are having a little power struggle."

"You are?"

"Oh, we have one daily, and I usually win. I think I lost this one. So how did it go?"

"I'm eating sugar cookies," he says, and I hear him chewing.

"Huh?"

"That's how it went. Rose made sugar cookies for Jimmy."

"They sound tasty." I wish he wouldn't chew in my ear. I'd rather he'd chew *on* my ear.

"They are. I'll bring you a few tomorrow if there are any left."

"Okay." Was that a gulp? "Um, Joe, what exactly happened?"

And then . . . he explains his miracles, and I explain some of my miracles—I leave out the little part about Crystal hating me—and I start dancing in the kitchen, and Junior's calling out, "Mama, you're making too much noise in there!"

"Hold on a sec, Joe." I return to the couch. "Isn't it past your bedtime?"

"Aw, Mama."

"You can finish watching it tomorrow. I need this couch. I cannot properly snuggle up with Joe's voice in that drafty kitchen."

He clicks off the TV and DVD player. "I liked y'all better when you were just talking online." He drops the remote onto the couch and goes to his room.

"You're having a power struggle over the TV?" Joe asks.

"Something like that."

"And wasn't that Junior's voice I heard?"

I sigh. "Yeah, it's complicated, isn't it?" I settle my head at one end of the couch, my feet digging under the couch cushion in front of me for warmth. And for whatever reason, my feet have become completely still. "Well, Joe, what should we do next?"

"We need to have a real family date now."

Joe and his family dates. "Or we could go out again, just the two of us." Where he can nibble on my ear and set me on fire a few times.

"You know I would like nothing better than to do that, but we need for our kids to get to know each other. We can't just dump all this on them and leave them hanging."

"Climb Ev'ry Mountain," that song from *The Sound of Music* trips through my head. Didn't Maria inherit a whole bunch of kids, too? "I know, I know." I hate to tell him that the list we made just won't do, but it has to be done. "You know that list we made?"

"Yeah?"

I look at the DVD box and get an idea. Thank you, Tyler Perry. "We could add a Gospel show to that list."

"A Gospel show?"

"Yeah." I jump up and rummage through the mail. "As a matter of fact . . ." I find the little flyer. "There's a Gospel show this Saturday night at William Fleming High School." God is in the U.S. mail, too. "Want to go?"

"A Gospel show, huh?"

I read from the flyer. "Advance tickets are seven dollars each, and kids twelve and under are free." Free. I like that word. It's how I feel, too.

"That would be . . . forty-nine for all of us."

I like his math skills. "I'll pay for them."

"I don't mind paying for them."

What day of the month is it? Five days until the rent is due . . . "I'll buy them, and you can reimburse me with forty-nine hot, passionate kisses."

"Okay."

Darn right it's okay. I get the better end of the deal. "And you know what?"

"What?"

"You can't fuss at a Gospel show." I'm sure you can, but

when the Holy Spirit is there, the only fussing is going to go on *inside* a few souls.

"Sounds good. Should we meet y'all there or take our van?"

If we're going to do this, we are going to do it right. "Why don't you pick us up? Think we'll all fit in that van?"

"It will be a tight squeeze, but I think we can manage."

Squeeze. I like that word, too.

"How should we dress?" he asks.

I laugh. "It depends on if you want to be seen or not. Some folks go all out like they're in Sunday church, getting their hair did, their nails did, their legs waxed."

"Really?"

"You'll see them in their great big hats. But y'all don't have to dress up. Just be casual and kind of churchy. There will probably be folks in blue jeans and T-shirts, too."

"Should I wear a tie?"

"No. A nice sweater ought to do."

"What are you wearing?"

I smile. "Now?"

"No, I mean to the show."

"Well, right now I'm wearing some very sexy sweats rolled up to my knees and a long-sleeved T-shirt. Oh, and I'm barefoot." Not very sexy, I know, but I'm feeling so goofy. "I plan to wear a simple dress to the show."

"Will you, um, get your hair did?"

I cackle. It sounds so strange coming from his lips. "Yes. Will you get your hair did?"

"I do need a haircut."

We're so domestic. "The boys, too." And I smile inside. I didn't say "your kids" or "your sons." I said "the boys," as if I'm already taking ownership. That's kind of cool.

"Great. We'll pick you up at, what, six thirty?"

Hmm. I'll be working until one on Saturday, rushing home, getting Crystal to do something with her hair, doing

Toni's hair, doing my hair, ironing, showering, shaving my legs . . . It's going to be close. "Six thirty will be fine."

"I don't mean to cut this short, but it's been a very emotional night, and I'm exhausted."

I pout, but I understand. "I miss you."

"I miss you, too."

And I'm about to fall over myself. "See you tomorrow for some hot coffee?"

"I wouldn't miss it for the world."

39

Joe

Six thirty. She said six thirty would be fine.

But now it's six fifty, and we've been waiting outside the Terrace Apartments for half an hour.

Maybe she said seven? No. Six thirty. She said it three times over coffee earlier today.

I look behind me at a spotless, vacuumed van and three mostly spotless children. Rose spruced up the boys in white church shirts, dark pants, and church shoes. "We look like Jehovah's Witnesses, Dad," Joey had said. They kind of do, but they look more like angels to me. Rose wears a mostly tasteful black dress with only two revealing thigh slits, white hose, and, yes, those red ballet slippers. She shouldn't stand out too much. If it's dark, that is. I put on a black knit sweater over a white turtleneck, which Rose tells me is "very chic," with gray dress slacks and my black church shoes.

"Call her, Daddy," Jimmy suggests.

"That will delay her even more, son."

I had already been to the door, only to be told, "Just a

minute" by Toni. Fleming isn't exactly around the corner from here, but Shawna had assured me that the Gospel show wouldn't start on time, so I'm not worried.

"How long is this thing supposed to last?" Jimmy asks.

"I don't know," I say. And I don't care because we will be traveling together as a family, attending an event where we can get to know each other, and leaving together.

"Here they come," Joey says, and he slides open the side door.

"Finally," Jimmy says.

Toni arrives at the van first, wearing a colorful red, pink, and yellow dress and shiny black shoes. Junior looks sharp with a white shirt, brown vest, and matching pants. Crystal . . . *whoa* . . . I didn't know she had that much hair. Are those stiletto heels? They have to be four inches high! And that tight mini-almost-there dress? That girl is beautiful, but she's dangerous.

And there's Shawna, wearing a black dress, white hose, and black shoes. I glance at Rose to see if she notices. Maybe Rose will make the connection. Shawna had called earlier to ask what Rose was wearing, I told her, and now Shawna and Rose are almost twins—except for the red shoes.

They are all standing outside the van. "Okay," I say, "Shawna will be in front, the boys will be in the back, and these beautiful ladies will sit in the middle."

The kids squeeze in and put on seat belts without a word.

Shawna gets in, leans over, kisses me on the cheek, and straps in. "You look nice."

"So do you."

She turns to the crowd behind us. "How y'all doing?"

More silence.

She leans over and kisses my cheek again, whispering, "Drive fast."

When we arrive at William Fleming High School, the

parking lot is full, forcing me to park at Ruffner Middle School next door.

"This is a pretty popular event," I say.

Shawna nods. "Gospel shows have a way of getting folks out of the house."

As the kids get out, Shawna hands out the tickets to all but Toni, who gets in free. My kids crowd around me while hers do the same around her.

It's an awkward moment.

"Shall we go?" I ask.

"Sure," Shawna says, taking my hand and Toni's hand.

We move toward the auditorium, my kids beside me, her kids beside her.

Still awkward.

Shawna stops, and we all stop. "Hold up," she says. "Look at us. Salt on the right, pepper on the left. We're already stopping traffic, y'all. The least we can do is mix it up a bit. Junior, you and Joey go on ahead and get us eight seats, preferably in the same row if you can."

They tear off.

"Crystal, you come around to Joe's side, Rose and Jimmy around to mine."

I have never seen active, healthy, vibrant children move so slowly. I try to move Jimmy and Rose more quickly with my eyes, but they don't get the message.

Shawna sighs softly and smiles. "Now, let's make us a grand entrance."

It's still a little awkward, but we make it by the ticket-takers and move down the aisle en masse—turning a few heads— stopping where Junior and Joey have been guarding eight seats, almost the entire row. Shawna purposely lets Crystal go in first, followed by Rose. Junior and Joey follow, then Jimmy and Toni, then Shawna, with me on the aisle seat. It's not exactly the arrangement I would have wanted, but I have to trust Shawna's judgment.

I look around. Shawna was right. It is a strange mix of dressed up and dressed down, many men and women dressed to the nines, and just as many dressed in their Saturday-at-the-park best.

"Ready to get your praise on?" Shawna asks.

"Yes," I say.

But are our kids?

40

Shawna

*L*ord, *I can feel Your presence, oh, yes, but I can also feel so much tension flowing from the other end of the row. Please, dear God, please, warm up those two young ladies. And, God, whatever You do, don't let those two tall, skinny women—*

Now Lord, of all the empty seats in this place, they had to sit right in front of Joe and me. Their hair is a mile high, blocking my view of the stage entirely. You know I'd move if I could, but I don't see eight spaces together anywhere. Lord, if You can, please keep those two skinny women seated—

Oh, the music's starting, and now the skinny twins are standing up and clapping.

I turn to Joe. "Don't you be staring at their behinds now."

"I can't, um, help it," he says.

It's true. They're up and shaking it, these two skinny black women with never-gave-birth behinds. So . . .

Up we go.

Sort of.

Joe and Toni stand with me, Junior and Joey next, but

Jimmy looks confused. I lean around Toni and tell him, "It's okay. Come on, Jimmy."

And Jimmy's up, looking all shy. He's not trouble.

"Put your hands together now, Jimmy," I tell him.

Jimmy starts to clap—*in rhythm*. Which is better than I can say for Joe, who is clapping all over the place in all the wrong places, but he's my Joe so he can be as uncoordinated as he wants to be.

I look down the row to see Crystal standing . . . and Rose sitting. Hmm. And Crystal's not clapping. She probably only stood to get away from Rose. Maybe we're rushing this—

Where'd the lights go? And why is the music so loud? We aren't deaf!

The curtain parts, revealing a small choir in blue and gold robes, and they start singing about cleaning my heart, Lord Jesus. *Yes, Lord Jesus. Clean a few hearts here tonight. Wring out all the dirt and fill those hearts with good—*

I look down the row. Where's Crystal? I lean around the skinny twins and see Crystal practically running up to the front. It's not time for the altar call yet, little girl! What are you—

Oh.

She has found a few of her hoochie friends. Lord, Lord. I glance at Rose, an empty seat between her and Joey and another empty seat on the aisle side.

I turn to Joe. "I'll be back."

"It's okay," he practically shouts over the music. "Maybe it's better this way."

"No, it isn't." I won't have any daughter of mine insult a future stepdaughter of mine.

I go out into the aisle, walk around the back of the auditorium, and make a beeline for Crystal. She isn't even clapping, just running her mouth with her friends. I stand behind her until she feels my breath on her neck. Wide eyes greet me.

"Your seat is back here."

"But, Mama—"

I stand on my tiptoes and get right on up in her ear, so close I could bite it off. "Until you leave my house, you will abide by what I say, now move."

"Mama, but I—"

"Now."

"But, Mama, I—"

I growl. *Not exactly a holy thing to do, Lord, but she wasn't hearing my words.*

Crystal sighs heavily. "See y'all later."

I follow her back to her seat, watch her sit, and then I get an idea. Instead of returning to Joe, I sit in the aisle seat on the other side of Rose. "How are you doing?" I ask her.

"I'm okay," she says without looking at me.

"Pretty loud, huh?"

"Yeah."

I need to get this child to look at me. "I just can't sit when I hear this music. Want to join me?" I stand.

Rose looks at me.

"Come on. We can sit on the slow songs."

"I . . . I don't know."

I crouch down. "Look, you're my twin tonight, and I'll look foolish standing up there in this dress without you." I look down. "I wish I wore flats. These heels are killing me."

Rose rocks forward . . . and stands.

Thank You, Jesus.

So, everyone's up but Crystal, but I don't care. God's going to deal with her during the show, and I will *definitely* deal with her afterward. I stare Crystal down. That's right. Sit there and feel all bad. All dressed up and making us all late because your hair wasn't right, and here you are—

Where's she going?

41

Joe

I see a ripple to my right.
Crystal is coming this way.

What do I do?

Shawna's face says to stop her, but I don't have the right. Crystal gets to me, the song swelling, the singers blending in a beautiful a cappella.

Toni grabs Crystal's arm. "Sit with me, Crystal."

Crystal looks down. Is that a tear on her cheek?

Crystal looks up at me. "Excuse me."

God, what do I do? "I, uh, I feel out of place, too, Crystal," I say, taking a tissue from my pocket, amazed that there's even a tissue in there. I haven't worn these pants— since the funeral. The tissues were for me and my children. I offer the tissue to Crystal, and she takes it.

"Thank you," she says.

I step out into the aisle as a woman dances by wildly, um, praise-dancing, I think it's called. If she *really* feels the Spirit, she could put an eye out with those long nails of hers.

Crystal takes a step, clenches her fists . . . then stands next to Toni.

And that's the way we attend the Gospel show until intermission, sometimes standing (so we can see) and clapping, other times sitting and clapping. The boys seem to be having a good time, and though Rose is standing and clapping, I doubt she's feeling the Spirit. As for Crystal, well, if ever a child didn't want to be someplace, it's her. I thought *I* fidgeted when I was nervous. This child is one tall, beautiful, dangerous fidget.

The lights come up during intermission, and while folks get up around us, our row stays put. I turn to Crystal. "I need to stretch," I say, though I really don't, since I've been standing for most of the show. I step out into the aisle.

"C'mon, Toni," Crystal says. "Let's go to the ladies' room."

"But, Crystal," Toni says, "I don't have to go."

Crystal glances briefly at me. "I need to fix your hair, Toni."

Toni touches her hair. "What's wrong with it?"

"C'mon," Crystal says. "I'll show you."

Crystal takes her sister's hand, and they wander toward the back. A second later, the boys zip by me. Oh, *now* they can move quickly. I walk past the empty seats to Rose and Shawna.

"Enjoying yourselves?" I ask.

"They need to turn down the keyboards," Rose says.

"You said it," Shawna says. "I can barely hear Tommy singing. Nicole, though. I could hear that child sing through a hurricane."

"She should do *American Idol*," Rose says. "She has as good a voice as any I've heard on that show."

I am having trouble breathing. These two are . . . talking. Conversing. Communicating.

Shawna fans the air in front of her. "This sure is a workout, isn't it?"

"Yeah," I say, only I'm not sure if she means the Gospel show or talking to Rose. Probably a little of both.

"Oh, Joe, please take off that sweater," Shawna says.

"Yeah, Daddy," Rose says. "You'll roast."

And now they're sharing the same ideas? I can't peel off my sweater fast enough, but I immediately wish I wasn't wearing a white turtleneck underneath. I'm practically shining.

Shawna whispers something in Rose's ear, and Rose smiles.

And now they're being secretive?

"What?" I ask.

"Nothing, Daddy," Rose says with a giggle. A giggle? What has happened? They've only been down here for maybe thirty minutes!

"Are you giggling at my massive physique?" I strike a pose.

Rose stands and plucks a dark tuft of sweater from my turtleneck and shows it to me. "You're, um, shedding, Daddy."

I look at all the dark fibers crawling like little snakes on my turtleneck. "I should put the sweater back on."

"Yes," Shawna says. "Please. Quickly."

I put it back on.

Shawna turns to Rose. "You let him dress himself?"

"Yes," she says.

Which is a lie! *Rose* dressed me tonight!

"Hmm," Shawna says with a smile. "We need to fix that."

"I've tried," Rose says, "but he's very stubborn."

"Well, he's only had one woman pestering him about it." Shawna winks at me. "Just wait until he has *four* women dressing him."

Rose laughs. She laughs! It's not a nervous giggle. It's a full-blown, honest-to-God laugh.

"We will not let him leave the house until we all agree that he is dressed properly from now on," Shawna says. "Deal?"

Rose nods. "Deal."

Shawna looks up at me. "You, um, have anything to say in your defense?"

"No," I say.

"Smart man," Shawna says. She looks at Rose. "We'll fix him. Now tell me where you got those shoes. My feet are killing me . . ."

I back away. I've disappeared completely. They're ignoring me already? It took *years* for that to happen with Cheryl and Rose. I don't know if I should feel hurt or overjoyed.

No. I don't mind this at all. Girl talk to the rescue.

Thank you, God, for cheap sweaters that shed.

42

Shawna

"But I'm always afraid of getting flat feet," I'm saying to Rose when Crystal comes over to us holding Toni's hand as the lights flicker before the start of the second half of the show.

"Hi. I'm Crystal, and this is Toni," Crystal says to Rose, then looks hard at me. "We weren't *properly* introduced."

Oops. I didn't introduce them. Shame on me.

"Um," Crystal says, "can Toni sit down here with us?"

Oh, I get it. Just the girls. I have to make sure. "Can I join you?"

And then they hit me with that eye thing girls of every race, color, and creed do when they want to be a-*lone* and a-*way* from a-*dults,* like they're scared little bunny rabbits looking at each other and twitching their noses.

"I was just kidding," I say. "My men need me." I bounce off a few boys' knees back to Joe.

"What happened?"

"Just another miracle," I say.

This is a good place for miracles. Even if the music is too

loud or the tree people in front of us have hair as high as Mount Kilimanjaro, miracles have happened.

Like the miracle sitting next to me holding my hand during "I'm Ready."

Yes, Lord, I am so ready.

43

Joe

I wish that all our family outings this spring had been like that Gospel show. We used my lame list with mixed results. The hockey game wasn't too bad, but Toni hated it, saying it was too cold and asking a million questions, like "Where are the cheerleaders?" and "Why aren't they arresting those two men fighting?"

Shawna says that if Toni didn't talk, she couldn't breathe. I believe it.

We tried to go to a Roanoke Dazzle basketball game, and though it was exciting and the Dazzle won, Rose tuned out the world, Jimmy didn't win a dress-up relay at halftime (a kid half his size smoked him), Junior and Joey talked about some math problem the entire time, and Toni asked (and got) whatever she wanted to eat. Crystal dressed so provocatively that I was surprised she didn't stop play on the court. And after the game, we had to wait until Crystal got some autographs from some of the players.

"She's probably getting phone numbers," Shawna said, "and if she gets any calls, I'll call block every last one of them."

Shawna had to call-block a *lot* of numbers.

We tried Thunder Valley to ride the go-karts and play a round of laser tag. What could be more fun than racing each other for "family" bragging rights or more exciting than to shoot light beams at your future brothers and sisters? We paid all this money for them to have fun together and eat a couple pizzas, but only Toni and Jimmy rode the go-karts, played laser tag, and ate pizza. The "high schoolers" were too cool for all that, preferring instead to waste forty bucks in tokens on video games, some I remember playing back in the old days. We spent close to one hundred dollars in two hours.

I am definitely in the wrong profession.

"Expensive date," Shawna said. "At least I got to beat you in Ms. Pac-Man."

I'm *still* upset over that. That used to be *my* game!

On senior night for the girls' basketball team, which went an abysmal 4-14, Shawna wanted me to help escort Crystal to center court, but Crystal wouldn't have it.

"I hope you don't mind if just my mama is with me," she said.

"I don't mind," I said.

And I don't—really. She's not my stepdaughter yet. However, I did mind minding the rest of our crew in the stands during the ceremony. They were excessively loud, almost rude, in their admiration for Crystal. I was almost embarrassed, the kids were yelling so loudly and drawing attention to themselves.

Oh, who am I kidding?

All of this—the headaches, the open hands asking for money, the empty pockets at the end of the night, the stress of squeaking by every month in the bills department, the yawns—*all* of this has been the most fun I've had in years. My kids seem alive again, and we actually have a future in mind. After Cheryl died, we couldn't see past the next minute.

Now, we're talking about the wedding, what it will be like to have a fuller house, and—except for Crystal—where each is likely to go to college.

Shawna and I still haven't had a real romantic date by ourselves, but that's about to change tomorrow.

"Rose is babysitting for us at my house," I had told Shawna yesterday during our lunch break ritual.

"She is?"

"Yep. They'll be baking cookies, eating popcorn, and watching videos while we are going to be sitting in the audience at a movie at Valley View Grande after sitting for a couple hours eating at Ruby Tuesday . . . without the kids."

Shawna's eyes had softened. "Without the kids?"

"Yes."

" 'Without the kids,' " she had said with a smile. "That is one amazingly calming phrase. Without the kids. The phrase doesn't work without the 'without.' 'The kids' sends a shudder through me."

They send a shudder through my wallet, too. They are eating machines. Three Extra-Large Papa John's pizzas— bought with coupons, of course—are not enough. They are money machines. Quarters cannot stay in their possession for more than a second before disappearing down some slot. They are time machines. They have a "need" for this or a "need" for that on every shopping trip, and they have to have it "*Now,* Daddy" or "*Now,* Mama" or "My teacher *said* I need it for school *tomorrow*" or *"All* the kids at school have them *already."*

And, they have no conception of the word "privacy," as in "I'd like some privacy while I'm on the phone with Shawna" or "I'd like some privacy while I kiss Shawna good night."

Shawna just shrugs over all this, saying, "We're just getting a taste of how it might be. How's it taste?"

Is "exhausting" a flavor?

Meeting the needs of three kids is hard. Meeting or trying

to meet the needs of six kids is flat-out tiring. I have barely had enough time (or money) to buy Shawna a proper engagement ring.

That I intend to give her tonight if all goes as planned.

And if I don't stop thinking all these thoughts and pay more attention while I'm shaving—

"Daddy!" Rose screams from downstairs.

Geez! I've cut myself. "What?" I call out.

"They're here!"

Just my luck. I've got a gusher, right on the jawline. I may need a Band-Aid.

I will look so . . . smashing for my first dinner date in twenty years.

44

Shawna

This is a nice place. Hardwood floors are nice. Shiny. I look down at my reflection. Hmm. With the right light you can see up my dress. Maybe too shiny. Give it time. Six pairs of children's feet screaming through here should cure that.

It'll be nice to be in a house again. I know I'll miss The Castle, but it's only right up the street and we can visit any time we want to. While Rose, Jimmy, and Joey give Toni and Junior a tour of where they'll live one day, I wander . . . to learn, you know? It's not being nosy when you're opening this or pulling out that in *your* future house.

The kitchen is nice and big with lots of dark walnut cabinets. Lots of closets and . . . no, it's a half bath. Right here off the kitchen? Decent placement if the food isn't decent. Hmm. We'll need to widen that toilet some. The Murphys have them some skinny behinds.

Where's Joe? I grab the first child running down the stairs. It happens to be Jimmy. "Where's your father?"

"Upstairs shaving."

I stroke the peach fuzz on his chin. "You'll be shaving soon, Jimmy."

He strokes what is almost there. "You think so?"

"I know so." In about two or three years.

"Cool." Then Jimmy takes off to parts unknown.

I check my watch. We're actually going to be early, so I don't mind waiting. I'm sure Joe knows I'm here. It'll give me time to check out the family room. Nice fireplace with a mantel. Golden clock surrounded by huge pinecones. Pinecones sure don't grow that big around here. They look out of place, though. Hmm. This is some old furniture. Claw feet? Solid wood? Plaid upholstery that doesn't match anything. We're going to need some slipcovers. Solid colors. JCPenney sells them. Pretty big TV with VCR and DVD built in. So this is the room I won't be able to recognize later on tonight.

What's taking him so long? Joe doesn't have that much facial hair. Actually, he does have quite a bit, but it doesn't grow uniformly on his face—or on the back of his neck. He's a furry thing before he gets a haircut.

C'mon, Joe! Let's go somewhere "without the kids"! I don't want to yell up the stairs, but, well, this is going to be my house so I may as well start acting like it. "Joe! You all right up there?"

Joe comes to the top of the stairs holding a tissue to his neck.

"What happened?"

"It's almost stopped," he says.

I dash up those stairs. "Where's your Neosporin?"

"Hall closet."

I open the closet and find an amazing assortment of first aid accessories: Band-Aids of every size and shape, some waterproof, others latex free; four tubes of Neosporin; several Ace bandages; witch hazel; Ipecac; and those "smack 'em" ice packs. So this is what it's like to raise two boys.

"We're ready for anything, huh?"

I grab the Neosporin. "I'll say. Take off that tissue."

"It's a real gusher."

Blood has already soaked through. Nasty. "How'd you do it?"

"I was thinking of you." He pulls off the tissue, his blood not squirting on me.

"Just don't smile or you'll blind me."

I push out a little bit of Neosporin and take the smallest clear circular Band-Aid I can find, smoothing it over his jaw-line. "Remind me to take it off of you before we get out of my car."

"Okay. Um, before I go, I should read them the riot act."

"The what?"

He looks down. "It's what Cheryl used to call it, you know, the house rules."

"Oh." The riot act. Interesting. "I'm with you."

We assemble our brood in the family room, and they look so hyper! I pity this room already.

"Here's the deal," Joe says. "No running. The floors are slick, especially if you're wearing socks."

Oh, don't tell my kids that, Joe! That's a challenge. They'll be "stealing home" headfirst into the kitchen the second we leave.

"Don't answer the front door unless it's the Domino's man," Joe says.

"You ordered pizza?" Jimmy asks.

Joe nods.

"How many?" Jimmy asks.

Joe looks away from me. "Five mediums."

Oh, no, he didn't!

"Which is one for each of you," Joe adds.

My baby can't eat a whole pizza by herself! That's a waste of money!

"I'll have my cell phone," Joe says, producing his, "but only call us in an emergency, okay? No funny stuff."

Oh, *now* we are going to get slaughtered with calls. I'll have to remind him to put his cell phone on vibrate at the theater.

"Rose is in charge," Joe continues, "so you do whatever she asks you to do." He turns to me. "Did I forget anything?"

What *didn't* he forget? We're going to have to work on his riot acts. "Just behave, y'all, okay?" I plead. "I don't want to be worrying the entire time about you on our first real date. Only call if the house is on fire or someone is hurt and needs an ambulance. I want this house to look *exactly* like it does now when we return. Clean up your messes, and be nice to each other."

"Mama," Junior says, "we'll be fine, now just go."

"We'll be back around eleven," I say, and I practically run to that door.

"Boys, mind your manners," Joe says behind me. "No unusual bodily noises, okay?"

Oh, that's just perfect. His house is going to be full of boy funk when we get home.

Usually Joe drives us everywhere in that van, but I'm the chauffeur tonight, and since I'm directing this vehicle, I get to direct the conversation. "Joe, why did you tell them all that? You know they'll do the exact opposite of what you told them."

"And now they know I know they'll do it."

"Huh?" That almost made sense.

"I know all of that will happen, and if it doesn't happen, I'll be amazed. It will be kind of like coming attractions for your kids when they move in."

"Who are soon to be *our* kids, right?"

"Right."

But before any of that can happen, I have to get a ring for this handsome finger. When am I going to get it? Rose told

Junior, who promised not to tell anyone, who naturally told Toni, who also promised not to tell anyone, that Joe had bought me a ring. But that was weeks ago!

"Did you just feel a load come off your shoulders?" I ask.

"Yes. About four hundred pounds' worth."

I do the math. His kids weigh that much? They must have big bones.

"Do you think we'll make it through the evening without a phone call?" he asks.

"I hope so," I say.

But I'm really thinking, *Not a chance.*

45

Joe

The first phone call comes as we're being seated at Ruby Tuesday. Jimmy is being especially vulgar, Rose tells me, and "We're almost out of air freshener." Should she light some matches? No, I tell her. "Put Jimmy on the phone."

"Yes, Daddy?" Jimmy asks.

"Cut it out," I say. Shawna is rolling her eyes.

"But, Daddy, I had burritos for lunch at school, and they're gaseous."

While I'm glad his vocabulary and his grades are improving, I cannot have him farting up the house. "Either stifle them or leave the room, okay?"

"Okay. Bye."

The second call arrives exactly five minutes later as we're sipping some rather unsweetened sweet tea, adding three packets of sugar to our glasses. I listen for a moment to Junior, then hand the phone to Shawna. "It's Junior."

"Uh-huh . . . uh-huh . . . uh-*huh*. The whole thing? Already?" Shawna covers the phone. "Y'all have some Pepto-Bismol in that cabinet?"

I try not to smile. "We keep it in the upstairs bathroom."

"There's some Pepto in the upstairs bathroom. Read the label and only give her what it says to. Good-bye." She puts the phone in the middle of the table. "You have extra toilet paper in the house, too, I hope."

"Yes."

"Toni ate her *entire* pizza already."

I cough into my napkin.

The third call happens exactly one minute later while we're about to order.

I listen a moment then relay the message to Shawna. "The boys want to watch *Mortal Kombat,* but the girls want to watch *Bring It On.*"

"Tell them to watch one and then the other," Shawna says.

"But the boys have stolen the remote controls and have hidden them upstairs," I say.

Shawna sets down her menu. "There are buttons on the TV. Tell them to use them."

"Rose, watch the movies back-to-back, and use the buttons on the TV." I listen some more. I sigh at Shawna. "Rose says the boys are trying to take over. They're hiding upstairs, and Jimmy's still farting."

Shawna reaches for the phone. "Gimme that."

"Rose, Shawna wants to talk to you." I hand her the phone while our server taps her order book.

"Hi, Rose, put Junior on. Thanks." She covers the mouthpiece. "How set are you about going to that movie, Joe?"

"I want to be alone in the dark with you."

Shawna's—and our server's—eyes pop. "Joe. Please." She uncovers the mouthpiece. "Junior? No, not you, Toni. Get Junior." She covers the mouthpiece again. "Why won't they leave us alone?" She uncovers the mouthpiece again. "Junior, what's going on? Uh-huh. Uh-huh. Well, you go on and watch your movie. The girls will get bored once you stop playing with them . . . They *will,* Junior . . . How's your sister? She's really okay? What was that noise? Well, go find out and call me back!" She hands the phone to me. "It isn't my house yet, but it sounds like something broke."

I drop my chin to my chest. "Broke?"

"Shattered is more like it."

The phone rings again, and this time I answer it. Our server is aging before our eyes. "Hello? What broke, Rose?"

"Nothing broke, Daddy. We've been careful."

"Uh-huh . . . uh-huh," I say. "Okay. Clean it up." I turn off the phone.

"What broke?" Shawna asks.

"She wouldn't tell me, but if you heard it break . . ."

Shawna throws her napkin on the table. "I don't believe this. I just don't . . . We have to get home."

I cough into my napkin again. "Are you sure?"

"They're tearing up *our* house, Joe. We have to go back." She turns to the server. "We're having a little emergency at home."

The server smiles. "Kids, huh?"

We nod.

I put a five on the table. "Will that cover it?"

"Sure," our server says. "How many kids y'all got?"

"Six," we say together.

Our server's eyes do somersaults.

It's the best part of our evening so far.

46

Shawna

Oooooooh, I am so mad I could spit nails and build a house!

On the night I am to get a ring for my handsome finger, those . . . monstrous little vermin have to—

"It's my fault," Joe says, interrupting my vicious thoughts as we climb into my car. "I told them all the things I didn't want them to do, and they did them anyway."

"No, Joe," I say. "It's another conspiracy. They all banded together to make us miserable. It's like they're trying to drive us apart by being so bad."

"You think so?"

How can he be so calm? "I know my kids. Junior may be quiet, but he's devious. And little Toni probably stuffed herself with pizza knowing she'd get sick and I'd have to come home. As for what broke, I bet they broke something expensive and right now they're at the house trying to cover it up."

"I guess we'll have to punish them somehow." He shakes his head. "But how?"

"Can we afford boarding school for the lot of them?"

Joe actually laughs!

"I wasn't trying to be funny, Joe. I was being serious."

"No, we cannot afford boarding school."

"Even if they had a volume discount?"

He laughs *again!* "Not even with a fifty percent–off sale."

"Joe, I wish you would take all this seriously."

I see him biting his lips. "Sorry."

I turn onto Wasena Avenue. "I guess that means we're stuck with them, huh?"

"Yep. They're one hundred percent ours."

And now he's throwing my words back at me! I know I'm putting more holes into this sidewalk on my way to the door. The *nerve* of these kids! They knew how important tonight was to us! We get so little time together, and now they had to go—

Joe's just standing at the door.

"Did they lock us out?" I ask. "Oh, they are in for it!"

"No. We're not locked out." And then he reaches into his pocket . . . Now? After all this? And here? At the door? Where's the romance in this?

He pulls out . . .

A key.

"Here's your copy, Shawna. Why don't you see if it works?"

A key? He chooses this moment to give me a key? It's a nice gesture, but . . . "Okay." I take the key, shove it in, turn it, and step inside.

The house looks the same. I even say it out loud. "The house looks the same."

"It should." He closes the door behind us.

"What do you mean it . . . should?" I don't hear a single sound. Oh, there's some ticking of a clock somewhere, and the faint smell of burnt bread, but other than that—nothing. "Toni, Junior!" I call out.

"They're not here."

"They're what?"

"They're not here, Shawna. Come into the dining room." He holds out his hand.

I take his hand. "Why aren't they here, Joe?"

But as I enter the dining room, I see the reason. There are lit candles on the table, two large covered silver platters, silverware, china plates, crystal glasses . . . And is that sparkling cider? "Joe, what's going on?"

"Surprise," he says, and he takes me in his arms and kisses the skin off my lips. "I made a deal with Rose."

Kiss me again. I don't know anyone named Rose.

"I let her take them to Putt-Putt, but only after they prepared our meal and did a few chores. They have promised to be gone until ten, so . . . won't you have a seat?"

He's not kissing me again. I pout and pucker until he resumes exploring my mouth with his tongue. I pull back to take a breath. "So all those phone calls were fake?"

"Every last one of them. They were all according to a script Junior and Joey wrote."

Figures. It's always the quiet ones you have to watch out for.

Joe pulls out my chair, I sit, and he slides me in.

"So Toni didn't . . ." Oh, those kids are *good!*

"They didn't have pizza. I'm not sure what they're going to eat. I hope I gave Rose enough money."

I look at all that glitters on the table. "So we're having a date . . . at home."

"Right."

A home date. That makes *no* sense at all. "While our *kids* are out."

"Right."

"That almost makes sense."

He smiles, sitting opposite me. "It does, doesn't it?"

"Shouldn't I be more worried with them out tearing up someone else's property?"

"Rose is an excellent driver. They'll be fine." He taps one of the huge lids covering the silver platters. "Well, let's see what they made us."

I put my napkin in my lap. "You don't know?"

"This part is going to be a surprise to me."

He lifts the silver lid, and I see . . . grilled cheese sandwiches, all the crusts cut off, a pile of chips in the middle.

Joe cracks up. I crack up. I lift the lid off another serving dish and see a bunch of purple grapes. How did they know about the grapes? . . . Unless . . . Rema. She must have told Junior. Ooh, I'm going to fix Rema when I see her again. "At least they hit all the food groups."

Joe takes a pair of silver tongs and waves them over the grilled cheese sandwiches. "Slightly burned or extracrispy, my dear?"

"Oh, crispy. I have to make sure my food is dead before I eat it."

He places two little triangular bricks on my plate. "Some chips?"

I hold up my little pinkie. "But of course."

He hands me the tongs. "I better let you serve yourself. I don't know how fresh the chips are."

I dig into those chips with the tongs and stop. Either the chips are extremely heavy with grease, or . . .

I've just found the box for my ring.

They hid the ring box in a pile of stale potato chips.

I can't speak.

Joe snatches the ring box from the tongs, pops it open, kneels beside me, and takes my hand.

My heart is drumming so fast!

"I hope I say all this right." He clears his throat. "*Baada ya dhiki, faraja.* 'After hardship comes relief.' "

And now my feet are running! Stop it! "I am relieved." And Swahili sounds so beautiful coming from Joe's lips. "Junior taught you that?"

"He and a fascinating young lady named Amina."

Junior and Amina taught him? "When?"

"The computer has come in handy."

So that's it. "You've been e-mailing little girls behind my back?"

"No. I've been e-mailing Junior, and she just happens to be there."

When I'm *not* around. I'm going to fix that.

"But I'm not done, Shawna."

That's right. The ring isn't on my handsome finger yet.

"*Mimi na wewe pete na kidole.* 'You and I are like a ring and a finger.' " He slides on an elegant, shiny, diamond ring with a gold band.

I name it "Mine."

"Will you marry me, Shawna?"

"Yes."

He reaches for and plucks a grape from the bunch, putting it in my mouth, and it is so sweet! *"Mapenzi hudumu ukila zabibu,"* he says. "Love lasts—"

" 'If you eat grapes,' " I say before he can.

"You know that one."

I pluck one and put it in his mouth, I stand, he stands, we knock a few good china plates around . . .

And a whole bunch more squishy grape kisses later, we leave the cardboard cheese bricks where they lie and head to the family room where I sit on the ugly—but strangely comfortable—plaid couch.

"Want to watch a movie?" he asks.

Nah, man. I want more grape juice kisses. I'm diving in for more when I notice a note in front of me on the coffee table. "What's this?" I read the note: " 'Shawna and Daddy: Hit PLAY. Love, Rose.' " I look at Joe. "You know what this is about?"

"No. Maybe they chose a movie for us."

I sigh. "I hope it's not *Guess Who.*"

He presses PLAY on a remote control. After some snow I see a woman lying in bed—

Oh, God, it's Cheryl.

And she looks so hollow, so pale, a bandana on her head . . .

Joe is crying, and now I am.

He presses the STOP button.

"Sorry, I . . ."

I hold his hand tighter. "It's okay."

"Oh, God. She and Rose must have recorded this while I was at work. The, um, the chemo—"

I squeeze his hand harder. "I know all about it, Joe. It's okay. You going to be okay?"

"I think so." He puts down the remote control. "This isn't the time to watch this, whatever it is. What is Rose up to?"

It's so hard to think! Calm down. Relax. Okay. Rose and I are getting along better and better. I don't think she's faking it. She's starting to care for me. This is obviously . . . "Joe, you have to play it."

"Why?"

"It's important to Rose. There's a reason she wants us to see it, *knowing* you were giving me the ring. She did know you were giving me the ring tonight, didn't she?"

He squints. "I did tell her. She knew. They all knew. But . . ."

I pick up the remote control and press PLAY.

"Is it on?" Cheryl asks.

"It's on, Mom," Rose says offscreen.

"Okay," Cheryl says. "Um, hi. I'm Cheryl, and you must be the new love in Joe's life."

I am a goose bump.

"I want to be the first person to congratulate you," Cheryl continues, her voice melodic and sweet. "I've instructed Rose to play this for you and Joe as soon as you become engaged, so I hope Rose doesn't forget."

I hear Rose sniffling. "I won't forget, Mom."

"I know you won't, honey," Cheryl says. "Well, there's so much I want to say to you two."

Cheryl reaches for some papers, her hands so thin. That could be Rodney's hand reaching for me.

She shakes the papers. "I wrote a Top Ten list of why Joe is a good man to marry, and I want to share it with you. Number ten: Joe doesn't snore. It scared me at first. I was always wondering if he was alive. If you're worried, just check his pulse. The pulse in his neck is easiest to find, and sometimes he wakes up." She winks. "Number nine: Joe has warm feet. Mine are icy, but his are fiery hot. Just watch out for his toenails. They can be sharp. Number eight: Joe doesn't drink or smoke. He should give you many years of good health. Number seven: Joe wears interesting underwear."

"Mom!" Rose yells, and the camera jiggles.

I hit PAUSE and look at Joe. "Are you going to explain? Or is this something I have to experience for myself?"

He can't take his eyes away from that screen. "Um. They're just boxer briefs."

Lord, this has to be so hard for him. "I like boxer briefs." Black ones, for some reason.

Joe doesn't respond.

I hit PLAY.

"Just kidding," Cheryl says. "They're not that interesting. They're sexy!"

"Mom!" Rose yells again.

"Well, they are, honey. Okay, okay, here's the real number seven: Joe works hard. You may have to tie him to the bed on Saturday mornings so he doesn't work overtime. Number six: Joe doesn't complain about my cooking."

"You're a good cook, Mom," Rose says.

"I try," Cheryl says. "It doesn't always work out, you know? I have to turn my pound cakes in that oven or they'll only cook through on one side."

I hit PAUSE. "I have the same exact problem. I've been doing that for years."

Joe is still mesmerized by his wife's face, so I hit PLAY again.

"Number five: Uh, Rose, could you leave the room for a minute?" Cheryl asks.

"Why?" Rose asks.

"I'm going to say something private, and I don't want you to hear."

The camera shakes a moment. "Oh, all right . . ."

Seconds pass, a door closes.

"I hope I'm in focus. That tripod is finally coming in handy, Joe. Number five: Joe is a passionate, tender lover who loves to cuddle. We could have had ten kids if we could have afforded them. Rose? You can come back in now, Rose."

A door opens and closes.

"You didn't hear what I said, did you?" Cheryl asks.

"No," Rose says.

But I can tell she's lying.

"Rose? Did you?"

"Okay," Rose says. "I did."

"I hoped you would, honey," Cheryl says. "That's the kind of man I want for you, too."

. "Ten kids?" Rose asks.

"Sure. Let's see, number four: Joe is very organized. Everything has its place. Wait until you see the Peg-Board for his tools. Every one of his tools has an outline around it."

I hit PAUSE. "Really?"

"Uh, yeah."

At least he's speaking.

I hit PLAY.

"Number three: Joe has good oral and physical hygiene. You'll need to remind him to shower on Saturdays, though. It's a manly smell, but . . . Remind him also to see his doctor for that checkup he's been avoiding."

I hit PAUSE. "Which one is that?"

He grimaces. "The one with the . . ." He sticks out a finger and winces.

"You're going next week," I say. "And I'll drive you."

He nods.

I hit PLAY.

"Number two: Joe loves his children. He's the first person they call when they've had a bad dream. He's the only person I call when I have a bad dream."

I hear more sniffles from Rose.

"And the number one reason you made a good choice: Joe loves the Lord with all his strength, his mind, and his soul. He's not a Holy Roller or anything like that. He just lives his faith. I have never doubted Joe for a second because of it."

The woman and I could be sisters. I let my tears fall freely.

Cheryl puts her papers to the side. "There's so much more I could tell you, but half the fun is finding it all out for yourself." She sighs. "I wish I could be at your wedding. Maybe God will let me drop in. Take care of my children, and take care of Joe. God bless you. You can turn it off now, Rose."

The screen fills with snow.

I am beyond stunned. Cheryl didn't shed a single tear, not one drop. She *knew* she was dying, and yet she took the time . . . to welcome me.

I feel so unworthy. I'm sitting in her house with her man, and I feel like an outsider.

Joe stands and turns off the TV, shoving his hands into his pockets. "I wasn't expecting that at all. Are you okay?"

I nod.

"It explains quite a bit about Rose," he says.

Why can't I find a single word to say?

"Are you really okay?"

I nod . . . then I shake my head. "No. I'm not okay." I stand and almost fall into his arms, burying my head in his chest. "I don't . . . Joe, she was a wonderful woman, and I'm . . . I'm not that . . ."

Joe squeezes me tightly. "You're just as wonderful, just as caring, just as tender. It's why God brought you to me. It's why God brought us together." He takes my hand. "Come upstairs."

He's kidding, isn't he? "The kids could be back any minute, Joe."

"I didn't mean . . . I want to show you something."

We go upstairs to a room at the far end of the hallway next to a bathroom.

"Is this her room?"

He nods. "You remember you heard some loud noises?"

I nod.

"The noises weren't in the original script. I'll bet it was because of this . . ."

He opens the door and turns on the light . . . to a *completely* empty room.

"I had the boys move all the furniture down to the basement, so I imagine they broke something, maybe a lamp or a lightbulb."

I am standing in a completely empty bedroom that used to belong to a woman who just spoke to me and is now up in heaven looking down on me looking at her completely empty room. I am still a goose bump.

"I'll have to refinish the floor, of course, but . . . I want you to do the rest. Curtains, carpet if you want it, furniture, bedding, comforter, the works."

I step to the closet, open the door, and then step *into* the closet. There isn't a stitch of clothing hanging inside. I look at Joe.

"Salvation Army," he says. "Good idea. They were so grateful."

"Wow," I say. "This is . . . wow."

"It was Rose's idea. Tabula rasa, she called it. A blank slate."

Rose has definitely lost all of her thorns with me now. "But where will you sleep until then?"

"I'll probably bunk with Jimmy for a while."

I stand in the middle of the room, not a shred of Cheryl anywhere. This isn't a blank slate—it's a clean slate. Rose is a wise child.

"So, what do you think?" he asks.

I smile. "I'll have to take some measurements. Um, you'll want a king size bed, won't you?"

"Whatever you want."

"It might crowd the room some . . . Maybe a queen size."

He holds me from behind, his arms around my middle. "The better to hold you, my dear."

I like the sound of that. "How about satin sheets?"

"Aren't they expensive?"

"Probably. I've never priced them." Two hundred thread count sheets are fine for me. "We'll need a fluffy down comforter, too."

"Keep talking."

"And lots of pillows, all shapes and sizes."

He kisses the back of my neck, and I almost wilt. "Is the closet big enough?"

"I could fit my clothes *and* my kids' clothes in there." I turn to him, draping my arms around his neck. "But that will give me space for all the clothes you'll buy me, right?"

"Right."

I kiss his chin. "Mirrored headboard?"

"Interesting."

"Candles everywhere, too?"

I feel his heart racing. "Shawna?"

"Hmm?"

"You're making me . . . excited."

My heart is racing, too, bouncing against his. "Me, too."

We kiss deeply, and just as we start to do a little slow grinding, we hear a beep.

"Their timing couldn't be worse," Joe says.

"Yeah."

But a few minutes later as I show off my ring to *our* kids, I realize that their timing or our timing isn't important.

God's timing is.

We have an on-time God.

47

Joe

After that, the days and weeks fly by.
And Rose gives me a hug every single morning.

And Shawna does drive me for that checkup, sitting in the waiting room for hours while the doctor prods, pokes, draws blood, and generally gives my body a thorough examination in ways that are uncomfortable and seem excessive. When all the tests come back—and there were so many!—we find that I am a healthy forty-year-old man who needs to work on his "bad" cholesterol level and lose a few pounds. And that's it. After all that *invasion,* I have to get one number to drop and I need to drop some weight. While I'm happy, Shawna is overjoyed. She hasn't come right out and said it, but I think she's glad that she's made a good investment. My body will give her many years of service. I know her joy, however, has a tinge of sadness. What if she had done the same for Rodney? Would it have made any difference in what happened to him? Would I even have met her or have the happiness I have right now because of her?

I try not to dwell on all that. I just know that God is in control, and I have to trust that He knows what He's doing.

My parents are thrilled I found someone. Even when I mention her race to them, neither "blinks" over the phone.

"As long as you love her and she loves you," Mom says.

"That's all that matters," Dad says. "I agree with your mother, Joe."

Dad always agrees with Mom. That's probably why they've been married for forty-six years.

Dad does add, however, that it would be best if Shawna likes to fish—"But that's just me," he says.

"Mama asked, 'When we gonna meet him?' and Daddy said, 'All right,'" Shawna tells me.

"That's all they said?" I ask.

"That's all," she says.

We both come from families who don't like to waste words.

Sundays we visit area churches, looking for a new spiritual home for all of us, then after lunch at our house we sit discussing the pros and cons of each. Too many old people, too many kids, not enough music, too much music, short sermon, long sermon, too much emphasis on money, not enough emphasis on the Bible, not multicultural enough—

We usually get eight different opinions.

My kids want to stay with "our" church, Shenandoah Baptist; her kids want to stay with "their" church, Pilgrim Baptist.

"We can't split up like that every Sunday," Shawna says. "We must worship together. We'll find the right church. It's out there. We just have to find it."

Both of our churches are willing to marry us—which is a blessing—but we're not expecting many folks to attend. Shenandoah's sanctuary is a cavern; Pilgrim's is just right, seating at most a couple hundred. Thus, we'll be married at Pilgrim. And of all the churches we've visited, from Rainbow Forest out in Botetourt County to Valley Word in

Roanoke County, I feel most at home at Pilgrim. The boys feel the same way.

Only Rose feels out of place.

"Daddy, I am the only white girl there most Sundays," she tells me. "At least Jimmy and Joey have each other."

"We're not there to be with our own race, Rose," I tell her. "We're there to worship God."

"I know. It's just . . ."

"What?"

"Truth be told, Daddy, the service at Pilgrim is just too long. I know, I know. God doesn't have a watch because He *is* the watch"—one of Shawna's favorite sayings—"but three hours? Doesn't God get tired of listening?"

Shawna has a solution, and although I don't think it will work, it does. Shawna and the girls arrive each Sunday "fashionably late" so the service doesn't seem so long for Rose. After a few Sundays of "being seen," Rose relaxes, and when we're all ready as a family, we will become members at Pilgrim.

On weekdays, Shawna and I often go on walks in Wasena Park, always with Toni as our chaperone, while the boys play basketball or hit the skate park under the bridge, and they "hit" the skate park often. We bring a cooler of ice and sandwich bags for their bruises, just in case. Crystal has yet to join us for anything but church.

"Freedom," Shawna says. "That's what Crystal wants, and that's what I've been preparing her for."

Though Crystal will be moving out after graduation, we're preparing the house for her just in case. We've added a full size bed to Joey's room, a bunk bed to Jimmy's room, and a brand-new bedroom suite in our room—but without mirrors.

"We're too old for that kind of thing," Shawna says. "Why look in a mirror when I can just look and see you?"

So, the house is ready, and the date for our wedding is

tentatively set for early September. Crystal has found a job at JCPenney and a roommate to share an apartment. Shawna is heartbroken about that, but she puts on a brave face, glad that at least Crystal is going to graduate without summer school, which is "another miracle," according to Shawna.

Life is coming together.

But.

But.

My mind is coming apart. I guess I'm getting cold feet. I've just had too many life changes in a short time, too many stressful life events. I'm thinking of putting off the whole wedding process for a few months, maybe even a year. Too fast. All this has happened much too fast for my mind to process. I want to slow down, consider all this prayerfully. And when I tell Shawna of my hesitation, she agrees.

Sort of.

"I didn't know you felt this way, Joe," she says. "You should have told me sooner or as soon as you started having these feelings."

"I'm sorry. It's, well, it's been on my mind for a while. I just haven't sat down and really thought about it that much. It's like riding the wind, and now that things have calmed down . . . I hope you understand. I just don't want to rush."

"How long do you want to wait?" she asks.

"I don't know," I say, and I really don't. "A few weeks. Maybe a few months, I don't know."

"A few . . . months." She's quiet for a long time.

"This will also give the kids time to digest everything, you know, get fully used to the idea."

"I guess . . . I guess I can wait," she says, finally. "Just don't keep me waiting too long, Joe Murphy."

And after that . . . things change.

We don't slow down as much as we quiet down. Our lunch meetings at McDonald's are shorter, more silence than conversation. The same is true of our phone conversations. I'm already doubting my doubt—if that's possible—so I call Arnie for advice.

"I am a wreck, Arnie."

Arnie laughs. "Moses started out as a basket case, too, Joe, so you're in good company."

"Very funny." I tell him all about my doubts, my fears, my hesitation.

"Do you doubt your love for Shawna?" he asks.

"No. I guess I'm just afraid of losing her, you know, like I lost Cheryl. I don't ever want to go through that kind of pain again."

"Let me get this straight," Arnie says, his voice getting gruffer. "You're backing away from a woman because you're afraid of losing her."

Just protecting my heart the only way I know how. "I know it makes no sense."

"Why would you hesitate when you obviously have a Proverbs 31 woman ready to marry you?"

Not that again. "Arnie, Shawna is not really—"

"Sure she is," he interrupts. "Everything about her says Proverbs 31 woman."

"You've only met her a few times at church, Arnie," I say.

"I am a good judge of character, Joe. Now tell me, can she sew?"

"Look, Arnie, I've read that passage in Proverbs, and—"

"Just humor an old man. Can she sew?"

"I don't know. Her kids are always nicely dressed."

"That counts. Does she get up early?"

"Every day."

"And stay up late?"

"I think so." We seem to have most of our main conversations late at night after all our kids are safely asleep.

"Does she garden?"

"She lives in an apartment, Arnie. She does have a few houseplants."

"Are they alive?"

"Yes."

"She can garden, then. Does she have strong arms and legs?" He clears his throat. "Not that it's any of my business."

"Yes. She's a good hugger and she stays on her feet all day."

"A good hugger. That's good, isn't it?"

"Yes, Arnie."

"Hmm. Is she charitable?"

"Yes." I tell him about Shawna's continuing work with LivingWithDeath.com. "And she loves me."

"You think you're a charity case, Joe?"

"Sometimes."

"Is she wise?"

"Yes, in a down-to-earth way. She can cut right to the heart of a problem in an instant."

He laughs. "Then you should be discussing all this with her, not me."

He has a point.

"Is she kind?" he asks.

"Always."

"Do her kids respect her?"

"Yes. Mine, too."

"Does she fear the Lord?"

"Yes."

"She's a Proverbs 31 woman, all right. You'd be a fool not to tell her that you've been a fool for having your doubts."

I *have* been a fool, but . . . "Arnie, I think I'm still in love with Cheryl. Everywhere I look in this house I see Cheryl. I see her in the faces of my children and hear her in Rose's voice. It's almost as if I'm cheating on her or something."

"You aren't cheating on your wife, Joe," Arnie says. "Didn't Solomon have a thousand wives? And David had a fair share, too."

Why am I *still* asking advice of a confirmed, lifelong

bachelor about all this? I see Rose hovering in the hallway. I mouth, "Do you need the phone?" She shakes her head, but she still hovers. Maybe she wants to talk.

"Arnie, I have to go. Thanks for all your advice."

"My pleasure."

I hang up, and Rose comes into the family room.

"What's up?" she asks.

That's usually what I ask her. Hmm. "Nothing," I say, echoing her usual response.

"Um, how's Shawna?"

And now she's asking about Shawna? "She's okay."

"Just . . . okay?"

"She's fine, Rose. What's on your mind?"

She shrugs. "I don't know. If I were her, I wouldn't be okay. I mean, she had her heart all set, and then . . ."

Rose has my attention. "And then . . . what?"

"Junior told me about this separation idea of yours, Daddy. I think it's silly and a waste of time."

"You . . . do? I thought you'd be all for it."

She shakes her head. "I'm not. She loves you, and you love her. You're lonely. It's time . . . you got . . . married again."

I blink. "Really?"

She takes my hand and squeezes it. "I have to be honest. I was . . . uncomfortable with Shawna as my future step-mother, but when I saw how happy she made you, how happy you've been, and how happy you *aren't* now . . . Besides, I have a whole new respect for you now."

This is one amazing young lady. "You do?"

"Yeah. You're being a rebel, Daddy."

"I am?"

"Sure. You're marrying outside your race. You're marrying a woman with three kids. You're marrying a woman your own age when most men your age would have a midlife crisis and marry a teenager." She grasps my hand with both of her soft hands. "Now I know where I get my rebellious streak."

"You think I'm a rebel."

"Yep."

"All this time I've been worried that you would never accept Shawna and that you might even one day leave us like Crystal did."

She punches me in the shoulder, like the tomboy Rose of old. "I'm nothing like Crystal, Daddy. Besides, someone has to take care of this house. Two parents working . . . I mean, who will make sure Jimmy does his homework every day? Who'll make sure Toni keeps her room clean?" She presses her shoulder against mine. "You need me around, Daddy. You need me to help make your marriage work."

"So, does that mean I have your blessing?"

She kisses my cheek. "Yes."

I wrap my firstborn in my arms and hold her close. "What was I thinking, Rose? I love Shawna. Why would I want to put off being with her?"

"The same reason I didn't want you to be with her. We both still love Mom."

"Yeah." I kiss her forehead. "What should I do now? Call her? No, she's working a double shift tonight. I could go visit her."

Rose shakes her head. "She'll be tired and cranky, Daddy. Why don't you . . . write to her? Have an e-mail waiting for her when she gets home."

"Would that be romantic?"

Rose nods. "It's kind of like you're at home waiting for her, you know?"

"Yeah. That'll work. Thank you, Rose."

"Any time, Daddy."

48

Shawna

I'm glad we're not that busy. I'm going through the motions anyway. Tonight this store isn't going to be all that clean. I just can't seem to motivate myself to motivate anyone else because Joe has thrown me a curve.

I really don't blame him, I mean, what was I thinking? I can't replace Cheryl, and I don't want to take up space. How in the world could I ever be a white housewife? How could I ever truly fit in Joe's world? Cheryl was a homebody, practically doting on her kids, the perfect stay-at-home mom. I'm not built that way. I've been getting a paycheck since I was sixteen, and I expect my kids to be able to fend and do for themselves. And in *her* house? I feel like a visitor there. I know I'd make some changes so it will be my house eventually, but . . .

"Dining room's swept," Chuckie says.

"All right," I say. "You can clock out."

Chuckie looks at me strangely.

"Go clock out, Charles," I say, and he bolts for the back. Normally I'd check his work or lack of work and make him do it again, but tonight I have some work to do in my mind.

Lord, I've been alone so long. I'm too set in my ways. Rodney and I jelled. Oh, it didn't happen overnight, oh, no. It took work, hard work, daily work . . . and eventually it became easy. Clockwork. Rodney and I were like clockwork. Do I want to go through all that trouble to whip another man into shape? I mean, Crystal hates him . . . although Junior respects him and Toni likes him. If I don't marry Joe, Crystal might come back home, and all my babies would be under my roof again, and then . . . and then . . .

I'd be lonely all over again.

I just . . . I miss Joe. My hands are getting sweaty just thinking about him. And sitting in church without him—he and his family went to Shenandoah last Sunday—was . . . lonely. As Pastor Reed likes to say, I was just "settin' on the premises instead of standin' on the promises." And Pastor Reed's sermon was . . . different. I'm sure Joe and I would have had a nice conversation about it. Who preaches from Habakkuk? "Write the vision," Pastor Reed kept saying. "Write the vision and wait for it, because it will surely come."

Write the vision. Write it down. So . . . I did. It took a *long* time to write and wasn't going anywhere until I used Pastor Reed's outline of visualization, anticipation, and manifestation. Pastor Reed likes to rhyme. That e-mail has been sitting in Joe's in-box for . . . geez, fifteen hours now. I wonder if he's responded.

49

Joe

I sit down to write to Shawna, and there's already a message from her in my inbox.

And it warms my heart.

Dear Joe:

Habakkuk 2:1 says, "Write the vision, and make it plain upon the tables, that he may run that readeth it."

Here is my vision: We are in our house. At the foot of our bed is a crib containing our child. Your arms are around me. The baby wakes, and we both get up to tend to him. I'm convinced we'll have us a boy. We bring him to lay between us, and we compare this miracle baby to each other. He has your nose and ears and my scary eyebrows . . . Get the picture?

Joe, I can see us growing old together. You're in my thoughts, my dreams, my heart, my soul. My hands and feet can't keep still. I believe with every part of my being that we are meant to be married. I want to make our love public for all the world to see.

Can you see my vision? Can you feel my anticipation? Do you still want to marry me?

I await your decision.

Love,
Shawna

And now, I'm supposed to run with this since I have readeth it . . .

Dear Shawna,

I can see us together. You always make me smile. Our child is golden. SHE has your eyes. You are in my prayers, my thoughts, my daydreams, my sleepless nights. Your smiles are a part of my bones. I hear your voice. I can see your hand in mine. I can feel your body next to mine. Yes, I want to marry you because

Because . . . why? There are so many reasons, but the main reason has to be:

God brought us together.

Thank You, Father, for doing that.

Shawna, I need to see you. I've only just realized that peace begins with your smile.

I love you.

Joe

I send the message, and then I runneth up the street to wait for Shawna to come home from work. I need to see her smile. I need to feel that absolute peace.

And when she arrives, her smile lights up the night, I start to cry, I run to her—just like those silly romantic movies.

"You read my vision," she whispers once I've stopped kissing those tender lips of hers.

"Yes."

"Did you write a reply?"

I hold her face in my hands. "I wrote something, but you can read it later. I want you to read this first."

And then I kiss her again, and in a few milliseconds, I feel peace wash all over me. All the worries about having five kids in the house and financing all that tuition—gone. All my doubts and fears about everyone getting along under one roof—gone.

Shawna pulls away first. "You, um, write very well, Mr. Murphy."

"Thank you," I say.

"Are you absolutely sure, one hundred percent, no doubts?"

"Yes." And I am.

"Okay." She smiles, and I get another shot of peace. "On the way here I got to thinking."

"You did?"

"I did." She smiles again. "I do that sometimes. I got to thinking how we can we live together before we live together."

50

Shawna

Joe's eyebrows wrinkle up. "Live together . . . *before* we live together."

"Right. And you know what I came up with?" I ask.

"What?"

"We need to go on a family vacation."

"Really?" Joe asks.

"Really."

"Think about it, Joe: Six sets of knees and elbows touching each other for miles on end, and I said *six* because Crystal will go. We'll be sharing our funk, sharing our stale breath—it will be perfect."

"Oh, yes," he says, nibbling on my left ear so gently. "It sounds more than perfect."

I don't think he believes me. "C'mon, Joe. A vacation is exactly what we need. A long family vacation in the van to meet my people and your people."

He blinks. "You're kidding."

"Nope."

He sighs. "It's nine hundred miles round-trip to Atlanta at

least, and it's sixteen hundred miles round-trip to visit my parents in Canada. At sixty miles an hour—"

"Yes," I interrupt, "it's a long time to spend knocking knees."

"Not to mention the cost of gas, the cost of meals on the road, the cost of at least two hotel stays, the cost of—"

I growl. "The cost of us not bonding is going to be more expensive, Joe. Besides, I haven't had a vacation in more than ten years. I deserve to get away." And I get to ride in front with all that leg room while the kids fend off each other's feet. "If that doesn't break us or make us, nothing will."

"Are you sure?"

I nod.

"Shouldn't we be making plans for the wedding?"

"I like how you think, Mr. Murphy, but we're old pros at weddings. We could probably plan a wedding in our sleep." I have already planned it out in excruciating detail on five full legal pads during our little "separation," and in August I will share all one hundred and fifty-seven items on my wedding checklist with Joe. But until then, we are going on a vacation.

"But can we afford a vacation *and* a wedding?"

It's always about money with Joe. It is with me, too, but this is a unique situation. "God will provide a way. And once we get to Atlanta and Canada, we'll have a free place to stay, right?"

"Right."

I can't wait to get up to Canada. Joe has said it's where God takes a vacation, and I want to be sure.

He sighs. "Yeah, once we get to my folks' house, they'll take care of us. They always have. Um, will Crystal go? I mean, will she *really* go?"

Crystal is certainly enjoying her freedom. She and LaTonya have done a nice job decorating their little two-bedroom apartment over near Valley View Mall. "Oh, she'll go. Two weeks is all I'm asking. JCPenney can do without her for two weeks."

"But . . ."

He's so negative sometimes. "But what?" I ask.

"We'll be traveling over twenty-five hundred miles in two weeks. Unless we drive straight through to Canada, we'll be on the road for six of those fourteen days."

I hadn't thought of that. "Then, my sweet man, we will drive straight through. We have, what, six eligible drivers?"

He closes his eyes. "Don't remind me . . ."

I rub the back of his neck. "You worry too much, Joe. There will be no problems on this trip, none whatsoever."

Later that night, after at least a half-hour "kiss good night" outside the apartment door, however, there's a big problem.

"Mama, I can't *possibly* take two weeks off," Crystal tells me from her new cell phone while she's driving around town with LaTonya in *my* Sentra wasting gas *I* paid for. "Especially in August with all the back-to-school sales. I can't go. I need those paychecks to pay for the rent, my phone, my car insurance, and my food. It wouldn't make sense for me to go."

Though I love to hear her talk "reality," I want her to know that she *has* to go. "Look, don't worry about the money end of things. Joe has agreed to cover it." Well, he will. I'll just have to buy some more grapes for us.

"But what if they fire me? I've only worked there a couple months. And I have to have six months' service before any of the benefits kick in."

Lord, how You can change a person so fast! I have trouble believing that this is the child who couldn't remember the days of the week when she was in first grade. "Tell your manager that it's a family emergency, that you can't help it, that you have to go, that it's a matter of life and death—that sort of thing. Then tell your manager that you'll work double shifts when you get back."

She laughs. "But, Mama, isn't it supposed to be a vacation?"

"So . . . it's an emergency family vacation. You understand why we're going, right?"

She scowls. "So we'll have some people to come to your wedding to give you wedding gifts."

Well . . . it *is* kind of true. Sad, but true. "That's not the real reason, Crystal, and you know it. We all need to bond, to go through something together that we will all have in common. It will give us strength. I mean, we've been doing a lot of family things, and I'm grateful you've at least come to church. It does my heart endless good when you attend church with us."

"You know I wouldn't miss going to Pilgrim, Mama."

Pilgrim is where she and her daddy would hold hands during the service. Now, however, it's some thugged-up "friend" named Tony and his tattoos, ripped abs, attitude, and silence. He's friendly enough, even polite around me, but he's so standoffish and cold—not like her daddy at all, at least from what I've seen.

"Just do this one thing for me, just two weeks of your life," I plead.

"Family emergency, huh?"

"Yes."

"When do I tell my manager?"

I almost say, "Don't tell her until we're on the road," but that wouldn't be very Christian. "I suggest . . . that you tell her the day before we leave. That way, when she calls to check up on your story, you won't be there."

"And you and Joe will pay for whatever LaTonya and I can't pay for?"

Say what? "Who said anything about LaTonya? You're *our* child. Her own people have to take care of her."

"I'm *your* child, Mama."

"See? That's why this vacation is an emergency. Y'all have to see that Joe is your father, too."

"I'll never see that, Mama. I'm not even going to try."

This conversation is taking a bad turn. I need to steer her back. "At least go with us down to Atlanta to see your grandparents and cousins. It will only be a few days, and you haven't seen them in years."

"I can drive down and see them myself whenever I want to, can't I?"

Shoot. I keep forgetting that she's an adult, but she's driving *my* car! "You'd drive over four hundred miles alone?"

"LaTonya would go with me."

LaTonya, the child who can barely pay her rent and still sleeps with her teddy bear, has a license? "That's not the point. That's my car you'd be driving."

"And?"

I don't have an answer for that one! *Grrrr*. I'm not thinking clearly today. Should I try reverse psychology? "Okay. Don't go. I wouldn't want you along on the ride anyway. Good-bye."

And then I hang up.

And wait.

And wait.

She's very stubborn, but I know I've made her mad.

I wait some more.

The moon is rising outside.

Did I mention that she's stubborn?

My phone rings. I check the caller ID. It's Crystal. I let it ring five times before answering. "Hello?"

"Mama, were you serious?"

"I'm really sleepy, girl. Is this important? Can't it wait until morning?"

"Mama, were you serious?" she repeats.

"About what?"

"About you not wanting me to go."

"Yep." I fake a yawn. "That will give everyone more room. Your brothers and sisters will love you for giving them more space. It will be a much more enjoyable ride. And anyway, why go where you don't want to go? You go on and work, and we'll go have us a vacation. I'll tell your grandma and your grandpa that you were too busy working at a mall to come see them."

C'mon, guilt trip. Work your magic.

"You wouldn't tell them that!"

"Yes, I would." And I *would*. Crystal knows my family well, and she knows we talk about folks who don't show up when they should. "And I'd also tell them that you plan to drive all the way down there one day, though I don't know when, what with your busy, busy schedule, and you'll be bringing LaTonya, who doesn't have a penny for gas money, who still sucks her thumb—"

"She does not!"

It was just a guess. "My mistake." I let her stew a few moments. "What could it hurt for you to go with us? What are you afraid of?"

"I'm not afraid."

I think I have her. *Please, Lord, let this work!* "Sure you are. You're afraid you're going to like Joe."

"What?"

"Yep. That's what I think. You know what else I think? I think you're not only afraid of liking Joe, but I think you're also afraid of everything about Joe."

"I am not!"

It's working! "Joe scares the bejeesus out of you, doesn't he?"

"He doesn't! I'm not afraid of him!"

We could go back and forth like this for hours, but I decide to cut to the chase. "Prove it."

"Prove it? How?"

"Come down to Atlanta with us. And if you want to hate him or talk bad about him the entire time you're down there, go on ahead and do it."

"And what will that prove?"

"That you aren't afraid of him." And she graduated a few months ago? Hmm. Diplomas must not guarantee logical thinking anymore.

"Okay then, Mama. I'll go with y'all to Atlanta, but I promise you this: I will *not* have a good time where Joe is concerned, and I will badmouth Joe with my every waking breath. I'll even talk bad in my sleep about him."

She's going! Yes! "Okay then."

"Good-bye, Mama."

"Good-bye."

It's not exactly what I was hoping for, but at least it's a step in the right direction.

51

Joe

The mechanics at Tire Centers Incorporated have assured me that the van will last at least another three thousand miles.

This does *not* give me a feeling of confidence. "Did you check all the hoses?"

They did.

"All the belts?"

They did.

"All the rivets and welds?"

They hadn't, but they had seen no rust.

"What about the starter?"

Fine.

"The battery?"

In the "good" range. A little corrosion, not to worry.

"Why isn't it in the excellent range?"

Because their gauge doesn't have an "excellent range" on it.

"It's trip-ready, Mr. Murphy," they tell me.

But is it kids-riding-for-twenty-five-hundred-miles-knees-touching ready?

"Where you headed?" they ask.

"Atlanta, then about two hundred miles northeast of Toronto to Aylen Lake."

That's when they look at each other with raised eyebrows and make little *Os* with their mouths.

I make them do another courtesy check, just to be sure.

Nothing, and I mean, *nothing* can go wrong with this van. We cannot break down, and we cannot have a flat because I am going to be with the kids for *forty* hours of travel. I love them all, don't get me wrong, but I doubt there'd be a lot of love in the air if we were stuck on the side of the road, say, during a heavy thunderstorm in the Pennsylvania mountains.

And with my luck, we'd be *exactly* halfway to Canada when it happened.

The idea of this trip is sound. We are going to throw together our kids in close quarters for two weeks to get them to bond. We're trying to give them all a common mind about something. They have made some wonderful connections. The boys call themselves "brothers from another mother," or something like that, but the girls . . . They just haven't clicked. Shawna thinks it has to do with their age difference, their life experience differences, the fact that Crystal is so beautiful, Toni is cute, and Rose . . . Rose is beautiful, but she won't let anyone see that anymore. And actually Crystal isn't beautiful—she's stunning. The child stops traffic. Rose is in her shadow. Well, Rose is in her own shadow, too. Rose just needs to come out in the sun, and I'm hoping she'll at least get some freckles up in Canada.

The fact that Crystal doesn't live at home anymore and won't join us when we finally blend it all together is a problem. The fact that Toni has no one her age to play with is a problem. She plays with me, and I don't mind, but I don't know if I'll have enough time to push a swing or to deal with "Watch this, Joe!" every day. We're hoping she'll play some rec league basketball this fall, just to give us an hour or two of peace every once in a while.

Since it will be hot, we are packing light for Atlanta. On our way back through Virginia, the idea is to drop by the house, exchange the Atlanta luggage for the Canadian luggage stacked in the hallway, and continue nonstop until we get to Aylen Lake, the Murphy family homestead. Shawna thinks I'm overplanning everything, but I have to. The van has only so many square feet, and the kids' feet are huge!

Yesterday, I handed her a list of what her kids should bring up to the lake, and she blinked at it.

"This is all they'll need?" she asked.

It is a very short list. "They'll be in their bathing suits for most of the time."

"As cold as it is up there?"

"Shawna, I keep telling you that it's not that cold, especially in August."

She rolls her neck, a sign that I'm wrong and she's right. "Seventy degrees is cold to me, Joe. And that lake will be colder than that, won't it?"

"It's refreshing." In, well, an Arctic sort of way.

"Well, you go on overplanning. I'll just have to *over-pack*."

And she did.

And they have.

And I am now staring at the Canadian luggage filling up our hallway. There is no way all of this will fit in the van, none whatsoever.

Shawna brings in yet another suitcase and has trouble finding a place to put it in the hallway, which is easily twice the size of the van. She balances the suitcase on top of two others. "Think it'll all fit?"

"If the kids don't go," I say.

She rubs my shoulders. She doesn't play fair. "We'll just have to get one of those cartop carriers."

"They're expensive, and we're already going to get horrible gas mileage." If we break fifteen miles a gallon I'll be ecstatic.

She keeps rubbing. I intend to win this little argument, but that feels so good!

"I want my kids to be prepared for anything," she says. "Is that asking too much?"

Yes, I want to say. "Is all this absolutely necessary?"

"Yes." She kisses my cheek.

Oh. Now she's bringing in the big guns, not that her lips are big. They're nice and soft and usually seal my fate in any argument with her. "Shawna, I will need a trailer for all this."

"So rent a trailer."

I think back to an old trailer memory. I see my father bending over a blown trailer tire, the second blown tire that day, on our way from Aylen Lake to Combermere—a distance of only twenty miles. That little trip took six hours. I could have walked to Combermere faster. Backward.

We used duffel bags once for a trip to Disney World, so . . . "I won't need a trailer. I'll just stuff my kids' clothes into duffel bags."

"And wrinkle everything?"

Don't all clothes get wrinkled, even in suitcases? "They don't seem to mind up there."

"Does your mama have an iron and an ironing board?"

"Of course."

She shakes her head. "Duffel bags, huh?"

"Yeah."

"And if we all used them, it will all fit?"

I nod.

"I have some army duffels at the apartment. Will they help?"

I kiss her forehead. "Yes, they will."

"Don't be kissing on me, Joe Murphy." She walks back to the van, which I've been letting her use for a couple weeks. "Kissing me on the forehead like he won something," she mutters.

I won?

I won.

Why don't I feel victorious, then?

Half an hour later, she brings the army duffels and tosses them onto the porch.

I pick up one and unzip it.

Shawna doesn't move.

"Are you . . . are you going to help?" I ask.

She's rolling her neck again. "You want *me* to help *you* wrinkle *my* kids' clothes?"

I smile. "Forget I asked."

She holds a hand behind her ear. "What? Huh? I couldn't hear you."

A few *hours* later, I have carefully placed the contents of ten large suitcases into six duffel bags filled to bursting, taking pains not to wrinkle anything too badly while Shawna watches my every move.

It is anything but fun.

"That's still a lot of stuff," she says.

"It'll fit."

I hope.

52

Shawna

While my clothes get crushed to death and wrinkled beyond repair, we leave early in the morning for Atlanta.

I hope Joe knows how to iron. And even if he doesn't, he is *going* to learn.

The first part of the trip is uneventful. The boys are wired into their Game Boys, Toni colors, Rose reads, and Crystal listens to her Walkman.

In other words, no bonding is taking place.

When we near Radford, about forty miles away from Roanoke, Junior breaks the silence with some Swahili.

"Pole, pole ndiyo mwendo," he says.

"You're not going to do that all the way to A-T-L, are you?" Crystal asks.

"Tell everybody what it means, Junior," I say, hoping it will start a discussion.

"It means 'slowly, slowly is indeed the long journey,'" Junior says.

"Kind of like enjoy the ride, huh?" I ask Jimmy.

Jimmy is already gone into the handheld video netherworld.

I smile at Junior. "Got any more Swahili you want to teach us?"

Junior beams and says, "*Ngalawa na iwe juu wimbi chini.* 'May the boat be on top, the wave below.'"

"This *is* a boat," Crystal says.

"The love boat," Joe *sings*. Badly.

Rose gasps, "Daddy, please don't sing."

I kind of agree, but . . . "Junior, do you have a saying for Rose?"

Junior looks at Rose carefully. "Hmm. Ah. *Yai halia tamii kuku.*"

"I'm not cuckoo," Rose says in a huff.

It sounded like cuckoo to me, too.

"It means 'an egg never sits on a hen,'" Junior says.

Ahh. I like that one. I don't get it, but it sounds . . . Oh. Oh, no. If it means "respect your elders," Junior is in trouble.

"An egg can't sit on a hen, Junior," Rose says. "It's impossible."

Junior raises his eyebrows. "You are the egg, and your dad is the hen."

Rose rolls her eyes. "Thanks a lot, Junior."

"Mseme kweli nana wajoli," Junior adds.

"Mama," Crystal says, "will you *please* make him stop? He's giving me a headache."

I ignore Crystal. I intend to ignore her this entire trip if she really plans on badmouthing Joe. "Junior, what's that one mean?"

"'The speaker of truth has no friends,'" he says.

So true! I have to get to Africa. Just setting foot there and learning these sayings will make me wiser.

"Mommy," Toni says in *that* voice, which can only mean . . . "I have to pee."

Jimmy looks up. "So do I."

Joe sighs. "The next rest area is in thirty miles."

"Mommy," Toni says in a shriller voice, which can only mean . . . "I got to go *bad*."

Jimmy leans forward and holds his stomach. "Me, too."

"Joe, find us a gas station, please," I say.

"Why?" Joe asks.

"Jimmy's holding his stomach."

Joe takes the very next exit, but not before Jimmy leaves a noxious cloud of funk behind him in the van. It's so bad that I still smell it all the way to South Carolina. When we stop for gas there, I buy several hanging air fresheners, but I still smell that funk!

After we're back on the road, once again, no one is inter-acting. Joe doesn't seem to mind. Traffic is light, the ride is fairly smooth, no one is fussing, no bladders are about to burst, no . . . aw, *geez!* What did that child eat?

Air! I need air!

My kids open or crack the window nearest to them while Joe's kids just sit there. They must be immune to Jimmy's bursts. I cringe inside, because it's only going to get worse when Jimmy eats Mama's cooking.

Jimmy will have to sleep outside and downwind from any populated areas down in Georgia.

We pass a strange-looking water tower or something that looks like a giant peach.

"Looks like it's trying to poop," Jimmy says, snickering.

"Jimmy," Joe says in a stern voice.

"But it *does*, Dad," Jimmy says.

"Ew," Toni says.

I'd say *"ew,"* too, but it does sort of look like a peach that will never quite complete a bowel movement. Maybe that's Jimmy's problem, too. We need to get that checked out.

During yet another period of silence after the "pooping peach," I ask Toni to ask Crystal for a CD to play.

"Mommy wants a CD to play," Toni tells her.

Crystal looks at me. "You're kidding."

"Toni," I say, "tell your sister that I feel the need to do a chair dance."

"Mommy says," Toni says, but Crystal cuts her off.

"I heard her, Toni," Crystal says.

"Oh," Toni says.

Crystal takes the CD out of her Walkman. "Tell Mommy to crank this. And also tell Mommy not to throw out a hip."

Toni hands me the CD, and I let her tell me all that Crystal wanted to tell me. She says "lip" instead of "hip," but I don't care. I slide the CD in the player, crank it as loudly as the van's little speakers can handle, and I start to groove.

"Uh-oh, uh-oh," the boys chant behind me. "Go, Shawna, it's your birthday, go Mama, it's your birthday."

I am an expert chair dancer, but when Joe tries to match me move for move, that's when the laughter really begins.

"Daddy, please stop!" Rose yells.

"I can't stop," Joe says. "I'm feeling the music."

"But you're not feeling it!" Rose shouts. "You're hurting it!"

The boys do a silly little line dance (while belted and seated, of course), looking like very short Irish River-dancers. And they're in perfect rhythm! Toni and Crystal are doing a little old-school routine from that *Thriller* video, and Rose is now saying, "Please! I'm trying to read!"

I reach back and snatch Rose's book from her. *Battle Royale?* What's this about? She lunges for her book, but I pull it farther back. "It's time to dance, Rose."

She throws herself back into her seat, crossing her arms.

Maybe I shouldn't have done that. Hmm. "Okay, y'all. Do what I do."

"Me, too?" Joe asks.

"No, Joe," I say, glancing at Rose, "you just drive."

Eventually, we are all bopping in rhythm together—even Rose, who is at least twitching her shoulders in time to the music—to some song with far too many cuss words. At least I think they're cussing. How can you tell with all that speed-mumbling? I look at Joe.

I told him to drive. What is he doing? When we're leaning to the right, he's leaning to the left, and the van is drifting that way, too! When we're rising up, he's dropping down.

But . . . it's funny, the kids are laughing, Crystal isn't fuming, and Rose even cracks a smile. It all breaks the ice, you know?

When the song ends, however, Crystal asks Toni to ask me for her CD back, the show ends, and I return Rose's book to her.

Well, what was that? Four minutes of bonding? Great.

I try to stare a hole in Crystal's head, but I can't get through. That child has some thick ice up there. Nothing Joe can do or say will make her like him. Even if Joe dropped her off right here and gave her bus fare back to Roanoke—where she'd obviously rather be than be with her family—she'd turn down his money and try to hitch a ride.

Joe turns to me. "Anybody hungry?"

The kids cheer.

At least they agree that they're hungry.

We stop at a Wendy's in Gastonia, North Carolina, and get some very long, hard stares. The black girl taking my order never looks me in the eye even once, looking around me to all the children—and to Joe, who is still trying to learn a few moves from Toni.

"Where y'all from?" she asks.

Earth, I want to tell her. "Virginia," I say.

"Oh," she says.

Maybe we're missionaries here, too.

Fed and happy, we putt along, but once we get closer to Atlanta, I, um, I get us lost, and we get to the I-85/I-285 interchange before I realize my mistake.

"Um, Joe?" I say. "We missed our exit."

"We did?"

"Yeah, um, it's been a long time since I've been down here. Did you see a Highway 20 anywhere?"

Joe's shoulders slump. "Yeah, about fifteen miles ago."

Shoot. I've just added thirty miles to this trip. "We need to go back."

"Okay."

"Kupoteya njia ndiyo kujua njia," Junior says.

And after almost four hundred miles, I'm almost sick of these sayings. "Go ahead, Junior."

"'To get lost is to learn the way,'" he says.

Ain't that the truth.

We turn around and go north on I-85, getting off on Highway 20, riding to Cumming through sprawling Atlanta suburbia to where my parents live right next door to my Uncle Raymond and his dogs. Most folks like to live apart from their kin.

Not my family.

Uncle Raymond moved in first, and with his Fred Sanford pickup and his barking bullmastiffs annoyed the neighbors into leaving, let my daddy know the property was for sale, and the rest is family history. There used to be a fence separating the two houses, but not anymore. In fact, and I'm sure they're breaking a few zoning laws, a single fence surrounds *both* houses so the dogs can run free on over almost two acres. As a result, there is little grass around both houses.

"Where's the lawn?" Joe asks as we pull up.

"You'll see why," I say.

Oh, Lord Jesus, protect us.

Here come the dogs.

53

Joe

Shawna had warned me about her family for days before we left, and if those slobbering, snarling dogs are any indication, I'm in trouble.

"My family is not saved, sanctified, holy, reverent, righteous, saintly, or devout," she had told me. "They're blessed, though, with the ability to drink too much, smoke too much, eat too much, and tell you exactly what they're thinking too much. You are going to see and hear and smell some amazing things. They're good people, now, but sometimes I wonder. Try not to judge them too harshly."

The Evans clan—and there are too many to count some nights—does not belie her description.

Most of her family is short and wiry, so Crystal stands out, being so tall. Rodney must have been tall. But I can see where Crystal found the need to tattoo and pierce herself. I see painful-looking ears loaded with earrings and studs, even a few impaled noses and eyebrows, and tattoos on arms, the small of the back, ankles, calves—just about everywhere imaginable.

We have cookouts every night of our visit, filled with hugs, handshakes, ribs, barbecue, greens, and potato salad. Men surround and "work" on Uncle Raymond's truck, which I realize is really an excuse to get away from the women to drink heavily, since that old truck hasn't moved in twenty years. "Try some-a this," they say, offering me an antifreeze container filled with something clear.

I don't try it. It might really be antifreeze.

Once the men see the van, they tinker with the van's engine over beers while the ladies fry fish and serve it to some drunk folks who holler long into the night.

But they're wonderful people.

Wonderful!

While I'm waiting in line that first night, a spread of food on picnic tables as far as I can see, a voice behind me says, "You better get yourself somethin' quick, cuz these folks can eat."

I turn and smile at the woman behind me, who is larger than life itself. I don't mean she's fat. She's . . . just . . . big. "She's gi-normous," Jimmy later tells me.

"Who you with?" she asks me.

"I'm Shawna's fiancé," I say.

After she finishes laughing and lights another cigarette, she whispers, "Nah, nah. Now who you *really* here with?"

"Shawna." I point out my kids to her. "Oh. I'm Joe."

She squints at them, and then she squints at me. "You and Shawna are gettin' married?"

"Yes." I step closer to the food.

"No kiddin'?" she asks.

"No. I mean, yes." I've never known how to answer that one.

The big woman slaps me on the back, and I feel a crown loosen on one of my teeth.

"You *still* better get you somethin' quick," she says, and she sucks on her cigarette. "Cuz like I said, these folks can eat."

Shawna appears beside me. "Hey, Aunt Sandy."

"Shawna?" Aunt Sandy asks. "Is this your man?"

She takes my arm. "Yes."

Aunt Sandy then starts coughing or laughing or both and walks away fanning the air in front of her.

"Aunt Sandy isn't related to a single soul here," Shawna whispers as we get our plates. "She once dated Uncle Raymond about forty years ago, and now she just hangs around drunk most of the time. She's harmless."

"You know what she said to me?"

"What?"

I tell her what she told me.

Shawna laughs. "She wasn't lyin'! You may only get one trip through this line tonight, Joe, so pile it high."

Later that night, Aunt Sandy offers me a cigarette and a sip of her beer, tells me I have a nice backside for a white man, drags me to the dance floor, which is a flatter section of the yard, and asks me again, "You with someone?"

During a rare lull in the action while games of bid whist break out all over the yard on card tables, Shawna takes me on a stroll. "My family hasn't left Georgia since they got here from Africa. While the rest of the black South went north, they stayed. My ancestors weren't lazy. They were just set in their ways. I mean, why leave your home for the unknown after you've lived in a place for a couple hundred years? All the ancestral graves are down here, too."

I look at the ground.

"Not here, Joe."

"Oh."

She sighs. "You were trying to be funny, weren't you?"

"No." And I wasn't. Who knows who's buried underneath all this dirt?

"Anyway, Daddy always says, 'Ain't supposed to leave no one behind.' So the Evans family is as much a part of this state as the clay, and we come in all shades of that clay, too."

I see some of the most exquisite blending of races here.

Cousin Ernie came back from Vietnam with a Vietnamese bride, and their daughter, Tai Lynn, who Crystal hangs out with, is beautiful, with wide eyes and skin a color Crayola doesn't make.

"Will, my second cousin, went to Korea and came back with Doris," Shawna says. "Her real name is hard to pronounce, so we all just call her Doris. The marriage didn't last, but the family still keeps in touch with Doris."

One night, Shawna points to one of the only women wearing a dress, the rest in jeans or shorts as tight as the ones Crystal wears. "That's Danika, a cousin I grew up with. Her husband, Phil, isn't here, but he doesn't come around that often because he's a black Republican. You know how rare those are?"

I don't, but I nod anyway.

"But we welcome her—and Phil, as long as he doesn't talk politics."

Inclusion. That's what the Evans family is all about. No matter how loud or quiet, skinny or huge, drunk or sober, everybody is included.

Only when we try to include them on some side trips we take around Atlanta, they don't want to join us. "Been there, done that," they say.

I don't argue with them. And after fighting traffic and construction and getting lost on several streets named Peachtree, I don't blame them a bit.

As a family—I like using that phrase—we put at least another two hundred miles on the van. We take a trip to Lake Lanier to swim in the bathwater there. It's not as warm as Smith Mountain Lake near Roanoke, but it's pretty close. We ride the MARTA downtown to go to an afternoon Braves game, shopping at the Underground afterward.

A major *ka-CHING*.

But the girls are happy, and by girls I mean Shawna, too. All four of them buy some kente cloth outfits in an Afrocentric store. My boys—all three of them—buy ebony wood walking sticks. Shawna holds up a kente cloth bow tie and positions it under my neck.

"For the wedding?" I ask.

"Nah," she says. "I just wanted to see." She puts back the tie.

"How'd I look?" I ask.

"Not your colors."

I try to quiz her on exactly what my colors are, and in a few seconds I'm reduced to brown, gray, black, and dark blue.

"And please, Joe, don't ever wear red."

Even Rose agrees.

What's so bad about a white man wearing red?

I'll never fully understand women.

Sleeping arrangements are, to say the least, interesting. I stay with Uncle Raymond in the "catchall room" of his house. "The bed should be somewhere in there," he tells me. It is, only it turns out to be a single bed with a mattress that hasn't been turned in years, a crease in the middle. The girls—again, Shawna included—camp out in the basement of her parents' house while the boys literally camp out in a freestanding screen-room with some of the cousins—and the dogs, which are truly sweet animals, especially if you feed them.

And count your fingers afterward.

So much happens at those cookouts that I don't get much of a chance to talk to her mother and father until midway through the week. The conversation I have with her parents is brief.

"So, you're marrying my daughter," Shawna's dad says.

"Yes, sir," I say.

"She's a good girl," her dad says.

"Hmm," her mom says.

"You take good care of her and them chirren now," her dad says.

"I will."

That ends our conversation, because Cousin Boo and Aunt Tawny show up. Shawna's parents immediately break out the cards . . .

I try to learn how to play bid whist, I really do, but it is so hard to concentrate when they are, as Shawna puts it, "talking stuff." All during the one game that I feel confident enough to play, Cousin Boo keeps saying, "Watcha bid, now, watcha bid. Too high, you'll be leavin' the table. Too low, you'll be leavin' the table. Don't think for a second you gonna warm up that seat none, cuz you are gonna be leavin' the table . . ."

Three hands later, Cousin Boo yells, "Next!"

There will be no "next" for me.

Shawna refuses to play as my partner anymore. "I have *never* lost so fast in my entire life! What kind of bids were those?"

"Bad ones?" I offer.

She is not amused.

54

Shawna

So Joe can't play cards well. I'm not worried. We'll practice nightly until he learns how to bid properly.

Aside from Aunt Sandy moving in on my man and Crystal sticking to "her kind" instead of Joe's kids, the visit goes
pretty smoothly.

Until my parents corner me the night before we're to
leave.

"That man needs to lighten up," Daddy says from his
La-Z-Boy, where he's been commanding family conversations for as long as I've been alive.

Mama laughs. "Lighten up? He already as light as any
body can be."

"He has freckles, Mama," I say. "He isn't all white."

"Nah," Daddy says. "Shawna's right. He a little yella, too."

I look at Daddy. "How is Joe yellow?"

Daddy leans forward. "He was afraid to marry you,
wasn't he?"

I never should have told Boo that Joe had cold feet. Out
of my mouth into Boo's ears and straight out of Boo's mouth

like wildfire, and now everyone knows. "Our separation was only a couple weeks," I say, "and it wasn't a real separation. We still talked to each other every day and saw each other often. I wish y'all would just let that go."

Mama looks at Daddy, and Daddy shrugs. This means they'll *think* about dropping it.

"He's also far too religious, Shawna," Mama says.

"The man's too stiff," Daddy adds.

"And quiet," Mama says.

"And them kids of his is uppity," Daddy says.

I sigh. "Daddy, just because they wouldn't eat greens doesn't make them uppity."

Daddy looks at Mama, and Mama shrugs. This means they think I'm wrong.

"Baby," Mama says. "Why don't you move down here? Your chirren are havin' a ball with their cousins."

"You been away from your family too long," Daddy adds.

"So, what are y'all saying without saying it?" I ask. "That you don't like him?"

Daddy flashes a look at Mama before looking at me. "Didn't say I didn't like him. Just don't think he's the man for you."

Daddy treated Rodney like a son. They used to spend hours working on Uncle Raymond's truck. They never got it running, but I don't think that was the point. They bonded over a couple tons of metal. Hmm. Maybe we'll get us an old hoopdy and put it in the yard for our kids to bond over.

"And if you haven't noticed," Mama says, "he ain't black. You want a white man raisin' your chirren?"

I count to five before responding. "I'll be there, too, Mama."

"All the time?" she asks.

"Mama, it isn't as if I'm going to raise Joe's kids to be black."

Daddy pulls the recliner's lever with a pop and stands.

"You shoulda been lookin' for a man like Rodney." He looks at Mama. "And that's all I have to say about it." He walks out of the room and down the hall.

I join Mama on the sofa. "Everybody misses Rodney. I miss him. But I have to go on living."

"Hmm," Mama says. I have never been able to tell if her "hmm" is a yes or a no.

"Joe is . . . Joe is godly, loving, and caring, as much if not more than Rodney was. I value that. So what if he's quiet? He speaks to me, even when he's not saying anything."

Mama shakes her head. "He can't play cards at all, Shawna."

I roll my eyes. "That doesn't disqualify him from me loving him, Mama."

She pats my arm. "You really love him, then."

"Yes."

"As much as you loved Rodney?"

Tough question, one I've been wrestling with myself. "I never thought I'd ever love anyone that much, and after Rodney died, I decided that I'd never even try to love someone that much."

"Hmm," Mama says.

"But, Mama, I'm going to try with Joe."

"Hmm," Mama says. "Your mind sounds like it's made up."

"It is."

She folds her arms under her chest and is quiet for a spell. "Well, as long as y'all visit more often . . . so I can get to know Joe."

"And," I add, "your new grandkids."

"They ain't never gonna be my grandkids, Shawna."

Ouch. I didn't mean to pluck that nerve. "Step-grandkids, then."

"Not even that," she says. "That youngest one, though."

"Jimmy?"

"Hmm," Mama says. "He's kinda like your daddy used to

be when he was a boy. Always into mischief, but he was always gettin' out of it cuz of that grin of his."

"Mama?"

"Hmm?"

"Will you work on Daddy for me?"

She blows out a breath, her lower lip turned down. "Got to work on myself first. Hearin' about it on the phone isn't like seein' it in the flesh. And you know how stubborn your daddy can be. That man's set in his ways like concrete. I can't teach that ol' dog any new tricks."

"Could you try?"

Mama closes her eyes and takes a deep breath. "You comin' down for Thanksgivin' or Christmas?"

"I don't know," I say.

"Could you try?" she asks.

More "saying without saying." That's what this family is all about. I've had to read between the lines and Mama saying "hmm" for so long. What Mama isn't saying is that if we visit more often, she'll soften up Daddy.

"Mama, I will definitely try."

55

Joe

I see so much good coming out of this trip, mainly from my own "chirren." At the Gospel show, it had been like an old junior high dance, with one side eyeing the other, lots of space between them, no one willing to make the first move. But here, they mixed it up from the second they stepped out of the van. Oh, except for Crystal. She pretty much stuck to the cousins she hadn't seen in so long. I can't blame her. Rose even put on shorts one day, reminding me of how beautiful she is under all that Gothic costuming. The boys must have played a hundred games of basketball and fifty rounds of horseshoes, and drank fifty gallons of sweet tea—real sweet tea, "so sweet any bug that'll bite you will overdose on sugar," according to Aunt Sandy.

Movement, laughter, fussing, cussing, smiles, food— Shawna's family. I know I've gained at least ten pounds in four days. No matter how outrageous Aunt Sandy was ("You get tired of that skinny, short *thang,* you give me a call"), no matter how long the argument ("You reneged, yo . . . I played spades three books ago, and you didn't have one then" . . .

"It is so touching the post! Boo, come here and see what this fool obviously can't see"), and no matter the hour ("Dag, is that the sunrise? Shoot, I got to work in the morning"), they did it as a family.

And my chirren was right up there in the mix, yo.

Shawna hates it when I talk that way, but I can't help it.

I've been infected by the Evans family.

56

Shawna

I am pooped.

I look behind me at Jimmy. Lord, I hope he pooped before he got into this van. I don't want a film of his funk on me for four hundred miles.

Everyone but Joe and I are asleep. No one slept on the way down, yet all of them will most likely sleep on the way back to Roanoke.

My family wore their little behinds *out!*

I reach over and massage Joe's right shoulder. "You okay?"

"Yeah."

"I can drive some if you like." Not that I really want to drive. I'm a little sleepy myself.

"Tell me that again in four hours."

In four hours, I will be out like a light. "So, what do you think of the Evans family now?"

"I felt right at home."

He's lying. "Really?"

"Really."

I don't believe this for a second. "Your home in Canada is like that?"

"Not really, but everyone down here made me feel welcome."

"Aunt Sandy especially."

"Yeah."

"I thought the heifer was going to corrupt you, offering you a cigarette or a toot or a sip. I am so glad she's not a blood relative."

"She's . . . something," Joe says. "Thank you for rescuing me so often."

"You're welcome. But next time we visit, you're on your own. I didn't play nearly enough cards."

Joe doesn't say a thing. He is wise. I have let him know how important card playing is to the fabric of the Evanses' family life, he has been found wanting in the bidding department, and no doubt they'll all be talking about Joe's bids at the cookout later tonight.

"Did you and Daddy talk?" I ask.

"Yes."

"Did you ask for my hand in marriage?" I know he didn't.

"I didn't have the chance." He winces. "Sorry." He adjusts the rearview mirror for the fiftieth time. He's always checking on the kids. I like that. "So, what did you and your parents talk about?"

I don't want to hurt Joe's feelings, so I decide to spare him their reservations. "As long as we visit more often, they'll like 'us' more."

"Fine with me."

"And as long as you learn how to play some cards."

"Was I that bad?"

I don't answer.

"I was that bad," he says.

"I will teach you. Nightly. Before we go to bed. And if

you don't learn to bid correctly, I'm turning out the light without giving you so much as a good-night kiss."

"Really?"

"Hmm," I say like Mama. "Oh, for a minute or so. I don't think I can be that mean to you. At least you tried to play cards and horseshoes." I wince. One time he pitched the shoe so badly one of the dogs snatched it up and ran off with it. Joe must have poor depth perception. Maybe he needs glasses.

"I like the way your family laughs," Joe says.

I massage my own neck. "It's kind of a two-edged sword, though. It is so hard to have any kind of a serious conversation sometimes. I think we use ESP or radar or something."

"Your family is close, Shawna. I like that."

"Your family isn't close?"

"Well, we live so many different places. My brother, James, is a missionary in Irian Jaya."

"Where's that?" It doesn't even sound like a real country.

"It's Indonesia's biggest province, right next to Papua New Guinea."

That didn't help much. "And where is all that?"

He smiles. "In the South Pacific, northeast of Australia. So James lives about ten thousand miles away, my parents live in Canada, and I live in Virginia. It's hard for all of us to get together. James is supposed to be up at the lake while we're there, but sometimes his plans change at the last minute." He smiles. "James has always bragged about his family, and now we're finally going to be even."

"How so?"

"He has six kids, all of them boys, named Matthew, Mark, Luke, John, Paul, and Timothy."

How biblical. It makes them easy to remember, I guess. I try to envision twelve children, nine boys and three girls, in one house. I can't. I won't. "How old are they?"

"They range in age from Timmy, who's nine, to Matthew,

who's . . . twenty, I think. And even with James's kids, my family is . . . quieter than yours."

"You don't have cookouts?"

"Some. Mom likes to cook in her kitchen."

"Will your mama let me help with the cooking?"

"Let's just say that she owns the kitchen. But we'll do the dishes. It might be the only quiet time we have up there." He adjusts the AC down a few clicks. "Unless we take a moon-light swim."

I adjust the AC *up* a few clicks. I am freezing! "I haven't put on a bathing suit in ages. It might not fit. Is the water warmer at night?"

"Relatively speaking," he says.

In other words, no.

"The air is colder," he says, "so the water feels warmer."

"As long as you keep me warm, I'll be fine."

He hums a little love song that almost sounds like . . . No. It doesn't sound like anything at all. I think my Joe is tone deaf, too.

He stops humming. "You might want to sleep now while it's quiet, Shawna."

How can I sleep now? I'm in the water with Joe, my bathing suit is slipping off, his hands are keeping me warm. But I *need* to go to sleep now. I *need* to have one of those wa-tery, sensual, erotic dreams that doesn't make me feel as guilty as when I'm having watery, sensual, erotic daydreams. Why is it that the lust I feel in my dreams is okay, while the lust I'm feeling right now isn't? *Lord, why did You choose to make us this way?*

I pout for a bit, try *not* to think of skinny-dipping with Joe, and in a few minutes, I am drifting off to sleep . . .

Ahh, this is nice. I'm in the water. A bathtub. Bubbles. Candles. Hands are caressing me, holding me, massaging my feet. Nice . . . Yes, right there . . . Oh, yes . . .

Oh, no! Why am I suddenly stepping off a curb? And why is there a curb in the bathroom? I hate this dream. I know that as soon as I put my foot down—

I flinch and wake up.

"You were out a while," Joe says.

"Where are we?"

I see the first of three exits for Salem, the town west of Roanoke. Wow. We're almost home. That was an extremely long bath. I wonder if my dream fingers are prunes.

I look behind me. Only Toni blinks at me, but her eyes are rolling, her neck barely keeping her head still.

"Has everybody been asleep the entire time?" I ask.

"Yep." He stretches an arm out to me. "And that means they'll be awake for most of the trip up to the lake."

That's not good.

When Joe opens his door in front of his—I mean, *our*—house, the lights in the van come on, and the groans begin.

"Everybody out," Joe says. "I have to unload and reload."

Rose slips out of her seat belt and comes to the front, draping her arms around Joe's neck. "Daddy, can't we sleep in our own beds for one night before we go to the lake?"

That's not a bad idea. I could use at least three or four more hours in the bathtub, I mean, in the bed.

He pats Rose's hand. "Sure. We can crash for a few hours and leave a little later."

After the kids troop into the house, Joe and I unload and reload the van. We step back and look at the back end of the van.

"It looks like a drooping lip," I say.

"And without us inside." He drops to his knees and measures the distance between the road and the bottom of the van. "It will scrape on the way in to Murphy's Unlimited."

"Murphy's what?"

"Oh," Joe says as he stands, "I didn't tell you. Mom and Dad's house is called Murphy's Unlimited."

Joe's parents have actually named their house. That's creepy.

"We may have to call for a water taxi," he says.

"They have those?"

"No. Dad will just bring the boat." He looks at the drooping lip again. "Dad may have to make two trips."

We walk inside and see kids sprawled all over the place on couches, chairs, the floor, and upstairs facedown on beds. We close the door to what will be the boys' room.

"We're quite a lively bunch, huh?" I say. I lead Joe to the bedroom. "You go on and rest. I'll—"

And then he kisses me right there at the foot of that bed, without grapes, even.

"Could you . . . cuddle with me for a little while?" he asks.

How can I refuse? But then I remember what Rema told me once I showed her my engagement ring. She warned me this might happen. "A ripe melon has to be eaten slowly," she said. I am that ripe melon, eight years ripe, but I don't want to rush the passion . . . that I desperately need! *Lord, could You maybe look away for a few . . .* No.

No. Not yet. It will be so much better if we wait.

"I'll cuddle with you," I say, "but above the covers, okay?"

"Sure."

I look behind us. "And with the door open."

Joe lies down. "Right."

I snuggle in behind him—just to be safe in case I can't control myself. I wrap my arms around him, and he takes my hands . . .

And falls asleep in seconds.

Without a sound.

Very creepy.

I check his pulse by putting my hand on his neck. Nice and strong.

This is going to take some getting used to.

Just as I'm about to step into my dream bathtub again, a flush in the bathroom next door wakes me. Who's up? I turn my head to see Crystal walk by and stop, dropping her eyes.

Oh, man.

Drama.

I slide quietly away from Joe, tiptoe out of the bedroom, and close the door, taking the stairs to the kitchen where I see Crystal peering into the refrigerator.

"Couldn't sleep?" I ask.

"No." She shuts the door with a little bang.

"Neither can I." I lean against the counter. "You okay?"

She hops up on the counter. "What do you think?"

After two days of avoiding Joe and me down in Atlanta, Crystal at least hung out with us on our trips into the city. But now that she's seen me with another man, and in another man's bedroom, I doubt she's going to continue on with us up to Canada. And for whatever reason, I'm okay with it.

"I didn't mean to shock you," I say.

"I wasn't shocked."

Sure she was, and if I give this room enough silence, she'll tell me she was.

"It's just that . . ."

Here it comes.

"Mama, I used to wake up you and Daddy, and you'd be spooning him just like that."

Spooning? What does she know about spooning? That Tony and her had *better* not be spooning, forking, cupping, or knifing at that apartment! They *can* go *bowl*ing, though.

"It made me miss him, that's all," she says.

I decide to break my silence. "Do you miss him or the waking-us-up part?"

She closes her eyes. "A little of both."

She's still in love with the idea of me and her daddy. I won't try to take that away from her. Besides, there's nothing I can say that will change those precious, simple memories.

"Mama, I'm keeping Daddy's last name."

I nod, even though it comes at me from left field. "I wouldn't want you to change it."

"*You're* changing it."

"Yes, I am."

"Well, why couldn't you hyphenate it?"

"Evans-Mitchell-Murphy," I say. "Murphy-Evans-Mitchell." I laugh. "That's too much of a mouthful, and if you throw in my middle name, I'd be Shawna Marie Evans-Mitchell-Murphy. People would brand me a mumbler, and you know I don't mumble." I inch closer to this child I want to hold so badly. "Besides, I don't remember any hyphenated people's names in the Bible." Besides El-Shaddai, that is, but the Lord can hyphenate whatever He wants.

She looks around me at the rest of the kitchen. "You really going to live here all cooped up like this?"

"Cooped up? Girl, this house is four times the size of our apartment with a much larger kitchen."

"But five kids, Mama."

"Yes. Five kids." I look into her eyes. "With room for six."

Those eyes change. "I'll pass."

Shoot. "Well, the door's always open. You never know how your life might change with a single phone call."

"Or an e-mail."

"True."

She sighs and shakes her head. "I just . . . Everything's so different now."

"How so?"

"I don't know. The way you're acting."

I know what's coming. "And how am I acting?"

"Like a thirteen-year-old."

I was close. I was shooting for sixteen in my mind. "I'm in love, Crystal. And I hope I keep acting this way for a long time. What else is different?"

"Do you have to . . . kiss him in front of me?"

I step back. "How often do I do that?"

"Once is too often."

"Well, I will be kissing him at the wedding. Are you going to look away?"

"I might."

Ouch. "Anything else different?"

"Just . . . Daddy's not here . . . to see you so happy. I mean, he was the one who made you happy before, and now . . . It's just confusing to me, okay?"

It's confusing to me, too. How can I, who had a man bathe me in happiness for so long, find yet another man who is willing to do the same for me? It's right confusing to be so lucky when so many other women can't even find one man to make them happy.

"I mean . . . Daddy just seems so far away from me now."

I walk up to her and take her hands. "Girl, your daddy is probably raiding that fridge right now."

Crystal looks at the refrigerator.

"And I'll bet he was there at senior night and at your graduation, too. What else does he have to do in heaven? I mean, you can only sing so many hallelujahs, you know."

She almost smiles.

"You still feel loved, don't you?"

"Yes."

"You still feel like the big sister, don't you?"

She groans. "Even more."

"Is that such a bad thing?"

She doesn't answer.

"Is it?" I ask again.

"No. One brother was bad enough, but three? It's going to take a lot of getting used to."

Did she just say . . . ? She did. She referred to Joey and Jimmy as her brothers. Can I make her say it again? "They're not such bad brothers, are they?"

"No."

Wrong question. Hmm. I'm too tired right now to think of one. "Will you promise me something, Crystal?"

"It depends on what it is."

She's growing up, all right. "Just promise to talk to me like this when I'm old and decrepit."

"I will."

Ouch!

She squeezes my hands. "And you're not that decrepit."

"Just a little, huh?"

"Yeah."

I pull her off the counter and hug her. "Thank you, Crystal."

"For what, Mama?"

I hold her out at arm's length. "For being."

"For being what?"

I touch her face, which has more Rodney in it than she'll ever know. "Just for being. I can't imagine my life without you."

"Aw, Mama."

She hugs me this time, and we stand in that kitchen just a-hugging away until . . .

"You're not just trying to butter me up so I'll go up to Canada with you, are you?"

Shoot. She's on to me. I sigh. "Please go, Crystal."

"No," she says.

I hold her back from me and just stare.

"What?" she asks.

"I say 'please go' and you say *no?* Just like that?"

"Yes."

I don't believe her. "When did you make up your mind not to go? Just now?"

She looks at her feet.

"Crystal?"

She stamps her foot on the floor. Ah, there's still a little girl under all this womanhood. "Mama, I was not going from the very second you said you didn't want me to go."

I blink. "Really?"

She nods.

I sigh. I knew this could happen. I just didn't think it would. "We'll miss you, girl."

"Yeah."

She didn't say she'd miss *us*. This freedom thing is a bear and a half to bare. "We'll, uh, we'll take lots of pictures to show you all the fun you missed."

She rolls her eyes. "Right. Um, I'll go get my things."

And a few minutes later, she's gone.

Taking a piece of my heart with her.

57

Joe

After I sleep for three hours, we herd the kids into the van at around 1 AM. The older kids walk like zombies, most dozing off before I carry in Toni, settling her next to Rose.

"Crystal's not going," Shawna says as I'm wiping the sleep from my eyes, and I only nod. I don't pry. In fact, I don't intend to pry into the female matters of our future family *ever*.

It seems safer somehow.

Before I pull away from the house, I check our ground clearance.

Four and a half inches.

We will not be speeding over any speed bumps.

I take Shawna's hand once I start up the van. "Let us pray," I say.

"Yes," she says.

"Oh, Lord, please help this van get us there. And, Lord, if You could help the kids sleep all the way to the border, I'd be especially grateful. Amen."

"Amen."

The trip up I-81 to Canada seems mostly uphill. Luckily, traffic is light for the first three hundred miles or so, and though I try to do the speed limit, the van starts shaking and the engine starts whining whenever I do. I stay five miles per hour under the speed limit, and when we go up long, steep hills I even have to put on my flashers like truckers do. Shawna finds a nice oldies station once we cross into Pennsylvania, singing along to monumental hits from the sixties and seventies. I love the sound of her voice, especially when she sings.

And she seems to like *not* hearing my voice. I'm no singer, never have been. Even humming gives me trouble. Actually, *I* have no trouble humming—my listeners have the trouble. Rose once compared my humming to fingernails on a chalkboard.

We hit Harrisburg before morning rush hour, which is wonderful, but north of Harrisburg we run into construction, eight miles of one-lane travel, mountains, and fog so thick I have to slow to twenty-five miles per hour or lower. I pray the entire time from Harrisburg to Hazleton, trucks doing seventy blowing by us and disappearing completely into the fog while everyone snoozes behind me. The fog breaks as we descend into Wilkes-Barre, and traffic lightens up tremendously once we get north of Binghamton, New York.

We're more than halfway there, I'm feeling fine, the sun is shining, and God has answered my—

"Are we there yet?"

Toni is awake.

"Uh, no, honey," I say.

Now, as long as Toni is the only one awake—

"Daddy, where are we?"

Jimmy is awake.

"Um, New York state," I say.

I amend my prayer: *Father, if you can keep the* rest *of them—*

Shawna wakes with the longest yawn I have ever seen. "We there yet?"

"No, not yet."

"How are you doing?" she asks.

"Fine."

She looks to the back at the kids. "Y'all hungry?"

Y'all? Who else is awake?

"Yes," Junior says.

I look in the rearview mirror and see Rose nodding.

"Let's stop at Friendly's, Dad," Joey says.

They're *all* awake.

"Let's stop, Joe," Shawna says with that sexy little pout of hers.

"There's a Friendly's in Cortland," I say. "About twenty more miles."

And then . . . silence. I like silence when I'm driving. It keeps me focused—

"What's a Friendly's?" Toni asks.

And then, everyone is talking at once about what they want to eat, how much they want to eat, how badly they're starving, how long ago they ate, what they ate . . .

Food and complaining about being hungry: another chance to bond.

Everyone is wide-awake by the time I pull into Friendly's, and soon after we get inside the staff pulls a few tables together. I'm thankful that Friendly's has an outstanding menu with more food than they can eat and at a decent price. The service is fantastic, the food hot, the Fribbles and Fishamajigs perfect, and as we chow down all I hear is chewing, slurping, and swallowing.

"We need one of these in Roanoke," Shawna says.

"I'd eat here at least once a week," I say.

"Every day if I could," Jimmy says.

Shawna stares Jimmy down. "Now, Jimmy, what are you trying to say about my cooking?"

"You're in trouble now," Junior says to Jimmy.

Jimmy looks at me for help, but I shake my head. He's on his own.

"I'm just saying," Jimmy says slowly, "that if I *could,* I would eat here every day."

"Boy," Shawna says, "I can fry fish better than this. Just don't ask me to clean the nasty, slimy things."

Let off the hook, Jimmy smiles. "Rose cleans fish."

"You do?" Shawna asks Rose.

"It's easy," Rose says.

"You let her?" Shawna asks me.

"It's a Murphy rule," I say. "Whatever you catch, you get to clean."

"I'll just have to throw anything back that I catch," Shawna says.

Jimmy shakes his head. "You won't want to, Shawna."

Shawna's kids jolt a little. It's the first time Jimmy has used her name.

Shawna doesn't seem to notice. "Why not?"

"Cuz catching fish is hard!" Jimmy's eyes seem more alive today than yesterday. "Besides, Grandpa, Daddy, or Rose will clean them for you."

"Really?" Shawna asks.

Jimmy shrugs. "Or I will. I don't mind. I like to know what they're eating."

The three young Mitchells don't look too pleased with our conversation, but luckily the meal ends.

Shawna takes the check. "I'll get this one."

"I don't mind," I say.

"Okay." Shawna checks the bill against what's on the table. "Just making sure."

Cheryl used to do the same thing. *Lord, You have brought another check-checker into my life. Thank You.*

* * *

From Cortland, through Syracuse, and past Watertown, I'm starting to feel younger again. Something about the trip, despite the exhaustion, takes years off my life. I'm going to my boyhood home, going back to a million boyhood memories. My kids have perked up considerably, chattering away about how much there is to do up at the lake.

"Okay, folks, make sure you're wearing your seat belts and look alive," I say. "We're about to hit the border."

"Why do we have to look alive?" Toni asks.

"You'll see." I turn to Shawna. "We'll need that folder now."

Shawna takes a file folder filled with birth certificates, passports, and an insurance certificate. After a short wait in line, we pull up to the customs booth.

"Citizenship?" the woman asks.

"All U.S.," I say.

She peers into the van, her eyes narrowing a little.

I hand her the folder before she can ask.

She flips through our files. "Purpose of visit?" she asks, handing back the folder.

"Bonding," I say. I feel Shawna's eyes on me. "Family vacation at Aylen Lake near Barry's Bay."

"How long will you be in Canada?"

"About six days." I wish it could be more.

"Anything to declare?"

I smile. "No, just that it's a beautiful day."

She almost smiles. "Enjoy your stay."

I turn to smile at Shawna as we pull away.

But she's not smiling.

58

Shawna

"Were you flirting with her?" I ask. That was some definite flirting. He was all one big smile with that squint of his.

"Anything to get through quickly," he says.

And he *admits* it!

"They can search through all our things without any real reason, and we could have been stuck there for hours," he says.

Wait a minute. "Hours?"

Joe nods.

Hmm. I guess flirting is okay, as long as it shortens the time we spend in this van. Jimmy's "pipes" have been kind to us so far, but I know that milkshake he sucked down is cozying up to his large intestine by now. I wiggle the air freshener on the vent, just in case.

We take a scary bridge, kids leaning right and left to look at the houses on all the islands, my kids pointing, his kids explaining. Yeah, this is more like it. This is bonding. They're all going to have the same memories. This is good.

The QEW (Queen Elizabeth Way) looks like any American highway except for the smooth ride and the Canadians flying by us at 130 kilometers per hour while we continue to putt-putt at 95 kilometers per hour.

"Are we there yet?" Toni asks with a giggle.

And now their bonding is causing trouble. "Which one of you kids put her up to that?" I ask.

All eyes land on Jimmy.

Jimmy looks around. "What? It's what I used to say. It's her turn now."

Ah. The passing of the "Are-we-there-yet?" torch. Cool.

I turn to Joe. "How long, Joe?"

"About a hundred eighty miles, so . . . four hours."

"Four hours?" I ask.

"The roads will change," Joe says.

And the roads do change. After driving north through endless farmland, we start hitting hills and curves and curvy hills, uphill, downhill, getting passed, often even on double yellow lines. The scenery is beautiful, though, and while the kids look for wildlife like bears, moose, and deer, I see blueberry stands, and combination gas station/post offices next to authorized Sears dealers, who also sell satellite dishes and live bait. Canada so far is . . . strange.

For long stretches through the mountains, we pass little lakes and cross a river or two and I don't see a single house.

"It's pretty remote out here," I say.

"Yeah." He raises his eyebrows. "Good place for a honeymoon," he whispers.

He has to be kidding. I don't want the kids to hear any of this, so I lean as far to the left as I can.

"No one to bother us," he whispers, "except for the bugs and maybe a bear."

Now I *know* he's kidding.

"And," he whispers even more softly, "without the kids."

Maybe he isn't kidding . . . "Joe, where are we going for our honeymoon really?"

"If you like it up here, and I hope you will, we can come up in September when the leaves are changing."

"With your parents here?" That's no kind of honeymoon.

"No, they're good Canadians from Ontario. They go down to Florida for most of the winter."

"Oh. But won't it be cold?"

"Sure will. I may have to keep a fire going in the fireplace or the woodstove continuously."

Hmm. Fireplace, cold, just the two of us, no kids, free lodging. Moose, bear, and bugs. "We'll see."

After a series of roads I will never remember, we end up on Highway 62 past some of the tallest, straightest pine trees I have ever seen. We pass a ski resort, the hillsides all grown up with greenery, and then we approach a town.

"Ladies and gentlemen," Joe announces, "we're about to enter the thriving metropolis of Barry's Bay, population twelve hundred for the last forty years. Look quick, now. Don't blink."

Barry's Bay reminds me of an old-fashioned American town, all the stores facing each other with cars parked in front of them, the main drag down the middle, only . . .

"Joe, they're parking on the sidewalk," I say.

"Yep."

I wait for the explanation, but he doesn't give me one. I guess parking on sidewalks is just what Canadians *do*. He stops at a little convenience store—at least it looks like one to me.

"Why are we stopping?" I ask.

"To get fishing licenses."

We pile out, stretching, yawning, and . . . Hey, this air tastes good. It's a little chilly, maybe seventy, but this air is nice.

We follow Joe into the store, all six of us, the kids fanning out to browse the snacks.

The lady at the counter doesn't even blink. "Hey, Joe," she says.

Luckily she's about sixty, or I'd have a problem with her knowing my man's name.

"Hey, Bonnie." Joe counts behind him. "We need five licenses."

"Seven-day conservation?" she asks.

"Yes," he says.

I tilt my head into his face. This means I need an explanation. I don't get one right away, so I ask, "What's seven-day conservation?"

"Oh," he says. "A limit of two fish each day. With so many of us fishing, we'll catch plenty."

"Mama," Toni says, "did Joe get a license for me?"

"You won't need one, Toni," Joe says. "You're young enough that you can fish without a license."

Toni pouts. "I'm not fishing, then, Mama."

"Why not?" Rose asks.

"I want a license, too," Toni says.

"But you won't need one, Toni," Rose says. "And it's so fun. I caught a five-and-a-half pounder two years ago. It's the biggest fish on the wall at Grandpa's."

I step closer to Joe. "You stuff them?"

"No," he says. "It's just a tracing of the fish on some newspaper."

"It's one of the biggest smallmouth ever caught at the lake," Rose says. Man, that child's eyes twinkle when she talks about fishing: "I caught it on a leech behind Turkey Island."

A . . . leech. Great.

Once we have the licenses, we buy three dozen leeches and two dozen worms. They travel in the back of the van with the boys. I just wish they wouldn't give me the play-by-play with the leeches: "They look like snakes . . . " "They only suck a little blood if they get on you . . ."

Joe will have to put them on the hook for me.

On Highway 60, we're stopped by construction, and I notice many of the workers are women, all dressed in jeans, boots, and flannel shirts. Where are the men?

Probably out fishing.

Joe slows to allow a logging truck to fly by, then pulls over entirely next to a pond. "That lake over there is where my great-grandfather got the foundation for Murphy's Unlimited."

"For what?" Toni asks.

Joe takes a breath. "Um, for the house, Toni."

"You named the house?" Toni asks.

Joe looks at me. "Um, yeah. It's kind of a tradition up here. Anyway, this is the place—"

"Can I tell it?" Jimmy interrupts.

"Sure, Jimmy."

Then Jimmy tells an amazing story. "Great-Grandpa George rowed all the way down the Aylen Lake. Two and a half miles. Then he put the rowboat on the bed of his truck and drove up the lake road, and it was really crummy back then. And then he drove here, put the boat in the water, rowed over to those rocks, loaded the rocks into the boat, rowed back, unloaded the rocks into his truck, put the rowboat on the back, drove back to the lake, reloaded the rocks into the rowboat, and rowed two and a half miles to the clearing, unloaded the rocks . . ."

I'm getting tired just hearing about it! Four times, he did this. Four times. All to build a foundation. Jimmy tells the story well, and I can feel the pride in this van.

At the top of yet another hill is a sign for Aylen Lake Road. It isn't really a road. It's more like a dirty washboard full of curves and speed limit signs we'll never threaten. Joe slows to cross a bridge over a little dam.

"There's some good fishing there, Toni," Jimmy says. "I caught my very first fish there."

Up a hill, bouncing over more washboard, over the top . . .

Wow.

God *does* vacation here.

Clear blue sky with fluffy white clouds hanging over

clear blue water, islands of pine, forests, mountains in the distance . . . It's the Garden of Eden North. I catch Toni's eyes. She's drinking it all in, too.

"Anyone need to use the restroom?" Joe asks.

Six voices say, "Yeah."

Joe needs to add more rest stops on the way back.

Then he pulls the van next to an outhouse—with both a men's side and a women's side!

"Is that what I think it is?" I ask.

Joe's kids get out of the van without any hesitation.

"Mommy, what's that?" Toni asks.

"The restroom," Junior says, and he gets out.

"Rose, can you take Toni to the restroom?"

Rose holds out her hand, Toni takes it, and they disappear around the other side of the outhouse.

As soon as they're gone, I ask, "Is it safe?"

"Yes."

He opens his door, and he goes, leaving me alone in the van with a buzzing mosquito. I swat at it, but it's too quick for me. And it is loud. And big! I get out just to get away from it, standing on some sandy, rocky ground.

Junior approaches. "They do have indoor plumbing, don't they?"

"I'm sure they do," I say, but I really don't know, and I'm afraid to ask Joe because I'm afraid of his answer.

After everyone but me has found relief, Joe goes to call his father at a pay phone while we wander about at the Landing, a series of cabins and docks and a gas pump. A big, fluffy, hairy dog—of a breed (or breeds) I'm not familiar with—comes out and plays fetch with the boys, and they're not using a stick. It's a log.

"Can we get some ice cream?" Toni asks, pulling on my arm.

"Where?"

She leads me into a little store where I can buy ice cream, fishing tackle, boat parts, bilge pumps, potato chips, and licorice. What a strange combination, like everything in Canada. I guess if someone up here needs it, they have it.

"Can I have some ice cream?" Toni asks again, practically drooling.

"I'm sure we'll eat lunch"—or dinner, it's so late in the day—"when we get to the house."

She pouts, but if I buy ice cream for her, I have to buy ice cream for four other kids, and anyway, I don't have any Canadian money.

Joe backs up the van to the largest set of docks, and he and the boys unload the duffel bags near an empty space at the end of the dock.

"There's Grandpa," Rose says, pointing out into the water at a huge green boat plowing through the water.

And suddenly I'm nervous.

"Like the color of Grandpa's boat?" Rose asks.

"Not particularly," I say.

"Jimmy says it's puke green," Rose says.

And that's exactly what it looks like.

As the boat nears, I get a clearer picture of what Joe might look like in twenty-five years. Joe's dad wears a fishing hat, jeans, and a black and blue flannel shirt.

Joey goes to the empty space at the end of the dock and catches the boat, tying it to little metal rings.

Joe's dad gets out and nods at Joe. He looks down at our pile. "Hmm," he says, just like my mama!

"Yeah," Joe says.

And that is their entire conversation, because Joe's kids crowd around their grandpa, giving hugs, shouting, "Grandpa!" and "How's the fishing been?"

Joe's dad looks from my kids to Joe. "All these belong to you?"

"Yes, sir," Joe says, and it makes me feel wonderful. "Dad, this is Shawna. And that's Junior and Toni."

"Isn't there another one?" Joe's dad asks.

"Um, she had to work," Joe says.

"Oh," Joe's dad says. "And who are these three pawing at me?"

"Ha, ha," Rose says.

"No, really." He looks carefully at Jimmy. "Who are you?"

Jimmy giggles. "Grandpa, you know who I am."

"You look like Jimmy, but the last time I saw you, you were only a foot high." He smiles at me. "Welcome."

"Hi," I say.

Joe's dad steps away from the kids, standing in front of me, looking every bit like Joe's older brother. "Not many of your kind around here."

Say what?

He smiles. "By 'your kind,' Shawna, I mean pretty." He hugs me. "Welcome to Aylen."

"Um, what should I call you?" And this is important to me. I don't want to call him the wrong thing.

"Yeah. Mr. Murphy might get confusing. What do we have, six or seven Mr. Murphys up here this summer?"

No way.

"You can't call me Joe either. There are three of those."

I turn to Joe. "You're a junior?"

"No. Seven generations in a row of Joes with different middle names."

Seven Joes in a row?

Joe's dad nods. "You can call me Kaz, short for Kazuby. It's a family name. Sort of a family joke, really."

I shake his hand. "Nice to meet you, Kaz."

Kaz looks over my head to Joe. "Now, what will we call your mother, Joe?"

"Mom?" I suggest.

"No. We have scads of those up here, too." He winks at me, and I feel . . . accepted. "You can call her Elle. Short for Ellen."

Loading the boat takes a degree in engineering and physics, but somehow the three Joes, Junior, and Jimmy (so many *J*s!) get all the duffel bags and us inside. We put a life vest on Toni, though she fusses with me the entire time.

"No one *else* is wearing one," she complains, but my eyes stop that complaint completely.

"We're going to ride low," Kaz says before he starts up the motor.

"We're used to it," Junior says, standing beside him.

"We might even swamp a skier or two," Kaz says with a smile. "That might be fun."

Joe unties us, Kaz backs out and guns it, and we all have to move to the front so the boat will "plane"—whatever that means. We plow through the water around Twin Islands— "Big bass there," Rose tells me—into open water. We see kids on tubes, skis, wakeboards, and boogie boards behind huge ski boats, a few sailboats, and a pontoon boat.

Toni is dipping her hand into the spray the boat is throwing up. "The water is cold, Mama."

God must like taking cold baths.

I look at my children's faces, and they have such wide eyes. Joe's kids, though, have soft eyes, eyes that seem to say "it's good to be back here."

I move as close to Joe as I dare. "Do all your kids ski?"

"Yeah. But now they're into wakeboards and dueling tubes. Crash, boom, giggle. You want to try to ski? I'm a good teacher."

In a bathing suit that might fall off? "Maybe next summer, after we *fly* up here." My riding-in-a-van muscles are sore!

Cabins and cottages, none of them quite a full house, roll by in all shapes, sizes, and colors. We see A-frames, ranches, A-frame ranches, a few sprawling cabin "estates," and no two are alike. I notice that all have walls of windows facing the lake. Fancy docks, simple docks, old boats, new boats, canoes, sailboats—there's just so much to see!

We slow to a single dock below a set of redwood stairs leading to a redwood house with a deck and a screened porch, an old brown boat tied up on one side, a canoe lying on the beach.

"Jimmy," Kaz says, "you jump out and tie us up as best as you can while the rest of us stay put." He turns to Joe. "I need to level and brace the dock again. Your mother has taken two unintentional swims."

"She fell in?" I ask.

"Dropped is a better term," Kaz says.

Oh, that's good. Not.

"If the dock isn't level and braced just right," Joe says, "it, um, opens up."

"We'll get her fixed," Kaz says.

Joe's mama or the dock? I hope she's okay.

"But just to be safe, let's do this nice and slow," Kaz says. "Go easy on the tonnage back there."

While Joey and Jimmy hand out our "tonnage" to Joe and Kaz, Elle comes to the top of the stairs. "I'm not coming down there until you boys fix that dock." She waves at me. "Hello."

"Hi," I say.

Elle is short, thin, pale, and wears a long-sleeved red and black flannel shirt, jeans, and hiking boots. Her outfit must be the national dress for Canadians.

My kids step gingerly onto the dock and run for the stairs. I get out of the boat with Joe's help, and the dock sways a little, bouncing me up as I take each step.

"How deep is it, just in case?" I ask him.

"Three or four feet, depending on the ice, rainfall, hydro . . ."

They don't even know how deep it is!

I hold the rail on my way up the stairs as the boys wrestle with our "tonnage," stopping in front of Elle.

"Joe lied about you," Elle says.

"He did?" Ouch! What was that? Something bit my leg.

"He said you were pretty," Elle says. "He should have said gorgeous." She hugs me.

"Thank you."

"Where's your oldest?" Elle asks.

"Working," I say. Ouch! Something is *still* biting my leg!

"Let's get away from these horseflies." She smiles. "I believe that God didn't create anything without a purpose, but horseflies and mosquitoes come close." She looks at my shorts. "You won't be wearing them much longer."

I swat something buzzing from my leg, and it's so big I think I bruised a finger. Between the stairs and the door to the screened porch is a distance of maybe fifty feet, but I get bitten four times by blackflies, mosquitoes, or horseflies by the time I get inside. I will wear long pants or sweats at all times up here.

While the kids fan out in the house to parts unknown, Elle offers me a cup of hot Red Rose tea. We sit at a picnic table covered with a tablecloth a few feet from a large kitchen.

She hands me my cup and sits. "We eat all our meals out here. Isn't it grand?"

It is. The porch is screened on three sides. Behind me is a shed and the woods. To my right is a view of the path and some towels drying on a cord tied between two massive pine trees. And right in front of me is a breathtaking view of the lake.

I scratch at lumps forming on my calves and ankles. "I need to change."

"Oh, the bugs are intolerable this year," Elle says.

"They seem to like me." A lot. I am, after all, so sweet.

"It's this heat wave," she says.

Heat wave? It can't be more than seventy-two out here!

"Joe brought some Cutter, didn't he?" Elle asks.

"Yes."

"Cutter helps, but I think the bugs use Cutter for an appetizer sometimes." She smiles. "As long as you keep covered, they won't bother you much."

I hear all sorts of noise coming from the rest of the house. "Shouldn't I be helping them get settled?"

"The men will settle everyone in. I've put all the girls upstairs where it's warmer at night. Hope you don't mind."

Of course I don't mind! "Will we all fit?" It doesn't seem to be that big of a house.

Elle looks up at the ceiling. "We can sleep eight comfortably up there."

"Really?"

"Murphy's can sleep sixteen comfortably, all told," she says.

Wow. But where? And how?

"You all like fish, don't you?" she asks.

"Sure."

She takes a sip. "Kaz has blessed me with a freezer full of bass. There's no room for ice cubes. We have to have a fish fry tonight."

The boys fly by in their bathing suits, shouting, "We're going to the beach!"

They disappear before I can make a sound.

"After you level and brace the dock, fellas," I hear Joe's voice say.

The boys, as expected, say, "Aww."

"I'll be down in a few minutes," Joe says from somewhere in the house. Where is he?

The boys troop by us across the deck and down the stairs to the dock.

"Sound sure does carry here," I say.

"Especially at night," Elle says. "You can hear people whispering across the lake."

Kind of like living in an apartment, only Canadian style.

"Joe told us about your husband," Elle says. "Seems like God can't stand being away from His best people. I'm glad Kaz has a little edge to him. You'll see. Kaz has a temper. If he can't anchor right away, he'll fume. If he loses a big one, he'll shout. Kaz is just bad enough for God to keep him down here with me so I can purify him. You'll like it up here, Shawna, I promise you. And if your kids are like Joe's, you won't see them much. You'll hear them, but you won't see them."

The boys are already in the water, splashing around and shouting, their shouts echoing into the woods behind me. Toni comes downstairs in a cute, colorful one-piece.

"Toni?" Elle asks.

"Yes, ma'am?" Toni asks.

"Toni, I highly recommend you wear a long T-shirt," Elle says. "The bugs are bad here, and they will eat you alive."

Toni holds up a bottle of Cutter. "I have this."

Elle squints. So that's where Joe learned to squint. "That Cutter will keep some of the smaller bugs away but not the horseflies."

"I'll be okay," Toni says.

When a child cries for a razor, I think, you give her that razor. I pull Toni to me and apply liberal amounts of Cutter and sunblock.

"If the bugs get too bad, you come back in," I say.

"Okay," Toni says.

Joe drops by wearing a T-shirt and a swimsuit that almost reaches his shins. Smart man. He kisses me on the lips in front of Elle. He didn't do that down in Atlanta. I wanted him to, but . . . I kiss him on the cheek.

"We'll have that dock fixed for you, Mom." He looks out to the dock, blinking. "Um, why isn't Toni wearing a T-shirt?"

"She'll be back for one any time now," Elle says. "She's too pretty a target for—"

"YOW!" Toni yells, and I even hear the echo from the woods behind me.

"Here she comes," Elle says.

Toni doesn't even look at me as she storms past us, returning a minute later wearing a long-sleeved T-shirt, a towel wrapped around her legs. She stomps down to the dock swatting at bugs flying around her head.

"Stubborn, that one," Elle says. "She could be a Murphy."

Joe leans down and whispers in my ear, "You need anything?"

I pucker up. He kisses me again. "Try not to get sunburned."

Joe opens the screen door. "I freckle."

"Well," I say, "try not to get too many freckles."

I watch Joe go to the shed—and is that an outhouse in the woods? I have to see if they have indoor plumbing, quick! Joe walks by with a large wooden toolbox, some boards, and a saw.

"Let me give you the tour," Elle says, rising. "You've already seen our dining room. We'll bring in some more chairs or put a card table out there for the younger kids, especially if James and his family get up here. Like our ceiling fan?"

"It's nice."

"We've been using it a lot this week because of the heat."

Where *is* this heat she keeps talking about?

I look at pieces of driftwood nailed to the boards in between the screens, a large cache of fishing poles and tackle boxes stacked and piled under a map of the lake. Before we can take two steps into the kitchen, Toni screams again.

She bangs through the screened porch door, her legs dripping wet. "Something bit me." She points to a spot on her leg. "Something in the water bit me."

Elle cackles. "Oh, that. It's just a little rock bass defending its nest. Completely harmless."

I look at Toni's leg, and I don't see any teeth marks.

"But it *bit* me, Mama."

"Oh, now," Elle says. "It couldn't be more than twelve inches long. Joe and the boys will probably net it and take it across the lake."

"When?" Toni asks before I can ask the same question.

"Soon," Elle says.

"Well . . . okay." Toni trips down to the dock again.

"I'm sure she didn't get bitten, Shawna," Elle says. "Bumped, probably, that's all."

I hope and pray they have a shower or bathtub! I am *not* taking a bath down there if Jaws Jr. is there.

59

Joe

Dad and I put away the tools after the boys and I had shored up the dock. It seems we do it every year, almost as if you can't truly have an Aylen summer without some kind of dock repair. We look out at the boys launching themselves off the end of the dock, Toni and Rose exploring along the shoreline, most likely looking for crayfish and frogs.

"So, how are you?" Dad asks.

"Tired, but happy to be here," I say.

"It's strange not to see Cheryl up here with you."

I nod. "Yeah. There's still so much of her here."

"We framed a few of her watercolors. They're hanging upstairs."

"Thanks."

"You look like you could use a long nap. I'll take the kids down to the beach for you. The bugs are pretty thick down there this year. Think Toni will go with us?"

"She might." Then I shake my head. "It might be better if Shawna or Mom asked Toni, though."

He nods. "I'll get your mother to ask. She can still make anyone do anything and like it, no matter how horrible it is."

He leaves me alone in the old shed, and I see more Murphy memories. Huge tin containers rest on shelves: Tritzels hearth-baked toasted pretzels, oven-fresh saltines by Keebler, Yuban and Maxwell House coffee cans, Cadet Pretzels. Paints, stains, varnish, hot-pipe black enamel, oars, winches, shovels, axes, boat batteries, creosote, instant-patch roof repair, ropes, wires, tools, kerosene cans, bait buckets, a hand scythe. The Murphys have been completely self-sufficient since, well, since time began, I suppose. During Y2K my parents had laughed. "The only computer in the house," Dad had said, "is the one in your mother's brain." They didn't worry a bit.

Wandering through the screen porch to the kitchen, I hear Mom giving Shawna the tour. Murphy's Unlimited is not a big house, but the stories about each room take some time to tell. This kitchen is practically an entire novel to tell. Ah, the Findlay Oval cookstove, still blacked and reliable. It's a pain to maintain, but it never fails us. Four kerosene lamps at the ready fill an entire top shelf. I open the fridge. Mom has stocked it with lots of bottled water. Nice touch, Mom. The well water, while pure, has been known to give visitors the runs. Mom boils any water she cooks with for at least half an hour when guests are around, just in case.

I move down the hallway to the Murphy Fishing Hall of Fame, really a series of tracings of some of the bigger fish we've caught, from a couple trout Dad landed in the 1950s all the way up to Rose's mammoth bass two summers ago. I touch Cheryl's first fish, caught at the dam almost seventeen years ago. That was something. She had the fish on before she knew it. She just reeled it in, and there it was . . .

Boy, we are running out of space. We'll need at least three more spaces for Shawna and her kids.

I step into the bathroom, as modern as any, I suppose.

Full shower and tub, toilet, wide sink, lots of storage for towels, sheets, and quilts. The same old sign hangs over the toilet: A fisherman with his "dame" in the back of the boat, him saying, "You gotta what?" I see a little needlepoint saying and smile. "If it's brown, flush it down; if it's yellow, let it mellow." Shawna's kids are going to forget. I usually do for the first few days. I sigh. One bathroom for nine people, though. The boys would use the outhouse, but . . . Hmm. We may have to label this the girls' bathroom.

I step into Grandpa Joe and Grandma Jenn's room, where I'll be staying, Shawna right above me. I see a knothole in the ceiling. I could probably wave at her toes. There is so much of my grandparents in here: a hamper, a walker, walking sticks, lots of hats, a plaque congratulating them on fifty years of marriage. I pick up an octagonal cookie tin, a poem on the lid:

> SOME HAE MEAT,
>   AND CANNA EAT,
> AND SOME WAD EAT
>   THAT WANT IT,
> BUT WE HAE MEAT
>   AND WE CAN EAT,
> AND SAE THE LORD
>   BE THANKIT.

They rarely threw away anything they thought could be useful. The room has five lamps, none of the shades matching, and a million hangers they couldn't bear to part with crammed onto an old water pipe. Old jackets, an easy chair that has been easy on the back for eighty years, two chests containing handmade quilts, and a card table in the corner nailed to the floor, Grandpa's Underwood portable typewriter on top. I touch the lone tie on Grandpa's tie rack. "Blest be the tie that binds," I say.

I step over to Grandpa's miscellaneous shelves. The first shelf contains a bullhorn, the rearview mirror for a boat, and a Coleman G.I. Pocket Stove with its original handbook. I flip through the handbook and read, "The G.I. Pocket Stove meant hot food for thousands of tired Yanks during the war . . . burns any kind of gasoline—white or leaded! Boils a quart of water in eight minutes." And I'll bet it still works. Things worked back then. The second shelf houses various batteries, an unused Zebco 33 Classic reel, a soldering iron, a thousand yards of eight-pound test line, Electrolux four-ply filter bags, and a stack of used mailing envelopes from as far back as 1956—to be reused if necessary, of course. I remember when Grandma reused "tinfoil" at least three or four times before discarding it. And sometimes, when all the stamps on an envelope weren't cancelled, she would steam off the "clean" ones. The top shelf contains some Flents sunguards for sunbathers, which, according to the package, "should not be worn while swimming." Yeah, these two were packrats, all right, two wonderful people prepared for anything and everything.

I walk into the great room, three ceiling fans whirring above two ancient couches, several cloth folding chairs, and Mom's latest thousand-piece puzzle displayed on a card table. The huge stone fireplace, pieced together by hand over fifty years ago, is the focal point of this room. Birch logs and pinecones fill the mantel, deer antlers above holding felt hats, fishing hats, and an old metal anchor. In the corner of the room is a display of Grandpa's "old-stuff"—his Peg-Board of ancient tools. I'll bet every last one of these tools still works. Above a series of old family pictures, Dad has hung an old-fashioned hand-painted sign:

"I PRAY TO HEAVEN TO BESTOW
THE BEST OF BLESSINGS ON
THIS HOUSE

AND ALL THAT SHALL HEREAFTER INHABIT IT
MAY NONE BUT HONEST AND WISE MEN
EVER RULE UNDER THIS ROOF"
—WRITTEN FOR THE WHITE HOUSE
BY JOHN ADAMS, ITS FIRST OCCUPANT

I stand in front of the picture windows that seem to hold up the front of the house. These picture windows are Mom and Dad's wide-screen TV. They can watch flowing water, the boats, the sunrises and sunsets, and the critters. And the "program" never repeats. There are no reruns up here of any kind. No TV, radio only at night, no car horns, no phones ringing incessantly. And the only news that really matters filters down through the woods to them by word of mouth, so they learn only what's worth learning, not the onslaught of death and mayhem and chaos that has become the news in the United States.

"Hey, stranger."

I feel hot breath on my neck. I don't turn. "Who's that?"

"Your woman," Shawna whispers. "Where are the kids?"

"At the beach, I think. Where's Mom?"

"Taking a nap."

Hmm. We may get a few minutes alone. "Settled in?"

"Not yet. I have a few things to show you upstairs."

I turn.

She beckons me with a finger.

We go upstairs.

60

Shawna

Though I want to have this man hold me close, I have far too many questions about my sleeping quarters than I was willing to ask Elle. I lead him up the stairs, each creaking a different note, and stop him at the top.

"What are you going to show me?" he whispers.

I point to a stack of hangers on the set of bunk beds we're not using. "Explain those."

"Oh, those." He starts to speak and stops.

I don't think I'm going to like this explanation.

"Whenever my parents are away for any length of time, they put hangers on all the beds to keep the critters from nesting."

I knew I wouldn't like his explanation. "Critters?"

"Um, yeah. What else do you want—"

"What kind of critters?" I interrupt.

"Um, squirrels, mice."

"You're kidding. Up here? *Inside?*"

He nods.

I look at where we will be sleeping. "There weren't any hangers on those beds."

He takes me in his arms. "Because Mom took the hangers off just before you got here."

"How can you be sure?"

He walks around, looking at the floor carefully. "I don't see any droppings."

Oh, lovely.

"And you probably won't see any." He holds me again. "If there are any mice around here, they're hanging around under the kitchen. It's why the toaster is upside down."

This is not comforting at all. "The toaster is upside down?"

"Just in case. It wouldn't be pleasant to have fur on your toast."

More loveliness. I'm not even having toast now.

Joe nuzzles my neck. "What else do you want to show me?"

I point above him to what looks like a hole in the roof.

"Oh, that. It's so the bats can get back out."

Surely he didn't just say . . . "The what?"

"We have bats up here."

"You . . . do?"

"They only come out at night to chase bugs. There used to be a mesh screen there, you know, for ventilation during the summer."

"Used to be?"

He sighs. "One summer Mom kept smelling this odor . . ."

I don't like the way this story is beginning.

"A bat had, um, gotten stuck in the screen and expired."

Peachy. "So you just let them fly in and out whenever they want to?"

"They don't come in that often, Shawna."

One time is enough for me.

"Dad doesn't like them much, so if you see one, call him. He'll get an old tennis racket and come up here swinging away. He has a nice backhand." Joe laughs. "His serve needs some work, though."

"Joe, this isn't funny!"

"Shawna, the only reason a bat would come in is to look for mosquitoes. There are millions of mosquitoes outside for them to—"

"You have a hole in your roof over me and my children. Won't the mosquitoes descend on us for a feast?"

"Not if you use Cutter."

I do *not* want to smell like Cutter for six days. "Joe, I want you to put the screen back up. I won't have bats or mosquitoes swooping down on my children."

"I'll put it back up." He then tries to swoop in on me for a kiss, but I'm not having it.

"So do it," I say.

"Now? C'mon, Shawna, the kids aren't around, Mom's sleeping . . ."

I cross my arms and frown.

He puts up that screen, adding twenty more staples than necessary with his staple gun because I asked him to. By the time he's finished, the kids have returned from the beach, the girls stomping up the stairs.

"Mama," Toni says. "I caught twenty tadpoles, and we built them a castle for them to swim in, then we let them swim out." I try not to stare, but the child's hair is a soggy, sandy mess.

"One of the tadpoles didn't make it," Rose says.

"Yeah," Toni says, "so we had to have a funeral for Bobby."

"Bobby? Who's Bobby?" I ask.

Rose lowers her voice. "The tadpole. Toni named it."

I look at Toni, and she seems genuinely sad. "Toni, Bobby's up in frog heaven right now."

"Frogs have a heaven, too?" Toni asks.

Joe slides by me with his ladder, nods to us, and leaves.

"Sure they do, honey." And I hope frog heaven is light-years away from people heaven. "Why don't you all get freshened up for dinner?"

Dinner smells delicious and fills the house from the foundation to the rafters. Sound carries in this house, and so do tasty aromas.

My first Aylen Lake fish fry isn't at all what I had expected. Elle stuffs and bakes the larger bass, pan-frying the rest, most of which still have bones in them. We spend most of the meal picking out bones and piling them on paper plates in the center of the table. It tastes wonderful, but you have to work at it. We eat baked potatoes, peach Jell-O filled with fresh peaches, corn with real butter, and yeast rolls. It is a feast. For dessert, we chow down on butter tarts and maple-walnut ice cream (which takes some getting used to) with maple cookies.

"As soon as you're finished eating, we're going on a scavenger hunt," Kaz says.

Joe's kids smile.

"What exactly is a scavenger hunt?" Junior asks.

"You'll see," Kaz says.

While Joe and I help Elle with the dishes, Kaz takes the kids down the path to collect an odd series of items: an American penny pre-1960, a Canadian coin pre-1950, one toothpick, one page of a newspaper, a mussel shell, a crayfish, a piece of driftwood, and a piece of fallen birch bark.

"It's mainly so the people around here can get to know your kids, or, in Joe's case, so they can see his kids again," Elle says.

"We could do a treasure hunt, too," Joe says. "It's a shame we missed the regatta. They would have had a blast."

"What's a regatta?" I ask.

"The whole lake gets together down at Ranger's Beach to have swimming races, canoe races, egg toss, spike driving . . ."

"Don't forget underwater banana eating," Elle adds.

"They haven't done that one in years," Joe says.

Gulp. "Someone . . . eats a banana underwater."

"Yep," Elle says. "You had to peel it and eat it without coming up for air."

"Sounds appetizing," I say.

"It isn't at all," Elle says. "Of course, that was back when you could drink the lake water."

Ick.

"We're not getting many of these dishes done at all with all this talking going on," Elle says, "so why don't you two go for a canoe ride? I can finish up."

I look at the incredible pile of dishes. "We'll help."

"No," Elle says. "Go on."

Joe has already put down his dish towel.

Is this a test? "We can go after we're done," I say.

Joe takes my towel. "Let's go."

Down at the dock, both of us wearing life vests, I complain a little more. "Joe, that's a lot of dishes."

"There will be more for us to wash tomorrow."

True.

He holds the canoe snug to the dock with his legs and helps me into it with a hand, telling me to stand in the middle before sitting. It's a tippy thing, but I get situated. He climbs in behind me, and with a few paddle strokes, we're floating free into the middle of the lake, the sun setting, the reflections on the water so beautiful.

"This is nice," I say, leaning back onto Joe's chest.

"Yeah."

"Did you take Cheryl out like this?"

"Yes."

And then he's quiet for a while.

"I'm sorry. I shouldn't have brought it up," I say.

He rests the paddle in front of me, a few drips of water hitting my shoes. "It's okay."

"Did Cheryl like to fish?" Why do I keep asking him about Cheryl? We're supposed to be creating some new memories of our own, not reliving his old ones. I just can't help it, I guess.

"Some," he says. "She preferred to go down to the beach and paint or read or help Mom. Up here is where she rested."

I am definitely going fishing a lot now. I have to do everything I can to separate myself from Cheryl. "You ever, um, make out in this canoe?"

"No. It's too tippy."

"We'll have to be careful, then . . ."

I turn as far as I can until my lips find his, and we kiss . . .

A siren goes off, startling me so badly I almost tip us over. "What was that?"

Joe laughs. "It's just a loon. Look." He points out into the water.

A black head like a periscope stares at me with beady red eyes twenty feet from the canoe.

"The loon must be our chaperone, huh?" Joe says.

With the worst timing. "Are there a lot of those out there?"

"I hope so. If there are a lot of loons, that means the lake is healthy for all the wildlife around here."

"And they just . . . pop up and go off like that?"

"Sometimes."

Rock bass that bite and loons that pop up and scream.

I may never go swimming in this lake.

61

Joe

The next morning a little after sunrise, when my mom and dad always get up, we eat a huge breakfast while Shawna takes a shower. I tried to get Shawna to take a bath with me in the lake this morning, but she wouldn't, and she wouldn't even give me a reason. "I'll keep you warm like I promised," I told her, but she still refused.

Junior tries to explain it to me over some Canadian bacon and Chelsea buns fried in butter.

"Anayeoga kwa hiari yake hatahisi baridi," Junior says. That Amina taught him a *lot* of Swahili. "It means that 'a person who bathes willingly with cold water does not feel the cold.'"

Ah. The water is too cold for Shawna. It does take some getting used to.

I watch the kids eat . . . and eat . . . and realize that they are all going to gain weight up here.

That van is going to hate us on the return trip home.

Jimmy, who always sits closest to Dad, asks, "We're going fishing, right?"

Dad leans back and squints. "The book says the best fishing is later this afternoon, Jimmy."

"Oh," Jimmy says, and he continues eating.

The "book" is a series of tables listing the best times for wildlife activity. I don't take much stock in the "book," and neither does Dad, but when you're tired and full and want to take a nap after breakfast, the "book" comes in handy.

"That book isn't always right, Grandpa," Joey says. "Especially up here."

Dad winks at me. Now I *know* he has planned to go fishing all along. "Well, I might be able to take out three ladies . . ."

"What about us?" Jimmy shouts.

I'm sure a few loons came up from the deep to check out the noise, too. All voices carry around here, but Jimmy's voice can be heard over in Ottawa.

"Your dad will take you out, Jimmy, and we'll have us a contest," Dad says.

Murphy fishing contests are the stuff of legends. According to my grandfather, "'Aylen Lake trembles whenever the Murphys compete for fish.'" He told me that when I was maybe five. "'Look, Joe, see all the waves? The lake is trembling.'"

"How about first fish, biggest fish, and most fish?" Rose suggests.

I smile inside. This is the Rose that's been in hiding for almost a year. Aggressive, competitive, passionate.

"Most tonnage," Dad says. "Only one category today. The boat that brings home the heaviest catch wins."

Shawna comes in looking so fresh and clean. "Morning, everyone," she says as she sits. "Mmm." She bites into a Chelsea bun. "Delicious." She turns to Dad. "Where are we going?"

"Fishing," I say. "And it's a contest."

"And who's my fishing guide?" Shawna asks.

"Grandpa," Rose says.

"Good," Shawna says.

"Hey now," I say. "What's good about it?"

"Your daddy is older and wiser than you are, and he knows the lake better than you do," Shawna says.

Dad smiles.

I wolf down the rest of my bacon. "Fellas, we have some fishing to do. Get your gear and meet me in the *Charlenor*. Jimmy, get us a couple dozen leeches and worms. Joey, you secure the poles. Junior, make sure there's an anchor in that boat."

"You're taking the *Charlenor*?" Dad asks.

"It's older than you, Dad, so it knows where the fish *really* are," I say. I stand and kiss Shawna briefly. After all, she has doubted my fishing prowess, and I intend to prove her wrong.

"What's the *Charlenor*?" Shawna asks.

Elle sighs. "That old brown boat down there, named after me and my sisters: Charlotte, Ellen, and Eleanor. We Murphys tend to name things we can depend upon."

I smile. "And you can depend on me, gentlemen, to find you some big fish today. Ladies, y'all are going to lose."

"Wanna bet?" Shawna asks.

"Most tonnage, huh?" I ask. "The boat with the heaviest catch—and they all have to be legal keepers, now—the boat with the most wins. The losers have to . . ." I look at Mom. "The losers have to sweep the house and do the dishes tonight for Grandma."

Mom smiles. "Ooh, I like this bet. I get the night off after dinner either way."

I turn to Rose. "Is it a bet?"

Rose smiles. "We'll, uh, leave the brooms out where you can find them."

And away we go . . .

I take the boys first to Wake's Rock, where we catch several keepers, most around a pound. Junior catches one on his first cast but stews when he can't add to it, getting hung up on the rocks. After a few minutes of inaction, we go to a shoal nearby. We feed a lot of little fish but catch nothing substantial. Joey suggests Ballet View, a little point with a shoal facing a wilderness ballet camp. I have never seen a single ballerina dancing on the beach, yet the name has stuck. As soon as I get us anchored, Jimmy has a big one on.

"It's a pig, Daddy!" Jimmy shouts.

It's so big, the fight loosens the anchor and we start to drift. We watch Jimmy struggling and whooping it up, Joey wondering when it's going to jump, me wondering where the net is.

"Whoa," Junior says when the fish finally breaks the surface, head shaking and backing away. "That's a pig."

Jimmy works it closer and closer to the boat as I ready the net. I hand the net to Junior. "Junior, you do the honors."

"Oh, no," he says, "I don't think—"

I put the net in his hands. "You can't miss something that big. You have him hooked hard, Jimmy?"

"I think so," Jimmy grunts. "Yeah. The pig is mine. I think he swallowed the hook."

Jimmy guides the bass closer to the boat. Junior misses on his first attempt but comes up with the fish on his second.

"Wow!" Junior says.

I reach into the net and grab the lower lip of the bass, pulling it out. "Easily four pounds." I look into the bass's mouth and see ovaries. "This pig is a sow."

"A female?" Jimmy asks.

"Yep. Swallowed everything except the sinker." I cut the line and add the fish to the stringer.

Junior still hasn't moved, his eyes fixed on the fish.

"Go on, Junior. There's bound to be a few more like that. Go to the front and cast towards shore." I see Joey about to do exactly that, but I mouth "wait." He winks and throws out into deeper water instead.

Junior casts a little shorter than I would have, but in a few seconds . . . "Something's after it."

I watch his line tightening and moving to the right. "Wait

for it, Junior. Don't set the hook too soon." The line snaps tight, and Junior's rod tip bends. "Now!"

Junior rears back and nearly falls, righting himself just in time, setting the hook probably into the bass's brain.

"You got yourself a pig, Junior," I say. "Take your time."

Junior's fishing style reminds me of Jimmy's when he first started fishing "with the big boys." He's excited, wide-eyed, grunting, laughing, and talking to the fish the entire time. "No, this way, come on, come on, is the net ready? No, not yet, come back here! Is he getting any closer?"

Five minutes of commentary later, Joey has the fish netted and in the boat. I lift it out of the net. "Jimmy, he may have you beat." Jimmy hands me the scale. Jimmy's "sow" weighs in at four pounds even. Junior's just breaks four and a quarter.

"Dang," Jimmy says. "By a quarter pound."

"Both of them go up on the wall," I say. I slide the fish onto the stringer. "Fellas, we're at our limit." Eight nice fish in less than two hours. Not bad. "Now if you want, we can stay here and catch bigger fish to replace some of these."

"Do you think we're winning, Daddy?" Jimmy asks.

I lift the stringer. "We may have fourteen pounds of bass here, gentlemen."

"Wow," Jimmy says. "The girls probably haven't even caught one keeper yet."

Joey keeps casting. "But what if Grandpa fishes, too? If they get their limit, they'll have ten fish. You didn't specify it was only the girls against us."

"So what if he does fish?" I ask. "Won't it be great to beat them *and* Grandpa? He'll have to sweep and do the dishes, too."

They all agree that having Grandpa do anything domestic is worth seeing since it is a rare event. He'll do massive maintenance on the house, but when it comes to dusting or vacuuming or drying a single dish, my dad is all thumbs.

I take the scenic route back to Murphy's, hugging the shoreline, looking at cottages, and cruising through Vanity Bay, so named because of the nice beach and the bathing beauties that usually hang out there. No one's lying out on the sand, but the boys make sure Junior knows what might be there later.

"Dad," Joey asks, "can we take out the *Charlenor* later?"

"To go fishing again?" I ask.

Joey's face reddens. "Something like that."

"Sure."

Jimmy jumps up and points. "Is that Grandpa's boat already at the dock?"

They haven't left yet? I guess it's possible. Shawna does take a long time to get Toni ready to go anywhere, but Dad wouldn't let that happen. No. They've already been out—and they're already back.

"I'll bet they got skunked," Jimmy says.

I don't have the heart to tell them that we probably lost. My dad would *never* come back that soon unless he has something mammoth for Mom to take a picture of to e-mail to every Murphy on planet Earth.

We're going to be doing some sweeping, all right.

62

Shawna

We kicked booty! I'd say "We kicked some bass," but that doesn't sound too Christian.

And my arms are actually tired!

After we all put on raggedy sweats and old fishing hats, Kaz took us to Ranger's Point, where we fished over a mass of underwater rocks, telling us, "Throw up on the rocks and reel in slowly. I'll get the net ready."

It was so calm he didn't even have to anchor, so we floated around—and caught some serious tonnage. Rose and Toni had fish on at the same time, I nearly got pulled over the edge of the boat, and we all lost more fish than we caught. Toni and I weren't setting the hook right or something. We were catching so many big ones that Kaz was continually weighing and exchanging smaller fish from the stringer. And then . . . nothing. Not a nibble or bite for thirty minutes.

"Not bad for an hour's work," Kaz said, holding up the stringer. "Has to be close to twenty pounds here."

"We won!" Rose said.

And then we went back to the dock, tied up, put the stringer in the water, and I went back to my bed to take a nap—after trying to get the fishy smell off my hands. Yeah, I held quite a few and almost took the hook out of one. Toni caught two "pounders," as Kaz called them, naming one TJ and the other JT.

An hour or so later, Elle shakes me.

"The boys are back." She holds two brooms and hands me two others. "They are going to need these."

I run down to the dock and see Jimmy and Junior holding up their stringer. They caught a lot of fish, too! But they couldn't have beaten us! Rose was so sure!

"Grandpa, did you fish?" Jimmy asks.

"I didn't have time, the girls were catching so many," Kaz says.

Jimmy's little face caves in.

"Rose," Kaz says, "could you lift our stringer up for them?"

"Gladly."

Rose pulls up the stringer from under the dock. The boys' eyes droop. They look like puppy dogs, the poor dears.

I hand a broom to Jimmy.

"But we haven't weighed them yet, Shawna," Jimmy says.

"Jimmy, just look at them," Joe says. "They have us by at least five pounds."

How they can weigh fish with their eyes I'll never know.

Joe takes the other broom from me. "You went to Ranger's, didn't you, Dad?"

Kaz smiles. "Uh-huh."

"C'mon, fellas," Joe says. "Grab a broom. We'll sweep the dock and the stairs first."

While the boys do the *worst* job of sweeping I've ever seen, putting more pine needles onto the stairs than were there in the first place, Rose and Kaz sharpen up some knives, Elle providing them with a roll of aluminum foil, a cutting board, and some paper grocery bags for tracing.

Toni points at the knives. "What are those for?"

Kaz drops down into the water while Rose lays a fish on the cutting board. "We have to clean the fish while they're fresh."

Toni looks at me. "But, Mama, I thought . . ." She looks back at the fish.

"What did you think, honey?" I ask.

"I thought I was taking TJ and JT home with me."

Now what? "Oh, honey, we can't take them all the way home. They'll die."

Toni's eyes fill with tears. "We can put them in buckets, and, and then we can get a big aquarium, and—"

"No, sweetie," I say, drawing her to me. "We caught the fish to eat one night."

Toni pushes me away and runs up the stairs.

"Toni?" Kaz calls out.

She stops but doesn't turn around. "What?"

"TJ and JT are too small to eat," he says. "Want to help me let them go?"

I nod at Kaz and mouth "thank you." So wise, even though her two fish are as large as most of the others. Toni comes back.

Kaz pulls a fish from the stringer. "We'll trace, uh, JT here—"

"That's TJ," Toni interrupts.

How can she tell? How could Kaz tell?

"So it is," Kaz says. "We'll trace TJ right quick, then let him go, okay?"

"Will he stay around the dock?" Toni asks.

"You know," Kaz says, "he just might."

Wonderful. At least I'll know the names of the fish that are biting my toes.

"Joey, Jimmy, Junior—any of you all want to trace your fish?" Kaz yells.

Junior and Jimmy come back, tracing their huge fish. Kaz traces TJ as best as he can while it flops around, the tracing at least an inch larger all around. They set their tracings in the sun to dry, and Kaz hands both fish to Toni . . .

And she holds them both up by the lip like an expert. "Bye, TJ," she says, and she *kisses* the fish! Lord, that's nasty! "Bye, JT." *Another* kiss. Then she drops the fish into the water, waving at them until they dart away into the deep.

I pull her aside. "Toni, honey, you shouldn't kiss the fish like that. They have germs."

She looks at me as if I were from another planet. "Fish live in the water, Mama, so they're clean."

I can't argue with her logic. Strange, but Toni watches Kaz and Rose cleaning the other fish with eager curiosity, maybe because those aren't *her* fish she's seeing dissected. I'm so glad she didn't name all our fish.

"Leeches and crayfish in this one," Rose says.

I don't stick around to hear the rest of the autopsies, instead floating up the stairs to watch my men—all four of them—sweeping the deck (and each other).

"You missed a spot," I say.

"Where?" Junior asks.

"As far as I can tell," I chuckle, "just about everywhere."

I turn and look at the lake. This place is just . . . heaven. That's what it is. It's heaven on earth. The air tastes good, the food tastes tastier, the sky is clearer, the bugs—*ow!* And right through the sweatpants, too!

I hurry inside and join Elle for another cup of Red Rose tea. I have to find this stuff when I get back to Roanoke.

We clink teacups. "To the spoils of victory," she says.

"Yes."

We watch Jimmy "accidentally" swat Joey on the butt, Joey "accidentally" swinging around and nearly taking off his head. Junior arrives in a pose right out of *Star Wars,* using his broom as a light saber. The brooms crack together, they pivot, and the battle is on.

That deck is never going to get clean.

"You all caught a lot of fish," Elle says.

"Beginner's luck," I say.

"I don't know about that," she says. "Not many folks who live up here year-round catch that many in only an hour's time. You might be a natural-born fisherwoman."

"Thank you."

She takes a sip. "Junior caught the biggest fish of the lot."

"He did?" He didn't tell me. I wonder why? I know he's a humble child, but beating Jimmy has to make him feel pretty good.

"Yep. He beat Jimmy's fish by a few ounces." She taps the. table. "That reminds me of a time Joe's brother, James, and he had a fishing contest. His wife called while you were napping, by the way. They'll be up late tonight with their six boys. It will be bedlam here tomorrow for sure."

Eleven kids and one bathroom is not bedlam—it's sheer terror.

"They're staying here?" I ask.

"Oh, no. James has a cottage across the way. They'll be here for Sunday lunch. Has Joe told you much about James?"

"Just that he's a missionary, right?" With six kids.

"To Irian Jaya. Anyway, before either of them was married, they must have been no more than twenty-three, they went out to fish, and whoever caught the smallest one had to do dishes for a week. Something like that. Well, Joe lands a big one, and James lands a big one, and neither of them has a scale. So they come home in the *Charlenor*, Joe driving, James in front all hunched down." Her eyes narrow. "James, the future missionary to Irian Jaya, lets Joe weigh his first. Maybe three pounds. James's fish weighs in at six pounds, an all-time Murphy family record. Joe can't believe it, and neither can Kaz, but as soon as Kaz shakes that bass a little, rocks and pebbles start popping out of its mouth." She laughs. "They are two of the most competitive people you'll ever meet."

"Rose is like that, too," I say.

"Yes. I've been worried about Rose, but seeing her up here the way she used to be all the time, I'm not worried anymore. This place brings people back to life." She touches my hand. "I'm glad you're here."

"I'm glad to be here," I say.

"And I sure am glad you're getting married this fall. We'll be able to stop by, see you hitched, then get on down to Florida early for a change."

I sigh. "There's so much to do when we get back. I don't know where to begin."

"Oh, weddings run themselves if you let them. And you've already had practice, right?"

"I didn't have my kids then."

"Or his," she adds. "It'll all come together. We had a wedding up here once, up at the chapel."

Joe had told me about the open-air chapel just a few cottages away, with rough-hewn benches and a view of Turkey Island.

"The bride wore a beautiful white dress and hiking boots." Elle laughs. "It was one of the most beautiful ceremonies I've ever seen. You'll see what I mean at chapel tomorrow."

The next morning, after the boys take lake baths and the girls take hot showers, we walk to the chapel. It's not a long walk, but the last part uphill is a killer. Someone had put benches to rest on along the way, and Elle takes full advantage.

The chapel has a shingled roof complete with skylights and a stained glass window in a frame hanging under the

GEORGE T. STEPHENS MEMORIAL CHAPEL sign. The wooden
benches, most under the roof and some out in the sunlight,
could easily seat two hundred or more. Carvings of a bear
and a wolf stand in the corners of a simple stage, a fish
carved right into the podium. Most folks dress casually in
jeans, flannel shirts, and sweatshirts, and the pine trees sway
out as if trying to touch us.

Yes, this would be a beautiful place for a wedding. The
bride wore hiking boots. I thought it was funny when Elle
told me about it, but now that I've walked up that hill . . . the
bride *had* to wear hiking boots.

The service is a Murphy family affair with Kaz leading
the singing, Elle playing the small electric organ, Joe reading the scripture, and James doing the sermon. Our kids sit
with James's kids, and we take up two full rows.

At one point in the service, Kaz says, "It is one of the traditions of the chapel to have the heads of the households in
each cottage introduce their families and tell us where they're
from."

Around the chapel we go, and people are up here from
everywhere, and most aren't from Ontario. There are people
from North Carolina, Illinois, Ohio, New York, Pennsylvania, and, of course, Virginia and Irian Jaya.

After all have introduced their families, Kaz steps closer
to our row. "My name is Kaz Murphy, my wife, Elle, is on
the organ, and we're from here."

"And Florida," Elle says.

"And Florida," Kaz says, and some folks laugh. I can tell
by his voice he much prefers being at Aylen. "And we have
with us Joe and his family up from Roanoke, Virginia." He
takes a deep breath. "There's Jimmy, Joey, and Rose, and we
have with us Joe's fiancée, Shawna, and two of her kids, Toni
and Junior." He pauses and smiles. "And yesterday, those five
kids—and Joe and Shawna—caught thirty-four pounds of
bass in a little under three hours."

Oohs and ahs. That's right. We bad.

"As a result, friends, there are no more fish left in the lake," Kaz says, and the audience really laughs this time. "Elle, do we have enough to feed everyone here?"

Elle stands and starts counting the people! She is so cute! "Almost. You'll all have to go out again on Monday."

"We'll let you know," Kaz says.

They sure take pride in their fishing up here. And in a way, Kaz has broken any ice that might be behind us. Folks won't see my kids as black kids. They'll see them as a young fisherman and a cute fisherwoman. That Kaz is pretty sneaky.

We sing lots of hymns, and then James, a taller, skinnier version of Joe, stands at the pulpit after we sing "Amazing Grace." He leaves his Bible on the podium and walks closer to us. "My dad is a great fisherman," he says. "He taught me and my brother, Joe, everything we know, and before I get into the scripture, I want to tell you a little story about . . . my brother, Joe."

After our scripture reading, I was expecting Jesus and the feeding of the five thousand, but now I'm not so sure. I squeeze Joe's hand, and he squeezes mine.

"Now I wasn't with Joe at the time, so you'll have to take this story with a grain of salt," James says. "Joe was at the Twin Islands using frogs for bait, back when they didn't cost an arm and a leg."

They fished with little frogs? How cruel!

"Joe got a strike on his first cast, but the bass snapped the line," James says. "Joe said a few choice words . . ."

Folks laugh.

James looks side to side. "I'm sure they were biblical."

More laughter.

"Anyway, he cast out and caught a big one. As Joe was trying to get the hook out of the fish, he saw a little frog's flipper in the fish's mouth. Using his hook disgorger—Joe has every fishing gizmo known to mankind—he opened the fish, and the frog crawled out into his hand. And he recognized the frog as the one he just lost when the fish broke his line. Being a true Murphy and not wanting to waste a thing, Joe put *that* frog back on the hook, caught *another* fish, and then he let that frog—which caught *two* fish—go."

"Is that true?" I whisper to Joe.

"All true," he says.

"Joe sent me an e-mail containing a picture of him holding those two fish, so I have to believe him. Do you?"

A few folks are scratching their heads, but most are nodding. That's how powerful the Murphy family fishing name is up here, I guess.

"That's one fish story I like to tell," James says, "but here is my all-time favorite fish story."

And *then* we get the story of Jesus feeding the five thousand that is so familiar to me. The Lord made a lot with a little. Sure, it was a miracle to feed that many with only a few fish and some bread, but the lesson James wants us to remember is much more practical.

"I've been a missionary going on twenty years. We often have to make a lot out of a little while trying to bring the Gospel to a land that has a million and a half people from two hundred and fifty different cultures, most of whom have existed there for thirty thousand years with no knowledge of the Bible. There are times when we don't even have a little to make a lot out of. As you all know, fishing is a game of waiting. Fishing requires patience. As a missionary, I have learned to wait on the Lord. 'God will make the feast,' I tell my kids. 'He'll bring the fish.' And He does. Not always when we want it, but He always brings it in time."

Nothing fancy, this church. Practical sermon, nondenominational, a focus on the Bible—what all churches could be if they tried.

* * *

Sunday lunch afterward is bedlam, indeed. Rose, Junior, and James's son Matthew sit at the "adult" table on the porch while the "kids"—the other *eight*—make quite a racket out on the deck as they eat on card tables. I haven't met many missionary kids, especially ones who have been raised for most of their lives outside the United States. James's wife, Kathy, tries to explain it (and them) to me.

"Six kids," she says. "I know. What was I thinking? And why? Well, it always gave us an excuse to come back to the States. All of them were born in the U.S. They're a little out of touch. I guess that's the right phrase."

"Mom, please," Matthew says.

"Oh, honey, but I wouldn't want you any other way," she says, putting her arm around his shoulders. "That's why we get up here as often as we can. It's so simple here. The kids can be curious and ask questions and not feel stupid because they don't know this song or that movie or because they don't wear the 'right' clothing."

All of James and Kathy's are extremely polite, and each has a "gift" of some kind, whether it is photography, chalk art, website design, flying a Cessna, drawing, or singing.

"It's been quite an education for them," James says.

Irian Jaya sounds almost exactly like The Castle, except without the crocodiles.

Matthew, a strapping boy with rosy red cheeks, tells us about his home. "Irian Jaya is beautiful. Dense tropical rain forests, snow-capped mountains, and beaches, too. The fleas are kind of bad, and it's really hot and humid, but the people are incredible."

"Most of them don't wear many clothes," Kathy adds. "That . . . that was a shock at first. At least the men cover their, um . . ." She looks around. "Oh, yeah. I'm at the adult table. The men cover their penises with hollowed-out reeds that look kind of like carrots, and that's how they come to church."

Interesting.

"They still farm with stone tools, their tribal elders often wear bones in their noses . . ." James's voice trails off. "I used to think Aylen was primitive but not anymore."

I look down to the dock because, suddenly, nine children are being quiet. "What are they doing?" I stand, and Joe stands.

All the kids have crowded onto the dock while Junior and Luke (I think) hold something.

"Oh, that," James says. "It's a slingshot."

It is the biggest slingshot I have ever seen.

"They'll launch just about anything just to see how far it goes," Kathy says.

"They claim they can hit Turkey Island with a potato," James says.

"We *can,* Dad," Matthew says. "We hit the point two years ago, remember?"

I sit, but when they release whatever it is they're firing and it disappears into the blue sky, I flinch. It makes me so glad that my kids only play with Game Boys and CD players.

63

Joe

I've been watching Shawna take everything in, and though some things bother her—the bugs, the bats, the rock bass, the cold water—most things don't. I'm glad. This is my ancestral home, and I want her to feel at home. I don't know what I'd do if she didn't like this place. I would still marry her, of course, but trips up here without her just wouldn't be as fun or fulfilling.

After James's brood leaves for the night, Elle, Rose, and Toni relax with another thousand-piece puzzle, the boys play tabletop hockey using a bottle cap for a puck, and Shawna and I flip through old photo albums, howling with laughter at what I used to look like.

"You were so skinny, Joe," she says. "And red-headed. What happened?"

"I have aged."

"You were cute," Shawna says.

I wasn't. I was skinny and had braces.

I play adventure guide the rest of the week, doing my best to exhaust the kids so Shawna and I can go off quietly into the woods to make out while mosquitoes buzz all around us or out onto the lake in the canoe to watch the sun set in her eyes. It hasn't been easy. These kids have more energy than I'll ever have again. We do dueling tubes at Ranger's Beach, and Rose is "queen of the tubes," mainly because she has such sharp claws. We go fishing every morning. We fish at night. We fish when the fish normally aren't biting during the heat of the day. We go to Blueberry Mountain to pick blueberries, giving up because it's been so picked over, instead floating around under the mountain in life vests. We even cliff dive there.

It isn't exactly cliff diving, though it's deep enough. It's more like cliff dropping. After climbing thirty feet up a rocky ledge, you step out to an outcropping, take one step, and plunge. We all wear old sneakers for this. The boys jump with abandon. Rose simply steps off and holds her nose. Toni can't make the climb to the highest perch, so she jumps in from around ten feet up. Even I go up—and jump off backward like I used to do when I was a kid.

Shawna isn't pleased.

"Don't do that again, Joe," she says. "My heart was in my mouth."

I join her in the sun as the kids plummet in front of us. "I can't wait to be with you," I whisper as more children fall from the sky into the water.

"Neither can I."

Like a lot of things, you never know what you're missing until it's not there anymore. My sex drive evaporated when Cheryl died, my energies diverted to my kids. Now that the kids are starting to recover—and starting to thrive—my sex drive has made a comeback with a vengeance. I want Shawna worse than I've wanted anything, and though that may sound un-Christian, I think that's God's plan. If more couples went about lusting only after their spouses, the divorce rate would plummet overnight. I *only* want Shawna, and she *only* wants me.

We try waterskiing one afternoon when the waves simply quit waving. The lake is a sheet of glass, perfect for teaching "newbies" how to ski. After Dad pulls Jimmy and then Joey around the lake with Toni inside the boat cheering them on, I prepare Junior, adjusting his skis and giving him some pointers.

"The trick," I say, "is to sit back and let the boat pull you up. You will want to stand up as soon as you can—don't. Stay in a crouch until your skis are on top of the water. Otherwise you might take a nasty spill."

Junior nods.

"I'll be in the water with you. If you fall and you're okay, wave your hands in the air."

"Okay," he says. "I hope I don't fall. Joey and Jimmy are so good."

"And they fell from the time they were nine up to the time they were eleven. Don't worry if you don't get up this summer. We'll be coming back."

He takes a deep breath. "I am getting up this summer."

I'll say one thing for Junior, he never gives up. While Shawna paces the dock and winces, Junior falls eight times in a row before he gets it, and once he gets it, he *really* gets it. Like most anything else in life, it's the getting up that's the problem. Once we're up, we generally do okay.

"I did it!" Junior yells once he's on the dock. "Mama, you're next."

I smile. "I'll get you some skis."

Shawna backs off the dock. "Ah, no. Maybe next summer."

I write in the air above my hand. "Cliff jumping and skiing." I close my hand. I open it and write something else.

"What are you doing?" Shawna asks.

"Making a list of all the things you're going to do next summer," I say.

She narrows her eyes. "I heard the first two. What was that third one?"

I only raise my eyebrows.

"Oh," she says. "Oh. That." She looks down. "I'm sure we'll do that, too, Joe, um, unless I've just had a baby."

The world stands still for a while, for quite a while, as a matter of fact. I vaguely remember seeing, of all things, my feet. "Shawna, I . . ."

She winks. "We'll talk later. Aren't you going to ski?"

I step closer. "You want . . . another?"

"Don't you?" she asks.

"Yes, but . . . Of course I do, but you see—"

She kisses me. "Good. Now, go on and show me something, but don't hurt yourself."

I won't hurt myself. I *can't* hurt myself. She wants another baby. And what better way is there to blend our two families together than having another child? I can't just ski now.

I have to *perform*.

"Be back in one second," I say.

"Where are you going, Daddy?" Rose asks.

"To the shed," I say.

"Oh, no, Daddy, *don't!*" Rose cries.

I don't answer her, because this is something I have to do. I run up to the shed to get the oldest, heaviest wooden skis I can find. I take them to the screened porch. "Mom? You still have any of the old suits?"

"I do. C'mon."

Five minutes later, I am standing near the stairs at the beginning of the dock on these ancient red wooden skis, the footings loose and wiggling, wearing a full-body wool bathing suit and a shower cap. I can't hear a word anyone is saying because they're laughing so hard. I have given the boys bait buckets to fill with water, and they're pouring the water onto the dock.

"Gentlemen, I will need water, lots and lots of water on this dock to assist me in my takeoff."

Dad backs the boat to the end of the dock where Jimmy steadies it. "You sure you want to do this, son?"

"Yes, Dad." I point at the dock. "More water. That's it. Keep pouring."

Toni looks from me to Dad. "What's he going to do, Grandpa?"

She called him . . . Dad doesn't miss a beat, though there's a little lump in my throat. "He's going to fly, Toni."

"Oh." Toni looks at me. "Don't hurt yourself, Joe."

I sigh. One victory at a time. "Y'all keep throwing water on the dock during my takeoff."

Jimmy brings me the rope, saying, "Be careful, Dad."

"I'll be fine," I say. I hope. I haven't done this in years. I turn to Shawna. "A kiss for luck?"

"Ooh," Mom says, struggling down the stairs with her camera. "Not yet, not yet. I have to chronicle this for future generations."

As Shawna kisses me on the cheek, Mom snaps the picture. "Okay," Mom says. "Go on and try not to hurt yourself too badly."

"You're so crazy," Shawna says.

"That I am," I say. "Let's do this."

While the boys, and now Rose and Toni, splash or pour water onto the dock, I squeeze the rope handle tightly. "Let 'er rip, Dad."

"Everybody pray," Dad says, and he guns it, the slack disappearing, the rope snapping, and . . . I am gliding (and screaming) over the slick dock and off the dock into midair and for some reason I decide to do a scissor kick and—

64

Shawna

That was the most *spectacular* wipeout I've ever seen. That would have made the number one Play of the Week on ESPN.

Joe raises both of his arms and waves his hands, the top of that wool suit billowing above his head.

Jimmy can't stop gushing. "Dad, that was *great!* Can you do it again?"

Joe swims in slowly, smiling. "I think I will *never* do something so crazy again." He pulls himself up on the dock. "Anyone else want to try?" He looks at me. "You couldn't do much worse."

"Next summer, I promise," I say.

As the boat drifts in to be tied up for the day, Toni says, "I wanna try."

"Next summer, baby," I say.

"Yes," Joe says. "When you're taller."

"As tall as Crystal?" Toni asks.

Both Joe and I nod our heads.

"Cool," Toni says.

Cool.

Oh, everything about this place is cool. I was so worried about the water, but after a few days soaking in it, it ain't nothin' but a thang. I could live here, I really could . . . from May to September, maybe. All that snow and the lake freezing six feet thick and the temperatures 40 degrees below zero—not for me. I'd be turned to ash in no time.

And the kids simply *love* it up here. These same kids who beforehand were fussing at me about no TV or cell phones and who are usually wired to something electronic have played more board games, card games, and simple games like darts and Frisbee than they've ever played before. It's as if they feel freer to play without all those electronic distractions. As a matter of fact, when we get back to Roanoke, they're probably going to be bored!

I don't want to leave! I have learned so much about Joe up here from Elle, and I don't plan to tell him what I know. While they're out fishing, she tells me everything. I asked her what a storm was like on the lake, and she turned it into a story about Joe.

"Oh, storms are awesome things," she tells me. "Waves four or five feet high, boats smashing into the dock, waves crashing and eroding the shore. We couldn't sit here on the porch, no sir. Rain blows right in."

"What if you happen to be out on the lake when a storm hits?" I ask.

"You don't want to be out on the lake in a storm—unless you're Joe. When he was eighteen or nineteen, he was out in the canoe, and the fishing was good. He had caught his limit. A storm came up, whitecaps, wind, the whole nine yards. He should have paddled directly to shore, beached that canoe, and waited it out. But . . . he wanted to bring home his catch to me." She sighs at the memory, looking across the lake. "We watched him through binoculars, when the rains would let us, as he rounded Green Point and paddled in place for at least a half hour. He could have cut to shore at any time, but, as you might know, he's pretty stubborn."

In a nice way.

"I was watching when that canoe dove headfirst into the water . . ." Her eyes glaze over. "And that canoe just . . . didn't come back up. I waited, counting to twenty, before Joe's head bobbed to the surface. He swam, pushing that canoe, all filled with water now, right over to Green Point where he should have gone in the first place. He lost his tackle box, two poles, and a seat cushion. But he didn't lose his paddle . . . or his catch. The storm subsided, he paddled home, he handed me his catch, we ate, end of story." She smiles at me. "But you have to admire a man who would do just about anything to bring his catch home."

And I'm his catch. I have been thinking about that story over and over again in my mind. Elle's point was so clear: Joe would go through hell or high water for me since I am, hopefully, his greatest catch.

He's not such a bad catch either, though he looks simply dreadful in a wool bathing suit. I can forgive him for that.

65

Joe

I never thought I'd see this.

All five kids are misty about leaving, hugging Mom and Dad an extralong time at the Landing. It seems a shame to go, and the weather today is supposed to be gloriously warmer, which Shawna would have enjoyed.

"We'd like to give you all an early wedding present if we can," Dad says once we've loaded up the van.

"Sure," I say, hoping it doesn't take up too much space in the van.

He puts his arm around Mom. "We'd like to be your baby-sitters when you two go on your honeymoon."

"Really?" Shawna asks. "That's wonderful!" She gives Dad another hug. "Are you sure?"

Dad stares hard at the kids. "They don't scare me."

The kids giggle.

Shawna hugs Mom. "Thank you so much for everything."

"Thank you," Mom says, looking at me over Shawna's shoulder, "for bringing my boy back to life." She kisses Shawna's cheek.

I hug both my parents at the same time. I wish I had bigger arms. "Thank you," I say, and I start to tear up.

"Just come back from that honeymoon," Dad whispers. "If you stay away too long, they might *begin* to scare me."

Mom takes a family picture of us with our backs to the lake. I hope it comes out. I want to frame it and hang it over the mantel back home.

Instead of being quiet, the kids talk all the way to the border, reliving the past few days at the lake. It's not the same as being there, but just to hear them talking about fishing and skiing and eating, it warms my heart.

Even when Rose says, "Girls rule," to start an argument, Junior says, "We'll get you back next year."

I hope and pray this lasts.

And to help it last, we stop at the duty free store at the border and buy matching CANADIAN GIRLS ROCK shirts for Toni, Rose, and Shawna. The boys, who do not want to match under any circumstances, get simple Canada sweatshirts, each in a different color.

As the skies darken north of Syracuse, I attempt to outrun a few thunderstorms while the kids start to doze. Shawna chooses this specific time to discuss the wedding.

"We only have a few weeks to prepare for this wedding, Joe," she says, "and we have so much to do when we get home." She rattles off a list of at least sixty things that must happen for our wedding to go smoothly, and that's only a partial list, and it's only for the girls. "Don't even get me started on all that has to happen before I let the boys attend our wedding."

"Don't worry," I say. "Black tuxes for me and the boys. They'll be my best *men,* if that's okay with you."

She doesn't speak, probably because I have reduced her "boys must do" list to one item.

"Are you okay with that?"

She shakes her head. "Why didn't I think of that? The girls should be my maidens of honor." She nods. "That makes perfect sense. Now, Pastor Reed is doing the service, and we'll have to pay him and the organist and the church. Oh, and the caterer. And the florist. Flowers, can't forget those. And my dress! I need a wedding dress!"

I wish we were closer to Roanoke. I don't want Shawna stressing for the next five hundred miles. "I know there's some superstition about—"

"I am *not* wearing my old dress, Joe Murphy. Don't you even suggest it."

Wedding dresses are far too expensive, in my opinion, for one day's work. If you break down a thousand-dollar wedding dress into the hours of actual use, it's like paying $250 an hour to look beautiful. "Why not?" I ask. "Why can't you wear your first wedding dress?"

"It's just not done, Joe."

"Why not?" I ask.

"I don't know why . . ." She sighs. "Maybe because it's full of memories."

"Good memories."

"Of course they were good. They *are* good."

I shrug. "So bring the good memories to the church. That dress obviously worked once, right?"

"Rodney didn't marry me for my dress."

I smile. "What *did* he marry you for?"

Shawna checks the kids, then whispers, "For my cooking, but that's not the point."

"Your cooking?" I ask. "You like to cook?"

"You know I do, and don't change the subject. I cannot—"

"I like the way you cook," I say, "and I am not just talking about food."

She seems about to say something, but I don't hear any words.

"You do like to cook, don't you, Shawna?"

"Of course I do," she whispers. "And not so loud. The kids might be listening."

"I like to cook, too," I say. "A lot. All day and all night if I have to. I'm just a cooking machine."

"I can't wait to cook with you, Joe."

I smile. "And this brings us back to that dress, Shawna. No matter what you wear, that dress cannot interfere with our cooking, because you won't be wearing it long."

She tightens her lips and widens her eyes. "Um, well, I guess I can wear that dress, I mean, if I'm only going to be wearing it for a little while."

We've just saved at least a thousand dollars. Hallelujah!

"I know I've shrunk, though," she says. "I'll have to be fitted."

I have a solution for that one, too. "Rose can do it. She sews."

"Ah." She nods. "That makes perfect sense, too." She laughs. "But, Joe, that means you had to assume I had more meat on me when I first got married."

"I know how children can suck the life out of you," I say. "I'll probably need a smaller tux, too."

I check the gas gauge. Almost on empty again? This van is sucking the life out of my wallet.

I pull into a Shell north of Scranton and fill her up. Luckily, none of the kids wake up to beg me for money for "American" junk food at the convenience store. But when I try to start up the van, the engine won't turn over.

"They said the battery was fine," I say. I try again, and I only hear clicks. "Come on, come on." I try once more, and I don't hear even the clicks.

A thunderstorm chooses this moment to dump about two inches of rain on the parking lot, and though we're under cover, the lot fills up with water and the wind sends sheets of rain against the van while I'm under the hood. Like my dad, I have this optimistic (though usually mistaken) notion that I can fix anything just by popping the hood and wiggling a wire or two.

I look at one of the battery posts and see some caked white powder clinging to it. I knock a crusty piece off. Corrosion. Hmm. If I dust this off, maybe . . .

I open the back of the van, searching for my shave kit.

"What's wrong, Dad?" Joey asks, yawning himself awake.

"A little trouble with the battery," I say. "No problem."

I find my shave kit and take out my toothbrush, returning to the battery—and Shawna, who is peering at the engine.

"You're going to fix the engine with a toothbrush," she says.

"Um, yeah."

"Y'all Murphys sure are resourceful."

I brush off lots of white, powdery dust from the post, blowing it away.

"And this will fix it?" Shawna asks.

"I hope so," I say. "Try it."

Shawna gets in, turns it over, and it starts. We switch places, I put the toothbrush, a vital tool for everyone's vehicle, into the glove compartment, and we continue on our way.

"Joe?" Shawna asks.

"Yes?"

"I don't want you to turn off this van again until we get home."

"I agree," I say.

And as the kids wake up, their motor mouths running in high gear again, I realize that families are just like engines. You have to keep them both running if you're going to get home.

66

Shawna

This isn't so hard.

Okay, it *is,* but it is not impossible to work double shifts at McDonald's, plan a wedding, shop for school clothes, buy a wedding band for my future husband, pack up the apartment, move Junior and Toni to Joe's house, make my incoming family comfortable at the apartment, squeeze Kaz and Elle in over at Joe's, and rehearse for a wedding, all within the span of three weeks.

I'm just going completely out of my mind, that's all.

And I'm loving *every* minute of it.

God has always been good, but I'm finding myself saying "God is good" more often these days. Those kids have been amazing, Joe has been amazing, and, if I can brag a bit, I have been amazing, too.

Actually, I have amazed myself in how I've been able to let go of things. I'm normally a hands-on person who owns and deals with problems on her own. Since Rodney died, it has just been me dealing with life head-on. Now that I have a "holy helpmate"—that's what Pastor Reed calls Joe—I am finding that I can delegate responsibility pretty well. "Let go, let God" is an old phrase I didn't understand until now.

Joe and I are letting the good folks at Pilgrim do our wedding, and all we have to do is show up on time. We gave them our ideas for flowers, food, and the order of the service, and they have taken those ideas and run with them. And— and this is *extremely* important—it will save us a *great* deal of money. Like many churches, Pilgrim gets a healthy discount on flowers, and, like most churches, Pilgrim has a ready stock of women willing to cook a feast for the reception. Pastor Reed is personally handling the program, our regular organist has agreed to play for free as her wedding gift to us . . . the wedding is set.

Right after we spent a few days in hazy, hot, and humid Roanoke upon our return from Canada, I set the honeymoon. We are going back without the kids for some alone time in the coolness at Murphy's Unlimited, where we'll build fires to keep each other warm. Even with the money we're saving on my dress and the wedding, we cannot afford to fly back to Canada. Joe said he has looked into it and found that for the cheapest fares, we'd have to drive down to Charlotte, take a plane to Cincinnati, switch planes and fly to Ottawa, and rent a car for the drive to the lake. "You don't want to know what that will cost," he says, "or how long it will take." Of course I ask, and when I find out it will actually take *longer* to get to the lake (and all that good loving!) if we fly, I say, "We're driving. Get that van battery replaced."

Rose has been an absolute whiz with needle, thread, and sewing machine. The girls' dresses of satin rose look amazing. And when I pose in my expertly altered dress for the first time in my bedroom at the apartment late at night after our Friday-afternoon wedding rehearsal (which went very smoothly since Pastor Reed was completely in charge), I feel right buxom. A new Victoria's Secret bra, courtesy of Crystal, helps, too. I'm actually kind of chesty. I just wish Crystal were here to see it. She's out . . . somewhere. I hope she shows up on time for the wedding.

"You look beautiful, Mommy," Toni says. "Joe won't recognize you."

"Especially when he sees your hair," Rose says.

I look at the bride in the mirror. I'm still a pretty woman. Not bad for a woman with three kids and three on the way . . . and maybe a fourth if the honeymoon does what it's supposed to do, I mean, I'm sure *we'll* do what *we're* supposed to do—

"Mama?" Toni asks.

"Yes?" I ask.

"Rose has asked you twice to take off the dress," Toni says.

I look at Rose. "Sorry, I was just . . . daydreaming."

I take off the dress and put on some sweats. I pose in the sweats, too, and I am still an attractive woman.

"The dress is old," Rose says to Toni, "and her hair will be new."

Yes, I'm going to have a little extra hair for Joe to have fun with. Not a whole lot, now. I want him to recognize me at the altar.

"Now," Rose says to Toni, "we have to find something borrowed and something blue for your mama."

"I have something you can borrow, Mama," Toni says.

"What?" I ask.

She pulls a thin light blue ribbon from her pocket. It can't be more than six inches long. "You could maybe pin it somewhere."

"It doesn't match anything, Toni," I say.

"So?" Toni says.

I kneel in front of her. "Where'd you get that?"

"Joey gave it to me," Toni says. "He showed me this box that had a lot of little ribbons and pictures of his mommy and buttons and bookmarks. He said I could use it for my hair, but it's not long enough."

So, Joey, the quietest child, has a memory box. I have one, too, under my bed, and it's filled with all sorts of little things that remind me of Rodney: movie ticket stubs, Post-its with "I love you" or simply his handwriting, receipts from our rare dinners out, his dog tags, some old pictures, a tie tack or two. I don't think I could ever give these memories away, but here's Joey giving Toni a memory of his mama. I connect with Rose's eyes, and she nods. She understands what Joey has done.

I take the ribbon. "I am going to wear this ribbon on my finger," I say. I tie it hastily to where my engagement ring used to be. I look at that ribbon as if it's purest gold. "Stylish, isn't it?"

Toni smiles.

"Now all I need is to borrow something," I say, and I look directly at Rose.

"I, um, I have a large collection of garters."

I try not to react, but most girls—most women, for that matter—do not have even a *small* collection of garters. "You do?" I ask.

"All colors," she says.

That surprises me, too, because I thought any garter she had would be black.

"You'll be wearing a slip," Rose says, "so even, say, a dark color won't show."

I have to ask the obvious question. "Um, and you only want me to borrow it, right?"

"Of course," Rose says, as if borrowing is the only thing you *can* do with garters.

"But I'm supposed to throw it to the eligible males at the reception, aren't I?"

Rose smiles. "You'll just wear two. One you'll throw, and one you'll return to me after the honeymoon."

This is twisted.

"I mean," Rose says, "I'll need it for *my* wedding one day."

And then I almost start to cry. In the space of fifteen minutes, the three of us have created a tradition, a new family tradition just for the girls. While each of the girls may not wear my wedding dress, each one will wear this blue ribbon. And while the thought kind of creeps me out, each one of my girls will wear two garters.

"Rose, I would be happy to wear one of your garters," I say. "You decide the color. Now, we need to get back to my party."

It isn't much of a party, really. We're just sitting around in a mostly empty apartment playing cards. I had invited all the ladies from McDonald's, but they all either had to work or had dates. I invited Rema, but she had to work overtime. I invited several ladies from Pilgrim, but they told me they were too busy cooking and preparing the fellowship hall for the reception.

Rose, Toni, and I walk into the kitchen where a bid whist game rages, all eyes on Elle. Earlier in the day, my mama had taught Elle the rudiments of the game, and Elle had picked them up quickly.

Elle throws down her last card. "Didn't think I could do it, did you?"

And now she's talking stuff, too?

Mama smiles and yells, "Next!"

Cousins Tina and Joetta, the only two cousins who could come up from Atlanta, don't move.

"Ten in a row," Elle says. "We are on fire! Who's next, who's next?"

"*We* are, for the tenth time," Tina says. "Now deal."

Elle beams up at me. "I just like saying that *so* much!"

"Listen, y'all," I say, "I am dead tired, so I'm turning in early. Don't be too loud, okay?"

I hit my bed and stare up at the ceiling, thinking of Joe, my daddy, Cousin Boo, and the boys, who are fishing down at Smith Mountain Lake. I'll bet they're catching lots of fish.

Hmm. They will all probably smell fishy at the wedding to-morrow.

It's going to be a pretty small wedding. Folks from Joe's work and my work will be coming. Folks from Pilgrim will be coming. And, of course, there are bound to be people that just show up, maybe by accident, going to the wrong wedding and just sticking around for the reception. I doubt I'll even look out at the pews, anyway. My eyes will be on Joe.

I roll off the bed and take out my memory box, a box that a can opener had come in a long time ago. It was probably a wedding gift. Inside I see Rodney's high school graduation picture, a couple wedding pictures, Rodney's high school class ring, and some other bits and pieces of Rodney I collected from our house after he died. I hold up the most recent picture of Rodney. He is standing in the second row of a team picture surrounded by six- and seven-year-old football players. There's Junior in the first row. Rodney was just starting his chemo then, but he wouldn't give up coaching his son.

"Hey, Boo," I whisper to the man in the back row. "You coming to the wedding? I know you'll be there. I still miss you, but I had to move on. I hope you understand. God blessed me with you, and He's blessing me again in spite of myself. I'm not about to argue with Him. God is good, God is great." Normally, I'd kiss the picture, but tonight . . . I don't feel the need.

I close my eyes, hearing Rodney's voice say, "There is much sense in what you say."

Good night, Rodney.

67

Joe

If Dad and Shawna's dad had their way, we'd be having a fish fry at the wedding reception. The seven of us caught enough bass and catfish to feed an army, Cousin Boo catching a nine-pound catfish from shore while we were just loading up the pontoon boat we rented for the day.

"We can't take this many fish back to Roanoke," I said, looking at *seven* stringers filled with fish, fish we caught in just two hours in front of a dam as the sun set.

So we had a midnight fish fry right there at a picnic pavilion. No bread, no potatoes, no corn, no salad—just fish.

I barely fit into my tux today.

These past few weeks, though, have been brutal enough that I've lost some weight. I don't see how Shawna has kept her sanity. I have been sick with worry and anticipation while she has somehow maintained her poise and sense of humor. I had to pick up her ring, which was supposed to have been resized five days ago, but was ready only two hours ago. Jimmy's shoes, which fit three weeks ago, don't fit today unless he goes sockless. Dad is supposed to be back any time now with a larger pair. I cut myself shaving again. I can't remember my vows, even though Junior and Joey have been helping me. I don't want to read from a piece of paper. I want it to seem natural and from the heart—which it is—but I can't get my heart slowed down enough to think clearly. I was worried that we'd be late to the church because of the boys, and here I am in the men's room at Pilgrim having trouble with the bow tie.

Lord, I need You.

Was I this nervous twenty years ago? I don't remember being nervous. Of course, back then, all I had to do was show up. I didn't have to house anyone or feed anyone extra or—

I'm getting married today. All that was yesterday. Today is what matters. Today is the—

"Are you ready, Joe?"

I turn to see Pastor Reed in his pastoral gown.

"Has the music started?"

I hear the organist beginning to play the prelude.

"You have a little time," Pastor Reed says. He reaches up and adjusts my tie. "That's better. We'll be waiting outside." He leaves the restroom.

I peel the piece of toilet paper from my chin, and it doesn't bleed again. Small miracle. After washing and drying my hands, I leave the restroom to wait with the boys in a small room near the front of the church. They don't look nervous at all. In fact, this is all just another good time for them.

As it should be. *Lord, help me relax.* I feel in my jacket pocket for the ring and the envelope. They're still there.

"You look great, Dad," Jimmy says.

"So do you," I say.

They all do, all spiffed up and creased. Mom is going to take lots of pictures of them today. It was so odd that both Shawna and I completely forgot about pictures, and we probably couldn't have gotten a wedding photographer on such short notice, anyway, but Mom has graciously accepted the job.

And now I have a job to do, one I have been stressing about for weeks.

I take the ring box from my jacket pocket. "Fellas," I say, looking at my shiny black shoes, "I've been doing a lot of thinking about who should, um, keep this ring safe until it's time for me to put it on Shawna's finger. All three of you are my best men, but only one of you can hold the ring for me." I look at Jimmy. "If we were having a fancy wedding, Jimmy, we'd have a little boy play ring bearer, but you're not a little boy anymore." I look at Junior. "You and your grand-dad are giving your mother away today, which is a great honor, so . . ." I hand the ring box to Joey. "Joey, I'd like you to hold the ring."

Joey takes the box. "Thank you."

"Now," I say with a sigh, "I am really nervous, so stay close to me. If you see me start to sway, catch me."

Pastor Reed sticks his head into the room. "Let's get married," he says.

I lead the boys out into the sanctuary, paying careful attention to putting one foot in front of the other, hoping I don't step on the backs of Pastor Reed's shoes. Pastor Reed stops, and we turn to face the audience . . .

There isn't a single empty seat.

Wow. Where did they all come from?

The "Wedding March" begins, and the audience stands. The girls walk in, Toni first, Rose second, Crystal third.

Wow. I have some beautiful daughters.

And when they get to us, each one of them kisses me on the cheek, even Crystal.

And now I'm about to cry at my own wedding.

Then I see Shawna and her dad . . .

Wow.

Breathe.

She's . . . wow.

I am lost in this woman's beauty. *God, thank You, thank You.*

And then things get a little hazy, except for Shawna's face and a little blue ribbon on her finger. What's that about? But I can't take my eyes off her eyes! Pastor Reed could be reading the entire book of Genesis right now, and I wouldn't know it. And then I'm suddenly taking her hand and it's sweaty, too, and I'm facing her, and it feels like heaven—

"Joe," Shawna whispers.

I blink.

"Your vows," Pastor Reed whispers.

Where am I? Oh, yes. I'm at my wedding. I clear my throat, and without even really thinking too hard, I say, *"Napenda kukuona mpenzi wangu ni furaha ya moyo wangu."*

Shawna smiles.

I love that smile. I want to see her smile like that always. Such peace that smile brings me. But now her eyes are narrowing. She's saying something like "the translation, Joe" through her teeth.

"Oh," I say. "It means . . ."

What does it mean?

How can I remember the Swahili and forget the English? I turn to Junior for help.

He steps closer and whispers, "'I love to see you, my dear.'"

Now I remember. I squeeze his shoulder. "I remember."

Junior returns to his place beside Joey.

I take a deep breath. "Sorry," I say, and it's then that I notice my voice bouncing around the sanctuary. There's a microphone here? Oh, yes. There it is in Pastor Reed's hands. I look at the audience. "I'm, um, sorry, y'all. I, uh, I just started looking at Shawna and was thinking how beautiful she is, and I forgot where I was."

She squeezes my hand and begins to tear up.

"I love to see you, my dear," I say. "You are the joy of my heart."

68

Shawna

Itold everyone I would be too happy to cry, and here I am crying!

Joe lifts my veil and wipes away a tear. And, oh, the audience is eating this stuff up. I even hear a few amens among the ahs.

"You have brought me joy, Shawna," Joe continues, "joy I didn't know existed. I promise to bring you joy for as long as we live. I love you."

Whoo. It's my turn.

"Joe . . ." I had this all planned out, I swear, but I can't say all that about love and cherish and hold on to each other now like at a typical wedding because we are not a typical couple, nor will we have a typical family. This has to be from my heart.

So . . . I wing it.

"Joe . . . Well, here we are."

I have no idea what I'm doing.

"I never expected to be here."

I have no idea what I'm saying.

"I never thought . . ." More tears. "I never thought I'd find another man to love me." I wipe away a tear. "Sorry."

"I love you," Joe says through a few tears of his own.

"I love you, too," I say.

Oh, now we're making folks in the sanctuary cry, too, lots of sniffling and men clearing their throats.

"Sorry, y'all," I say to them. "God has just been *that* good."

After some resounding amens, I look at my children, all six of them.

"God brought us all together," I say, "and though I don't know what's going to happen, whatever happens, Joe, I want it to be with you."

"Are you . . . finished?" Pastor Read asks.

I laugh. "I sure hope not. Joe and I are just getting started."

And then, at my second wedding in front of more people than were at my first wedding, I hear laughter, glorious, glorious laughter. In fact, I'm still giggling when Joey hands the ring to Joe and he slides it on top of the blue ribbon, I'm still giggling when I slide Joe's ring on, and I'm still giggling when I lay quite a tongue-twisting soul kiss on my man to seal the deal for all eternity.

"I now present to you, Mr. and Mrs. Joe and Shawna Murphy," Pastor Reed says.

And don't you know, we get us a standing ovation, and instead of just Joe and I walking down that aisle, all eight of us do a little marching, Elle snapping lots of pictures—and giggling a little herself.

It is *thick* at the reception, so thick I wonder if they'll be able to seat and feed everybody. Though Crystal thought— and probably still thinks—that having a variety of sheet cakes instead of a wedding cake is tacky, no one else seems to mind. We have all the bases covered, too, so no one can say no. We've got red velvet cake with white icing, yellow cake with chocolate icing, white cake with white icing, and carrot cake with sweet cream cheese icing. And the food selection is amazing. It seems as if every woman—and some men, too—at Pilgrim have brought a dish. I have to use two plates to contain it all, but I don't get a chance to do much eating, what with so many people to greet and hug—and a new husband to kiss.

"Mama," Toni tells me, "there are *so* many gifts on that table upstairs. Lots of envelopes, too."

Joe nearly falls out of his chair. "Oh, no."

"What's wrong?"

"Um, nothing." He reaches into his jacket and pulls out an envelope. He peeks inside and widens his eyes. "We have to go."

"Huh? Now?"

"Yes," he says.

I cover up Toni's ears with my hands. "I'm feeling pretty horny, too, but we can't just leave all these people."

Toni swats my hands away. "Mama, please."

Kaz comes up to our table. "It's here."

"What's here?" I ask.

Joe takes my hand, pulling me to my feet. "We don't want to be late."

"For what?" I ask. "I have to throw the bouquet, and you have to feel up my leg, man."

"Huh?" Toni asks.

Oops. I turn to her. "He has to take the garter off my leg."

"Oh," Toni says.

I turn to Joe. "And we still have to go back to the house, change our clothes, and pack the van."

"There's no time for that," Joe says. He looks out onto the crowd. "Your attention, please! May I please have your attention!"

I turn to Toni. "Do you know what's going on?"

She shrugs.

The crowd a little quieter, Joe says, "Shawna and I have to leave now, but we want you to stay and enjoy yourselves. Let's give all the cooks a big hand!"

And while the people clap, Joe tries to drag me away and out of the church.

"No," I say as I drop his hand. "I am throwing this bouquet."

"Okay," he says. "Throw it."

"But they're not lined up!"

"Hand it to someone then, Shawna. We have to go now." He walks to a window. "Look."

I look outside and see a black limousine. "That envelope in your pocket. Are there tickets in there?"

He nods.

"We're flying?"

"Only if we get there in time."

I tap Mary Simpson, a fortysomething single woman, who has been in the singles adult Sunday School class since the class began twenty years ago. "Mary, catch this bouquet."

She catches it. "Thank you, Shawna." She then tries to hug me.

"No offense, Mary, but I got to go." I hike up my dress right there at Pilgrim. "Get the garter quick, Joe."

Joe drops to his knees. "Which one?"

"Either, it doesn't matter."

I don't even feel the garter leaving me. Joe stands there holding it as I let down my dress.

"Well, give it to somebody, Joe."

"Who should I—"

I snatch the garter and hand it to Mary. "Girl, you take this and give it to the man you want. I got to *go*."

I didn't know I could run so fast in a wedding dress. As soon as we get into the limo, it takes off, and Joe shows me the tickets.

"We're really flying," I say. "But I thought you said—"

He kisses me. "I wanted to surprise you. You know how hard it is to surprise you with six kids snooping around? We'll fly to Pittsburgh, switch planes, land in Toronto, and drive up the rest of the way in a rental car."

Joe has been busy. "But . . . but what about our bags?"

"They're in the trunk."

I relax a little. "All of them?"

He kisses me more passionately this time.

I push him back. "*All* of them?"

"Uh, no. Just, uh, just what I thought we'd need."

I look at my dress. "I have to change, Joe. *We* have to change."

"No time," he says.

When we get to the airport, Joe takes *one* carry-on bag out of the trunk, hustling me to the ticket counter, my dress flowing all around me.

"There can't be enough in that bag for both of us!" I shout, but Joe isn't hearing me, checking us in and rushing us up the stairs to the main terminal.

"Our plane is boarding," he says, and we run.

And as we run, I see smiles and smiles and more smiles from everyone we fly by. If I weren't so upset about the bag, I might enjoy all these smiles. Joe hands our boarding passes to the attendant, and we dash down the little tunnel and enter the plane. I am sweating from the top of my new hair down to my shoes. We find our seats and sit.

And the folks on the plane start clapping for us, saying, "Congratulations!"

Joe hands me the bag. "Look inside."

I unzip the main compartment, see some silky some-things, and zip it back up. "Who packed this?"

"Crystal," he says.

I unzip it a tiny bit and peek again. "There isn't much in here, Joe."

"I know. Are you mad?"

How can I be mad at a time like this? I'm flying, not driving eight hundred miles in a van. I'm excited about the night to come. I'm still getting congratulations from people who don't even know me, a few even taking our pictures.

"The only thing I'm mad about," I whisper, "is that I'm still in this dress. You said I would only be wearing it for a few hours."

"You might as well get some use out of it, Mrs. Murphy, because this is the last time you'll ever need to wear it."

Flying, even with another mad dash in Pittsburgh to another plane, is wonderful. I get to hold Joe's hand, I get to whisper sweet nothings to him without a child overhearing, and I get to be beautiful for a little bit longer.

Customs in Toronto is fairly smooth, our rental car is ready, and we're speeding to the lake up some nice, flat roads, stars twinkling overhead. Despite my excitement (and some unholy anticipation—*sorry, Lord*), I fall asleep on the ride.

Joe wakes me gently, and instead of being at the Landing, we've parked right behind Murphy's Unlimited, the shed and the outhouse barely visible in the darkness.

"It's so quiet," I say.

All we hear are the waves lapping on the shore and our footsteps as we search out a place to sleep. We have our pick of any room in the house, but Joe guides me upstairs to the bed I slept in so well before, my dress rustling on the wooden steps and floor.

We stand at the foot of the bed, the carry-on dropped to the floor.

More silence, though my heart is making lots of noise.

"It's been eight years for me, Joe," I say.

"Three for me," he says.

I didn't know that. Cheryl must have been sick a long time. "We don't have to tonight . . . if you don't want to."

He hugs me. "I was about to say the same thing to you. I'm so nervous."

"Me, too."

For the past eight months, I have lusted after this man, and now I don't know what to do!

"Have you ever slept with a man in a tux?" he asks.

"Am I wearing the tux or is he?"

"I meant . . ."

I swat him on the butt. I can do that now since I'm his wife. "I know what you meant. No. Have you ever slept with a wedding dress–wearing woman?"

"No."

"So why don't we . . ."

And that's what we do on our first night together. We lie together in that bed wearing our wedding finest, watching the sun come up over a crystal-clear lake, snuggling and snoozing. So many colors . . . so many beautiful colors . . .

But later, I wake up alone and smell smoke.

"Joe?"

I hear Joe on the stairs. "Good morning."

I gather the covers around me. "It's cold."

He's still wearing his tux. "The temperature's dropped, so I made us a fire."

I throw off the covers and walk on my knees across that bed. "Is it going to be hot down there?"

"Yes."

"Then I won't need this." I take off the dress, leaving me only with my Victoria's Secret bra, some matching panties, and the other garter. "We may need a quilt or something."

Joe removes his jacket and starts working on his shirt buttons. "I'll keep you warm."

I help him with those buttons.

"Won't we need a quilt because of the windows?" I don't

want people walking by to see us, since I have a feeling we're going to attack each other.

He kisses me, running his hands down my back. "They're boarded up for the winter."

"So there's no view?"

He picks me up, one arm securely under my thighs. "I can take one or two down later . . ."

Eight years I have waited for this moment, even when I didn't know I was waiting for this precise moment, this bliss. A roaring fire, a passionate man, my body still remembering what to do and how to move, his body performing so well, our eyes sharing tears, our mouths sighs, our skin glowing, and me eventually wearing nothing but that garter.

I cannot possibly give that garter back to Rose now. The things it has seen!

But our lovemaking is holy. It is the way it should be. I am Eve, and he is Adam, and we are alone in The Garden of Eden North . . . and it is *good*. And not just the lovemaking. It is *all* good. The timing. The place. The man. The season. Maybe Ecclesiastes 3:1 isn't so morbid after all. There *is* a time, and a place, and a season for everything.

And if we keep this up, all the clothes in that carry-on are going back to Roanoke clean.

69

Joe

"You think we made us a baby?" I ask.

"I hope so," she says.

God, she is so beautiful. We haven't left this spot beside the fire in at least five hours.

"Boy or girl?" she asks.

"Triplets will give us a baseball team," I say.

She grabs my butt. "And triplets will give me a hernia. Boy or girl?"

"Girl."

Shawna pouts. "I wanted a boy."

"Twins, then. One of each."

"Oh, all right." She slides on top of me, resting her elbows on my chest. "We have to name them. The girl first."

"How about . . . Joshawna Elle."

She blinks. "Joshawna?"

"Joshawna."

She squints, looks up at the ceiling, wiggles her lips . . . "Not bad. Joshawna is okay."

"What's our boy's name?" I ask.

"Shawn Joseph," she says immediately.

"I like it."

She crawls even higher, putting her head on my shoulder. "Maybe we can name her or him Shawnjo Kazuby."

I laugh. "Really? It sounds African and Polish."

"It's a nice blend of cultures, right?"

I nod. "I like the way we, um, blend."

She sighs. "Me, too. I was so nervous that I'd forget what to do."

"Just like riding a bicycle."

She plucks my ear with a finger. "No, it isn't."

"No, not exactly. Generally speaking, when you ride a bicycle, you put on the brakes a lot. We, um, we haven't put on any brakes."

She kisses my ear. "Sorry for plucking you."

"I'm, um, I'm ready to go on another little trip if you are."

She rolls off me and lies on her back. *"Embe mbivu yaliwa kwa uvumilivu."*

"I'll take that as a yes." I move over top of her. "What did you just say?"

"'A ripe mango has to be eaten slowly.'"

Whoa. "Are you, um, ripe?"

She nods and pulls me closer. "Ripe and ready. Let's make us a baby for real. . . ."

70

Shawna

We *had* to have made a baby.

It is peak time for me, just before my period. It is definitely a peak time for Joe fishing inside me, and I'm not leaving this fireside until I've had my limit. My body's saying, "Pull up anchor and get back to sleep!" But my mind just can't get enough of this man.

That's when I hear chainsaws buzzing outside.

Close to the house.

As in out on the deck on the other side of the boarded windows.

And banging metal.

And hoots and shouts.

Not a good thing to happen when you're wearing nothing but a garter.

"Joe, what's going on?"

Joe sits up, and he smiles! How can he be smiling at a time like this?

"Oh, my goodness," he says. He wraps himself up with a blanket and goes to the window, looking through a thin sliver of light between the boards. He turns to me, laughing. "We're having a shivery."

"A what?"

"We need to get dressed. You need to put on a pot of hot water and get some teacups ready."

"What for?"

The racket outside gets louder.

"It's a shivery. It's a tradition up here. The men are going to take me away from you while the ladies console you and sip some tea."

"You're kidding."

"I've only seen it done once, so I'm sure there's more to it. I know I won't be gone long."

"A shivering?"

"A shivery."

I'm already feeling cold, and I'm sure that racket out there is waking up the entire lake.

"I better tell them we're getting ready," he says.

I throw off the blanket. "Joe, I look a mess!"

"No, you don't." And then he stares hard at my body, making me kind of shy all of a sudden. I wrap myself in a quilt that will one day wrap our grandchildren and great-grandchildren and follow him into the kitchen.

"Mom knew this was going to happen," he says. "Look."

Elle certainly has it all ready for me. On the counter rests a large silver tea set complete with a bowl of sugar and packages of Sweet'n Low. All I have to do is boil water and add some Red Rose tea. Joe unhooks the window over the kitchen sink, pulling it up and latching it in place. He knocks on the boards covering the window, and the chain-saw stops.

"I'll be out in a few minutes!" he yells. He kisses me, and I almost drop the quilt. "Can you do without me for a few hours?"

"Hours?"

"Honestly, Shawna, I don't know how long this thing lasts."

That's comforting. "Do I at least have time to take a shower?"

The chainsaw roars to life again.

"I'll take that as a no," I say. These Canadian women and their need for tea!

I rush around to put on deodorant, perfume, layers of clothes—anything to mask our lovemaking. I spray air freshener around the fireplace and the kitchen.

Joe goes out the door we came in, and I see a group of . . . *old* men and women, *ancient* old men and women, older than Kaz and Elle, even. They help him take off the boards from the picture windows, the screened porch, and the door to the deck while I boil some water and ready the Red Rose. Joe gives me a kiss, I open the door to the deck from the inside, and the ladies troop in to the screened porch, all of them smiling ear to ear.

Oh, joy. They know *exactly* what we've been doing. Are we supposed to talk about it or what?

The men push and prod Joe down the deck stairs to the dock and a barge of a boat. They all get in and motor off, leaving me with six ladies pushing ninety. I carry the platter to the table and pass out the teacups.

"So this is a shivery," I say.

Six nods, smiles so broad their wrinkles are disappearing. Ah, I get it. This is to make *these* women feel younger for all the memories of *their* honeymoons.

After they introduce themselves to me, I have to know. "Were you, um, outside very long?"

"No," Opal says.

"Not too long," Helen says.

"Maybe ten minutes," Bet, short for Betsy, says.

I am so embarrassed!

Mary Anne smiles. "You look absolutely radiant."

It's the sweat from our lovemaking mixed with the anxiety this shivery is causing. "Thank you," I say.

And then . . . these ancient ladies get ancient with me, telling me stories about the lake from *way* back in the day.

"Remember Gordon?" Joan asks Joyce.

"Do I ever!" Joyce says. "He was once a beau of mine."

Helen leans forward. "Back when the train was still coming to Aylen on the Opeongo Line."

"But," Bet says, "didn't Gordon fall in love with that Indian girl?"

"Oh," Joyce says, "he wasn't in love with her. Just smitten. That brother of hers wouldn't let their romance blossom, remember?"

Eventually, through their many voices, I hear the story of Gordon Frazier and the Indian girl at the Lodge, where lumbermen would live and eat while working the forests around Aylen Lake. It isn't a very long story, since both Gordon and the girl disappeared a long time ago.

"Some say," Bet says, "that Gordon is at the bottom of the lake still wearing that tool belt of his. They say that he got drunk—he *was* a heavy drinker—they say he got drunk and stepped off his boat thinking it was his dock and sank to the bottom."

This gives me yet another reason not to swim in Aylen Lake.

"Oh, I don't know about that," Opal says. "I've always hoped that they ran away with each other and found true happiness somewhere."

I hate to interrupt, but . . . "Um, when will they bring Joe back to me?"

"You miss him already?" Helen asks.

"Yes."

Mary Anne nods. "That's the whole point of a shivery, dear. Just when you and your husband have"—she looks around the table—"consummated your marriage . . ."

"Made whoopee," Helen says, twitters floating all around.

"Yes," Mary Anne says. "But you don't have to be so blunt, sister."

Helen and Mary Anne are sisters? Hmm. There is a slight resemblance. They do have an infinite number of wrinkles.

"What my old-fashioned sister is trying to say, Shawna," Helen says, "is that a shivery makes you want your man more. I was at one shivery that lasted four hours."

"A very bad sign, very bad," Opal says.

More twitters and cackles.

"I don't think those two *ever* had any children," Helen says.

Even more twitters and cackles.

"Well," I say, "I want my man back now."

Opal checks her watch. "Twenty minutes. You will have many children together."

I smile. "I already do."

Their eyes pop.

"I mean, I have three children from—"

"We know all about you, Shawna," Joan says. "We weren't born yesterday."

"What day was yesterday?" Joyce says with a smile. She pulls out a walkie-talkie. "Gene? Come in, Gene."

The walkie-talkie crackles, and I hear Gene's voice. "Who is this?"

"Who else would it be, old man?" Joyce says. "Your wife."

"Oh," Gene says.

"Where are you?" Joyce asks.

"Just past Houghton's Point," Gene says.

"They haven't gotten very far, Shawna," Helen says.

"Well, you can bring him back now," Joyce says.

"Will do," Gene says.

Joyce puts away her walkie-talkie. "It'll be twenty minutes at least."

I can wait that long. "More tea?"

Then we sip tea and smile for twenty minutes. When we hear the barge approach, we get up and go down to the dock to greet them, the sun almost completely set, the Northern Lights appearing as a ribbon in the sky. It's strange, but it's as if the men are bringing the conquering hero home to his bride. It's sweet, and in a way, we have just become bonded to all these people—although I doubt I'll remember any of their names tomorrow. I'm sure they're related to Joe in some way. It's another village taking care of its own. Not the way I wanted to spend an hour on my honeymoon, but just seeing Joe again after this little separation makes me want him so much more.

"Normally," one old man says, "we'd carry Joe up to you, but . . ."

Joe gets out, helping the ladies onto the barge.

"God bless your marriage, Joe and Shawna," Joyce says.

Joe puts his arm around me. "Thank you. Thank you all for coming."

As the barge backs out and moves away, I turn to Joe. "I want you now."

"Here?"

I look into the water. "Is that rock bass still under the dock?"

"I doubt it."

Oh, Lord, I can't believe I'm about to do this. It's dark enough. "Joe, have you ever made love in this lake?"

"No."

I'm shivering already. "Then let's do this now before I lose my nerve."

We strip, Joe diving in immediately, me holding myself and shivering at the end of the dock. "Is it cold?"

He grits his teeth. "Yes. Hurry."

Oh, Lord, oh, Lord! I jump in feet first, and every pore of my body slams shut in a millisecond. Joe swims to me, and I latch on to him.

"You'll have to be quick, okay?" I ask, teeth chattering.

"I'll try."

At first, all I think about is the cold and the icy fingers of water surrounding me. But after a minute . . . then another . . . then several more, I don't feel anything but Joe's love for me . . . And after that, I make Joe go get us some towels and soap so I can take my first bath in Aylen Lake. I soap him, he soaps me, we rinse each other off . . .

It's as if I've been baptized again.

Much later (and much warmer) in front of the fire, my head resting on Joe's chest, I think about those old men and women, who are still together after all those years, fifty, maybe even sixty years. There's something about the water in Aylen Lake, all right. Something holy.

I'll bet God takes baths up here on His vacations, too.

71

Joe

My parents told me they played Monopoly on their wedding night, Mom winning and Dad stewing . . . and they've lasted forty-six years.

Shawna and I haven't even opened a single pack of cards.

I wonder how long we'll last . . .

We watch every sunset and a few sunrises, the ones we're awake for. We cruise the lake in the *Charlenor*. We bathe. We cook simple meals for two. We even take the rental car down a dirt road to the west end of Aylen, parking and hiking to Wilkins Lake. So many colors. Just the two of us walking hand in hand through the woods, Shawna worrying about wolves and bears. We find moose tracks, collect more huge pinecones for our own fireplace mantel back in Roanoke, holding each other as if we're the only two people in the world. And standing on the shoreline of Wilkins Lake, the mountains and rocks perfectly mirrored in the lake, we *are* the only two people on earth.

"What are you thinking about?" Shawna asks.

"Just you."

I get a kiss for that one.

"This place cleanses the soul, Joe," she says, huddling closer to me. "We will come up every year, even if it's just the two of us." She laughs. "*Especially* if it's just the two of us."

I rub her stomach. "Which won't happen for eighteen years or more, right?"

"Maybe."

What were we thinking? Shawna is convinced she's pregnant, and I don't doubt her. She says her body is sending her messages that there's a child inside her waiting to be born. And all this thinking about Shawn Joe (or Joshawna) gets me thinking once again about my parents taking care of six kids back in Roanoke.

"Do you think the kids miss us?" I ask.

"I hope they do." She turns to me, draping her arms around my neck. "You have given me a whole new set of memories, Joe Murphy. Thank you."

"Same here, Shawna Murphy. Thanks."

She buries a cold nose into my neck. "Do we have to go back? I want to make some more memories."

"I wish we could stay here forever."

"Me, too. I'm going to be so sad to leave."

I hold her tightly, kissing her soft ears. "But another adventure awaits," I whisper.

"I know." She takes my hands, and we swing them together like teenaged lovers. "Um, when we get back I'll, uh, buy a test to make sure that I'm pregnant, but how should we break it to the kids? A family meeting?"

I blink rapidly. "Those don't always go over so well."

"Maybe the two of us can run one just fine," she says.

"It might cause some pain, but it will get feelings out in the open."

She smiles. "You remember that?"

"I remember everything about you," I say. "I think I have every square inch of your body mapped."

"No, you haven't. There are a few places I want you to visit tonight."

Yes! "We better get back, then."

We walk through the woods again, and this time Shawna doesn't jump at every stump. "Okay," she says, "who'll be the happiest about the new baby?"

I think a moment. "Toni. She won't be the baby anymore."

"That's what I was thinking, too. And she'll have a little sister or brother to boss around." She stops and bumps her forehead against my chest. "But Crystal is going to have a problem with it."

"Maybe she'll surprise us," I say. And I hope I'm right.

"I know her. She's going to have a problem with it because she *can*."

72

Shawna

And baby makes seven.

Or more, if Joe and the ladies at the shivery are right. I hope he isn't, but if it's God's will . . .

God will just have to help me take care of them.

At least I'll have several babysitters—who I don't have to pay—to choose from so Joe and I can go out once in a blue moon.

If the tester in my hand is correct . . . it's official. I am about to become a twice-married mother of four and stepmother to three. A positive test. Hmm. *Lord, You obviously want this child to join us, but I was just getting back into the swing of things in bed with Joe.* Now I'm going to balloon up and not be as desirable. Joe assures me that we will always be able to, um, cook. We'll just have to turn out all the lights after the fifth month.

I go immediately into our bedroom and begin nesting, moving furniture around to make room for a crib. Joe, the pack rat, has already located Jimmy's crib in the basement, saying that it will need a little work. He wants to bring it upstairs and let the kids discover the news on their own—the man *really* doesn't like family meetings—but I don't want that. We have to treat them like the little adults that they are. But we'll feed them first. Maybe happy stomachs will give them happy thoughts.

At our first *full* family meeting after more magic meatloaf than I have ever cooked before (I may have to start calling it a "magic meat-log"), we sit around the kitchen table on benches Kaz found at a yard sale. They are almost identical to the ones up on the screened porch at Aylen. But we're not having the family meeting yet because we're waiting for Crystal to get off work.

Since I hate to waste any time, especially when the kitchen needs work—and it always needs work—I point at the chore list, one *I* made and intend for them to keep.

"But we're having a family—" Jimmy starts to say, but I stop him with a stare. "Okay, okay."

"Go," I say, and I watch them do what I taught them yesterday, my first full day back from Canada—and my first full day as their mama.

The dirty dishes already stacked in the left sink, Rose puts in the drain plug, turns on the hot water, and pours in the dish soap. Junior uses the dishrag to wipe off the counters before laying out five dish towels. As soon as Rose washes an item, Junior will rinse it, laying it on those towels. We will have no broken glass or plates in this house. Joey will dry them while Jimmy sweeps the floor and Toni wipes off the table.

"Uh-uh, Jimmy," I say, pointing to his feet. "Take 'em off."

Jimmy looks at Joe for help, but he's not going to get any. Jimmy takes off his shoes.

"And the socks," I say. You cannot properly sweep a kitchen floor with shoes or socks on. You have to be able to feel the crumbs.

We watch the assembly line cranking along, when the doorbell rings.

"I wish she'd just come in," Joe says. "It's her house, too."

Joe answers the door, and Crystal moves in, looking so tired.

"You look beat," I say.

She sits at the table, little circles under her eyes. "The Christmas season has begun."

And it's barely October. Those stores should be ashamed of themselves.

Crystal watches her siblings making my kitchen spotless enough to pass a health inspection. "I got here at the right time," she says.

"You could help Joey put some of the dishes away," Junior suggests.

"It's okay," I say. "She's a working girl. She's had a long day." And I want her in as good a mood as possible for our news.

After I check thoroughly for the least speck of crumb and the tiniest drip of goo, I pronounce the kitchen "acceptable."

I don't want to build them up too much. They actually do a fantastic job. Having more kids comes in handy sometimes.

"Ladies and gentlemen," Joe says to start the meeting, "we have an announcement. We are going to have a new addition to the house."

"We're building onto the house?" Jimmy asks.

"Another bedroom?" Rose asks.

"A game room?" Junior asks.

We should have scripted this. "By 'addition,' your father means . . . another child."

Silence.

Joe told me about the mantel clock, and it's clicking loud and clear right now.

"I am pregnant," I say with a smile, "and I am due in June."

More silence. A second ago they couldn't shut up.

"So," I say, "what do y'all think about that?" I hear Crystal panting and turn toward her. "Crystal, do you have something to say?"

"Did you *mean* to?" Crystal asks.

What a question! "Yes. We meant to."

"At your age?" Crystal asks.

Two mean questions in a row! "Girl, I'm not yet forty. Plenty of women are having children at my age."

"But the complications increase the older you get," Crystal says.

I look at the rest of the kids, who obviously don't know what to say. "Then y'all will just have to take extraspecial care of me, okay?"

"I'll help you, Mommy," Toni says.

"Thanks, sweetie," I say. I can always count on Toni.

"But how," Crystal asks, "how can you all even afford to have another baby?"

This is the ultimate unanswered question. I look to Joe for help.

"Yes, it's going to be tight, but it won't be crowded," Joe says, not even addressing Crystal's question. "The baby will stay with us in our room."

"That's not what I asked you," Crystal says.

Joe sighs. "As for our financial situation, it's going to be a little different for a while."

"How different?" Rose asks.

Uh-oh. *Two* children are fussing with Joe, but at least Rose had modified her Goth look since her return, wearing jeans with dark T-shirts and those red ballet slippers.

"Well, Shawna and I are going to level with you," Joe says. "We've decided that there will be no secrets in this house, especially when it comes to finances."

I am *totally* against this. I don't believe children should have to know all the gory financial details. Joe, though, was raised a lot differently. "I want you two to know the worst so you can behave your best," Kaz had told him and his brother when they were old enough to understand money. In a way, I guess, that's good, because Joe is a financial whiz—except for his credit cards. I have one I use only for emergencies, and somehow he keeps four maxed out. As a concession to me, we are going to spare the kids the credit card debt, because at the present rate of repayment (we're only paying the minimums), we'll be paying on those cards for about forty years.

Joe pulls out a piece of paper listing most of our assets and liabilities. It was so scary making that list because the assets are so few and the liabilities so many, especially with Junior and Rose going off to college this time next year and Joey following the year after with, hopefully, Crystal going to Virginia Western or a college or university someday . . . Four kids in college at the *same* time.

I am praying that someone goes into the military! But actually, with what's happening in the world, particularly the Middle East, I don't want that at all.

"First, the good news," Joe says.

I am against this order, too. Why not *end* the meeting with the good news?

"We've paid off the van and Joey's and Junior's orthodontist bills," Joe says.

They have perfect teeth now, but we're still paying on them. I'm lucky Crystal's teeth were fine, but Toni's are starting to scare me, one tooth seeming to grow behind the other.

"Both Shawna and I make enough to meet most of our long-term bills and debts, and we should get a nice tax refund this spring."

How nice, we're not sure, but it has to be a chunk of change with all these kids.

"On the other hand," Joe says, shifting in his seat, "we have college funds to contribute to including the baby's." He pauses for anyone to argue. No one does. "Everyone here is going to college. Everyone."

And Joe said it just like Rodney had to me all those years ago. Maybe there's a "go-to-college" gene in all good men.

"We have a mortgage on this house," he says. "We may have to refinance that mortgage to make sure we meet all our ends."

I am checking offers daily online. It's all so confusing that even Joe scratches his head.

"And as you know," he says with a sigh, "we will have five drivers to cover under our insurance."

Luckily we don't have enough vehicles to go around, but I'm sure they'll be some fussing about who can drive and when. We've already upped the collision deductibles on the van and Crystal's Sentra. We will be doing a *lot* of praying while we drive.

"We don't have enough money for another vehicle right now," Joe says.

I watch Junior's and Joey's shoulders sag slightly. Rose just shakes her head.

"Our food bills," Joe continues, "have become legendary, despite our judicious use of coupons and finding all the sales."

We have to fill two carts every week just to feed them. I feel like a train conductor at Kroger and Food Lion.

"All of you are still growing—"

"I'm not," Rose interrupts.

I have to say something. "You two know what he means. Buying clothes for y'all is a backbreaker. Y'all are especially hard on shoes."

Joe takes a deep breath. "We are going to need your help to make it through."

More silence. The clock ticks.

"Um, Daddy, what do you mean by that?" Rose asks.

I sigh because this is the hardest part.

"We're going to need each of you to contribute in some way," Joe says.

Rose's eyes pop. "Dad, this is my senior year. Junior's, too. Are you saying that we'll have to get jobs?"

"And I have my own bills," Crystal says. "You can't expect me to set aside money for *this* house, too."

I can't believe this child, saying these things after we had just paid for her half of their September rent. So ungrateful.

"Just hear me out, okay?" Joe asks. "Sometimes contribution means other things, other more important things." Joe looks to me, but I look away because I can't soften any of this any easier than he can. "Here's the deal. We're all going to have to make some sacrifices to save every penny we can. Shawna and I will be working longer hours and taking fewer or no vacation days so we can both be off when the baby's born."

I am praying for no complications, too. I will have to work at least six days a week through the seventh month of this pregnancy, the eighth month if the Lord lets me.

"With us being away from the house so much," Joe says, "you all will have to cook for each other, clean for each other, do the laundry for each other, and take care of each other."

I glance at Crystal. She sure looks smug. Joe has just given her a list of all the things she *won't* have to do.

"From now on," I say, "if your shoes fit and aren't falling off your feet, you will wear them. No new shoes or clothing at least until Christmas. We can manage with whatever you have in your closets and drawers and hand-me-downs if necessary."

Oh, God, I hate saying this since I lived in hand-me-downs from my cousins for years.

"You boys share most of your clothes now as it is," Joe says, "so it shouldn't be a hardship."

The real hardship is washing and ironing them. We will have to do an average of two loads a day, everyone pitching in, but only Rose, Junior, and I are qualified—or allowed—to iron them. I plan to teach Joey in the hopes that Joey can teach his father. I tried up at Aylen and gave up after Joe put more wrinkles in a T-shirt than were there before.

"I can't believe this," Rose says.

"Yeah," Crystal adds, "didn't you two consider this before you got married?"

To be truthful . . . no. We knew it would be tight, but we didn't have all the numbers then. The numbers in front of us now are scary, and we have to do something to make them less scary.

"We knew it would be difficult at first," Joe says, "but if we all work together, it will work out."

"I want to help," Toni says.

I smile at her. "Thank you, Toni."

"Mama, how is she going to help?" Crystal asks.

"By trying not to grow," I say, and the boys laugh. The girls don't even move. "I'm kidding, Toni, but . . . Listen, like Crystal said, I am a bit old—just a bit, now—a *bit* old to have a baby. There may be complications, and I may not be able to work as long as I want to. And Joe and I both agree that if you older ones do decide to get jobs—"

"You mean," Rose interrupts, "that we don't *have* to get jobs?"

"No," I say, and Joe nods. "It's strictly voluntary. If you do get jobs, that money is yours to do whatever you want with it. Joe and I are going to provide the basic necessities. If you want to keep or get your own cell phones, for example, you'll have to earn the money to pay for them."

"Our contract with Verizon ends in December," Joe says, "and we do not intend to renew it."

And this will save us close to one *thousand* dollars a year for surplus phones and charges.

Rose is still mad. "How am I going to get any calls in this house? If I didn't have my own cell phone, I wouldn't get a single call."

That is so true. Joey has started talking to a nice Hispanic girl named Alexa, and Junior and Amina are still going strong. A little boy keeps calling Toni, too, though after the last time I talked to him, I doubt he'll be calling her back. I was, well, a little blunt, saying, "Don't call my daughter! She's only nine!" Jimmy is probably the only one who gets no calls, but as handsome as he's becoming, it won't be long.

"Rose, you are just going to have to find other ways to communicate." Joe smiles at me. "E-mail, for instance. There's a computer in each of your rooms, and you will all still have access to the Internet."

Joe, Junior, and Joey have rigged the whole house as a wireless network, so no matter where I am, I can get on the Internet, even in the kitchen. Don't ask me how it works. Joey tried to explain it to me, and he lost me when he said "cable modem," "wireless router," and "USB network adapter" in the same sentence.

"How can I make some money for the family?" Jimmy asks.

Jimmy is such a sweet boy. I hug him every day for no reason at all, and he hugs me back, despite the fact that students at his school tease him for having a black mama. At first, he would fight back with his fists. We've spent a few days together at home because of that. Now he fights back with smiles, using these very words on anyone who torments him: "You're . . . just . . . jealous."

It makes me proud to be his "black mama."

"You can help us by staying out of the hospital," Joe says. "All of you. Stay healthy."

"We want you kids to concentrate on your schoolwork," I say. "If you feel you can swing a job, even a weekend job, go on and do it. We're not making anybody get a job." I sit up a little taller since they've almost completely calmed down. "We just cannot waste a single penny until this baby is born."

"What about Christmas?" Rose asks.

There's that clock again. I'm worried about Christmas, too.

"What about it?" Joe asks.

"What will Christmas be like, Daddy?" Rose asks.

"It will be different, and that's all I can say," Joe says. "From now on, we will buy what we absolutely need, not want."

More ticking. I am beginning to hate that clock.

"So ask for a raise, Mama," Crystal says. "You've been working there long enough."

"Yeah, Daddy, ask for a raise," Rose says. "You worked all those Saturdays. That has to count for something."

We will be hinting at raises from now on, but we're not crazy enough to push it too hard. We need both jobs at our present salaries to make it through to June.

"Shawna and I aren't counting on raises any time soon," Joe says, "but we'll be asking, when the time's right."

"How big will the tax refund be?" Junior asks.

We have played with those numbers so much my head still hurts, running it all through a tax program on Joe's computer using last year's tax laws.

"It should be sizable enough to cover the new baby's arrival and *maybe* another vehicle," Joe says.

"Yes!" Rose whispers under her breath.

"I said *maybe,* Rose," Joe says.

"I know," Rose says.

"Babies are expensive, y'all," I add, and I stare down Crystal especially. I have a feeling that she and her thug man might be doing a little more than attending church with us.

And before she leaves for the night, she drops a huge bomb.

"Mama, I'm . . . I'm pregnant, too."

After I pick up my heart from the floor, I can only think to ask, "How far along are you?"

"I'll, um, I'll be a few weeks after you."

Good . . . grief. Mama and grandma within a few weeks of each other. *Lord, Your mysteries are indeed incredible to behold.* "Are you . . ." I can't think! "Are y'all thinking about getting married?"

She looks at her hands, and I see a tear fall. She shakes her head. "He, um, he wants no part of us."

"Move back home," I say.

"There's no room," she says.

"We'll make room. There's always room in a home. That's what makes a home a home. There's always room, Crystal. Come home."

She shakes her head. "I don't want to be here . . . pregnant like that. I'm too ashamed."

I can't fault her logic, but . . .

"And I want to see if I can make it on my own first, Mama. I mean, you've been on your own with three kids for eight years."

I hold her hands. "Girl, I haven't been on my own. I thought I was—at first—but then I realized that I needed other people. I have a good friend in Rema. A strong, caring church family. God. You."

She sets her jaw. "If you can do it, so can I."

So hard-hearted, this child. "Crystal, honey, please let me be your mother again. At least until the baby's born and you're on your feet again."

"But you'll have your own baby by then."

"So I'll take care of two. You and Junior are only a year apart. I've had practice."

She looks down. "I'll think about it." She closes her eyes. "So you're not mad at me?"

What a question! Of course I'm mad—at Tony, at her, at me for letting her leave. "I have to confess that I'm sad. You're not going to college like your daddy wanted you to, you're not living with us, and now . . . this. I'm just . . . sad." I sigh. "I am a bit ticked at Tony. I will definitely remind him of his duties as a father. He *will* be around to help you, I can guarantee you that."

"I don't want him around, Mama. This is my baby, not his."

My prayer list just got a whole lot longer. "Well, do you . . ." No. I can't ask that question.

"Do I what?"

Oh, well. "Do you want a boy or a girl?"

"Oh," she says with a slight smile, "definitely a boy. Girls are so much harder to raise."

And then . . . the tears come, and after a few moments, I don't know who's crying more. "All in God's hands and plans," I whisper. "All in God's hands and plans."

Lord, I don't pretend to understand Your will in all this, and I know I'm not supposed to lose my mind trying to figure it all out. Help me to accept this and go on.

And Lord, if you can bring my baby—and my future grandbaby—home, I'd really appreciate it.

73

Joe

The kids aren't grumbling (audibly), but I'm sure our financial situation is finally becoming real to them.

But since Shawna and I keep them so busy with chores, they don't have much time to grumble. There's always something to be done with the yard: planting fall grass where the summer sun has created little dust bowls where grass used to be, pruning trees, planting bulbs, weed-eating, even painting the playhouse and staining and sealing the deck. And the interior of the house needs constant attention since it seems to rain dust everywhere, collecting in corners, behind doors, and under beds. Our windows have never been cleaner, our wood floors never shinier.

The house is coming back to life again.

Shawna decided that she wouldn't make any major changes in décor right away, and for that I'm glad. It's her house as much as mine now, but she also realizes that my kids will be more at home if we don't change too much. We went through all the Canada pictures Mom sent down, choosing several nice family and action shots to enlarge, frame, and place over the fireplace mantel. "Shared memories," Shawna calls them, "for them to look at every day." Other than reorganizing all the shelves and drawers in the kitchen ("So I can find the doohickey I'm looking for," Shawna says), she has left Cheryl's kitchen as is. "I like it," she says. "Cheryl had good taste."

And our baby is coming to life, too. The ultrasound picture showed a little . . . something. We don't know if it's a boy or a girl, and the girls are lobbying for Joshawna to even up the balance of power in the family.

"We *have* to have another girl," Rose says.

"As if Joshawna will be able to vote," Junior says.

Yes, they've almost forgotten about Crystal. But in my mind, she's still a part of us, even if she isn't here. I catch Shawna spacing out during meals or as she watches the kids leave in the morning. I know she's thinking about Crystal.

I wish I could figure out how to get Crystal—and her unborn child—to come home to us. God will figure it out, I know, but I wish I could do something. And I also wish I could figure out how to have Christmas in style.

That's yet another miracle I'm praying for.

74

Shawna

While Joe wishes the weather would change for the worse so he could "meet more people by accident," I work as many shifts as I can. But that's taking its toll because I miss my kids. I'm working these hours to give them a Christmas to remember, but if I keep working sixty-hour weeks, they won't remember who I am and I might start forgetting their names.

"You have to slow down, Shawna," Joe says. "The Lord will provide. Wait on the Lord, right?"

Wait.

Right.

I look down at the scale I'm standing on. I've been waiting on *weight* to come, too, but I've been rushing around so much that I haven't gained but five pounds in the last month and only ten pounds overall. My doctor also says I need to slow down, take time to rest. And he doesn't come out and say it, but he's really telling me to fatten up for winter. I try to eat a lot, but I work it off so fast.

Of course, the doctor is responsible for giving me plenty

to worry about. "Older mothers-to-be," he tells me, "are generally in good health and have good health habits, but there is still a risk of high blood pressure, gestational diabetes, low birth weight, and Down syndrome." Add to this that 20 to 25 percent of pregnant women my age miscarry and many need a C-section, and I am flat-out hurried and worried.

"C'mon," I say to the scale, "give me at least a half pound more today."

The needle doesn't budge.

I come back to bed, snuggling up with Joe, who has been giving the calculator another workout. "No change," I say. "I'm going to give birth to a skinny baby, a skinny, *hungry* baby." I look at my little breasts. "I'm going to be in trouble."

"You'll be fine."

"I hope so. So, how do we stand?"

Joe holds up a spreadsheet. He prints out everything, when just a little notepad would do. He's just being thorough. "We'll have approximately . . . three hundred extra dollars . . . *total* . . . to spend on Christmas."

Only fifty dollars per child? My heart can't sink any lower. "That's not enough for a proper Christmas, Joe."

"I know." He sighs. "Our first Christmas together should be memorable, but not for what they *didn't* get." He shakes his head. "I guess we should take up one of those loan offers."

"At those high interest rates? Forget it." It is so weird that I am beginning to sound like Joe already. I never used to worry about money before—never. A loan would be a solution, and we could have a nice Christmas, but the entire time I'd be thinking about paying back that loan. Borrowing is like a wedding, but paying back is like a funeral.

He massages my back, and I relax a little. "My bonus will cover the loan."

I bury my head in the pillow for two reasons: one, because Joe gives a much better backrub if I lie flat, and, two, because Joe won't receive his Christmas bonus until early January. Why call it a Christmas bonus if you can't get it until after Christmas? Drivers in Roanoke are not wrecking enough to give us a happy holiday. Shame on them!

In the midst of my grief over what is looking like a lean Christmas, I go back into that bathroom later that night and cry. It's the first time I've wept since Rodney died. I feel so helpless. We keep a Bible in there for, um, longer visits, and I read a chapter or two once I've calmed down. I stumble when I read the verse "God loveth a cheerful giver."

But Lord, I pray, *we don't have much to give! How can I be cheerful when these children, who have pulled together and sacrificed and done without . . . so much . . . how can I be cheerful giving them a few little presents under the tree? That tree should be surrounded by gifts, even buried by them. Lord, provide a way. And while you're at it, Lord, I have three more requests. Please keep all those holiday catalogs from making it to our mailbox. They arrive by the ton and waste so much paper. You're a recycler, aren't you, Lord? The kids get the mail before I can, and by the time I get home, I walk into the house and see them reading those catalogs. Jimmy reads the Eastbay catalog as if it's the best novel he's ever read. Please . . . give the mail carrier a hernia or something, I don't know. Also, please make the folks who come into McDonald's this holiday season cheerful. They all come in tired and cranky from shopping for* their *kids while I'm crying inside over* mine. *And last, Lord, bring Crystal home. Amen.*

I know it is a selfish, whiny prayer, but it is from the heart. Neither Joe nor I need any gifts this year, since we have each other and six living, breathing gifts who love us. We may exchange some Christmas lust, but that doesn't cost either of us a thing. Okay, it costs Joe a few scratches, but . . .

Hmm. Maybe we ought to knock that off for a while. I might be losing the weight I should be gaining because of all that friskiness.

Nah. I need me some hot Joe in the morning.

But for the first time in my life, I think I'm depressed. I shouldn't be. I have every reason not to be. I have a nice home, six smart, polite children, and the most loving of husbands. I know many single women with children out there who have none of the above. I thank God every day for His mercy on me, but the gloomy clouds hanging over our finances and Christmas make me so sad. Even the clouds in the sky seem to hang just over me, following me wherever I go, leading me to puddles only my feet seem to find. The Lord could at least give us a white Christmas, but the forecasters call for either clear and cold or unseasonably warm and rainy for the rest of December. Yet they're rarely right. If I bring my umbrella, it doesn't rain. If I wear my boots, it doesn't snow.

I am a jinx, I guess.

A week into December, I have just about had it. I'm stewing and fussing inside about our general lack of money, customers are fussing and generally lacking manners, employees are wanting days and weekends off to go shopping, the weather is turning colder and contains no snow or sleet or anything dangerous, and the work schedule looks dangerously thin for such a busy time of year.

To top it off, employee contributions to the Angel Tree Fund are practically nonexistent. Since I became a full manager, I have set up a tradition with the Angel Tree. There are trees at the mall with little cards in the shape of an angel, and each card represents a child who wants to have a nice Christmas. On the card are the child's age, gender, shoe and clothing sizes, needs, and wishes. I usually take two cards, one for a boy and one for a girl, the employees donate more than enough, I go shopping with Toni, and we wrap as many needs and wishes as we can. This year I chose *six* children, and so far, my employees have barely donated enough money for only half a child to have a nice Christmas. How am I going to help the other five and a half kids have a decent Christmas? I can't just go around begging my employees or customers for money, and the gifts are due tomorrow to the Salvation Army. I don't know what to do! And I especially don't know how to pray about it. I want my *own* kids to have a nice Christmas, yet these Angel Tree kids have so much less than my kids already have.

I look at the pitiful sum of money in the Angel Tree envelope at the beginning of my shift. *Lord, You did a whole lot with a little to feed all those folks. Please . . . I'm trusting that You will do something for my kids, and, Lord, if it's in Your will, fill this envelope today for these angels.*

I immediately feel guilty.

I'm sorry, Lord. Help these angels first, okay? Help the last people folks think about at Christmas come first for a change. Amen.

I set the Angel Tree envelope in a prominent place near the back entrance and get to work, leaving God to control it all. I find myself drifting to the back to check that envelope every now and then, and it's not getting any fuller. "Um, today is the last day for Angel Tree contributions," I tell the crew as I work breakfast.

No one contributes a single penny.

This is weighing me down, and I can't have this on me while I'm working the lunch rush. I give Joe a call. "I need to see you," I say.

Ten minutes later, he arrives. "Are you okay?" he asks.

"Physically, yes," I say. "But mentally . . ." I tell him about the Angel Tree Fund, and he nods.

"Our United Way contributions are way behind, too," he

says. "Folks just aren't as giving anymore for some reason."
He smiles. "You know what we could do?"

"I'm open to suggestions."

He opens his wallet, and I see . . . six fifty-dollar bills. "I
went to the bank today to take money out of savings for us to
go shopping this weekend." He widens his eyes. "It's Tuesday, Shawna. Why would I take out this money for the weekend when it's Tuesday? You know I'd leave this money in the
bank all the way until Friday for it to draw another few pennies of interest." He laughs. "I think I took out this money
today for your angels."

"Oh, Joe, I don't think . . ."

He hands me the money. "It's Christmas, Shawna. If we
can't have the merriest of Christmases, let's at least help
these angels. Our kids will understand."

"But what about Christmas for our kids?"

"We'll figure out something." He kisses my cheek, right
there at the counter in front of the crew and a few customers.
"Or God will."

I wish I had this man's faith. "Are you sure?"

"About God? Always." He winks. "I have to go. City bus
versus Cadillac. No injuries, but with a Cadillac . . ."

"I love you," I say, squeezing the life out of that money.

"I love you, too," he says.

As I'm walking that money to the back, I pray hard. *Lord,
You answered my prayer, and I thank You, but You only answered part of it.* I put the money into the envelope. *Answer
the other part, okay? Please?*

And for whatever reason, the Lord chooses to send every
person in Roanoke to my McDonald's right after that. I have no
time to rest. The parking lot is full, the drive-thru line never
seems to end, the only empty seats are outside in the play
area, the ketchup dispensers are squirting in all the wrong
directions, the milkshake machine goes on the blink again,
and we run out of, it seems, a different soda at the self-serve

every five minutes. In addition, one of the cash register drawers gets stuck, the dining room is an unholy mess, and we never have enough fries ready.

On top of all this, Crystal shows up out of the cold gray sky during an epic lunch rush that is sure to set a record, the lines full of parents and their children, children who can never decide what they want.

"You have a break coming up?" Crystal asks.

I look at the throng in line. "Give me about fifteen to twenty minutes," I say. I point to a booth that a family of four has just vacated. "Want something?"

"No. I'm fine."

After twenty-five furious minutes of yelling, flashing my "get-your-booty-in-motion" eyes, and *telling* children what they want to eat, I pour myself a cup of decaf and join Crystal.

"Y'all are getting slammed," she says.

In many more ways than I could even explain. "What brings you out here today?"

"I was just in the neighborhood," she says. "How, um, how is everybody?"

This is a switch. We haven't seen Crystal much since she told me she was pregnant. We talk on the phone often enough, but . . . "We're doing fine." I know I just lost another pound this morning, and Christmas is going to suck, but . . . "We're fine. How are you?"

Crystal looks away. *Oh, Lord, don't You let this child tell me she's had an abortion! I'm already having an awful day. Don't make it my all-time worst!*

"Tony, um, I convinced Tony to do right by me, and he has promised to try."

Thank You, Jesus.

We sit for a spell not speaking. While I'm glad Tony will be around, I sense an unspoken sadness in Crystal.

"You know, Crystal, there's a house full of folks who love you."

"I know."

"They miss you, Crystal. I miss you. You need to come around more often." *Mainly so I can stop cooking so much food! I always cook enough for eight people just in case Crystal drops by, and the fridge is bursting with leftovers by the end of the week.*

"About that," she says with a wince. "LaTonya has decided to move back home since our lease is up, and though I *could* pay all the bills since I'll be working full time over break—doing inventory, yuck. I hate doing inventory."

Lord, is she saying what I think she's saying? Please let it be true.

"Can I come . . . live . . . with y'all for a little while?"

Whoo. I have to hold my tongue a few seconds so I don't sound too eager. "Of course you can." But I have to ask her, "How long is 'a little while'?"

"Oh, at least until I go off to a real college next year. After the baby's born, of course."

Lord, please don't have me breaking down crying during my break. If the crew sees it, they won't respect me. "Um, which college?"

She smiles. "I was kind of hoping that Virginia Tech would give group discounts."

Three kids at *once* at the *same* school? Has it ever been done? I'm sure it has. I'll have to go online to find out how they paid for it all. "Are you sure, Crystal?"

"About Tech? Sure. It's a good school."

"I mean," I say, a little waver in my voice that I cannot control, "are you sure about you coming home?"

"I am, Mama. I'm sure."

"I mean, well"—my feet are dancing under this table!—"Toni has gotten right particular about her room." *Toni has*

WNBA posters everywhere. The child can play her some basketball. "You might not like the décor."

"I've seen her room, Mama. It's okay, but I should be rooming with Rose."

I blink. Could a piranha and a shark ever share the same room and live together in harmony? Wait. Putting a piranha and a guppy on the verge of becoming a barracuda in the same room can be dangerous as well.

"Mama?"

"Just doing some thinking." I sigh. "Please don't take this the wrong way, and I am overjoyed you are coming home, but I'm not sure Rose would want you to—"

"But she does," Crystal says. "She even suggested it."

No way! "Are you and Rose even on speaking terms?"

"Yes. Why wouldn't we be?"

I can think of a few reasons. "I mean, well, she used to be, a freak, remember?"

Crystal shrugs. "She's not a freak anymore, Mama. Now that I know her better."

"But she called your friends . . ."

"Oh, that." She rolls her eyes. "We talked about it."

"When?" I can't remember the last time I've seen those two speak.

"A while ago."

"How?"

Crystal pantomimes using a phone. "I told her that I didn't agree with her choice of words but that I understood her frustration. She apologized to me, I forgave her . . . We're cool, Mama."

I have to be sure of this "coolness." "What if Rose slips and says it?"

Crystal smiles. "Rose told me, and I believe her, that that was the first time she ever used that word. It embarrassed her, Mama. 'I wasn't raised that way,' she said. She still regrets saying it, wishing she could take it back."

"What about your friends?"

Crystal blinks. "What about them? Once they see me with her and realize she's my friend and my stepsister, they'll come around. And if they don't, they weren't my friends in the first place."

I nod. "Maybe once they get to know her . . ."

"Yeah."

I sit back. "So, you and Rose have already talked about you moving back, and *behind* my back!"

"Get used to it, Mama," Crystal says. "Sisters keep secrets."

I like the sound of this. "So what does Rose think?"

"Rose said that Toni should have her own room since she likes it so much, and I agree. Toni's never had her own room before, and Rose has never had a roommate, so . . ."

Lord, You do move in mysterious ways, even behind my back when I am more than completely exhausted. Thank You.

"Um, when can you move in?"

"Is today too soon?"

Today . . . *today!* I love the sound of that word!

"What are the boys doing?" she asks.

I will my eyes to swallow their tears, but they aren't co-operating. "Whatever it is, Crystal, they're *not* doing it now. They are going to help you move." I want to hug her so bad, but there's a table between us, and the little chaps inside us might get squished. My stomach rumbles for good measure. "Girl, I am suddenly hungry. I need to get me a couple apple pies. You want some?"

"No." She stands. "When will you be home?"

Lord, she keeps calling it "home." I don't deserve Your blessings, Lord, but I sure am going to take them. "I'm getting off at the regular time today."

"No overtime?"

"No." I smile. "Toni and I will be shopping for the angels today."

Crystal smiles. "You're still doing that?"

"Yes."

"Well, maybe I can help you do the wrapping when you get back."

I nod. "We'll have lots to wrap. We're doing six angels this year."

"Wow." Crystal smiles. "So, I'll see you at home?"

There's that word again. "Yes, Crystal. You'll see me at home."

"Great. Can I borrow the van for all my boxes?"

We exchange keys, and then it hits me. "You already packed?"

"Yes."

"What if I said you couldn't move back?" Not that I *ever* would.

"I knew you would. You're still my mama. You can't stand to be away from me. See you."

I float from the dining room to the crew behind the counter, and they scatter in search of something to do, probably because they've never before seen me smile so much. I even fix that stuck cash drawer with a tap of my hand.

And every customer who steps up to that counter for the rest of my shift gets a very nonpolitically correct "Merry Christmas!"

75

Joe

Having Crystal in the house is like having two Shawnas around. The house has never been cleaner, each bedroom neat and orderly, the meals have never been tastier, and the kids have never seemed happier. We are all together now. We are a unit. We are one.

We also have *less* hot water, *fewer* leftovers, a *longer* wait for church, *less* room at the table, and *more* phone calls per hour than any house on earth should. Our MSN mailbox is overflowing with correspondence from folks needing help from LivingWithDeath.com, and every night, long into the night we answer them. We make a mighty powerful team, and I've lost count of the number of folks we've already helped with their grief.

All this amazes me, but I'm most amazed by Crystal and Rose. Crystal moves into Rose's room, and it's as if they've been rooming together all their lives. They share clothes. They do each other's makeup. They style each other's hair. They giggle. They stay up late talking. They're . . . sisters. And when we visit Shawna's family the week before Christmas, they room together there, too. I can't praise God enough for this unexpected miracle.

And despite my earlier gloomy prediction for having little money for Christmas, we "find" money—or have money find us—in the strangest of places. Several library books the kids had lost over the years and we had already paid for turn up during a cleaning of all closets. The school refunds the money. Roanoke Gas gave us the option of applying our surplus budget funds for natural gas to next year's payments, or, the letter read, "We can refund the surplus in time for the holidays." We had them cut that check. My insurance company has an unusually good year and refunds a sizable chunk of our auto and home premiums. My parents send us a check for six hundred dollars, the note from Mom reading: "The Lord put this amount on my heart." The more we give, the more we get, and we even sponsor another Angel Tree child as a family.

The Lord is providing us with a simply awesome Christmas.

Shawna and I decide to blend our Christmas traditions. On Christmas Eve, my family always opens the gift from the family member who lives farthest away. This year it happens to be a package from my brother, who is back in Irian Jaya for their summer season. It is a pretty big box, and we let Jimmy and Toni open it.

Jimmy holds up a wooden mask, turning it over. "This is for Rose," he says.

He and Toni hand out a different intricately carved mask to each child. I get a woven carry-all only about a foot deep "for the next fish you catch," according to the note. Very funny, James. As if I'll catch a fish that small. But we all crack up when Shawna holds her . . .

We have no idea what it is. It looks like a long, skinny shell wrapped around a horse's tail.

Toni finds another note at the bottom. " 'Greetings from the Dani Tribe,' " she reads. " 'Thank you for the TP.' "

I laugh. "They got it." Everyone is looking strangely at me. "I told Dad to send them a care package loaded with toilet paper. It's like gold to them there."

"Uh-huh," Shawna says. "Keep reading, Toni."

" 'The masks are made by the Asmats, and each is unique, no two the same,' " Toni reads. " 'Just like you six are. And the fly swatter' "—she looks at Shawna—"you're holding a fly swatter, Mama. It says it's made out of a bird's leg bone and the bird's feathers."

Shawna swats the air. "I'm taking this up to Canada next year."

My brother. Every gift has meaning. Our children are different, so he sends each a different mask. Shawna had trouble with the bugs, so he sends a fly swatter. I am a better fisherman than he'll ever be, so he sends me a joke. It is amazing how carefully selected gifts can bring the givers right into your family room.

We all attended the Christmas Eve service at Pilgrim, one of Shawna's traditions, and on Christmas morning we line up on the stairs for a family picture—a Murphy family tradition, since the beginning of photography, I suspect. We first open the stockings. I am surprised the mantel held up under the weight of eight stockings. Then comes breakfast (waffles, eggs, and bacon), and then . . .

"Joe and I have decided to use the Murphy family tradition of opening gifts youngest to oldest," Shawna says. "Any objections?"

Of course there aren't any, and several *hours* later, we still aren't through. Shawna and Crystal have enough unisex clothes for several babies. Rose has her prepaid cell phone. Junior has a new web design program for the boys' computer. Jimmy has his "fierce" new bike. Toni gets new clothes so she won't have to wear any hand-me-downs. Crystal gets a whole Virginia Tech wardrobe: sweats, hats, T-shirts, and even a coffee cup. I get a few "outfits" picked out by Rose, Shawna, and Crystal that "won't embarrass us in public," and Joey gets all the books he's been putting off reading—and a special box from my dad. I already know what's in it since I packed it in the van when we were up at Aylen. He opens it . . .

"It's Great-Grandpa's typewriter," Joey says. Of my three, he knows the most about our family's history, mainly because Cheryl drilled it into him.

"Joey," I say, "it's Grandma and Grandpa's way of saying they're proud of your writing, and they hope one day that maybe you'll write about them—and us, too."

"Does it work?" Joey asks.

"Find out," Shawna says.

Joey slides in a piece of wrapping paper and pecks away. "It works."

There are six envelopes on the tree left to open. I'd purposely placed them low on the tree behind the presents so no one would notice.

"I didn't even know they were there, Joe," Shawna says. "Who are they from?"

My kids, who had usually received them from Cheryl, look at me.

"They're from me this year," I say. "Toni, I want you to hand them out."

Toni hands them out, and I watch each open his or her letter. Without fail, they each look at the check first, and then they read the letter.

"What do they say?" Shawna asks.

"Good things," I say. "I, um, I got my bonus early."

"You did? And you didn't tell me?"

"I just wanted it to be a surprise."

I had to threaten to quit to get that bonus, and I was almost out the door, too, I was so frustrated. But it turned out that someone somewhere in the company had a heart.

One by one, the children, *my* children, all six of *my* children, come to me, waving their bonus checks, and give me hugs, saying, "Thank you," and "Merry Christmas, Daddy," and "Merry Christmas, Joe."

Crystal is last. "But, um, Joe, this is way too much."

I take her hand. "It's okay. Buy yourself a car or something."

She nods, and a single tear slips down her cheek. "Thank you." She hugs me.

That hug was the best Christmas present I ever got.

76

Shawna

I have to read one of these letters, but before I can get to one, Joe takes an envelope from his back pocket with "Honey" written on it and hands it to me.

"You're going to make me cry, too, I can feel it," I say.

"Open it."

I open it and read:

Honey,

I love you. I don't say it as often as I should. I'll try to say it to you more often. I love you. You have brought me back from sorrow and given me new life. I thank God for you every day. I cannot wait to see the life we have made that is growing inside you. I hope he (or she) has your eyes. I could look into your eyes forever. Please accept this small token of my love and use it for something you really want.

All my love forever, Joe

I look at the check. Three hundred dollars? That was some bonus! And that was . . .

That was all we had just a few short weeks ago.

God is good. God is great.

"All I want is you," I whisper, giving him a juicy kiss. I look at the children, who are looking at Joe . . . with awe. There's no other way to describe it. "How much did you give them?" I whisper.

"I split it all up," he whispers back.

What? "You divided up your entire bonus?"

He nods. "Kids," he says a little louder, "and Shawna, you are the reason I earned my bonus. You're the reason I work so hard. Everything . . . everything I have is yours."

I don't know if it's a tradition in this house to gather around for a group hug with the man of the house, but that's what we do. If only someone could have taken a picture . . . Priceless.

"Oh," Toni says. "I almost forgot." She runs upstairs and comes down with a thin present, handing it to Joe. "I got you two something."

"Oh, honey," I say. "You didn't have to get us anything."

Toni's eyes fill with tears. "I know."

Both Joe and I open it, and in the most exquisite jade green frame is a picture Toni drew . . . of me and Joe, with her in the middle holding both of our hands.

All she ever wanted was a mama *and* a daddy.

Lord, crying a lot is yet another Christmas tradition around here.

"You like it?" Toni asks.

We cradle that child between us, lavishing her with tear-filled kisses.

"Murphy Christmas, everyone," Joe says.

Yeah, it's silly, even cornball. But "Murphy Christmas" means so much more.

77

Joe

The winter months fly by. The government is very good to us with our tax refund—five digits' worth—and heaven is practically shining down between what we make and what we owe.

Well, not exactly.

We have already sent down payments for three kids to go to college next fall at Virginia Tech, which is not what Cheryl and I had envisioned happening when we planned our family at two-year intervals. It's probably not what *any* parent ever envisions. By my calculations, we'll be paying college bills for the next *twelve* consecutive years, or until Toni graduates from Yale—or wherever future leaders of America go who love to talk. Then, after a six-year break, we'll put Shawnjo/Joshawna Kazuby and Crystal's baby, who she'll name either Rodney or Shanté, through medical school. All told, for the next, oh, *thirty* years, Shawna and I will know the ins and outs of every federal student-aid form in the country. We are fortunate that the financial aid folks at Tech have a heart, because they found work-study and some obscure scholarships for all three kids and even waived Crystal's nonrefundable application fee.

I took the family out for ice cream with that money. Banana splits at Bruster's. Very yummy. Shawnjo/Joshawna and Rodney/Shanté liked them, too. Lots of wonderful kicks.

Because of all these future bills, we will most likely drive the van and the Sentra forever. I wonder what the record is for mileage in a van. I know we can break it.

With everyone's help, once the weather turns from gloomy spring to sunny spring, we turn the playhouse into a gardening shed for Shawna, complete with trowels, spades, potting soil, hoses, and shelving. "I'll just add to what's already here," she says, looking at all the crocuses that Cheryl had planted now bursting into the sunlight. "I'll just mingle my flowers with Cheryl's and see what grows." She loves working in her garden, so much that one day she comes in with tears in her eyes, saying, "I missed this . . . creation." She also says that eventually I won't have to cut the grass because there will be flowers covering every square inch of both the front yard and backyard.

I can live with that.

Shawna, my favorite gardener, is a ripe mango, healthy and plump. Shawn Joseph (we know that for sure now) is right on schedule for delivery in the last week of June, two weeks before Crystal is to have Shanté Tonia. I go with both women to their checkups, and while other women might cringe at their weight gain, Shawna rejoices, saying, "Shawn is not going to be skinny now!" We still take walks around Wasena, just at a slower pace, and we still get frisky.

After all, we *are* newlyweds.

With six kids and one on the way.

And a grandchild on the way.

And two kids graduating high school.

Where has this year gone?

* * *

This year is moving too fast! Life is moving too fast! Rose was just a baby a minute ago, and a second ago, I was taking her prom pictures. Now, I'm taking cap and gown pictures of Junior and Rose at the Roanoke Civic Center Coliseum. I must have blinked or something.

Once again, we take up a full row in the stands, all of us eager to hear Junior's salutatory speech, which will be the third salutatorian speech of the day. The first two are all right, a little heavy on the platitudes, but Junior's is by far the best, and not because he's my stepson.

It's the best because Junior actually has something to say.

"Akilini mali," Junior says, repeating the Swahili phrase several times.

He repeats it until the audience joins in.

"Now I will tell you what you have been saying. *Akilini mali* in Swahili means 'use of brains begets wealth.'" He pauses, and I see Shawna's lips pause as well. They had worked so long on the speech that she has it memorized. "Use of brains begets wealth. I have been blessed with brains."

Shawna mouths "by God," a phrase the "censors" at PH removed so no one would be offended.

I'm offended that they removed the phrase.

"I have been blessed with brains by my father and my mama . . ."

Junior pauses, and Shawna tenses. "This pause wasn't in the script," she whispers.

"I have also been blessed with brains by God."

Yes! What can they do? *Nothing.* They can't keep a salutatorian from graduating because he has morals. I hear enough amens to drown out any possible reprisals, and I pray the *Roanoke Times* prints large excerpts from this speech.

"I was not supposed to say 'by God,' just now." Junior looks at a woman behind him on the stage furiously flipping through several sheets of paper. His "censor" is about to have a conniption. "But I would not be here if it weren't for God's love, God's grace, and God's holy power."

More amens.

"That's my son," Shawna says, fiercely gripping my hand.

Junior looks back at his censor. "I will return to the speech now. Page two."

A ripple of laughter circles the Coliseum as the censor "finds" page two, and the senior class is actually paying attention. They had been playing with a huge beach ball during the other speeches, and now they're listening to my son.

"Can you have wealth without brains in this country?" Junior asks. Another pause. "I can think of a few people who have." He looks back at the censor. "I would list them all for you, but that might get me in trouble."

Nice laughter.

"But wealth is more than money, and that's what I want to talk to you about today." Junior nods. "I have been raised by the smartest woman I know."

"He's going off script again," Shawna whispers, "as he *should*. I'm so proud!"

The "censor" has just about had it. We can actually hear her sighing!

"I used to think I was poor," Junior continues. "I used to envy other kids for what they had, things I only had dreams of having. But now I realize that I am the wealthiest person I know because of my mama."

Shawna cries, but they aren't tears of sorrow.

Junior looks over the heads of the seniors to the teacher section behind them. "I know I should be thanking my teachers for all they have taught me, and I do thank them, but I can't give them all the credit. I need to give credit where credit is due. I stand here today because of my ancestors who fought, and bled, and died, and marched so I could be here."

Junior pauses, many heads nodding.

"I stand here today because of my father, who fought for this country . . . and died in my arms almost nine years ago."

Now our entire row is crying. Shawna hands out tissues.

"I stand here today because of my mama, who has raised me to be a man. I stand here today because of my sisters, who have schooled me daily on my behavior."

More nice laughter.

"I stand here today because of Shawn Joseph, my little brother who is not yet born, who *I* will school one day on *his* behavior. I stand here because of my stepsister and stepbrothers, my sister and brothers from another mother, who have accepted me as . . . their older brother."

Lord, this is as good as life gets.

"I stand here because of my stepfather, who, I hope, will help raise me to be a better man."

I take two tissues from Shawna. *Lord, I sit corrected. This is as good as life gets.*

"I stand here today because my God is good, and my God is great."

Applause! People standing! Cheering!

"That," Crystal shouts, "was the all-time greatest shout-out I have ever heard."

Junior waits for folks to sit. "Ralph Waldo Emerson once said, 'Speak what you think today in words as hard as cannonballs, and tomorrow speak what tomorrow thinks in hard words again.' That's the way my mama raised me. I heard her hard words, and I listened when she said, 'I live as I can afford, not as you wish.'"

So much wisdom surrounds me!

"Emerson also said, 'Whoso would be a man must be a nonconformist. He who would gather immortal palms must not be hindered by the name of goodness, but must explore if it *be* goodness. Nothing is at last sacred but the integrity of your own mind. Absolve you to yourself, and you shall have the suffrage of the world.'"

Shawna and I compare goose bumps. She has more, and we're all out of tissues.

"Pole pole ndiyo mwendo," Junior says. " 'Slowly, slowly is indeed the long journey.' Our journeys have just begun. *Haraka, haraka, haina baraka.* 'Hurry, hurry has no blessing.' On our journeys, we must take time to count our blessings." Junior locates our row and counts with his finger seven times. "Those are my blessings, back there in row B, section seven." He steps back from the lectern and starts clapping for us.

I feel the eyes of the world on us.

"Thank you for listening," Junior says, and he sits.

I can't get to my feet fast enough, and I am not alone. So humble, so inspiring, so much his mama's son—Junior. It is a blessing just to say he lives in my house, at least until August. *Lord, I don't know how I can make him a better man than he already is, but help me try.*

After I make sure that Rose and Junior's diploma covers contain diplomas, we splurge on a huge meal at . . . Golden Corral. It's all-you-can-eat, it's reasonable, and the kids love the rolls and the dessert selection. While we eat, perfect strangers come up to Junior to shake his hand, telling him, "I was there, young man," and "God bless you and your family."

And now, the third Saturday in June, life is just plain *good* out here on the back deck where I'm sipping lemonade while the kids are at Wasena Park and Shawna is resting in her bed trying not to go into labor even a second too early. Even Crystal and Tony are walking around Wasena. I would be lying next to Shawna, but she says I distract her from keeping the baby inside her "to finish cooking."

I am so glad Shawna and the kids have been healthy. I
don't know what we would have done if anyone had gotten
sick. I have ended every prayer at dinner with "and keep us
safe and healthy" since I was a child, and God listened especially well this year. He does hear us when we cry.

And this lemonade is *good*. God makes good lemons, too.
He—

"Joe, honey, it's time."

I jump from my chair and see Shawna holding her stomach. "Yeah?"

She smiles. "Ooh, yeah. We got to go. I was just dozing
and then . . . Joe, he's about to kick his way out."

I whip out my cell phone, a Father's Day present, using
the walkie-talkie function. "Come in, Rose."

"Rose here."

"Code Shawnjo, code Shawnjo, I repeat, code Shawnjo."
I snap the phone shut. "They're on the way back from the
park. You are to lie on the middle seat of the van. Junior will
drive the boys in the Sentra. The girls will go with us." I
check my watch. "We should be at Community Hospital in
less than fifteen minutes if the kids run fast and we hit all the
lights, twenty-two minutes if Toni can't keep up on the run
up the hill and we hit all the lights. Rose is calling ahead to
Dr. Peavey. Your overnight bag is already behind the back-
seat of the van. When did you eat last?"

Shawna's mouth drops to the deck.

"Shawna?"

78

Shawna

And to think he used to be so unorganized around the house!

"Who packed my overnight bag?" I ask.

"You did, three weeks ago."

Oh, yeah. I did. What did I put in there? I can't remember. "Well, come help me to the van."

And just as Joe had rattled off to me, we get to the hospital in only seventeen minutes, hitting just one light.

Ten minutes later, I'm in a birthing room with Joe, holding his hand, grinning, sweating, feeling so fine, so fine—

"He's crowning," a nurse says.

"He is?" I ask.

"Yes," the nurse says. "You got here just in time. As far as I can tell, you've been in labor for a couple hours." She pages Dr. Peavey.

"But I'm not feeling the pain," I say to Joe. "I should be feeling—"

Oh.

Ow.

There it is.

Oh . . . *God help me! . . .* This . . . *hurts!*

"Is your hand okay?" I ask Joe.

"Just keep squeezing it," he says. "I'll be fine."

Dr. Peavey arrives, checks me out down there, and looks at me. "Um, here we go."

"Should I push?" I ask, and I am really feeling this chunk now. *Jesus, help me! My other babies were so skinny!*

Dr. Peavey looks up at me. "You mean you aren't?"

I shake my head.

"Well, here he comes," Dr. Peavey says.

"Should I push?" I ask, the most excruciating pain tearing through me and then . . .

Ah.

I hear the cry of a baby.

Shawnjo has arrived.

Dr. Peavey can't believe it. The nurses can't believe it. *I* can't believe it. Joe . . . Joe doesn't care because now I'm holding our son, and *I* don't really care because Shawnjo has Joe's squint already and a firm grip on my ring finger and—

"Can our kids come in here?" I ask.

Dr. Peavey goes and gets them, and as all six file in, I watch the nurses' eyes growing wider and wider.

"We need a bigger room," Joe says.

Shawn Joseph Murphy is *so* precious! And a chunk, too, weighing in at eight pounds, seven ounces. None of my kids weighed more than seven pounds, and here he is . . . in the flesh among us. *Thank You, Jesus, for a healthy baby.*

But mainly, thank You for a quick delivery. How did You arrange that? I was set for a thirty-hour fight, an epidural, ice chips, a fainting husband, and maybe a little unholy cussing. Thank You for sparing me that. You really know what's best for us, don't You?

Oh, that new baby smell!

Sorry, Lord. But this child smells so good.

I turn to Joe. "I want another one."

As I expect, the kids cry "No!" and "Where will we put her?"

Yeah. I want a little girl just like this one.

Joe certainly seems willing. And since we're going to Aylen Lake again this summer, I'll bet we can make us a little Joshawna, too. Something about the air up there must make me fertile or something.

"Oh, little boy," I whisper as he looks up at his mama, daddy, and six brothers and sisters, "I would give *anything* to know what you're thinking right now."

79

Shawn Joseph
"Shawnjo" Murphy

Who are all these people?
   Do I belong to them all?
I hope I do.
Are the colors right?
White, black, red . . . or is that pink?
I can see them all just fine.
Look at all those teeth!
I hope I get some soon.
What's that smell?
Oh, that's me.
What's this feeling?
It feels good!
What's this feeling?
"He has your face . . . Shawna's eyes . . . Daddy's squint . . .
Grandpa's Murphy's chin . . . Grandma Evans's ears."
Wow.
I have so many parts of so many people.
Did I come fully assembled?

What's that smell?
Oh.
Me again.
Oh, there's that feeling again, too, and that word.
"Blah blah blah blah love. Blah-ditty-blah-blah love you."
Love.
Yeah.
That's what I'm feeling.

Meet executive assistant Shari Nance: She's smart, sexy, talented—and excitingly fed up . . .

Shari is past done with letting her uber-incompetent boss, Corinne, steal her ideas and get the big bucks and promotions. So, why not pose as Corinne, work a major ad account, and prove who's the real talent? And if that means competing with a rival agency's top executive, well, Shari can't wait to take him on. But when the man turns out to be her boss' ruggedly-sexy boyfriend, his agenda has the kind of sizzling moves Shari can't trust *or* resist . . .

Tom Sexton couldn't be happier about Shari's deception. He's been aware of her abilities for as long as he's been getting sick of Corinne's ego. And helping her will give him a chance to start the agency of his dreams. But keeping their double game under control is only making Tom want more of Shari in every way. And as the stakes get thrillingly higher, he'll do whatever it takes to show her they're the perfect partners, in the boardroom *and* the bedroom . . .

**Please turn the page for an exciting sneak peek of
J.J. Murray's new novel
I'LL BE YOUR EVERYTHING
coming next month!**

Chapter 1

An elderly white woman with a fancy camera around her neck waits alone at Tillary and Jay in downtown Brooklyn. I wish I had a digital zoom camera like that. At first, I think she's a lost bird feeder from one of the nearby parks because she wears a brown wool jacket, matching frumpy hat, and brown corduroys. But she's out here at 7:30 a.m. in this gross, misty, dirty, frigid weather that screams, "Brooklyn is too cold for people to function in November."

Tourists are getting as hardy as the trees in Whitman Park.

She steps in front of me and asks, "Will this bus take me to Times Square?"

I want to tell her that any bus will take you anywhere eventually, but she seems so needy. I squint through my misted glasses at the oversized blue sign. B51. I rode that bus once and hated it. A bus is no way to see the world unless you have a window seat and the person next to you isn't big-boned. I didn't have a window seat that day, decided to save my money and the hassle of feeling like a sardine, and haven't ridden a bus since.

"It might take you to Times Square eventually," I say to the tourist, wiping mist from my lenses and returning my glasses to my face. "But don't take my word for it. I don't ride the bus enough to know."

"You ride the subway instead?" she asks.

Also once. Not a good time. Though I'm five feet tall, slim, and can squeeze into just about any tight space, that trip on the subway gave me major claustrophobia. The fumes, men in suits oozing thick, cloying cologne, little bruises on my booty from slamming into the poles as more people crowded my little body, the intermittent darkness— not my idea of a good time. I kind of miss the booty bumps caused by some random briefcases held by some of the men supposedly reading the *Times*. I never knew briefcases could get so fresh.

"No, ma'am," I tell the tourist. "I walk."

She cocks her head to the side. Maybe she's hard of hearing. Either that or she has to move her head occasionally to focus a wandering eye. "You walk?"

"It's only a few miles."

To MultiCorp, America's number-one multicultural ad agency fifteen years running, and that's why I'm walking. I can *afford* to walk. I've been an administrative assistant at MultiCorp for *five* years. I *know*. Five years is a long time to be kissing anyone's booty. I've had a couple of bumps in pay, and I even earned a bonus last year, an IKEA gift card that I redeemed for a storage combination with three bright pink buckets that hold whatever comes out of my pockets: keys, receipts, Post-its, and change. But mostly, I survive the daily grind. Walking keeps me in my $1,500-a-month apartment that has a "window office" (a cherry desk and my laptop), a narrow kitchen with a skinny oak table and two skinnier oak chairs, and a view of the Statue of Liberty if I put my face flush to the window and squint just right after the sun goes down.

"Well, thank you anyway," she says, stepping back.

"Anytime." I turn to leave then remember my Virginia-born manners. "Um, enjoy your visit to Brooklyn."

The woman leaps in front of me. "I'm in Brooklyn? I thought *this* was Manhattan." She points in a westerly direction. "Isn't that Central Park over there?"

Manhattan was my favorite Woody Allen movie. I can afford to *rent* that. I work in lower Manhattan, and I even like eating Manhattan clam chowder, but I could never afford to live in Manhattan or anywhere near the big ad agencies on Madison Avenue like Young & Rubicam, Doyle Dane Bernbach, and Harrison Hersey and Boulder.

"No, ma'am. That's Whitman Park. This is, um . . ."

How do I make her feel better without confusing her and ruining her vacation? Wait. She's touring Brooklyn, which she has mistaken for Manhattan, in November. What kind of a vacation is that? At any rate, she seems lost enough as it is. Nothing I say is going to make her feel any better.

"This is Brooklyn *Heights,*" I say. Sort of, but not really. It's complicated. You have to live here. "Tell the bus driver you want to go to Times Square, and he'll hook you up." Again, eventually. I don't tell her that she'll probably have to switch buses during the craziest time of the morning in Manhattan.

"I was so sure *that* was Central Park." She still points over toward Whitman Park. "It looked just like it does in the movies. I got some wonderful pictures that look *just* like they came from that *Law & Order* show. Is Manhattan far from here?"

There's a loaded question. I want to tell her that it takes forever to get to Manhattan and stick around. "It's only a few miles," I say. It's only a few miles as the crow flies, but there are few straight lines around here.

I check out her shoes. Comfortable black Brooks walkers. I love her corduroys. Her whole outfit is a statement. What that statement is, exactly, I don't know.

"We *could* walk together," I tell her. "It will only take half an hour or so, and it may even be faster than taking the bus."

She squints.

Ah.

The lack of trust inherent in out-of-town people whenever someone from Brooklyn stops to give them assistance. I was the same way when I first arrived and spoke good, southern English to people who sometimes spoke English. I now speak Brooklynese with a slight southern twang. I squinted a lot back then, too.

Hmm.

The Good Samaritan in the Bible just went on and did his thing. I should just grab her arm and get her some exercise. But I had home training, and I don't twist anybody's arm—not even my own.

"I work on William Street in lower Manhattan." Seventeen floors up. "A few blocks from where they're building the Freedom Tower."

No bells. She blinks.

"Um, near where the World Trade Center used to be."

A bell. She nods.

"William Street is about . . ." Again, how do I make her feel better for mistaking Brooklyn for Manhattan? Can it be done? This situation is why people write online blogs. "It's about a cab ride from Times Square."

"That close?" she says.

Wow. And I thought I was naïve and spatially challenged. "Yes. That close."

"Well, I think I'll wait for this bus anyway. Thank you for your help." She steps back.

I continue walking.

At least she said thank you. So many people don't. Especially ignorant people, but ignorance is bliss, and she sure seemed quite happy to wait in her version of Manhattan on a rainy Friday morning in Brooklyn.

What people *don't* know about the world or where they're going keeps them happy.

Bliss is being lost in America.

I doubt anyone will ever quote me on that one.

Chapter 2

A ll this brings me to my job again. Why do I think so
much about my job? Oh yeah. I have to pay $1,500 a
month for a four-hundred-square-foot "space" in downtown
Brooklyn in a skinny silver rectangle made of glass, metal,
and concrete that rises fifty stories into the gloom. On a clear
day, you can even see the ocean from the Beach, an outdoor
space on the fifty-first floor. The Brooklyner—they brain-
stormed about half a second when they named the place—is
kind of like a shiny graduation pen stuck into a big brown
and black asphalt pencil holder. I still have my silver graduation pen from high school. It worked for about two years
before the ink ran out seven years ago. Crazy, but I have a
graduation pen on my desk at MultiCorp that reminds me
that I'm twenty-seven. It does look good on my desk,
though. It reminds me to stand tall and shine brightly every
day.

Even if *I'm* out of ink.

All the leaves have given up and jumped to their collective deaths over at Whitman Park. I wish it wasn't raining. Those piles of leaves would be fun to kick around with old Walt Whitman himself. But I'm walking late because I helped Miss "Isn't This Manhattan?" take the bus she was going to take *anyway* before I tried to help her.

Some people just need full confirmation of their foolishness.

That quote is going up on my fridge.

What was I thinking about before? Oh yeah. Ignorance being bliss. What people don't know about the products they buy won't hurt them—until the recalls and the lawsuits, I suppose. That happens way too much these days. The only things recalled when I was a kid were cars and cribs, and now car companies are becoming extinct and cribs are houses and penthouses of the rich and infamous. I'm sure there's something ironic about that. "Cribs" cost more than cars these days—at least on MTV.

What a conflicted job I have. I help advertise products that people don't really need or want—at first. "We create the need and the want" is MultiCorp's grandiose and over-exaggerated slogan. If we were doing ad campaigns for milk, flour, eggs, hand sanitizer, toilet paper, Vaseline Intensive Care Lotion, Blended Beauty Curly Frizz Pudding for my BB3 spiral curls, hiking boots, and used paperback books, I could see the point of advertising, but . . . no. Most of the products MultiCorp represents aren't necessary for anyone. No one *really* needs the products we promote, and in a way, all advertising does is confirm the American public's foolishness.

Maybe I'll put that quote up at work. I doubt anyone will notice.

All this foolishness does give me a job, though, and for that I'm thankful to almighty God, especially in this economy. Working at MultiCorp is like stepping onto the stage of a wonderfully absurd comedy most days. No. It's an absurd comedy *every* day because the ad account executives take everything so seriously. "We have to sell this overpriced, shoddily built, ozone-killing, ice cap-melting, and lawsuit-begging whatever-it-is if it's *the last thing we do!*"

I trip a lot at work. It seems we do "the last thing" daily while promoting the "next big thing" that, again, no one really needs.

I'm finally hiking up to the somewhat level part of the Brooklyn Bridge, about two miles to go. Whenever it snows, I try not to follow in the footsteps of others. A few years ago, sixteen inches of snow fell, and I was the first person on the bridge. I wonder if anyone followed in *my* footsteps. I wouldn't recommend it because I have small feet. During that snowstorm, the wind blew so much that I experienced complete whiteout for the first time in my life. It was as if I were floating in a sea of cotton.

It was kind of peaceful, actually.

Man, I am running a few minutes behind. I better start power walking.

Today the air smells like a cross between cat litter and cheap wine with a hint of seagull poo and a trace of old pennies. How many times has this bridge been bought and sold? I think this just about every time I walk across, and I still don't have an answer. Foot traffic is light at 8 a.m. today. It must be the rain. Thank God for Gore-Tex and my blue North Face waterproof jacket. I once used umbrellas on rainy and snowy days until I lost or forgot about five of those umbrellas at work when cloudy, wet mornings turned into clear, starry evenings. I wonder where lost umbrellas go. Not *inside* somewhere, obviously. I hope they're not out wandering aimlessly in the street. Maybe the black ones show up at movie funerals and the red ones show up on insurance ads.

But back to ignorance. If ignorance is bliss, does that

make the opposite true, that knowledge is pain? It has to be. It has—

"Hey! Stay to the left!" I yell at the bicyclist who veers into and out of my "lane" and speeds past. The nerve! Man, that's got to be the same guy who has buzzed me a few times before. Jerk!

Nice booty, though.

Where was I? Oh. It has been a royal pain for me to take classes online to get my MBA through Long Island University *and* to hold a full-time job—and live in downtown Brooklyn. And to walk twice across the Brooklyn Bridge every day. And to take time out to help clueless tourists who think Whitman Park is Central Park because it looks *just* like it does in the movies. And in just three years—man, that's a long time—I'll have that MBA, and I'll use it to do *exactly* what I've been doing, probably. If MultiCorp wasn't paying for half of the tuition, I wouldn't be trying to get my MBA at all because there are so many people who have MBAs out there who are still looking for jobs. And even if I get the chance to interview for something better, I can hear the interviewer say, "And where did you get your MBA, Miss Nance?" Um, LIU. "Next!" No, I would beg, I was on the *Brooklyn* campus of LIU! That's the nicer campus!

Knowledge *is* pain.

I'm halfway across the bridge now, and I'm catching up to a bottleneck of people. Five years ago, there was only a smattering of people walking. Now, there are literal human traffic jams, because of the economy, I suspect. It's getting windy, not that I have much hair to muss or that I care if it gets mussed. I've gone completely natural since coming to Brooklyn, and my hair is finally growing out.

There's a whiff of the ocean in the air today. Might be the Long Island Sound. Or a fish market. Not much boat traffic today either. Where's the sun? Not that it matters to me. I'm shady enough as it is. I could just use a little golden sunlight today, you know? That would make me happy.

Now, what do *I* believe about happiness and bliss? I believe that bliss is an uncluttered heart and an open mind. So far I've maintained both. I'm kind of lonely about the heart part, though there is a guy down in Virginia named Bryan who has been after me since we were kids, but Bryan's there, I'm here, he's somewhat happy there, I'm somewhat happy here, case closed.

Until he comes to visit again. I used to like it when he came to visit. We're friends first and lovers every once in a blue moon, but his last few visits weren't much fun. We had spent the day at Coney Island, and there he was on his knees on the hardwood floor in my bedroom later that night. I thought he was going to propose and effectively ruin our friendship, so as soon as he said, "Shari Nance," I tackled him and started kissing on him. I didn't give him a chance to finish. That was the only time the neighbors complained about the noise. I may be small, but I can shout. Bryan might have been asking me to turn off the light or to help him find his shoes. He might have been asking me to fix him a sandwich, I don't know. But he was on his knees in my bedroom, you know? Not many men ask for a freaking sandwich when they're on their knees and vulnerable like that in a woman's bedroom.

That was three months ago. Since then Bryan has been pestering me in e-mails and during phone conversations to "come home where you belong." I blame my parents for that. They used to say that to me, too. And he keeps saying "home" as in, "Shari, it's time for you to come *home* before that place makes you crazy" and "The folks back *home* miss you so much" and "Girl, you need you some *home* cooking." *This* is my home now, I told him, and if you really want me, you will come to *my* new home. Home is where the heart is, right? So if Bryan's heart is with me, then he should come up here and stay here with me in my home.

I might have confused him with all that because he hung up on me.

And I wasn't mad.

At all.

I'll bet he felt me shrugging my shoulders all the way from Brooklyn.

He didn't call me for a week, and when he finally did call, he told me that he was planning to visit me for the Thanksgiving holiday. To do what? I asked. "To be with you, Share." He calls me "Share," as if we're still in middle school. Having a visitor would be nice to break the monotony that is my life, but the holidays are such a romantic time of year, and I'm worried he'll drop to his knees, say, "Shari Nance" again, and I'll be too far away from him to knock him down before he pops the question. Not that I would accept. It's just that I don't want to give him an answer that would ruin our friendship.

Always keep men ignorant of your intentions. It makes them crazy, and they pay so much more attention to you, as if they're trying to earn something.

Speaking of ignorance . . .

If ignorance is indeed bliss, then using my earlier definition, *ignorance* is an uncluttered heart and an open mind. That's kind of edgy. So that means the opposite of ignorance—knowledge—is a *cluttered* heart and a *closed* mind.

That is so true!

And *that's* the wench I work for.

Chapter 3

Corrine Ross, my boss, is knowledge personified, only her knowledge comes from management seminars, hardback books, Harvard, an upper-middle-class upbringing in New Haven, Connecticut, and other out-of-touch places. "It should work," she tells me whenever we're working on a new ad campaign. "I have a hunch, Shari dear."

Her hunches are butt ugly, gristly, snaggletoothed, and always dead wrong. I *gently* correct her with a well-placed newspaper story or magazine article placed *gently* on her desk, bring her *gently* back to reality with the rest of us in the real world, or I simply ask her straight up, "Have you thought about doing *this?*"

And then she un-gently uses my ideas as her own.

Oh sure, *we* get accounts, but only her bank account prospers. She gets the glory and the ridiculous five-figure yearly bonuses, and I get little shoulder squeezes and the phrase, "Go team!"

Life as I know it goes on slowly, like the drain in my tub

that finally *glug-glugs* in about half an hour and ends with an audible burp and a sigh.

I am finally off the bridge. I can't wait till it ices up or snows so I can see if these new Chippewa boots can hack my morning commute. Look at that! I can see my breath. At least I keep my eyes up when I walk to work. The "movers and shakers" around me only look at their shoes. Wait a minute. They can't be movers and shakers if they're walking alongside me into lower Manhattan, lower Manhattan where people aren't Park Avenue old money and actually have to work for a living. While this city can be so cold and while faces of every slice of the American rainbow can often look icy, most folks I've met in this city are survivors like me with warm, multicolored hearts.

I stand in front of my building on William Street, looking up like a tourist. Man, this job sucks so hard. How hard? Imagine you've dropped your keys into the toilet. Okay, maybe not your keys. They'd fan out and get stuck in the hole, especially if you have a lot of keys. You'd probably flush a few times until the water was completely clear, and then you'd reach in and rescue them. Okay, imagine your cell phone or BlackBerry plummeting into the toilet as soon as you push or pull the lever. You want to reach into that nasty water immediately to rescue what is essentially your life, I mean, your cell phone, but you shake your head and watch as it gets sucked away in the swirl.

That's how bad this job sucks.

Dreams are only one flush away.

I may post that saying in the ladies' room where my boss spends an inordinate amount of time primping.

Hmm. I have to face it. I don't just hate my boss. I loathe her. I abhor her. I abominate her. I detest her.

One day, Corrine Ross, the honeymoon's over. *Pow*. Right in the kisser.

Just not today. Today is payday. I'd like to eat for the next two weeks. I'll have to play nice today, and since she's returning from a three-day business trip to LA, I'll have to play even nicer since I have a hunch it didn't go too well, and *my* hunches are usually right.

It's hard being nice when you're seventeen floors up and surrounded by food you have to *fetch* for your boss. Bennie's Thai Cafe is in smelling distance. Corrine usually has me get her dumplings stuffed with ground chicken and shrimp, bamboo shoots, dried mushrooms, and shallots. I get an egg roll because only chicken should be involved when it comes to dumplings. Corrine gets a burger and sweet potato fries at Zaitzeff, but I get nothing but a burger because sweet potatoes should become pies, not fries. I sometimes go to Les Halles to get Corrine eggs Benedict, which, in my humble opinion, is the luxury version of the Egg McMuffin. John Street Bar & Grill provides me with my quesadillas. I *must* have them. Corrine won't touch them because they're "too ethnic." Sometimes I go to Pound & Pence and splurge on their baked mozzarella and onion soup with these cool ale bread croutons on top. Yoro Restaurant on Fulton Street, though, is Corrine's brilliant idea of nutrition. It isn't mine. Fish should be breaded, cooked, and have bones you pick out with your teeth. Sushi and I do not mix. Corrine, however, loves Yoro's designer maki series, which includes avocado, shrimp, crab, and vegetables in sticky black rice. I don't call that lunch. I call that a night in the bathroom. The Libertine Restaurant is where Corrine takes us for caramel cheesecake whenever we've "sealed the deal." We haven't gone there lately. Hmm. She's on a cold streak as long as her extensions, mainly because I've been keeping my mouth shut and not giving her any ideas to steal lately.

All this food is within my grasp, and it's why I need those twice-daily power walks. The folks at MultiCorp eat a lot, at odd hours, late at night, all day, in fact. I know I would put away three thousand calories a day at least if I ate like some of them do. Instead, I sip my Honesty Tea from Soma by Nature, the nicest oasis in the building far away from the seventeenth floor, and I use no sugar or cream, just the straight stuff, because I am the antioxidant queen.

Because I'm running late, I step into the elevator instead of taking the stairs, all two hundred and thirty-eight of them. I have toned, tight calves, thighs, and booty from climbing and descending over one *million* steps in the last five years. This elevator is still stank. I look around at people trying not to touch each other but most likely secretly wanting to. I used to have a crush on a tall Hispanic guy who used the stairs a lot. I called him "Tool Hombre." He had this huge toolbox and hands as big as my head. I'd smile, and he'd grunt. I'd smile some more, and he'd grunt some more.

We were regular conversationalists.

I smile all the time on any elevator, and these real New Yorkers around me think I'm crazy. While they give careful nods at people they *think* they know or that they think know *them*, I just smile. No winking at any time, though. That could lead to a sexual harassment lawsuit in the wink of an eye these days. Hands at sides, feet together, eyes front—I'm a good little MultiCorp soldier.

The elevator doors open and . . . "Welcome to Multi-Corp."

I smile at our main receptionist, Tia Fernandez, sixty-five, widowed, fiercely Cuban, and who still salsa dances every Friday night at Cuba on Thompson Street. She thinks I'm a shorter version of Lauryn Hill, and I think she's a *younger* version of Eva Mendes. Other than me, she is the nicest person here, and like me, Tia trips every day here at MultiCorp.

"Hi, Tia," I say. "Don't you look sexy today."

Tia rolls her eyes and smiles. She has to be the prettiest woman I have ever known. I hope I look half as good as her when I'm her age. She has the smoothest brown skin, always smells of sage for some reason, and other than me, wears the loudest clothes, preferring bold oranges, vibrant yellows, and electric greens. Today, though, she's business casual with a pair of tan slacks, old-fashioned earth shoes, and an oversized white sweater.

"It is Friday, Shari," she says. "Payday."

I smile. "You're making me look bad with that outfit."

"I am not dancing later," she says, adding a few dance steps anyway. "But you will be dancing soon, because Miss Ross is back from Los Angeles."

My heart falls to my stomach and instantly biodegrades. "Miss Ross is here, as in here early?" I whisper.

Tia shakes her head. "She is due back from LA this morning." She points behind her at a master calendar the size of Wyoming. "Her plane should have already landed, but knowing Lady Di as we do, we should not expect her anytime soon."

I smile. Everyone in the office has a different nickname for Corrine. Some call her "Diana Ross." Others call her "Die, Anna." The latest nickname floating around is "Corrine-cula" because one of her front teeth is kind of, well, pointier than the other. I secretly call her "Miss Cross" since I bear her all day and sometimes bear with her even on weekends.

I walk behind Tia's "edifice," which isn't a desk so much as a building partition the shape of a flying vee with a rolling chair behind it. I check Corrine's mail slot and find yet another catalog from Neiman Marcus.

Corrine and her Cinderella dresses. "It's a Tahari," she told me once about a brown outfit she modeled for me. As I nodded and showed my false approval by forming a little *O* with my mouth, I wondered why an old game-system maker would diversify into dresses. "You like my Kay Unger?" she asked one day. I'll bet it looked better on Kay. "Paisley is the new black," she once told me while wearing a jade-green dress. Why can't the new black *be* black? Before a date with her longtime boyfriend, Tom "Terrific" Sexton, an account executive at Harrison Hersey and Boulder, Corrine changed at work from a hoochie-kootchy Gucci to a Michael Kors sheath dress, which, I found out later, cost as much as my monthly rent. The rip up the side of that dress was, to be blunt, a rip-off. They must have used the fabric they cut out at the bottom to make the rest of the dress. And Corrine routinely drops five hundred bucks for scary-looking stilettos. I'd like to see her get those spiky heels stuck in a pile of pigeon poo on the Brooklyn Bridge.

I would pay to see that. I'd even film it and upload it to YouTube.

But back to MultiCorp. There are wide-open spaces on this floor and no cubicles anywhere. Only our founder and CEO, Mr. Dunn, has an actual office because "we are a family with no secrets." Thus, we have no privacy, and our phones don't buzz or ring and only light up. As a result, everyone whispers around here, and at first it drove me crazy. I'm used to it now. Except when people have gas. I will never get used to that.

Because of all the glass and lack of walls, I get decent views of Brooklyn and the Brooklyner, which is nice most days, but sad on cold, rainy days. It just shows me how far I have to go after I tidy up Corrine's career, I mean, accounts and affairs by, oh, seven o'clock. I haven't left at five since I started here five years ago. If I ever billed MultiCorp for all those extra hours, they'd owe me over $50,000.

Hmm. Why don't I bill them for those hours? Oh yeah. I'm on salary. Still . . .

MultiCorp is the largest minority-owned, full-service multicultural advertising agency on the planet. We do TV, web, print, radio, billboards, and whatever else you can advertise on, including T-shirts, kids' meal toys, mugs, pens, and boxer's backs. We reach out to the dispossessed, the tired, the hungry, and the poor. Okay, technically we reach out to clients who want to *take* money from African-American, Hispanic, and Asian American urban consumers.

Thus we try to convince Grandma Millie to shop for her eggs, bread, and butter at Kmart instead of Walmart. We want Hector and Juan to join the exciting U.S. Army instead of the boring U.S. Air Force. We urge the New Dons and OYG street gangs to buy their throwaway cell phones from AT&T Wireless instead of Verizon. We want America to shed tears and act indignant about our public service announcements concerning teen pregnancy and spouse abuse. Those are always so uplifting. We want people with no disposable incomes to frequent casinos as often as they can. The U.S. Census Bureau is one of our major clients, and it makes so much sense to use MultiCorp the more multicultural this country becomes.

We also represent Jamaica. No kidding. We represent an entire country. "Come to de islands, mon." That's about all we need to say because folks *go* to the islands. You really can't screw up advertising paradise. Okay, hurricanes sometimes turn Jamaica into a giant mass of windblown palm trees and knee-deep mud, but essentially, keeping the Jamaica account has been a no-brainer and therefore perfect for my boss.

Yeah, um, perfect. When Corrine and I first heard we'd be working on the Jamaica account, I said, "Come to de islands, mon." She didn't make the connection. I had to explain it to her *five* times. Corrine then told me it was a silly idea, that good advertising ideas take time to develop, and that no one would take "Come to de islands, mon" seriously. She said she would think of something "much more upscale and erudite," yet *my* slogan is out there on billboards, in magazines, on the radio, on every bus in the city, and all over the TV. The Jamaican man who did the TV ad and who has lived in New Jersey his entire life (so much for realism) has even been on a few talk shows. Naturally, Corrine took full credit for my idea and got the big bonus and the free vacation to Jamaica. Mr. Dunn has been calling her his "rising star" ever since.

I can't afford to go to Jamaica or to live too long in my disappointing past, so I go to my desk, which is within whispering distance of Corrine's "space," as she calls it. I have vowed to stop whispering because I'm making her too much money. Luckily, Corrine is gloriously late this morning because of her trip. I do a happy dance, my boots spraying water on the plastic carpet protector under my rolling chair. Now I can get so much more work done because the boss isn't around.

Somebody has to work around here.